JumpStart

JumpStart

Champagne Universe Series
Book 1

By A. K. Brown

Squid Publishing Edition License Notes

Copyright © 2016 A.K. Brown

ISBN-10:0-9945412-1-X

ISBN-13:978-0-9945412-1-5

Acknowledgments

I wish to thank my wife for her tireless support and understanding while I worked to write this book.

To my longtime friend, Nicole, for preparing the foreword and her encouraging words of wisdom.

Special thanks go to Celia and Tam for all their editorial efforts and advice.

Finally, credit to the pushers; those quality friends who have that unique gift, the ability to encourage the artists among us. Their spirit giving us reasons to believe we can roll boulders up mountains: Shirley, Wylie, Anna, and Gillian.

Foreword

Many years ago when I first met AK we both talked about writing a book sitting on the back verandah overlooking the national park under the stars. Things have changed since then. There is now a cover on the verandah so it's good for all months of the year and not just the balmy summer ones. Gone are the shaggy comfort chairs where we would make wild predications about our future and what we'll do; none of which have come true, as someone who was listening to our conversation would have predicted.

So it somewhat surprised me when AK said he had started writing a book. It surprised me more when I began reading it and that I wanted to keep reading. I suppose we never really see the hidden talent that people keep locked up while life is moving on in its customary way. So it has been a blessing that AK's life had a speed bump. Otherwise, the talent that he kept hidden for all these years would still be hidden.

I think that AK's theme of fighting a war against seen and unseen enemies is particularly relevant in today's world. As we experience life we are sometimes our own worst enemy, we don't question our thinking patterns that create this. We go from day to day not questioning our impact on the world or the effect that we have on each other. I think that AK having the courage to change direction means that we all might just be able to find our own nth dimension.

Nicole Swan

Chapter One

Dr. Stevenson's Lab, Washington DC

It is not often that one can say with absolute certainty that the world had irreversibly changed. John stared at the wall clock enthralled as the second hand of this new reality ticked slowly by. Clamoring for attention in his peripheral vision, the computer screen flashed those fateful words in large green letters, '***Simulation Successful!***'

John scrunched his eyes shut before taking a deep breath from flash pain in his lower back. The last round of tests had been particularly gruesome. His head pounded from long hours of sustained concentration and copious amounts of caffeine. John rubbed his temples and the fragile skin under his thickset glasses that always burrowed into the bridge of his nose.

Resetting his Buddy Holly black frames on his nose, John opened his eyes. He stared at the computer screen and knew that when others discovered this new reality, they would stop at nothing to control it.

Developing a working theory was one thing, applying it to build a prototype is something else entirely! Leaning forward, John focused on the monitor. The words were still there... blinking loudly, taunting him. His thoughts strayed momentarily onto the devastating implications if his discovery fell into the wrong hands.

Eventually, casting aside those weighty notions, he focused on his achievement; a smile crawled across his face to settled into his '*happy-campus*'.

He was experimenting with matter transportation through the nth dimension.

What started out two years ago as a random thought experiment, had led to this astonishing discovery. Matter, in theory, could be transported outside of space-time from one location to another. Instantaneous travel was theoretically possible!

John's unrestrained laughter echoed off the sterile lab walls. In a spontaneous moment of joy, he jumped up and started dancing haphazardly around the room. Lost in his own merriment, he miss-stepped badly to come crashing down onto the floor, still shaking with mirth.

He was taken by surprise when the lab door flung open framing a petite, wide-eyed brunette sporting a pristine white lab coat.

"Are you ok?" Jen asked.

"Ha, ha ... I've never been better ..."

Jennifer looked down at him with a frown. *Is he some crazed psychopath?* Shaking her head, *she should have checked the other tenants to this lab facility before she moved here!*

Jen stood there frozen, with the door wide, caught in John's line of sight, undecided as to inquire further or just leave. John lay on the floor laughing while he struggled to regain his composure.

"Are you sure you're OK?" she said with a nasal Australian accent.

"Yes, yes, I just had wonderful news."

Jen waited for him to elaborate further, nothing. Then finally she prompted him, "You just won the lottery?"

John laughed, "No. Something much better."

Slowly, he got to his feet and straightened his glasses. His face flushed as he noticed how beautiful Jen was. Her crinkled forehead and smiley crow feet eyes betrayed her concern at his spontaneous outburst. Her interest flushed his crimson cheeks even more.

After an uncomfortable moment of silence, Jen realized that John was not going to be any more forthcoming, so she half-smiled and turned to the door.

"Crazy Americans," Jen muttered to herself, as she turned away and left the room.

John shook his head. *Damn! It was obvious that he needed to brush up on his social skills; that wasn't half awkward, she must think I'm nuts. She did have a nice smile though.*

◆◆◆

Jen walked back to her lab trying to refocus her thoughts after the annoying interruption of her apparently crazy neighbor. She needed to get some work done as time was running out.

She had recently moved house leaving Sydney to live in Washington DC. Since getting her doctorate, she had been struggling to find work in Australia. Her big break had come when an American research firm headhunted her to bolster up their research profile. As quickly as her big break had come, it had mysteriously disappeared.

Once the company had secured the tender for some fat Department of Defense contracts, her services were no longer needed. Rightly annoyed she'd sent letters and emails to anyone who would listen, but to no avail. Knowing the injustice, and proving it, were two entirely different things.

Her right to work in the States was quickly becoming a problem, her visa required her to have active long term employment. In a last ditch attempt, she called in a favor from a friend she'd met at the university for some medium-term contract analysis work. She had hoped this would be enough to circumvent the visa restrictions, but more importantly, solve her immediate money problems. Nevertheless, she was far from convinced it would be sufficient; She needed something else... A backup plan, a plan 'B'.

◆◆◆

John finally calmed down after his outburst and reseated himself at his desk. Focusing his attention back on his computer screen, he clicked through his nth dimensional model checking its parameter inputs once again. He had to be absolutely sure of all his calculations. One wrong calculation and he could rip a hole in space-time. He wasn't sure what would happen then. All he knew was that it would be bad, *very* bad.

Working late into the night, John eventually pushed his chair out and turned off his computer. He decided it was time for an impromptu celebration. Realizing it was quite late, he discounted calling his longtime reservist friend Elvis. His real name wasn't actually Elvis; he had acquired that nickname when he was in the Army. Elvis like to hum the lyrics to one of his namesake's song, 'A Big Hunk O' Love'. It invariably annoyed the rest of his unit when he hummed it loud enough to be overheard by their NCO; who gave them all demerit calisthenics each time. John tried not to laugh at the sexual innuendo, but sometimes, army peer pressure just forced the humor out.

Searching his pockets for the lab key, John walked through the entrance and quietly closed the door. Bright light escaped from under Jen's door into the dark corridor. John smiled at the opportunity fate brought before him. Striding up to her door he knocked briefly. Soft tapping from inside stopped, and an echo of stiletto footsteps made their way towards him. John straightened his glasses and blurted out his invitation as Jen slowly opened the door.

"Thanks for your offer of help before, I don't usually go around acting crazy like that." She couldn't disguise her annoyance of a caller at such an hour, and their temerity to interrupt her train of thought. John immediately realized he was intruding, but it was too late to take it back. The bright lights from inside the lab coupled with Jen's agonized expression couldn't take away the tempered beauty he saw framed within.

Irritated by the intrusion, but after seeing the dilemma on John's face, Jen smiled and shook her head at their earlier encounter. *It was kinda funny seeing a grown man wallow on the ground in obvious delight.*

"As long as you don't make a habit of it. You know, I thought you were going to clean the whole floor with your back with all that giggling." Her crinkle laughter lines smiled even further.

"Ha, ha... I had a small breakthrough," John said nervously.

What? Giggling, John grimaced inwardly, like a girl? Hrrummm.

After a short silence, he continued, "It's getting late, and I just thought ... I hate celebrating alone."

Jen looked at him for a long time trying to determine his motives before nodding briefly.

"There's a pub, 'The Flying Jack' that I sometimes go to, it's just down the street," said John.

Jen remembered the bar, she had passed it on her way to the lab that very morning. The joint was not too shabby, there was a rustic feel to it. The tacky playing cards magically stuck to the walls at odd angles as though launched from a full pack by a dealer. Their color strewn all over set a festive mood, making the place look somewhat, *inviting*.

It could be worse she thought, *after the day she'd had, she could use a drink.*

"OK, but no crazy breakthroughs."

"Deal," John said smiling.

♦ ♦ ♦

Ten minutes later, the two were sitting at a corner table in 'The Flying Jack' nursing a couple of drinks. The late hour had stilled the other patrons. The subdued lighting complemented the Jazz playing softly through hidden speakers. It gave the room a dreamy understated atmosphere.

"So are you going to tell me what we are celebrating?"

John was decidedly uncomfortable with her innocent question. Jen could see he was debating with himself, he finally took a large gulp of scotch and whispered, "I think I just worked out how to teleport matter."

"Yes, well very funny!" Jen replied. *Obviously it was too hush, hush.* "I understand. Forget I asked."

"No, it's true!"

Jen just smiled. It was a hazard of the industry they worked in; secrets were a necessary evil.

"Well then, you can beam me up another drink Scotty."

Chapter Two

John was a self-proclaimed inventor. He had had a few careers in his life bouncing from one job to another, which was surprising given his middle-class American family upbringing. His childhood was almost devoid of any unusual occurrence until his teens. It was a singularly mediocre existence that was suddenly turned upside down when his mother upped and left. She disappeared without a trace. There was no note of explination, there were no transactions on the bank statement, there was just... nothing.

His father, Andrew Stevenson, was a nervous man that had plied his only skill, 'Financial Consulting', to their family's ruin. It was not that the man was bad at his job; he endured life with a circular depressing resolve after his wife had disappeared. Sadly, lacking any of life's motivation, he fought the dangerous nature of economics and big business to no avail. The nest-egg they had put aside was squandered on indulgent self-pity.

He had never gotten over the emotional loss she had inadvertently wrought on the family. It was more the not knowing than anything else. Being the dutiful father, he'd attempted to take on both parenting roles, but unfortunately overcompensated and made a hash of it. He eventually found a niche for his skills in a nefarious money laundering operation with the nasty Massioni family from the New York underworld scene.

Where John lived, sons usually followed their father's profession. The furtive looks from neighbors and the not so silent whispers from school mates ensured he spent most of his teens avoiding what his father had become. Finally, to escape the vicious cycle, he confronted his father. In a final act of contrition, his father forced John to spend the remainder of his schooling living with his Aunt Grace. She had been awkward, antisocial and sometimes downright mean. But ultimately, they'd come to a rocky understanding.

When he finished his schooling, and real adulthood threatened his tiny existence, he roamed the streets lost like brush weed dancing from one place to the next driven by winds of laconic pleasure.

His life changed radically after one hell of a night of copious amounts of drugs and alcohol when he found himself in front of a judge explaining why he had put a goat into the co-pilot seat of a helicopter he took on a joy flight. It struck John as funny that the first thing the judge asked about was the goat and not that he was seventeen and didn't have a pilot's license. His only answer to the judge was, "Well... I needed a radio operator, and he could talk just as well as those in the control tower." The whole courtroom burst into laughter, except the judge.

The judge sentenced him, to either two years in the military or ten of community service, for his lack of judgment and reckless endangerment. John couldn't see himself doing the time helping grannies across the road, so he took what he thought was the easy option, a stint in the army. He sometimes mused that maybe if he had brought the goat in as a material witness, the sentence might have been different.

◆ ◆ ◆

Several days later, John was at his desk reminiscing on the impromptu celebration he had had the other night with Jen. He had found out how she was treated by her previous employer and was appalled. He thought that workers had at least some rights, even those from overseas.

Focusing back on his model he realized he would need to build the field generators so that he could manipulate the fields to replicate his model. It was necessary otherwise he couldn't create the nth dimensional portal. There had recently been stunning advances in not only detecting Higgs

Bosun particles but in manipulating them and their energy state within the Higgs field.

Once again he started to make a long list of equipment, scribbling items on the pad he kept on his desk. Time seemed to disappear into a vortex. John had this uncanny ability to focus absolutely on something when he needed to. It was one of the reasons why his scientific endeavors had been so successful.

After his stomach had growled for the tenth time, John walked out of the building to the nearest cafeteria. He noticed Jen sitting in the corner tucking into some steaming hot soup while managing to spill droplets of stark orange all over her pristine lab coat. Smiling and waving, she motioned for him to take a seat.

"How's the analysis going?" he said.

"Just finishing up ... It's only a small job," she replied after gulping and slurping a mouthful.

From what John remembered of her description the other night, it was a complicated analysis of laser burn rates on armor plating and theoretical shielding using fields theory. For her to finish so quickly meant she was either a fool or a brilliant analyst. He could tell she was no fool.

Jen continued to slurp her soup looking at John over the top of her thin-rimmed glasses. She was thinking of the celebratory night. *This guy was some seriously quirky scientist.* Although long ago she had realized that she liked quirky. *Well, some quirky, a girl had to have standards.*

"I saw all the deliveries to your lab earlier," Jen said with an intensity of curiosity which surprised John. *The deliveryman had nearly knocked her over twice.* She was contemplating whether to say something about the bruising on her ass.

"I'm nearly ready to test my modeling," John said tentatively.

Jen looked directly at him, disarming him with her smile. She chuckled to herself, thinking of the teleportation joke he made the other night.

"How long do you have here?" John asked about her work status, as he nodded to what looked like immigration papers. She had been looking at the complicated forms strewn across the table with spills of soup all over them. Her nose crinkled at the complexity of bureaucracy. She had lost count of the number of forms that she'd filled in. It was a silly game she played with herself, to distract from the actual act of filling forms in.

"A month maybe, two and a half at most," she said.

"Then what will you do?"

"If I don't find work soon, I'll have to return to Sydney."

"Is money that tight?"

Jen just smiled, trying not to make a big deal about it.

"Not exactly," she finally replied. "I have to justify to immigration that I have a job to comply with my work visa," she said as she sipped more soup. "No work ... no visa."

The waitress arrived at the table with a small pad and pen in hand, interrupting the two.

"Nachos and a Fanta please," John said staring up at the dark haired woman standing there expectantly.

The waitress scribbled in the shorthand they do and stiffly walked away. Her ill fit uniform caught John's interest, despite her precise presentation topped with a smartly positioned cap.

Jen frowned a surprise at John's interest in the elderly waitress.

"I may have something for you...," John said without thinking.

"Really?" Jen looked at John with curiosity written on her face.

Thinking quickly, "I need some analysis on a targeting mechanism."

Jen stared directly at John.

What the hell am I doing? Is it the crazies? John thought.

"Oh ...you do?" Jen said non-committal. She resumed eating her soup to give herself time to think. Finishing the spoonful, she smiled.

John was flabbergasted at himself.

Seriously, what the hell am I doing! She left him hanging there awkwardly with just slurping noises, without responding.

He had essentially offered her a position, but even more than that, a way to stay in the country and all she could do was to eat soup!

Damn her smile.

"I'll be finished in a week. Umm, I'll report for duty on the following Tuesday, if that's ok?"

John had never had to look after anyone in his line of research work before. He had commanded many soldiers in the Army and the Reserves. He was, however, sure it would be different with civilians.

Why was he doing this again? Oh yeah, that damn smile.

He was comfortable alone in his little world testing theories, making models and then building the prototype to on-sell it to manufacturers. He had done this numerous times before. That's how he had gained his small fortune, which was just enough to allow him to do the things he wanted. He sold his ideas as full-scale inventions to corporation's then reaped the royalties. He was definitely not interested in the business side of manufacture and sales / distribution.

But now he was taking on employees... sigh.

"Excellent," was all John could manage.

◆◆◆

Just over a week later John sat at his work bench calibrating the unusual mixture of equipment. Totally engrossed, he didn't notice Jen enter the lab and walk around the counter to lean in looking carefully at what John was doing.

"What power setting are you using to set the field?" Jen asked curiously.

Startled from his deep concentration, John quickly straightened up. Seeing her right there made him smile. He was thunderstruck, she was wearing an unusual fragrance; flowery with the smallest hint of zesty fruit. Her glasses framed her slightly oval face. Her mousey brown hair was set back behind her ears with the remainder in a ponytail. She figited under his scrutiny by straightening her now pristine lab coat. All the splotches of orange pumpkin soup from the previous day had magically disappeared.

Walking over to his admin desk John drew out a sheaf of papers.

"I have some paperwork for you to fill in," John said handing over a weeks' worth of forms. He had unfortunately contracted his lawyer who drew up a non-disclosure agreement that was surprisingly thick. His other major pit stop was his accountant where forms seemed to sprout from his hand.

"The government has its weird employment ways," his accountant confessed.

Jen reached into her own bag and pulled out a sheaf of paperwork of her own. Handing them over she said, "If you don't mind filling these out to say that you're employing me so I can extend my visa, that would be beaut," she said with laughter in her eyes.

Her sheaf was bigger than his.

Taking the papers with an inward groan, John briefly scanned them looking at all the detail he would need to fill in. "I'll need a copy of your resume...," John asked belatedly. A tinge of red airbrushed his cheeks. At least with that it will make filling in the forms that much simpler. John sighed as *bureaucracy, and red tape reared its ugly head again.*

It would take weeks to finalize all the paperwork. John had been both anxious and pleased at the prospect of working with Jen. However, he was a little apprehensive about including her on as paid staff given the unexpected outlays to cover her employment. His accountant had been more than thorough giving him every detail of expense and tax. He almost thought the accountant delighted in his misery. But then recoiled realizing it was only the accountant's enthusiasm that had boiled over. Although his previous inventions had given him a steady stream of royalties, he wasn't exactly overly flush with funds. However, he did have a solution if she went for it. *Fingers crossed.*

"Look we didn't actually discuss your salary. I've not got bags of money."

Here we go... Jen thought.

"What I can offer you is a small starting salary with a proportion of the royalties. If ... No I mean **when** we market this new invention, I believe that you will be more than handsomely compensated."

It was a surprise and not what Jen was expecting. She had never had an invention let alone one developed to the point of being sold. She thought about it and realized it was just another form of employee participation scheme companies would use to get the best productivity from their employees.

"I need at least enough to live on till the millions just start rolling in..." Jen said with a smile. John just melted again.

Over the next couple of hours, the two negotiated Jen's employment contract, finally settling on 5% of the royalties.

Jen signed the contract and nondisclosure declaration with a flourish.

"So boss... what's next," Jen said as her glasses slipped to the end of her nose giving her a demure librarian look.

"Please unpack the projector parts and set them on that bench over there, while I pull together an overview for you."

Jen left to fetch the boxes as he marshaled his thoughts into some semblance of order. *It was complicated*, he thought, as he shifted through concepts in his mind to make what he was building understandable.

I hope this isn't a mistake, John thought.

His accountant had advised him to hire an investigator to check out Jen's background. John was surprised he had the PI on speed dial as he vouched for the veracity of his investigator, as well as his discretion. John had told the PI he only needed to know whether she was an honorable person.

Before their meeting, the elderly detective gave John an unusual response.

"If she were my daughter I would be proud of her." John thought about this answer and smiled. The PI had given him exactly what he needed without compromising what he considered was her privacy.

He realized it was an unusual position to send the investigator spying on her and yet claim he'd kept her privacy. He rationalized, if he didn't know her background and the PI was not involved further, then her privacy was still intact. John chastised himself, as an employer, he had a right to know. He guessed he just didn't like the employer bit of the working relationship. He resolved to tell Jen that he had contracted an investigator to do a background check.

It took hours of discussion for John to explain his findings. His ideas and models flowed through her, captivating every fiber. When he had finished, the startling realization struck her between the eyes like lightning. Her hazel eyes stared intently at the model on screen then into his.

"Oh my God! You weren't kidding. You actually have developed matter teleportation!"

John smiled at her incredulity.

"Once we set-up this equipment we should see if the modeling matches reality."

Jen's eyes widened as she sat back stunned at the discovery, *not only modeling but prototyping.*

A tense excitement ran through her in waves of warmth.

She'll be at the forefront of this world-changing innovation. She also felt a real sense of honor and gratitude towards John for picking her to participate in the groundbreaking work.

Then in the next instant, had doubts. Biting her bottom lip, she wondering why he had picked her! There were plenty of highly qualified people here on campus that were excellent, it's a university where they study particle physics for Christ's sake.

Jen turned abruptly back to John, he had started talking again.

"... So, I'll need you to look at the nth field targeting so when the object dematerializes from here, we can rematerialize it there. I believe your work with the shield field harmonics will come in handy allowing us to target and rematerialize the material correctly."

Jen was instantly relieved; he had chosen her for her professional work rather than something superficial like her looks.

As the week progressed Jen was a rack of nerves while all the immigration paperwork was being finalized. The whole employment process smacked of something not quite right. She had doubts and ugly suspicions. She had already been conned once. *It was all too good to be true*, she told herself. Perhaps that's why immigration took so long to respond. She chastised herself a hundred times for the negative thoughts she had, especially those demeaning John's character.

It didn't help when John mentioned *private bloody investigators*. She would work herself up second-guessing this royalty thing. *What if all he's got is a theory? Just a theory? She would get nothing!* Biting her bottom lip, she mused at her own insecurity. *Was this guy really on the level?* She could see that what he said conformed to the data, but part of the scientist's job is to question it all. *That's just it though, he's not a scientist, he's an inventor!*

So to distract herself she thought about how the teleportation system would apply to this new field being generated by the projectors.

"How do you propose to get enough power needed to rematerialize the object?" she asked.

"Once the power reaches the breach point the new target location is set. The power cut off should snap it back to this dimension."

Jen was still looking confused, so John continued.

"Let me explain it this way, each place in space has a specific harmonic resonance. If you imagine two musicians in an orchestra, say a violinist and a harpist. We start at a point in space where the violinist sits. Our reality is harmonized to that location. We then create a bubble in which we alter the harmonic resonance to reflect that of the harpist. Then suddenly and instantaneously you are transported to the destination of the harpist.

It's a little more complicated than that, but basically, we need to map the harmonics in three dimensions from here and at our target destination point."

Jen thought about what he was saying. "The calculations to compute the resonance from one place to another must be astronomical. To take initial resonance from here and then propagate it through to another location to determine the resonance there."

"Yes, you're right... I purchased one of the few SR 17 quantum computers," John said matter-of-factly.

Jen was stunned looking around the room for one of those incredible machines. Quantum computers had developed in leaps and bounds. Their calculation capacity was phenomenal, as was their size, currently about that of a household fridge / freezer. They were still exorbitantly expensive, really only the domain of large corporations and governments. How John had gotten one; *he was just full of surprises.*

"I have set up a secure link to it. Currently, it's sitting in one of the data comms secure storage data houses off campus." His modeling and targeting could only have been possible with the computational power of the new quantum computers. Calculating the harmonics of different locations required its unique multiprocessing capabilities.

◆◆◆

John sat at his desk staring at the sender field of an email that had dropped into his inbox. The unopened email, from Andrew Stevenson, blinked several times before it disappeared into the trash unopened.

He hadn't spoken to his father in several years. Why now?

The email had come via the university domain. His father must have been keeping tabs on him. John shrugged inwardly and tried to put it out of his mind.

◆◆◆

John gripped the bench until his knuckles went white. He surveyed the equipment assembled there and recounted in his mind each of the objects before him. Like a massive jigsaw puzzle, each piece of equipment contributed to making the roadmap for the teleporter. They needed this to be able to target from one place to another. Building this roadmap was an important first step in the teleportation process.

When all the preparations were completed, they were checked and double-checked. John flicked the on switch. An annoying whine boxed at their ears as the projector targeting equipment warmed. Slowly the intensity built to a crescendo. A piercing high-pitched metallic sound screamed through the lab loud enough that it would have been heard from across the road.

Doctor La Perouse, a researcher from next door, rushed up and banged on the lab door yelling.

"Keep it down will you Stevenson! Some of us have real work to get on with!"

John just looked at the closed door without commenting. He had had his troubles with the rotund researcher ever since he had moved into the university lab complex.

La Perouse had accused John of stealing his ideas for an invention he was working on for the DOD. It was something to do with sonic devices. John hadn't bothered to find out. It seemed like every week the researcher had some gripe against him.

John eventually had had to placate the University Administrator, whom he could tell was getting tired of the situation. John knew that his contract with the University would be the one that was terminated rather than La Perouse's. The DOD would no doubt take precedence even with La Perouse at the pointy end. Every time that La Perouse blew up, John was sure the administrator would make some subtle move to encourage him to placate the Frenchman. John borrowed the expensive equipment from and the Lab Administration at minimal lending fees. *But for how long?* La Perouse was shaking the apple cart. It annoyed John no end. They would need to mute the sound.

Jen frowned not saying anything while looking over at John. After they had suspended work on their mapping to install some serious sound-proofing, they worked away the hours calibrating the protectors then mapping the harmonic resonance of reality. Hours turned into days until it became a regular rhythm. Each day the two would break for lunch and discuss the targeting or some other aspect of the project. Then they would return to the lab for a repeat of the morning. John's quiet yet commanding demeanor was offset by Jen's sharp wit and inquiring curiosity. Both found a comfortable tempo set in.

Chapter Three

In a nearby star system aboard the Squishy Pirate Ship, Kator

The Kator, shuddered as large pieces of the freighter's engines exploded in an expanding bubble of energy. The plasma ball accelerated out creating a shock-wave that buffeted against the Kator's shields. The wrecked freighter spun out of control off the port side.

Kazorr, the weapons officer, sat with his slobbery mouth gaping open at the main view-screen. His eyes turned on their stalks towards his commander in a plea for mercy.

"Kazorr you idiot! You have blown the engines," Commander Kane yelled.

They had been slowly trailing the freighter for over a week, waiting for the ship to drop out of FTL. It was pure luck that they had caught up, and Kane was not one to ever miss a golden opportunity to expand his wealth.

"First the Patrons wipe-out our home world, now you blow any chance of us making any credits," Kane said in his gruff sinking voice. His irritation was highlighted by a jet spray of multicolored ink with negative chunks of hard pheromones aimed towards his tactical officer. The Commander's aim was off sending it messily over the back of the sensor officer's bulbous head instead.

The unintended victim squealed in surprise.

"Damn," the commander muttered under his breath.

He knew that he wasn't fair, but if it made his crew more efficient after his wrath, then he would use it, and abuse them. Sometimes he thought he got too much pleasure out of it, but laughed it off as childish musings.

The Squishys were an intelligent flamboyant species of sentient Octopi.

"That's coming out of your share Kazorr!" Kane bellowed. His two side tentacles quivered then wound around the coral pedestal in the middle of the *Kator's* bridge. His suckers pulsed angrily as he reassigned Kazorr's share of the prize.

Kazorr cursed his bad luck under his breath without taking his two stalk eyes off the main viewer. His eyes had telescoped out of his head. The rest of his normally flexible octopus shape sat rigid to the chair. Kazorr's eyes always seem to pop out on their stalks when he was under stress, like a nervous twitch. His schoolmates had played cruel games tormenting him to see how many times in one day they could stress him then squish his eyestalks back into his head. Kazorr hated it. He would never forget the high pitch squeals of laughter from his classmates.

His two mid-tentacles wound around the tactical station chair holding him tight, as if in response to those heady schooldays. The tuberous elongated head started to change color taking a stressed induced pale shade of white as he listened to his commander. His two fore-tentacles squelched and sucked the control console betraying his tension.

Kane turns around looking for his next victim. "Drakmok! You're our salvage expert! Get out there and see what's left of that freighter that we can salvage," the Commander roared.

Drakmok could only stand aghast. The chaotic spinning of the engine-less wreckage would make it almost impossible to retrieve safely. His left appendage had only just regrown since he had lost it on the last salvage. He didn't want to go through the pain of regrowth again.

◆◆◆

The Squishys were an unusual species in that their make-up was similar to that of a Terran octopus with a few significant differences. The first and foremost being, that these octopi had an extra pair of lungs so that they could breathe air directly; however, they still had gills inside their mouths that absorbed oxygen through water under pressure. The second major difference was that the back two tentacles were much larger than the others and could be stiffened as hard as stone enabling them to walk on their hind tentacles. Terran octopi do crawl on land, primarily using their hind tentacles to propel them to new hunting grounds, but they required salt water spray while they traverse from one pool to another. Squishys would not be found far from water. Even their starships had generous salt dipping pools throughout their interiors.

Their tall, scary appearance was contrary to their flamboyant and often childishly chaotic natures, which with their chameleon-like abilities, meant they morphed into endless displays of color and. Hide and seek was a favorite game they played well into their adulthood. Their communication was a baffling mixture of speech, and colorful, dramatic body poses. Tentacle posture was often used as an accent to emphasize their points of view. Their lives seemed to revolve around the senses, with smell seemingly the least used... their body odor was disgustingly fishy!

The Squishys were only one of many younger races in this arm of the Milky Way galaxy. Intelligent species were forcibly aligned within politically unified blocks to the older advanced space faring Patron species. The Patrons brutally enforced their edicts over their subjugated dominion.

Chapter Four

Ferntree Hill Observatory

The newest and most sophisticated space sensor built by humans, the Tachyon Sensor Array (TACSA) at Ferntree Hill Observatory, Los Alamos, ran silently monitoring FTL particles from neighboring stars to determine their make-up. The emissions piqued from the explosive flash that signaled the fateful demise of the defenseless freighter.

Deep within the Oval Office, the President sat in his favorite comfy chair nursing a scotch neat. The Science Advisor and Secretary of Defense sat opposite him sipping their own drinks.

"Mr. President, it's been confirmed that the TACSA picked up nuclear denotations in outer space. It looks like we are not alone after all," pronounced the Office of Science and Technology director.

"Has it hit the newswire yet?" the President asked.

"I believe there's been some blogging and twitters. However, since it's been confirmed officially today, the stories will undoubtedly be picked up by the mainstream news and media. The Ferntree Hill Observatory Director is planning a press release."

President Avery Kennedy, turned to his friend Brad Wellington the newly appointed Secretary of Defense. The older secretary spoke out, "Shall I put together a special meeting with USSTRATCOM?"

The President furrowed his brow, "Is that the bit of the military that looks after space defense?" asked the President.

The Defense Secretary smiled, "Yes Sir, Space Command and Army Space Missile Defense Command."

President Kennedy just shook his head before speaking up, "Ok, but make sure the Joint Chiefs are included. I'm sure they'd get their knickers in a twist if they weren't."

It was Brad's turn to shake his head. "Mr. President, you can be too flippant sometimes. I wouldn't want the press to get hold of that."

The President smiled with a crooked grin, "Brad, you worry too much. Just get that scheduled, we need to work up a response to this," said the President waving his glass in the air.

"Yes, Mr. President... Avery." The President then laughed aloud at his friend's uncommon use of his first name.

Chapter Five

Ready Set Go ...

John pulled back surveying the equipment set up over the three benches in the lab.

"I think we're finally ready to test the teleporter. We have enough mapping to the local area to get a decent target profile. Let's start the next phase afresh in the morning."

Jen looked at John and just nodded. They could barely contain themselves that evening having a restless, sleepless night.

In the morning, John got into the lab early to setup the harmonic emitters and power generator. When Jen arrived, he had already moved on to the power conduits apparatus.

John threw Jen a pristine green apple.

"Use that for our first test subject. Let's see if we can transport it from this bench to that bench," John said as he motioned towards the two benches.

Without been directed, Jen placed the apple on the source bench platform and cleared the target platform location. John smiled as she got straight to work on calibrating the targeting.

Twenty minutes later as the clock struck 8 AM, John raced over and turned on the video camera before lining up beside his computer terminal.

"Are you ready?"

Jen made one final adjustment on the target matrix then nodded.

Pointing to a second pair of goggles while John repositioned his own pair, he took one last quick look at Jen and smiled with anticipation.

"Right, here we go." Leaning forward to watch their equipment intently, John pushed the 'Enter' button on his console.

Suddenly a violent implosion flung both of them off their feet forwards towards the remnant of the bench and back onto the floor. The source apparatus stood in ruins. Smoke billowed from the edges of it where there was a sharp sphere shape cut-out of the bench.

The two disentangled their limbs from each other to stagger upright, only to see their half destroyed lab obscured by all the smolder. Both of them waved their arms to dispel the smoke and heat out the window. They were further startled by the brash clanging of the fire alarm as it started up. A minute later, a torrent of water came pouring down through the ceiling sprinkler system, drenching them and their equipment.

"Holy Crap!" mouthed Jen.

"Where's the apple?" John said aloud. It wasn't on the destination bench platform.

John stared at the spherical cut-out in the source bench grinning.

A few minutes later, they could hear sounds of a huge ruckus from emergency services sirens echoing up through the window. The two turned to each other and rushed towards the opening. Their eyes wide and mouths agape despite the smoke. They stared across the car park at the wreckage of a very expensive BMW. Pieces of debris lay scattered over the surrounding vehicles and walkways. Nestled in the middle of the ruined sports car, stood a pristine spherical cut-out of a bench with an unmarked delicious green apple sitting centered atop of it.

John couldn't contain his joy and started giggling, which quickly became infectious. Soon both of them were in full swing doing-the-crazies. Each time they'd stop, one would start again until their eyes watered. Jen yelled out above the noise of the sirens and pointed at the debris, "Oh no, was that old Grumpy Bum, La Perouse's' car?" The realization that their annoying neighbor's car was in pieces brought on another fit of laughter.

By the time the two had made their way down the stairs from the lab and entered the car park, the place was an anthill of activity. The police were busy trying to cordon off the area. Bomb disposal units made sure that what remained of the car was safe while the fire brigade stood off stunned like the rest of the crowd.

La Perouse was arguing fiercely with a detective attempting to get the story straight. John could hear only muffled sounds over all the commotion. From his left, two policemen walked by discussing how weird the debris pattern from the bomb blast was. The singularly important question, 'How could a bench just appear in the middle of the car so soon after the blast?' Someone had removed the apple and was riffling through what was left of the bench draws. La Perouse then spotted John and started gesticulating madly, pointing directly at him yelling obscenities in French.

John took that as a sign to scat out of there. Grabbing Jen's hand, he pulled her through the crowd off the street and back towards the lab. Holding her hand felt comfortable. He could hear the scuffle of boots on the ground running after them. Worried it was La Perouse and the police, they quickly ducked into a small side alley.

Jen sidled up to him and whispered … "Why are we hiding?"

When John didn't comment she continued, "Seriously, La Perouse is an idiot."

"I'm not worried about La Perouse. I'm worried about the DHS (Dept. of Homeland Security) assuming some terrorist set a bomb off in downtown DC. Bomb Disposal officers were trawling through the car and bench. If they think we're working on a new type of bomb…"

Scarcely a minute later two policemen walked past the entrance of the alley. John moved closer to Jen almost touching face to face. Looking at her lips he lowered his voice further, "If they think that we're responsible, they'll shut us down quicker than you can change your lipstick."

◆◆◆

University Carpark, Washington DC

Michael O'Brien was a dangerous looking person with a street scarred face. Twenty years on the police force and more in the DHS had hardened him to the extremes of human nature. His typically cranky demeanor hadn't changed for the better this morning since receiving the report of an explosion near the University … in Downtown DC no less. The last few years had been tough on him since his wife was killed in the London bombings. He'd made a lucky escape, but his wife sitting not two feet from him hadn't been so fortunate. Survivor's guilt trailed him like a shadow. Changing jobs to the DHS hadn't helped. So he spent many an evening at the local pub trying to forget that damned holiday to the U.K.

"What do you mean there is no explosive residue?" O'Brien queried the forensic investigator as the two walked around what was left of the BMW as other investigators took samples and pictures.

"We found no trace," reiterated the investigator shaking his head. "What else is strange is that there's part of a bench at the flash point, right in the center of the wreckage."

The investigator then pulled out a sample bag with a green apple in it. "You're going to like this …" the investigator said with a smile, "this was sitting on top. It's without any blast marks on it, so must've been placed there after the explosive was detonated."

O'Brien stared at the apple then the wreckage. "Who would put a desk in the middle of an exploded car?" the agent said shaking his head in disbelief. In all his time on the job, he had never come across such bizarre behavior.

"It's a bench... Not a desk," interrupted another investigator. "It's like something that's used in a lab."

"And the apple?" O'Brien queried.

"It's a green Crispin, you can buy that locally here at any greengrocer. We have dusted it for prints and DNA."

The agent walked around the remnants of the car once more trying to piece together some motive but shook his head without an answer.

He then caught the attention of the officer talking to a very round animated man. O'Brien had been on the job many years. He could tell the civilian was an intellectual and given the university's close proximity, this guy was probably a scientist or lecturer.

The Officer walked over to O'Brien eyeing his DHS credentials hanging loosely out of his suit pocket. "That is Dr. La Perouse. All this wreckage is his car, or what's left of it."

"Dr. La Perouse? Medical?" O'Brien said.

"No, scientific. He works at the University down the road. He's currently under contract with the DOD on weapons research."

"Great, just what we need, more weapons!"

The two officials walked back to the scientist. "Doctor La Perouse, my name is Agent O'Brien. I'm from the DHS..."

"Yes, yes!" he broke in impatiently. "What are you doing about my car! I just bought it last week and now look at it. What am I going to tell my insurance? You need to write a report for the insurance company..." he said visibly working up to a tirade.

"Doctor," O'Brien cut-in with a loud bark. "I'm not here to write reports for insurance companies so you can get your little toy back." The doctor stood with his mouth agape.

O'Brien had at this stage, only one possibility that seemed unlikely, '*Was the doctor stupid enough to blow up his own car given his secret weapons research?*'

"Can you think who would want to kill you?"

"No... No," he said. A person clearly came to his mind.

"Doctor, need I remind you of the seriousness of the situation. We have a possible terrorist threat. Someone with the means and the motivation to use it."

Two smartly dressed suits walked up to the doctor. "Are you alright Dr. La Perouse?"

"And you are?" O'Brien said as he turned towards the newcomers.

"My name is Thurston Hughes. I am the Administrator for the University, and this is my assistant Miss Jenkins."

"Doctor, I would rather you didn't say anything till our lawyers get here," Thurston said to La Perouse.

La Perouse looked angry. "There is someone who has been stealing my ideas..."

"Doctor there is no evidence of that..." Thurston retorted.

"Dr. Stevenson," was all the Frenchman said.

O'Brien took the cue and called his Admin Support Staff to do a background check of this Doctor Stevenson. Returning to the Administrator, he said in a gruff voice that brooked no argument, "Administrator, I would like to see this... Dr. Stevenson."

"Fine," Thurston replied reluctantly.

♦♦♦

Lt Colonel Dan Prior picked up the phone and listened for a few minutes before calling out to his adjutant. A bright looking young lieutenant entered smartly, saluted and stood at the ready for orders. Dan saluted and spoke up, "One salute in the morning is sufficient. Otherwise, we won't get any work done at all.

"Book me on the next transport to Andrews. Then get me what you can on a civilian... a Dr. La Perouse and his colleague Dr. Stevenson. I believe La Perouse has some small business DOD contracts with us based in Washington DC."

Dan then sat down and flicked through pages and pages of the latest sonic devices. Could this doctor have developed a new sonic weapon? The call from the Director of Air Force Research and Technologies had been disturbing. Dan had specialized in weapons research after bouncing from one scientific program to another. The unique nature of his job ensured he was quickly promoted through the ranks.

He was surprised that the pompous Dr. La Perouse had made what appeared to be some breakthrough. He recalled contracting the rotund scientist with serious reservations. Although now the plot thickened as he accused a colleague of stealing his ideas. Is this colleague a danger to the U.S.? The whole business was starting to leave a very bitter taste in his mouth.

Within the hour, Dan was in the air flying towards Andrews Air Force Base near Washington D.C. and this latest incident.

◆◆◆

John and Jen made their way back to their lab, avoiding any further police or government officials. The lab was a mess. Equipment was strewn all over the place with puddles of water from the fire sprinkler system.

There is no way in hell the university will let me stay now, John sighed.

After a few moments surveying the room John spotted the laptop and backup data storage units. Directing Jen to pick them up while he moved to retrieve the targeting sensor and field generator. Glancing out the window, John saw the University Administrator and his young assistant trailed by two enforcement officers walking across the grounds towards his building.

"Time to go," John said.

They rushed out of the room and down the southern stairwell, their arms heavily laden with singed equipment. They made their way quickly through to the back of the building and outside where a white station wagon stood. He thanked his lucky stars he had brought the extra heavy duty conduits in that morning. The cable's bulk had forced him to park in the small parking lot close to his lab's rear exit. He stowed the equipment on the back seat while Jen jumped into the front passenger side. Quickly driving to the exit boom gates of the university, John saw in the distance the gray uniform of the pudgy guard manning the guard box.

Jen started to bite her bottom lip with nervous tension as they pulled up to the boom gate.

"Hello Dr. Stevenson, hold up a minute."

"Yes?"

The guardhouse phone then started to ring. John's foot hovered over the accelerator.

"We have a problem," the guard said, "I had to turn back the delivery truck holding equipment you ordered."

"What do you mean?" John gripped the steering wheel tightly, his hands turned white under the pressure, "Why?"

"Did you hear about the bomb in the main parking lot? The Administrator ordered that no deliveries are to be accepted today until the police have finished their investigations. I suggest you contact your supplier to get the order redelivered in a few days after all this mess has been sorted."

"Oh! Of course," John said letting his breath out slowly while shifting his foot.

The guard then turned and pushed the gate open button as he answered the phone again.

John immediately accelerated out of the grounds into the traffic almost hitting a passing car.

"What are we going to do? They are going to know it's us." Jen said. "I can't afford to lose my work visa. I'll never be able to work here again."

"I think we have a slightly bigger problem than your work visa, like getting charged with terrorism."

"And you think that running way will help?" Jen snapped.

"No, not in the long run. But I need a bit of time to figure out what our next move is."

"What do you mean? Going to the police is the next move!" Jen countered.

"No, we can't," John said while turning the wheel. "The research we have done is not yet legally protected. We could lose everything."

"But isn't this sponsored by the Physics department? Isn't it University protected?"

"This is not a university-sanctioned project. I lease the lab and their equipment. The work here is my project, not the Uni's."

Jen stared at him for a long time before replying. "Fine, but this is our project!"

Relieved, John made a mental note to increase her share of the royalties, if they ever happen to get any, she was taking on much more risk than she had anticipated, it was only right.

◆◆◆

John drove his car south towards the outskirts of Arlington city and pulled into a diner. Covering the computers and equipment, they got out of the car and made their way to the tables inside. The place had a deserted look about it. The only patrons, a few trucker types that sat up at the counter eating an assortment of greasy foods while the television blared in the background announcing the latest update to the terrorist bomb attack in Downtown DC. The distracted waitress walked over to their table and announced with her eyes glued to the screen.

"Specials for today are Big Don's Meat Burger and Spicy Tofu bratwurst for the veggies," she said with a pleasant voice automatically.

"Veggies?" Jen looked towards John with a frown.

"For vegetarians," John said.

"I'm certainly not a veggie. I'll have the Big Don's Meat."

The waitress turned and regarded them properly for the first time. Jen, realizing what she had said blushed and amended her order, "The Meat Burger please."

John stifled a grin. "I'll have the Don's Meat Burger too," then to Jen, "I didn't realize you are such a connoisseur of our brawn burgers," John said with a deadpan face. Then to see her blush even more was priceless.

"So smarty pants... What now?" Jen said.

John thought for a minute before responding, "I think a buddy of mine will help us. He has a place in Alexandria, we should be able to hold up there for a bit."

"How do you know him?"

"We served together in the Army Reserves."

At that point, John pulled out his notebook and started to scribble a list of items. Jen looked at the list and added suggestions of her own. The two quickly wrote down ten pages in his small notebook, pausing just as the waitress arrived with their order.

"Someone order a hunk?" she said grinning as she placed Jen's order on the table laughing. Jen just looked at her rolling her eyes with an *'everyone's a smartass'* look.

While the two tucked into their meal, they interspersed it with brainstorming items for another lab. A picture of an enraged La Perouse yelling at a policeman appeared on television. The story shifted to an image of John and Jen with the caption, 'Wanted for questioning'. Jens' eyes widened as she nearly choked on her food.

"Better be quick," John said as he started to wolf down what was left on his plate. Fortunately, nobody took the slightest notice of them.

"I'll meet you at the car." He then took off towards the counter to hand over some money.

"Thanks, Keep the change." John turned about face and headed for the door.

The waitress took her eyes off the TV mentally calculating the tip realizing it was a lot more than normal. She took another look at John exiting out the door then quickly turned her head back to the TV in recognition. Without pausing, she reached under the counter for the phone. Ordinarily, she couldn't care less about the everyday rough nuts that ate at the diner. But they were saying terrorists and bombs on the TV, which scared the hell out of her, so she dialed.

◆◆◆

John quickly got into the car and drove out of the car park and headed North towards Ronald Reagan Airport.

"I think she recognized us," he said.

"Damn!"

John tapped the hands-free phone on the dash calling his mate Elvis.

"John is that you?"

"Yes. Hey, buddy, I need to use your pad for a few days is that cool?"

"Yeah, no problem. Hot date huh."

"Something like that" John replied trying to avoid talking about the explosion.

"Just don't leave any handcuffs around. I had no end of problems explaining that one to Veronica."

Both John and Jen chuckled, for entirely different reasons.

"Who's that with you? You know, you're on speaker."

"Elvis, this is Jen."

"Jen the Hottie?"

John went beet red while Jen just giggled again.

"Hi Elvis," Jen said, then realized what Elvis would think? John just asked to use his pad.

"Have a GOOD time. I have to go... See you later." Then hung up.

Jen looked at John appraisingly "Handcuffs... really!" she said with a smirk.

Twenty-five minutes later they pulled into Elvis's apartment visitor parking.

♦♦♦

The University Administrator and his assistant stepped inside the door then stood aside letting Agent O'Brien and the police officer enter Dr. Stevenson's lab.

"Oh my God," said Thurston as they surveyed the devastation. O'Brien just stood there and called in for more support.

"I want an all-points bulletin out on Dr. John Stevenson and Ms. Gale for suspected acts of terrorism. He may be dangerous so approach with extreme caution."

♦♦♦

Elvis's apartment was small but comfortable. Jen settled into the patchwork fabric couch while John checked the kitchen. "I'll just go out and get some food." The fridge was bare except for a solitary beer, and last week's lasagna. Elvis was never good at keeping house, even when he was hooked up with Veronica, who was a chef.

A few minutes later John walked into the local convenience store picking items from the shelves unaware the in-store CCTV cameras tracked his every move. Unbeknownst to him, the new camera system was the latest in neighborhood security. It linked all Supreme Security customers to the local police station for a security check and affordability rating. Although the system had been expensive for the shop owner, the insurance premiums had been worse this year. After three robberies in a row, the premiums would be astronomical next year.

The owner had gone all out and purchased the diamond package. The would-be robber's image was scanned then sent to the massive data collation center in downtown Washington where they passed it through facial recognition programs and debt credit ratings.

◆◆◆

A bell sounded in the police data collection center alerting of a *'Person of Interest'* match. The officer pushed his chair to the console to investigate the hit.

'Terrorists suspect – Dr. Stevenson wanted for questioning regarding Acts of Terrorism Washington D.C.' floated across the screen.

He placed his donut down on the desk and dialed dispatch giving them the details of the grocer and Dr. Stevenson's last location, isle three. A red flag was automatically routed to Agent O'Brien's message drop-box detailing Doctor Stevenson's pending apprehension.

Opening up the red flag on his phone, an evil grin spread across O'Brien's face. Grabbing his badge and stuffing his pistol in his back holster, O'Brien pulled on his crinkled suit jacket and headed for the Alexandria police station.

Chapter Six

The U.S. Department of Homeland Security, Washington Office

John sat opposite Agent O'Brien in a pristine police interrogation room.

"I'll have you in prison by the day's end. They'll even throw away the key, you treasonous terrorist prick." The agent said in his gruff hardened manner.

"That's right. We're charging you with terrorism against the United States. Doctor La Perouse was working for the DOD so he can be considered an agent of the United States."

John just smiled a smile that he did not feel, as he stared back.

O'Brien deliberately paused for effect.

"We retrieved your workbench in the mess of what's left of Dr. La Perouse's car."

O'Brien barely staved off a coughing fit as he took another draw from his cigarette. "Who were you going to sell it to? The Chinese?"

John frowned while Agent O'Brien stubbed the last of his butt against the table top, only to take another cigarette from his pack. Lighting it up he then placed the pack and English lighter on the table. Glancing at the Union Jack on the handle, his face grimaced for just a second before his eyes narrowed, zeroing in on John once again.

"We know it was your bench ... the one in the car. The University Administrator has confirmed it. The bench number correlates with the one assign to you in your lab. Oh, wait, your bench has a missing tabletop, from you know... *the destroyed lab.*"

John merely stared silently at O'Brien's bloodshot eyes and yellow stained teeth as the agent smiled menacingly, curling his upper lip. "You've outdone yourself, two wrecks in one day. Well...?"

John made no response, willing his jaw muscles tight as a spring to show a deadpan face. Beads of sweat started to form on his temples.

"Tell me how you got it there, you know, the bench in the car so quickly?" O'Brien's face was genuinely curious.

John's face gave nothing away. "I respectfully request an attorney."

"Why the hell would you put a bench inside a car? What moronic scheme are you pulling?" O'Brien queried.

The door burst open interrupting the two, as a tall man in a dark blue pressed U.S. Air Force uniform marched into the room. The officer inspected the disheveled O'Brien with a cigarette in hand and equally unpleasant breath, and said, with authority born from years of command, "I'll be taking it from here."

O'Brien looked at the clean cut hair and then the silver chevrons on his shoulders. "Colonel this is my suspect. The military will have to wait in line."

Lt Colonel Dan Prior just looked at the man and his yellow stained teeth. "Agent O'Brien. I'm from the AFSR- Air Force Scientific Research, which is a part of the joint committee on terrorism response. A word if you will." Dan turned and left without waiting for an answer.

John just watched the spectacle as the DHS Agent left the room angrily.

Through the door, John heard O'Brien's angry muffled retort *"No bleedin way."*

Ten minutes later the Lt Colonel entered the room again and said "Stand. You're coming with me."

John had a terrible sinking feeling that being interrogated by O'Brien may have been better.

♦♦♦

Space Command, Peterson Air Force Base

John inspected the well-appointed conference room as Dan sat down. He was immediately drawn to the man's blue air force jacket where there was a multitude of colored ribbons and a space ship looking emblem below. He watched Dan carefully place pictures of the University and its parking lot on the table.

John was expecting a windowless room with hard metal chairs designed to make the occupant uncomfortable, like the medical examination room for 'Nurse Ratched', but not this. Not these plush surroundings. He had seen newspaper articles where officials claimed a terrorist act then suddenly the victim is never seen or heard from again. John's mind raced forward, and he wondered if there was even going to be a trial in his case?

"You did it, didn't you?" Was all Dan said, crashing through John's reverie.

"Did what?"

"You made the sonic weapon," he replied. "We know it was you and your assistant Miss Jennifer Gale."

John shuffled in his chair. *Sonic weapon, what sonic weapon?*

"The good Dr. La Perouse says you stole his design. Is that true?"

John snorted at the 'good' and 'La Perouse' oxymoron but said nothing still not knowing exactly where this was going. John then realized La Perouse must've been working on some sonic weapon. *Did the Colonel drag him here about a security breach?*

"Doctor La Perouse has made more than one complaint ... to Mister Thurston Hughes, the University Administrator. The Administrator has confirmed that deafening noises have been heard coming from your lab." John recalled been summoned to Thurston's office over the noise levels. They had quietly struck a deal over a case of nice 25 years old Scotch whiskey. John would keep the noise down, while Thurston would turn a blind eye. Once again John smiled, the sample whiskey had been excellent.

Dan looked at John for a full ten seconds before continuing. "Doctor La Perouse has been working on this project for over three years, and he says he's on the verge of a breakthrough. Did you steal his research?"

"Asking the same question will not alter the answer. La Perouse is nothing but a self-serving bore, who couldn't find an idea if it hit him in the face."

"What about if it blew up his car?" John's eyes darted to Dan's unwavering gaze. Shrugging his shoulders, John wasn't surprised and couldn't help give a smirk. Dan eyed him carefully then smiled. John's own smile dropped when he realized the Colonel had confirmed his own suspicions.

"I don't know what's gone on between you and Doctor La Perouse, for you to leave a calling card in the blown out shell of his car. Frankly, I don't care. What I do care about is defending this country with the best weaponry I can lay my hands on.

"John, I know you are a patriot. You were a Captain in the US Army then the US Army Reserves. Despite your links to the *Doomsday Preppers*. I know you're loyal to the US."

"What... what do you mean? Doomsday...?" John said as he straightened up.

"Your association with Mr. Randy 'Elvis' Watts. You served with him didn't you?"

"Yes...?"

"Well then..." John just phased out for a minute, *Elvis what are you into.*

"... Mister Watts is a senior member of the Preppers. They have built up enough firepower that they have become an organization of interest to the government. They've been under surveillance..."

Damn Elvis, John thought, not even listening to the rest of the Colonel's statement.

The Colonel looked at John quizzically. "Let's get right to it John. We want that weapon, and we are prepared to drop the terrorism charges if you hand it over."

"The sonic weapon?" John replied thinking quickly. "You can't do that... you don't have any real evidence that it was me, let alone Jen."

"Come now John... We have enough to put you away for the next century. The good doctor's statements, your military background, and links to a disreputable paramilitary group. But most importantly an apple!" The Colonel said with a huge grin.

"An apple?"

"An apple from a burnt out wreck of a car with yours and Miss Gales fingerprints on it."

John stared at the Colonel for a moment. "Alright... I'll co-operate, but I want some concessions."

"Like?" the Colonel replied.

"I know the DHS will just patent it so when they get their grubby hands on it, I want the royalties. You get one of your small business associate enterprises to build the weapon, we get 40% of the total royalties."

"20% and you provide a week's worth of training in its use," the Colonel replied.

"I'll not release the product till all the bugs are ironed out!" John said, *which could take a hell of a long time. Enough time that he was sure that he could think of something. Hopefully, before even more shit hit the fan.*

The Colonel agreed and smiled, remembering the state of the car and John's lab from the on scene pictures.

Two hours later after signing hastily prepared contracts, John was escorted to a taxi with his mind floating in disbelief. He had just negotiated to provide a weapon that he had no idea about, let alone how to build! *Geez, I am in deep shit!*

Making his way up the stairs to Elvis's apartment, he was confronted with Jen, hands on hips giving a Xenia Warrior Princess look.

"Where have you been, it's been hours?" There was a scolding tone to her voice, but it was laced with concern in the corners of her eyes.

"Signing my life away," was John's only response.

"Where is the food?"

John fell onto the couch too tired to respond.

John and Jen were bone tired after spending days tidying up the devastated lab before the university re-modelers moved in to fix the benches. There had been numerous interruptions from Dr. La Perouse, which hadn't been pleasant but more importantly one from the University's Administrator, Mr. Hughes. He was rightfully annoyed that his lab was a total wreck. Only when offered promises to restore the lab to its original condition and provide the cost of a new coffee machine for the staff room was he placated. Thurston was still unconvinced until John pulled out the clincher, a contract with the US Airforce. John couldn't help but admire Thurston for his savvy bargaining.

John chortled when he mentioned with a wink the destruction of a motor vehicle on campus, and that John should watch out for any student carrying out dangerous experiments.

The next day John set about ordering replacement lab equipment and one brand new top of the line coffee machine. He had decided to treat the faculty given Thurston's lenient attitude to the whole matter. He realized it could have been far worse.

Clearing a space on the one remaining bench, John pulled out his laptop.

"So how did we happen to target La Perouse's car? Let's go over the calculations once again," John said to Jen's groans.

Two hours later after rechecking all the calculations. Jen stood waving her arm and smiling. She flagged John to what she found. I think it has to do with the power control mechanism. The source power was too variable. Once it started, it had a cascade effect on the rest of the calculations. I think we need finer control here and here," she pointed to the computer model.

John stepped back from the computer screen contemplating the changes Jen was suggesting.

"Well for that sort of control we are going to need some serious power flow controller and conduits. Yes, the controller will even out the power oscillations to target it accurately. Nice work, Miss Gale," she smiled in response to John's playful formality.

John added those items to the ever growing shopping list.

Chapter Seven

Randy 'Elvis' Watts was sitting on his couch in nothing but his underwear cleaning his .22 caliber assault rifle. He was hopeful to use it this weekend at Sugarloaf Mountain with his friends in the Doomsday Prepper Group called, 'The Extinction Survivalists'. His now ex-girlfriend had introduced him to the rowdy crowd. He enjoyed the survival challenge offered by the Preppers weekend warrior training after his time in the Army Reserve. It made him feel like he was at least utilizing the skills he had acquired in the Reserves 'Crunch' training. It didn't hurt that after the sessions, they would all congregate at the Hog's Breath on the outskirts of town for some serious liquor debriefing.

All of a sudden the front door to his apartment exploded splintering inwards as a dozen masked troopers with 'SWAT' emblazoned on their Kevlar jackets charged into the room shouting. Elvis's mouth gaped open as he sat frozen to the couch. Their disciplined demeanor was incredibly effective as they brandished wicked looking assault rifles and sub machine guns. The first two officers yelled out "Gun! Gun!" in unison.

"Put the weapon down! On your knees face down! Now!" The officers yelled.

Despite his training, all Elvis could do was sit watching the procession dumbfounded. Then as if struck, he realized his predicament and didn't need to be told twice to get on the floor. The smaller officer held Elvis down with a swift knee to the back. She tied his hands with a cable tie as another kicked Elvis's gun out of reach while targeting Elvis with his own.

Amidst all the drama, the Agent O'Brien walked into the apartment brandishing a glock pistol unchallenged. He was quietly pleased with himself that he had managed to bludgeon his way onto the first response SWAT team for this operation. If he couldn't have Dr. Stevenson, then he would have to settle for the next best thing. *Mr. Elvis Bloody Watts.*

"Planning a little war are we Mr. Watts?" O'Brien said with barely concealed contempt.

◆◆◆

It had been several days of hard work in the lab once the all the remodeling had finished. Jen was holding up well after all the stresses of the previous week, so John put her to work refining the power control for the targeting while he worked on making the fields bigger. John and Jen rebuilt their prototype transporter with the improved power control systems.

"I think we are getting close to testing again," John declared.

"So shall we try for La Perouse's new car?" said Jen laughing.

The rotund La Perouse had cajoled the insurance company into giving him a replacement car, while they sorted through the meaning of, 'An act of God' in relation to self-exploding vehicles. True to his word, O'Brien refused to write any report for the insurance.

John smiled back with a mischievous grin.

"As much as it would give me the greatest of pleasures, I don't think our DHS friend will see it the same way. Let's find a large open space to test this," John said.

He then picked up his mobile and dialed his buddy Elvis to see if he was up for a trip to the desert. John frowned putting the phone down after he'd had no response. It wasn't like Elvis to ignore him. He had called a dozen times over the past week with no response. John was starting to get worried given all the government agencies floating around.

"OK. Are you ready for a trip to Texas? I was thinking of the Trans-Pecos in the Chihuahua Desert. It's quite beautiful but more importantly sparsely populated."

"Oh, goody. I haven't seen much of the states yet," Jen replied.

The following day John hired a truck to carry all the equipment with enough room in the front cab to comfortably seat three people. It was going to be a long 2 to 3-day trip just to get there. They spent the rest of the day loading the truck with the equipment and a few small personal items.

Early the next morning the two in the hire truck headed out of the University grounds and took to the streets, turning southeastward they made their way through central Washington towards Arlington and then southbound to Alexandria.

"I just want to pop in to see Elvis."

"No problem," replied Jen, "you still haven't heard from him?"

"No," John replied, worried.

They drove in silence through the streets each in their own thoughts till they pulled up outside Elvis's apartment. Climbing the two levels to his front door, John cried out, "What the...?"

Across the remnants of his friend's front door was yellow, '*Do Not Cross*' tape. The jagged zigzag pattern of tape screamed out 'crime scene'. What was left of the door lay splintered in pieces on the floor begging any crook to come in. John ran to the tape and yanked it away in one swift motion, "Elvis?"

The two strode into the lounge room where they found the place a shamble. Overturned chairs and books lay strewn all over the floor, while cupboards and drawers hung open in a haphazard way with clothes scattered all around. An old photo album lay open on the kitchen bench with some blank spaces where pictures had been removed. John turned some pages only to set his focus on a snap of him and Elvis in Army fatigues attempting to piece together a tent without a clue. His brief smile was replaced by a determined grimace.

John started rifling through his wallet for the card the Air Force Colonel had given him.

"Dr. Stevenson, what can I do for you?"

"Colonel, I agreed to help you, and now I find my friend's missing, no doubt taken for interrogation. This treatment won't get the sonic dauber wacky any faster," said John angrily.

"Dr. Stevenson... What are you talking about?" Dan replied in a controlled fashion.

"I'm talking about you taking my friend Elvis!" John countered.

"Despite what you might think of me Doctor, the Science and Technology arm of the U.S. Air Force doesn't have a habit of kidnapping US citizens."

"He's missing. His place has been destroyed. It's taped up with that official yellow boundary tape."

"You mean the ones used by the police or DHS?" Dan responded.

"DHS... Damn!" not those bastards again. Dan couldn't fail to hear the anxious tone in John's voice.

"I'll see what I can do. No promises."

"Thank you, Colonel."

As John hung up, guilt and trepidation hung over him. Not only did he feel sorry for his friend, but the deception against the Colonel with this imaginary sonic weapon was playing on his mind.

Turning to Jen, who stood in the kitchen looking through the photo album and said, "Can you call a local handyman to get this fixed," as he pointed to the broken door. "We can't leave it like this. I need to make a few more calls to my favorite DHS agent."

Twenty minutes later Jen had a carpenter and a new front door delivery organized for the afternoon. Meanwhile, John had little luck tracking down Agent O'Brien let alone his friend Elvis. All of a sudden his mobile rang. "Colonel...?" answered John.

"Doctor, the DHS anti-terrorism group, has your friend in lockup while they investigate the car bombing."

"But you and I both know it's no terrorist act. Right!"

"It will take a while to convince them of that, because of his links to *'The Extinction Survivalists'*."

"What... You're kidding me! The yahoos he goes camping with each month?"

"Well, they're a little more than that. They're classified as a paramilitary group."

John was struck speechless for a minute.

"Well, I need him out because he's my consultant engineer," John said making it up. He knew Elvis had an engineering background.

"I see..." was all Dan said.

"We are currently on our way to Texas to test the equipment, and we need him," John said as an enticer.

"What sort of tests? Maybe I should come along," said Dan.

"No. It's not ready yet." John countered quickly as his guilt deepened with the deception. He couldn't allow his buddy to be treated like a terrorist because of his experiments.

After an awkward silence, Dan said, "Very well. Where in Texas?"

"El Paso. We are heading to the desert."

"Just don't blow up anything that could be difficult to explain. I'll send your engineering support as soon as he's released."

"Thank you, Colonel, I appreciate it," John said as he hung up the phone.

Dan couldn't shake the feeling that something wasn't right. He knew that there was a military base just outside of El Paso and, if needs be, he could call on them to intervene

♦♦♦

John and Jen hung around Elvis's apartment until the new door was replaced then headed West, Far West to El Paso, Texas.

Elvis was surprised to be released from lock-up by an Air Force Colonel. He was happy to see the back of the grumpy old DHS agent O'Brien. He even smiled at O'Brien's profanities when he was forced to release him. Although, he was annoyed with John for embroiling him in some fantasy terrorist plot he was smart enough to keep his mouth shut at the sketchy story that he consulted for John on his experiments. His friend was always a little secretive regarding his work, so to find out that he was working on weapons, made him reevaluate his long-time friend. He had thought John was a relative pacifist. Even after his stint in the army reserves. He always knew John had a strong sense of patriotism, but something more than that, the ability to sacrifice anything for a specific goal was a useful skill in the army.

Despite all the danger and the real threats, he had gone through, Elvis got a small kick out of mixing with true professionals. The S.W.A.T. team had the cool kit. The up close and personal experience was an eye-opener on their tactics and, in a strange way, Elvis had enjoyed every minute of it. Especially the young SWAT woman who kneed him in the back.

♦♦♦

O'Brien was furious. Twice now the Air Force had swooped in and taken his collars. He had thought the kindergarten soldier boy, 'Elvis', was in the bag with his links to Dr. Stevenson. He even had a of the two with army weaponry in a photo. Then there were his regular training sessions with the paramilitary group '*The Extinction Survivalists*'.

"Elvis" was nothing but 'an offense' on two legs, in O'Brien's eyes. Even his name was offensive. The tinker toy soldier offended the name of his one and only true music icon. He scowled to himself. He wouldn't be able to listen to his favorite Elvis songs without thinking of the smarmy little sod.

O'Brien could only sit and watch the young Air Force Colonel walk the prisoner out of his grasp. Grinding his teeth, he turned back to his computer console, cigarette in hand and attempted to write a report explaining to his bosses the wasted resources used to capture and detain his latest suspect.

◆ ◆ ◆

When Elvis finally returned home, he found himself in front of a new door. There was a note taped to the eyehole with his name on it.

"Elvis, Pal, Buddy, Mate, ..." The letter started. *"Mate!"* he thought. *He's obviously been hanging around that Aussie girl too much. Maybe Aussies had a different definition of a 'Mate'.*

Elvis read on only to discover the two had left DC on a road trip to Texas, of all places. John was urging him to come out to El Paso. He understood the need to keep this charade up, but he also had a few strong words he wanted to tell John in return.

Chapter Eight

John and Jen pulled into a small Motel parking lot on the outskirts of El Paso. The heat washed over the expanse of hot asphalt warping the horizon in a heat haze. The motel air-conditioning would be a relief from the boiling cabin of the truck. John would be having words with the hire company since the air-con broke down at the Texas state border. The two pushed through the purple painted door, to reception and a quaint little office. Fake cedar paneling and tacky white plastic clocks adorned the back wall. The clocks were set to the differing time zones across the world as if it suggested something of the hotel's clientele. John smiled at the young dark-haired Hispanic receptionist and booked two rooms with extra towels.

Later that afternoon when the heat had lost its sting, John ducked out to the local real estate agent. He had spotted a property on the net and was intent on seeing if it suited his purposes.

Pointing to the ad in the window, 'New Listing of the "TEXAS Ranch" big enough to get lost on your own property'

"Is that true?" John asked the real estate agent. The picture certainly seems to suggest it. A desert landscape where the property straddled a secluded dead-end valley with surrounding countryside. It was a huge 6500 acres. There were no neighbors in sight. There would be no stray BMWs here. Nestled in the center between a couple of squat mounds was a small farm cottage made of roughly hewn stone and corrugated iron. Rust colored dirt-clotted over the walls hiding its profile. A large work shed with late last century metalworking tools and machinery were scattered gathering rust. The land was perfect. The only sticking point was the price tag. Just on 2.5 million.

In the same desert landscape backing onto the Texas Ranch was a smaller land parcel split off from the original ranch and for sale for a fraction of the larger block.

John had never been too caught up with money. He saw it as a tool to be used to create choices. Jen was surprised when John returned with the receipt for a deposit on the purchase of the smaller block from the realtor. He arranged to meet him the following morning to finalize the sale.

Martinez Mendez, the only real-estate agent this side of the border, couldn't believe his luck. That was the quickest sale he had ever made. Although there was a mountain of paperwork he had to do before tomorrow, he knew the quick sale of the gatehouse block lead to the prospect of selling the "Texas Ranch". He would celebrate tonight.

John and Jen kicked at the small dirt clods while standing in front of the rundown newly purchased boarded-up gatehouse cottage.

"You have to be kidding! I'm not spending the night in that. Who knows how many redback spiders are around!" Jen said indignantly.

"We don't have redbacks in the States; however, we do have lots of scorpions," John replied.

Jen just looked back with a withering look. "There's no way in hell."

A loud mechanical roar cut through the slight desert wind. Dust billowed and split along the access road as a sleek black sports Ducati 750cc motorbike pulled in and stopped next to the two, bringing with it a small cloud. The short athletic rider dismounted and took his helmet off revealing a grim-faced balding man. Several faded tattoos adorned his arms as he took off his leather jacket and gloves revealing a sweaty sleeveless camo tank top. Despite the heat, Elvis wasn't going to ride his bike without leather protection.

"Elvis!" John called out.

"Geez John, I thought they were going to put me in front of a firing squad!"

"Yeah, sorry. I hadn't expected that."

"I knew you were a scientist, but I thought you were a pacifist. I didn't know you went for developing weapons."

"What!! What weapons?" Jen exclaimed as she eyed John.

Elvis turned and focused on Jen. She was his height with mousy brown hair. Some dark sunglasses hid her small delicate features. The loose fitting top couldn't conceal her trim body with a faded suntan. The woman standing there was not the woman that John had described when he said, scientist.

"You must be Jen, the Aussie."

"You must be the infamous Elvis," Jen replied. Then she said to John. "What weapons?"

John looked decidedly uncomfortable and a little sheepish. He then recounted the story of his meeting with the Air Force Colonel and subsequent deal to produce a sonic weapon for their release.

By the end of it, both Jen and Elvis were so incredulous they both started giggling then wound up splitting their sides laughing.

"So we have to build this sonic thingy we have no idea how to make!" Jen said.

John just nodded.

"Geez, John! It's a wonder why I like hanging out with you. Not a dull moment!" Elvis remarked which started another fit of laughter.

"So what's the real experiment if it's not the sonic weapons," Elvis said with a snicker.

John looked at Jen and took a breath and launched into a rehearsed speech. He had decided to include Elvis in the inner circle of patent holders, especially after what he had just been put through.

"So this thing-a-me does, what?"

Jen cut in, "It's like *Star Trek* and beam-me-up, Scotty."

Elvis looked back and forth between the two, "Damn, are you kidding me... You've developed a transporter?"

"Yes."

"I want you to be part of this. I need someone with engineering skills to translate my rough-edged scientific based designs into something that works solidly. There is no upfront money; there is no guarantee that it will make any money at all. Are you in?"

"Are you serious? You're offering me a share in this discovery?" Elvis knew that John was generous but given this device, any share even a small share, would turn into millions. "Guess?"

John smiled at his long-time friend, then proceeded to say, "I need you to first work on stabilizing the power flow regulation..."

All John could see was Elvis's grin, from ear to ear.

The following morning the three made their way from the hotel to gather in the far corner of the local diner for breakfast. The brainstorming session was fast becoming a regular feature of their day. The three of them discussed improvements and applications that the transporter could be put to. The relaxed, casual atmosphere made the days turn into a blur. The three were almost in a dream state enjoying each other's company and the challenges that the project brought up...

"The more I think about all the possibilities for this technology, the more scared I get." The others turned to stare at John, waiting for him to elaborate. "What if someone was to use this for evil purposes... Say transport someone into the sun. Or worse bring the sun here to Earth, it would be devastating, an immediate extinction event. There are so many ways that this can be used to cause cataclysmic destruction. Nuclear weapons are children's toys compared to this." Elvis and Jen became reticent. Jen bit her bottom lip while Elvis just stared at John unblinking.

"Maybe we shouldn't develop this technology?" Jen said out loud.

John knew this was decision time. He couldn't take his eyes off Jen and her seemingly innocent question.

Behind Jen the television on the wall switch to its favorite news storyline of late, aliens.

"We need to develop this technology. Even if we put strict controls on its deployment and implementation. However, we can't let this technology get into the wrong hands, ... but we definitely have to develop the technology."

"I don't want it to be another Oppenheimer's atom bomb," declared Jen.

The three sat there staring at each other.

John whispered, "A lot of good came out of Oppenheimer's experiments. Can we afford not to develop this technology? We can't patent this technology or even have records of how it works once it's refined if we go ahead."

Elvis then said, "I think you're kidding yourself if you think that the secret won't get out."

"I don't believe we have a choice. If we don't, someone else will, and I'd rather set up the best controls we can from the beginning. There will be no direct royalties whatsoever from this project."

Elvis blew out the breath that he was holding then spoke, "So, you're saying if we don't develop this technology. Obviously, we won't get any money, and if we do develop the technology we still won't get any money cause it's too dangerous to patent it.

"Well hell John, if we had the first transporter we could make millions just doing stuff with it... like contracting to dispose of nuclear waste from power stations. We could transport it into the sun."

"Or we could clean out all the gold from Fort Knox," Jen said giggling, while Elvis smiled and John frowned.

This was crunch time; will they still stay with the project given that there were no direct, immediate monetary returns in sight?

"This technology is too powerful to leave under-utilized. I do think we can use this technology as a stepping stone to other things." It was John's final bid to convince Jen and Elvis.

Jen stared directly into John's eyes and delivered her ultimatum, "I want your promise that we will destroy it if we can't develop reasonable controls to keep the technology out of the wrong hands."

Phew, she's still onboard for now, John thought. "You have my promise we'll put as much protection in as we need," John said to reassure her. "Elvis?" John said staring at Elvis waiting for his answer.

Elvis nodded without hesitation.

Jen smiled briefly.

"So a teleporter auto-destruct?" Elvis blurted out. "Excellent, I get to play with explosives." John and Jen just looked at Elvis with concern.

Elvis, seeing what was written on their faces, laughed aloud turning the waitress' head to scold the three for disturbing the peace.

"Elvis can you also look into how technology can be safeguarded physically from being reverse engineered,"

John turned to Jen, "Jen, can you look into ways to use the teleporter to get itself out of trouble. For example, if there is tampering, the machine activates and teleports itself into the sun or back to base."

Jen didn't look wholly convinced that developing the technology was the right thing to do. However, she nodded ever so slightly.

The discussion then moved off the security issues and onto setting up the gatehouse property to transform it into a research base. John had spotted labs that were built inside cargo container so as to make them transportable.

"I found a company that converts containers into reinforced labs. I already rented a couple of labs and a housing unit. Once the converted cargo containers arrive, we can dedicate the different experiments in each container."

"Containers? Why transport containers?" Asked Jen.

"They're steel and reinforced. They'll protect us from explosions."

Both Jen and Elvis stared at John. "You're serious are you?" Elvis said.

"I think he is," said Jen. "Did you see the car?" she directed at Elvis.

"I thought that those pics were some interrogation tactic. That was real?"

Neither Jen nor John said a word while they thought about it. Both knew the metal was not going to stop a materialization, the BMW was metal.

"Shit John. You don't do half measures do you?" Elvis said with a tinge of unease.

"Anyway, they are easy to transport if we have to move in a hurry. Besides, we won't always be in the cottage block here."

Four days later they were directing the delivery trucks, which arrived with their containers.

John thought they were fantastic.

A week later the group had all the equipment set up in each of the containers and one for a temporary living unit. Jen still wasn't convinced to stay out near scorpions. She never stayed overnight in the makeshift accommodations. She stated one day that three stars were her absolute minimum. The only thing missing were the utilities and transport of the quantum computer. It was John's biggest concern as it was a delicate piece of equipment that required fragile handling and constant temperature control.

Testing at the makeshift research base started in earnest. Loud cracks could be heard echoing up and down the countryside. Fortunately, no one but old man Sykes was there to hear it. Even then, the man's hearing aid was usually turned off as he didn't want to waste the battery. By the end of the week, they were able to teleport items all over the small block. There had been two tests with explosive results. Elvis thanked John's foresight for including the reinforced cargo container to protect the three. Although each test took several hours to set up, they were making slow but steady progress.

On the twelfth day, an old man approached the makeshift camp with a dog barking in a cage held at arms-length. The man was unshaven with a mean look and wore a permanent ingrain scowl. His clothes reflected his demeanor; ragged, harsh and crinkled. The man walked to the center of the camp and dumped the cage on the ground. The caged dog growled at the old man's cruel treatment.

In a rough voice, he said, "Please keep your pets on your property."

Jen, who was incensed cut in, "That's not our dog, you can take it back." Her voice ended in a crescendo.

"Well, this tag says it's yours." The old man looked down at the label and started reading, 'Urgent delivery to The Ranch Gatehouse'. That rusty bucket is the gate house," the man said pointing to the small dilapidated building.

Jen was about to rebut the man when John stepped up and took the animal.

Elvis jumped in, "Geez, John."

Jen added, "Nooo, you can't be serious! We're not ready for that!"

The scowling man just stood there with a raised eyebrow. What a strange bunch, he thought. The tension was palpable between the three over the rascal dog. The old man had very few vices left in life after his doctor had tried to blackball his smoking and drinking. He never listened, he usually ended up grimacing to himself when he left the surgery. One thing he did love was soap opera TV and late-night shows. The tension between the neighbors had stirred his interest. The three of them out here in the middle of nowhere with transport containers storing God knows what. That was unusual, to say the least. Like a child with candy, each new revelation thrilled the old man no end. His head turned, switching his attention from one to the other like a tennis match.

"We have to, eventually," was all John said.

Jen stormed off while Elvis just stared at John not knowing what to say.

John realized the old man was still there watching the whole drama unfold. So he thanked him and escorted him to the front gate.

The man reluctantly left, still curious as to what was really going on.

The following day, Jen refused to talk to John all through breakfast, because of their disagreed over the dog. He was, however, not deterred by her petty, childish silent treatment that was distasteful and juvenile.

When they returned to the research base, John gave the dog treats while petting it. Eventually, he placed it on the launch-pad commanding it to '*sit*'. The dog followed John's orders and received another biscuit for his obedience.

Jen and Elvis although sullen, reluctantly took their stations to prepare for the live subject test. All their previous tests to this point had been with inanimate objects and some small insects. Some objects had admittedly been quasi-alive, such as fruit. The results were still remarkable; the cellular structure remained unchanged. The transport or jump process seemed to create a bubble where everything within the sphere was taken from one place to another. Jen finally indicated that her calculations were all complete. Elvis flagged he was also all set to go.

All John said was "Make this count."

The generator started at a low buzz as the power built up in the capacitors.

"How's the power flow regulator settings, is it working at the higher output?" Jen nodded at John then at the dog, her eyes starting to tear up. The dog sat on its haunches in the center of the platform, dead still. Then, as if it knew something momentous was about to happen, it jumped to its feet and paced back and forth on the launch-pad. The high tension between the four was palpable, reaching a breaking point. Jen was shaking as her hand hovered over the execute button. She took one last pleading look at John, standing there like a granite statue, impervious to her silent appeal. Jen had always loved animals, in most cases, more than people. Their immutable trust-filled holes in her hidden hurt from broken relationships.

They had done so many tests, Jen rationalized. She knew that she was desperately trying to reassure herself. She wasn't a religious person *per se;* however, this was one time in her life that she thought that she could call on the God Almighty to hear her plea. 'God, please let this work'.

At the last minute, Elvis raced over to the dog and gave it one last pat rubbing its head and ears. Smiling and saying, "Good boy." The dog seemed to settle a little sitting on its haunches observing the three.

John hated himself at that point. He knew the test had to be done but, why this dog! Knowing deep down, it didn't matter which dog it was. He would feel the same with any. The best he could do was to make sure the process ran as smoothly as possible.

The generator finally reached a fever pitch, then Jen pushed the button; a loud cracking sound split the air, and the dog disappeared only to reappear twenty feet away on an identical platform.

An audible gasp broke the silent aftermath of the transport. The old man from next door had snuck back onto the property. His body was half concealed while bending the branches so he could view the anticipated continuation of the previous day's confrontation. He had had little to amuse himself lately since they had taken Jerry Springer off the TV.

The dog yelped after being momentarily stunned from the transport. It jumped up high in the air to land back onto the platform with its legs splayed for balance. It quickly looked back and forth at each of the curious humans standing there.

Elvis ran over to the platform grabbing the mutt's head shaking it playfully. It yapped while he scratched it behind the ears. The dog shook off its confusion enjoying the attention Elvis was lavishing on it.

"I think I'll call you Scotty," Elvis said with a rueful smile. Relief and smiles mirrored all around when the bushes suddenly parted as the old man ran out covered in dirt and twigs.

"That was damn brilliant! Nothing like what we went through in the war, but damn brilliant," the old man shrieked in barely concealed excitement.

"What the hell are you doing here?" John challenged.

"I was concerned about, the animal," the old man said, blustering.

"Well, you can see its fine. Now leave! You're on private property!" John said. Once again he directed the old man off the block.

When he returned the three of them sat down together to discuss what to do about it. The old man was a grave security risk.

Chapter Nine

We are not alone...

"It's Official," the television announcer was saying. "There are little green men in outer space. The Ferntree Observatory Director has confirmed what the UFO enthusiasts have been saying all along. The astronomical community can now say without a doubt, that there were nuclear explosions in outer space that cannot be natural. They are even going as far as to speculate that a blast like that is either a very good or a very bad thing. In other words, a massive accident, like some alien forgot to turn off the gas after cooking their breakfast *or* some aliens are holding a very large nuclear grudge party to which we hope we are NOT invited."

The announcer then took a more serious tone.

"There has been a mixed response from the White House. One official has been heard to say, 'It's only a matter of time before they are forced to reinstate the defunct Space Shuttle program'. We have been advised that there is no official comment from the President's Office and that he's in a meeting with the Joint Chiefs. We can only imagine what, if anything, will be their response."

Space Command, Peterson Air Force Base

Ever since the discovery of aliens in outer space, Lt Colonel Prior had been inundated with requests for information on the state of the US's space-based defense capability. The requests although not always answered came from various government officials and the military high command. The most disconcerting were the ones from the President's office.

"Colonel, tell me we have something that we can use against space-based attack?"

The President listened to Dan's response. Then replied, "So, correct me if I'm wrong, we are woefully unprepared for an attack from outer space. We have X37 space drones about one-tenth the size of the shuttle, launched from a rocket. These drones barely reach orbit."

"Yes, sir."

The President continued, "We have ICBMs that can be modified to eliminate or redirect smaller meteors on a ballistic course towards Earth. But to attack a moving combat ready spaceship, we have nothing."

"Sir, we have a laser targeting system that you're aware of, commonly known as the Star Wars system. We can re-task it to face outwardly. The ICBMs that we have can be modified to fly in outer space. However, they would only be able to fly on a ballistic trajectory at this point. We are working on changing that. As you're aware, the space shuttle provided a platform to send a large payload into orbit. The program is now defunct unless funds are directed to reinstate it. We currently use Ultra 5 rockets to deploy the payloads.

"Some other space faring nations have programs. The Chinese have gone ahead in leaps and bounds. We believe they have anti-satellite stealth technology that may be able to be used; however, that is still unconfirmed. The Europeans are working on their smaller space shuttle and are likely to be complete within a few years. Right now, they have about as much reach as us. Lastly, some private enterprises have a space-based capability. You may recall Virgin Airlines now have a space arm. There is another private group in the European Union that is close to completing another commercial space plane design. Each of those private enterprises has faced their own difficulties of exploding ships and fuel tanks. Finally, there is Space X that services the IIS."

"Can we turn the International Space Station into a weapons platform?" The President asked.

"It may be possible sir; however, even the slightest thing shot at it would destroy it. It has no shielding, no armor. It would be like standing in front of a cannon with a pea shooter. I think it would be insulting to them... The aliens I mean."

The President chuckled despite the grave nature of the discussion.

"Okay, well I'm going to approve this rail gun technology research. They tell me it may be possible to shoot something with enough power to exit Earth's gravity. Given that people won't be on board, it seems plausible. We will also fund more on the X37 project to make them combat ready. I would, however, like your recommendations for further weapons development."

Chapter Ten

Would you like pancakes with that?

"There is nothing we can do about it," John was saying to Jen and Elvis at their morning breakfast meeting. The intrusion of the old man had turned John right off his food. Even the diner's usual 'Big Lucky' all you can eat breakfast didn't sway him. Elvis was, on the other hand, still tucking into the three sausages, two eggs, and three hash browns laced with pancakes and syrup.

"Can we pay him to keep quiet?" Jen countered.

"I don't think so. He doesn't strike me as the sort that would honor it, besides that riles me in principle."

John and Jen just looked at each other as Elvis munched on his slowly disappearing breakfast. Then Elvis's eyes were drawn to the television on the wall above the counter. Once again the Observatory director was going through the results of the TACSA scans and the recordings of the nuclear flashes.

Elvis spoke up, "That guy loves all this limelight. Pity he knows squat about what actually happened."

John stared at the television with a phased-out look. Elvis smiled to Jen as he nodded in John's direction with his eyes in a 'bugged out' look. Jen followed his lead crossing her eyes also just as the waitress came to the table. Elvis laughed out loud as Jen's face turned beet red. John then looked at the two with a frown, which made both the waitress and Elvis laugh even harder as Jen turned crimson with embarrassment.

They all returned to their meals as Elvis thought on what he suspected John was thinking. They had been friends long enough for him to have a pretty good guess. Shortly, the sound of crunching bacon was drowned out by another story on alien sightings.

John sat in silence alone, staring at the fat brown envelope on the cottage kitchen table. His mind churned with the knowledge that his father still lived, even though he received an email from him several weeks ago. Maybe it was subconscious wishful thinking.

"What's that?" Elvis said as he strolled in to top up his coffee.

"It's nothing. Just a useless gesture," John said scooping up the packet and walked out of the room.

Elvis' eyes trailed him out of the kitchen as Jen walked in.

"Hey," Jen said.

Elvis just stared at the exit where John left not saying a word.

"What's going on?"

Elvis just shrugged shaking his head.

♦♦♦

Back at the makeshift laboratories, John and the other two sat around the kitchen table discussing the testing protocols to make the teleportation experience safer. Teleporting of Scotty the dog had been an incredible milestone in the development of the machine. Since then they had witnessed no discernible change to the dog after its dematerialization and rematerialization. They had, much to Jen's disgust, teleported Scotty over a dozen more times. The dog had taken it on as a game. They would teleport him 20 to 50 meters away to which he would then race back to the group yapping with delight.

"No, no, the best way would be to have a box or a barrier to stop something from hitting you after you teleport. You don't want to teleport in the middle of something and have it instantly crush you or run into you," John said.

"So, we need protection from the elements and physical objects. Maybe something like a small airplane in case you end up in the air. Something that can glide," Elvis replied

"How fast can we reset the transporter? If we can set it quickly enough, we won't need to fly, we just need to transport to the ground," Jen put in.

"Or we just use two," John said, "and we'll have a backup then." He was a big believer in redundancy. The 'just-in-case' ran strong in his veins.

It became apparent to the three that teleporting an individual was entirely possible but very dangerous unless they were protected by some sort of craft. No one wanted to be accidentally teleported into space without a suit.

Elvis then said, "We need to get a computer guru onto the team to develop the procedure to auto target reset." After thinking a bit, John realized that any automation required computer technology. Elvis was right; they would need a tech specialist.

"I'll contact the University Administrator, he may know of someone," John scribbled in his notepad.

Then it was Jen's turn, "I think we need some laser targeting for the short direct transports, as this will increase the accuracy and speed of setting the navigation when we move within line-of-sight. It could be set like a point and click transport. It will help to cut down some of the manual targeting calculations."

"That's a great idea." John furiously scribbled some more. "I think we will have to go military grade, I might be able to get our laser targeting system from our family friendly Air Force Colonel. I am sure he will want to help target his 'sonic weapon'." John said with a grin.

Elvis could only shake his head.

"OK. What about the field shape, can we shape it to be more efficient?"

"We will need more projectors to form the field more precisely..." Jen said.

The discussion continued for several hours as the three of them got hyped up on the instant coffee and stale rock hard biscuits.

"We'll need to use a petrol generator linked to some batteries, we'll have to work out how to get rid of the exhaust if we are inside the box."

"It needs to be fully self-contained: air, water ... beer," Elvis grinned.

"I should be big enough for all of us, with room to spare." Jen countered with a smile.

The discussion continued back and forth as they steadily built up the jump box specs.

The following morning the trio set out in the truck to the regular breakfast strategy and brainstorming session in town. John decided to take a different route out of interest. As they passed several older properties, the landscape slowly changed from the secluded scrub valley to flatter dust bowl farmland. Many of the local farms had a spent look that cried out in anguish, they had seen better days. The buildings were often dry, dusty and run down or in ruin.

"Stop!" Jen yelled.

John immediately pulled off the road. Jen pointed to a dirty grain silo marked with a huge for sale sign. Close by was a shabby 1930's style cottage with the faded name 'Riley' on the mailbox.

"I think I have just found our box!" She said with a smile. The tall silo was raised off the ground allowing access underneath. A second tube on the side ran the length to the top. The silo was relatively new but had a weathered unused look.

The surrounding farm had a tired, unkempt feel. Not far from the silo stood a tool shed; run-down like the rest of the farm. Its walls scuffed with paint peeling from its trimming. The building, once proud, now leaned like an old man hunched over a stick. John turned their truck around and drove slowly up the driveway to stop near the old pickup. The vehicle rested near the front of the cottage unused, grassy tufts grew up around the tires. Surprisingly, the cottage itself was tidy even though it was rundown. It was as if a handyman stopped mid-job fixing the yard.

A lazy dog with large floppy ears lay draped over the porch near a tatty door. Without a flicker of interest, the dog turned towards the sun and his doze.

John yelled out, "Hello?"

The dog opened one eye, briefly annoyed at the noise, then returned to its sun-induced slumber.

An elderly woman emerged slowly from inside the house and shuffled out onto the porch. Her clothes matched her cottage, worn but tidy. The three looked at the deep lines on her face that told a story of hardship.

"Excuse me, Ma'am," Elvis said as he walked towards the woman coming to a halt five feet away. "Forgive me for sayin', but your silo looks to have seen better days."

"Well, since my Frank died... I haven't used it."

"Would you be interested in parting with it for a fair price ma'am?"

"Eighteen hundred dollars," the woman said immediately.

"May we inspect it further first?" John asked.

"Don't matter to me." The woman replied and just stood there. Jen looked closer and saw small tears forming in the corner of her eyes.

"How long have you been living here?" Jen said.

"All my life. My grandpaw used to own a lot of the farmland round here. Well, t'was the way til the depression of the 30's. The creek dried up an' it ain't been the same since," She said in her Texan drawl.

"It must have been tough times," Jen replied.

"Where you from girl? You ain't American."

"Australia ma'am," Jen said taking the lead from Elvis.

John returned after circling the silo.

"Looks in good shape," John said. "I'm John Stevenson, ma'am, and I'll be happy to give you the asking price."

"Scarlet Riley's the name if we be doin' business," the older woman replied. Jen could see the relief in her eyes at the thought of the sale.

After a little more chatting, the three said their goodbyes with a promise to return soon with the cash and to arrange the removal.

When they returned to the research base, John received a call from the University Administrator who gave him some names that fit the profile 'super computer geek'. He mentioned one in particular because of his background in computing and astrophysics. Max Tyler just happened to be an avid sci-fi fan and was probably in Austin Texas at the sci-fi expo nearby.

John looked up the background of the candidates on the net and decided Max was, in fact, a good fit.

John returned the following day to Scarlet Riley's farm to hand over the asking price of the silo and a little extra for some tools she had scattered in the shed. He called a salvage company based on Scarlet's recommendation to help deliver the large silo in one piece to his ever increasing lab facility.

The removers, who bore a striking resemblance to the old lady, were somewhat amused at John's request to put the silo on its side. Clearly making it useless as a grain storage the way it was originally intended. But John just smiled and thanked them as they left. They had been courteous and fairly priced. A refreshing posture the local business took, as opposed to the highly motivated profit driven city trades.

Once the curious onlookers had departed from the property, the trio entered the silo visualizing the interior. They guessed at each of the different components that would make it an independent vehicle with the teleporter or 'jump drive' as its mode of movement; the first ever 'JumpShip'.

◆ ◆ ◆

Old Man Sykes was watching trash TV reruns when an old news story regarding a terrorist plot in Washington blared out of the TV. The reporter described an unusual new weapon that had the authorities baffled. Mugshot pictures appeared on the screen. His eyes widened as he recognized the profiles of Elvis, Jen, and John.

"Damn foreign bastards," Sykes's usual response to any offensive behavior. But he felt justified this time, especially given Jen was obviously not American, she wasn't even Canadian.

Sykes thought briefly about notifying the authorities but reached for his shotgun instead. It was well after four in the afternoon when Sykes arrived at the makeshift research base. The old man was a little surprised to find a huge silo on its side. Didn't the city folk know anything, he thought with a sneer.

Sykes pulled the gun off his shoulder as he walked towards the work area near the barnyard entrance. Jen was hunched over the computer controls while Elvis adjusted the throttle on the petrol generator. The pitch of the generator drowned out Sykes's heavy footsteps until the dog's insistent bark broke through the noise, alerting the two to his presence.

Elvis started to walk over towards Sykes just as he raised his shotgun. Elvis's eyes widened as the glint from the two barrels pointed straight at the chest.

"I don't know what yer planning, but yer ain't going to git away with it."

"What do you mean?" Elvis yelled at him in return over the strum drum of the generator. Elvis's tension set Scotty into a dangerous and menacing growl.

"I saw you terrorists on TV," continued the old man, his voice harsh.

Jen shifted the transporter targeting from the platform to Sykes' location with a subtle tap on the keyboard. The old man was too distracted by Elvis and Scotty to notice.

Continuing to prime the transporter Jen started charging the capacitors. The old man suddenly catching the movement in the corner of his vision waved the firearm in Jen's direction. She instantly stopped eyes wide as she held her breath.

Scotty growled even louder, flashing his canines at Sykes's. The old man shifting his attention back to Elvis, swinging the weapon to point squarely at him.

"I'm takin' you in..." Sykes yelled so he could be heard over the generator as its pitch changed once again.

Elvis started to say, "We're not doing anything ...," when Scotty lunged at Sykes. The old man had surprisingly quick reflexes; he aimed the gun at Scotty and firing in one swift motion, just as Scotty snapped towards his gun arm. There was a deafening roar as the weapon went off. Pellets flew out of the barrel at nearly 800 mph crashing into Scotty's open jaws.

The force of the buckshot flung the flying bundle of fur backward into the dirt. Blood sprayed through the air splattering the surprised Elvis in the carnage. The dog was a mess, half his jaw and chest blown off as he lay unmoving on the ground.

Deep red gore was everywhere as Elvis looked on stunned.

Without hesitation, Jen pushed the starter button causing the transporter to whine. Suddenly there was a tremendous crack as Sykes's body disappeared before their eyes. The air thundered rushing in to fill the space where he had stood. Most of Sykes's body had vanished leaving two legs standing like pillars alone in the dirt. The legs were sheared just below the knees.

Jen sat there dazed, staring at the rough old brown boots, its leather scuffed and calloused just like the old man.

Elvis was shocked, his eyes bulging and mouth agape speechless a second time in as many seconds. Belatedly he gasped "holy crap!"

Jen just stood focused on the boots, biting her lower lip. Anguish flashed across her face as she turned seeing the remains of poor Scotty. She then doubled over, and a stream of vomit sprayed the ground before her.

Elvis sank to his knees with a stunned look on his face mouthing noiselessly to no one in particular, "Holy Crap. Holy Crap."

John came running out from behind the last container as the noise of the shotgun caught his attention. He stopped in his tracks as he took in the havoc. Seeing all the gore he rushed over to Elvis. Blood covered his face and shirt but after patting his friend down, he eventually realized the blood was not his, it must've been that of the dog's. He then raced over to Jen to check her for injuries.

John was no stranger to gore. He had seen combat when serving in the army on tour in Iraq and on a peacekeeping mission in Somalia. He had been a pilot in a chopper Evac squadron assigned to one of the MASH units. There was plenty of gore from warlords who fought everyone for God knows what.

Jen raised her head lost. She had a deep searching look in her wild eyes, grasping at reality, pleading for its return. It was an expression that John had seen before. He watched as Jen's face transformed, leaving a hollow blank look. All he could do was hold her as she stared unfocused into oblivion until the shocking blackness slowly receded. John could do nothing as tears ran unheeded down her face.

The International Space Station in close Earth Orbit

"Did you see that?" the Russian communication's specialist exclaimed as he pointed out the glass portal.

"What?" the commander asked as he turned to face the burly Russian.

"I thought I saw an old man waving a shotgun."

The Commander stared at the Russian for a minute, then leaned over to check the oxygen mix of the station air. They couldn't afford carbon dioxide poisoning.

◆◆◆

Research Base El Paso, Texas

After tucking an old blanket around Jen and leaving her on the couch in the office, John carefully gathered Scotty's remains. He took them out to the largest tree on the property to bury them. John's anger grew with the physical exertion of driving the spade into the hard stony ground. *Why was the man there! That old coot just couldn't mind his own bloody business.*

When John returned to the makeshift base of transport containers, Elvis had decided to remove the old man's legs by teleporting them to his property, but a mile underground. The crack of the teleport, all at once seemed so very final.

Chapter Eleven

The Hog's Breath

Later that evening, the trio made their way to the Hog's Breath Bar & Grill just out of town. A few strong local beers dulled the trials of the day. The sullen mood was interrupted by a news item on the TV. The latest theories on the nuclear blasts in space speculated that they were the result of massive space battles between aliens. Various lobby groups were getting in on the act creating political pressure to push government spending towards space defense research. Xenophobia seemed to be gripping the country. The human race was coming to terms with its insignificance and vulnerability. 'Earth Defense' was becoming a catch cry. The US government was expected to make a decision on the funding issue shortly.

Elvis downed his beer then went to the bar and returned with three more passing them around without comment. The talk show host finally concluded that the mystery would stay just that until someone went out there.

The trio looked at each other and started to smile as the germ of an idea hit them all simultaneously.

John then spoke up, "How far do you think we can teleport?"

They both looked at him, thinking about the possibilities.

Elvis said, "Do you think we can go that far?"

"Even if we could, should we? It would be dangerous," Jen responded.

"What... More dangerous than to dematerialize and rematerialize?" Elvis countered.

"Let's see what we can come up with," John said finally.

♦♦♦

Over the next weeks the trio set about transforming the jump box (silo) into a wondrous new *Jumpship*. It was to be no ordinary craft; it would be one of contradictions. The vessel would be cutting edge yet hopelessly vintage. It was unlike other ships that had to travel through space to get to their destination. It was not like they would be out there forever. The trio was new to building Jumpships (spaceships), so any idea was opened to the group for discussion on its own merits.

The ship would have the first 'Jump Drive' ever made and yet would be barely more than a grain silo with a few racing car seats for comfort. The power source, a few car batteries and petrol generator for a speedy recharge. It would not even be pressurized; the crew would be in space suits the whole time they used it. It made sense to use space suits, they didn't have the facility or expertise to build an environment module; not to mention it would be a lot cheaper.

John returned to Scarlet's place to see about contracting more local trades for the construction and fit-out of the *Jumpship*.

By John's third visit to Scarlet for local workman recommendations, she had, after a fashion warmed to him giving him some homemade oatmeal biscuits that nearly broke his teeth the first time he tried them. After that, when John visited, they sat on the porch where she insisted on having coffee with the infamous rock biscuits. Both knew the rock cakes were teeth crackers, but were unconcerned. It was the ritual that drew out their tête-à-tête. Scarlet would just smile knowingly and tell stories about the good old days with her Frankie.

The week crawled by slowly transforming the ramshackle bunch of containers into a hive of activity. Welders fashioned a large hatch into the base of the silo exposing the cavernous insides. A control room was built at the nose of the silo to house the computer panels and seating. John went all out and bought top of the line sports car seats for comfort. If racing car drivers could sit in them for hours, it should be no problem for them. Portals were cut into the front and sides. A makeshift deck and bracing were built to hold the jump drive, batteries, and a sealed unit with its own air bottles to feed the petrol generator. Oxygen tanks and various tools were placed throughout the *jumpship* in cabinets or tied to the walls.

John raced to pull Jen to her feet. "Stand up straight, arms and legs out like a star." Jen was starting to get curiously suspicious now. John's orders were getting weird.

He just laughed out aloud and reached around her waist. "I'm measuring you for a space suit," he said smiling.

Elvis then piped up, "I want Jen to measure me. I'm sure John will put an extra couple of inches around my waist." John and Jen cracked up. Elvis kept himself in very good trim and was the fittest of the three.

The days drew into weeks. The locals started to see the *Jumpship* take shape. It was a haven for exotic and unusual scuttlebutt. The contractors laughed at the crazy foreigners and their farmyard ship.

The jump drive testing was done out of sight. The noise created by the drive and the generator, however, were hard to conceal. The contractors were immensely curious. They all knew that spaceships couldn't fly in space with big holes in them. The ship didn't have a big rocket on its tail like the shuttle. How ridiculous is that! He would often smile to himself when he overheard their wild and curiously bizarre guesstimates as to their undertaking, anything from circus entertainers to film studio sets. It was hard not to share the secret details with the locals as they exuded so much excitement like a family expecting a newborn.

◆◆◆

John kept a close eye on Jen and Elvis. The shocking reality of the old man and Scotty's demise played heavily on the three of them. Would the old man be missed? Shouldn't they go to the police? It would be seen as self-defense surely. The old man seemed cantankerous and nosy, but he didn't deserve to die and disappear without a proper sendoff. So many times the discussion around the cottage table revolved around notifying the police.

John contacted the private investigator he employed to check up on Jen.

"I would like you to check up on an old man called Sykes," John said over the phone. John gave him what details he could, and left it in the PI's hands.

Before too long the dark secret bound the three together.

The PI reported that Sykes was the last of his line and alone. The three then took an oath on his memory to make a yearly donation to the returned servicemen foundation. Sykes had been a veteran of more than one war.

Elvis's became moody and overtly extroverted, Jen on the other hand, internalized her anguish, and barely spoke of the incident directly.

She had told them that she'd only meant to transport him to the outer edge of the property. With tears in her eyes, she admitted that in the chaos of the moment she had forgotton to change the height of the transporter pickup and destination location was a computer setting that was stuck in its memory from their first suborbital jump.

John realized it would be a long time before Jen forgave herself if ever. Her quiet nightly sobbing could be heard through the paper thin walls.

♦♦♦

The Jumpship's first tentative steps

"So are we ready for the first test flight?" John asked.

"Yes, almost there, just give me one more minute. I need to check the backup jump drive and the two computers." For general ship operations and preexisting jump settings they brought a standard laptop. That way they could keep the quantum computer turned off until it was needed for new target calculations. It would minimize damage from shocks. Getting the quantum computer into the silo was a challenge in itself. In the end, they settled with a separate sealed container braced with heavy shock absorbers to protect the delicate instrumentation. Mounds of insulated shielding to protect it from the elements.

Yellow warning lights flashed on the console until Elvis finished his checks. One by one they turned solid green. The critical of these was showing the power levels of the batteries and output of the generator.

"Did you check how much petrol we have for that generator?" John yelled over a shoulder.

Elvis replied with a thumbs up.

Everything seemed ready. John ran through each of the systems once more on his console voicing their status out loud. "Jump drive alpha is green. Jump drive Bravo is green,"

"Batteries fully charged,"

"Spacesuit one status," John looked down at his sealed helmet arms and oxygen supply connection, "is green."

"Spacesuit two status?" John looked at Jen who nodded, "is green."

"Oxygen tanks status is green, and doors are locked."

Elvis then rushed to the final open seat in the cockpit. He buckled in and connected his oxygen then checked the power levels of the generator one more time. He signaled John that his spacesuit was status green.

"Spacesuits three status... is green," John said out loud.

"We are all ready. Green across-the-board. Okay, Jen is the target locked in, with a clean cache?"

"Affirmative, target is locked."

"Okay ladies and gentlemen please buckled your seats we're jumping in five, four, three, two, one. Mark!" John pressed the jump button.

The tension was immense, one minute they're sitting in the valley in Texas then the next second they were 40 feet further from their start jump location.

"Oh my God! That was incredible!"

All three were grinning with absolute joy.

"Jen, how is the jump drive?"

"Jump drive is good."

"Elvis, the generator and batteries?"

"The generator is running to recharge the batteries. The batteries are down to 5%."

"Jen set the next target location at the end of the valley. We will jump in half an hour when the batteries are recharged, and Jen has recalculated the new harmonic." It took them closer to two hours before they were ready to jump again. Most of the previous calculations were made when the computer and the targeting were fixed in a location at the research base. The point of reference had now changed to their new location 40 feet from their original launch position.

"Target location, locked and ready" Jen replied

"Jump in five, four, three, two, one Mark!" Once again there was a sudden crack and the ship disappeared 40 feet from the makeshift research camp and reappeared deep at the other end of the valley. A slight jarring was felt as the *Jumpship* crashed to the ground from a height of 2 feet.

"Is everyone okay?" They both answered "yes". Jen realized she should have used the laser targeting to confirm the height difference between their departure and arrival.

"Okay, systems check. Jen, Elvis?" John said as he unbuckled to check on the computer and that the batteries were being recharged.

Jen got up to check on the projectors alignment.

After a few minutes, they all signaled that nothing was damaged.

John gave the all clear, "Let's transport home."

An hour and a half later Jen announced, "Targeting complete."

The ship disappeared to reappear in the research camp.

"Let's use jump drive Bravo and repeat the tests in a few days after we get heavy duty shock absorbers in the landing struts."

The three tested the jump ship hundreds of times within the valley walls, each time becoming more confident in the process. At the end of the week still amazed at their accomplishments they downloaded the logs and the readings they took during the testing so that they could find tune the whole process. The target harmonics of the entire valley ended up been mapped and stored in the computer memory. Once mapped all they needed to do then was to import those coordinate harmonics in the field generators that responded creating the appropriate field setting.

John brought two bottles of champagne and placed them on the table set up near the nose of the silo.

"I know this project did not go as smoothly as I had planned. However, I would like to go forward and christen this our first ship." He said as he poured out four flutes of champagne on the table. "In honor of the fourth member who was paramount to our discovery and whom will never be forgotten, I christened the ship the *Scotty*."

In some way, each of them felt a kinship to the courageous mutt. Each of them smiled raising their glasses in salute.

Chapter Twelve

Squishy Pirate ship Kator in outer space

Commander Kane sat in his pedestal chair in the middle of the bridge twiddling his four forelimbs. The crew edged further away from him as his fidgeting screamed of frustration at the slow progress of the salvage. Things had gone wrong from the start, first the engines were destroyed which meant they couldn't pilot the vessel to their hideout let alone sell the freighter as a working vessel. The wild spinning of the wreck in space added extra complexity to the salvage operation. They had been sitting in this backwater sector of space for the better part of three cycles now, which was far longer than he had planned for.

The idiot Drakmok had gone and lost another limb while attempting to secure their latest prize delaying the salvage even further. Kane was sure that all of Drakmok's seven mothers forgot the coordination gene. Casting his eye storks around the bridge he focused on the weapons officer. He was sorely tempted to send out the diminutive officer in Drakmok's place.

"Do we know what the manifest is of this freighter yet?"

"Commander, it's mostly farm machinery, road works, religious icons and frozen foods."

"Damn it! What about the biologicals, the crew, can we enslave them? What species are they? Are they fit and healthy?"

"They are bipedal trader lizards that are pretty weak with only a small amount of fat and musculature. These particular reptiles are not aggressive like the warrior caste; however, be careful of their spit. It's acidic and will quickly eat through to your brain if you get it in your eyes," the Trade Officer said.

Kane's eye stalks straightened with fear. "A lizard ship..."

"Yes, Commander. But it's the trader caste. Nothing to worry about."

Kane didn't look convinced. Nobody messes with the lizards for good reason.

The trader officer continued with his report, "A standard male-female pair would value 1500 credits at the slave markets in the carnivore states. A child would fetch nearly 2000 credits on its own... They're a delicacy there."

Kane's eyes widened with this last comment, "Tell me there are children on that freighter," he asked avariciously, all fear forgotten.

It was not uncommon for transport ships to be run by family units. The Trader Officer answered reluctantly, "There are two." He was uncomfortable with the whole concept of child slave labor. But especially child ingredient labor for the Carnivore States. Dealing with that civilization was always tricky, as one never knew whether all your crew would return with all of their limbs. The Carnivores saw Squishy limbs as delicacies served best with GoGo juice.

Kane said to no one in particular with a gleam of satisfaction. "This prize just may be profitable after all." As he looked around at the bridge crew's discomfort. You can't live out here in the backwaters without trade, whatever type of product it is.

◆◆◆

When the Squishy crew completed loading the first cargo container into the *Kator's* hull, Kane was finally pleased with the progress of his salvage operation, despite Drakmok's lost limb. The fishbait had come through and stabilized their prize with only five limbs. They had secured the four bio cargoes, he had to laugh at his own deviousness when he made Kazorr responsible for the two child lizards. By the noisy rasping sounds of the child lizards throughout the ship, Kazorr was being punished well and truly.

The pirate ship was not a large vessel; the waterborne environments took up a lot more space than straight air-breathing creatures needed. One of the cargo holds was wholly dedicated to a pool and sauna spa, which meant they would need to return several times to plunder all of the freighter's cargo. With their own cargo area full, they set out on the return voyage to their hideout with their spoils.

Chapter Thirteen

Here comes Max

The three in the command team sat in the kitchen of the old cottage which had been completely refurbished as a meeting place. One of the rooms had been set up as John's office and the other as a secure storage. Construction had already started on some larger buildings within the property.

"So where do we stand now. We've tested both jump drives, checked the power settings, projectors, and the targeting." Before he continued John received a telephone call from Max accepting the job offer. John provided him with the address of the lab and asked him to start as soon as possible. After hanging up, John continued with their meeting.

"You may have noticed around the perimeter, that we now have security staff patrolling to keep out unwanted guests. There is also electrified fencing going up around the perimeter."

Jen and Elvis stared back at him with concern. "Yes, I know about fencing. It's not even enough to wake you from a deep sleep. But it gives us the opportunity to say '*Warning Electrified Fence*'. A little bit of misdirection never goes astray. You will also notice that Scarlet's contractors have built a new gatehouse where the guards can doze off while they are on duty. Here are your new ID cards, treat them well." John handed out photo IDs with the big letters T.N. on the back.

"I have also added extra security around the mobile labs; some motion detectors and other bits and pieces. So please be careful where you stand, step or pee. Let me know if there are any further security measures you think we should take."

The following day Max Tyler arrived in his clapped-out old VW Combi van. Although those vans have a reputation for running forever, Max's sounded decidedly ill. The billowing smoke and dying breath may have given it away. He was almost turned away by the overzealous new gate security when John raced up to Max letting him in. The Mexican guard just looked at John in a confused manner with his limited English. John had the distinct impression that there was a serious communication difficulty here, or maybe he had better start learning Spanish. John made a mental note to inform his new security of any new arrivals that were expected.

Max was a lanky fellow, one of those sorts of people that could eat a million different fatty foods and not gain a single ounce in weight. John hated that ... His eyes were framed in 1950s Buddy Holly Black rims. In contrast his thin build and long face accentuated his rather large eyes making him look alien. Not that John would ever say that out aloud...

"Max Tyler, my name is John Stevenson," John said as he held out his hand. "May I call you Max?"

"Of course Dr. Stevenson."

"Please call me John we don't stand on ceremony here."

He typified the classic computer geek with his reserved, shy personality that bloomed when he forgot his surroundings. After a few minutes conversation, John couldn't help but smile as he spotted Max's Star Trek uniform. The red and black command line outfit was lying openly on the front seat of his clapped-out van.

"I want to thank you for coming so quickly; I understand you were enjoying the sci-fi convention and had to cut it short."

"... mmm yes it was cool," he replied slightly embarrassed as he noticed he'd left the uniform in plain sight.

"I've always wanted to go, but I never seem to have the time," John said trying to ease his embarrassment. "Max, you come highly recommended by Mr. Hughes. How do you know the University Administrator, what is your relation with him?"

It took Max a minute to recognize whom John was talking about. "Oh, Thurston. I have done some projects for the University. I first met him when I was doing my second degree in astrophysics. He introduced me to Dr. Polansky, who was at the time developing the new TACSA tracking system for the observatory in New Mexico." Max shrugged, "I was able to help."

John was impressed with Max's modesty, as he knew from Thurston that Max had written all the code for it. The two moved inside to the conference area and sat and talked about Max's experience in computing and astrophysics. The more that John found out, the more he was sure of his decision to invite the computer geek into their little group.

"Max, for this job you will need to do a full physical." John placed some forms on the desk in front of him including a rather lengthy non-disclosure agreement.

"I thought you were hiring me for my computing abilities, what does that have to do with taking a physical."

"This job requires you to go on site to which there may be significant dangers. I can't tell you exactly what they will be but be assured it will be hazardous."

Max's eyes widened, but he said nothing.

John continued his sales pitch. "I can assure you that you will be very well compensated for any risks that you will be facing."

Max thought that over. "And you can't tell me what sort of risks?"

"No. I can say that when our work becomes public, you'll be kicking yourself for missing this opportunity. I know that may sound hollow and manipulative, however in this case, it happens to be true because it's an opportunity of a lifetime."

Max looked at John trying to gauge what he'd just heard. Employers weren't normally that openly honest. In the end, he trusted that Thurston wouldn't give him as a recommendation to someone whom he didn't trust. All of

Max's dealings with Thurston had been well received. Given his young age, Thurston had always acted fatherly, and that indefinable bond pushed Max to make a decision.

He pulled out a pen and signed the nondisclosure agreement and the employment contract.

"Welcome to our little party." John stood holding out his hand and shook Max's. "Trust me, with your interests you are going to die when you see what we do." All the secrecy and build up was making Max very nervous but also hyper excited.

"Let's go meet the team." John led him out to the labs and introduced him to the others.

He was dumbfounded when they first told him of the transporter. He was then floored a second time by their recent test jumps with the *Scotty*. Max was so excited he was running and jumping over every part of the silo spaceship. Despite *Scotty's* spartan look, Max was grinning from ear to ear, until finally, he came to the quantum computer. Third time lucky he passed out on the deck. Jen had to rush out and get half a cup of water to splash on the lanky guy's face.

Over the next few days, Max walked around in a daze as he slowly familiarized himself with the various jump and power systems. His first jump nearly sent him on another fainting spell. John thought to himself he must have smelling salts on hand whenever they make a jump with the funny geek.

Max finally got used to the jumping process and started work on automating the target and power controls. This was exactly what John had hoped for. His background in astrophysics was a major bonus in identifying astronomical objects and simplifying the whole process of targeting locations. However, it still left the niggling problem of targeting for new locations. Each site still had to be mapped out. No one wanted to jump into the ether without knowing where they would land. It was a very disquieting and real fear that they carried with them on every jump. Time progressed, and tests continued in a regular fashion.

One afternoon when the team was sitting around the dining table John declared, "Let's make our first jump into orbit."

"Are you sure John?" questioned Jen.

"Yes, I have a sneaking feeling that time is running short. We need to test the jump to space quickly. Then work out how to jump to where that blast came from. That explosion in outer space was not that far away in stellar terms. If we can detect the EM blast, then I'm damn sure they will be able to sense Earth's electromagnetic signature. It's only a matter of time before they come here. I don't want to be defenseless when they arrive."

This was the first time that any of the others had heard John talk like this. All the talk so far had centered on finding out what had happened out there. Not what was happening or going to happen over here if the aliens came *here*. It brought home to everyone for the first time that the Earth was potentially in danger from another species. It also brought with it an urgency. They all knew that Earth had limited and pathetic space defenses. Half of them didn't believe that the Star Wars defense system was even real. Government, politics, and secrecy all seem to go hand-in-hand muddying the truth.

"I totally agree; we need to get cracking. The implications of *Scotty's* abilities could be a game changer," said Elvis eventually. Max nodded his head in agreement. Then they all looked towards Jen.

"Okay, okay," she said with her hands up, "But we jump straight home if they're there. The *Scotty* is not exactly a warship." There was silence as they each thought about what they had committed to.

Chapter Fourteen

Orbital Adventure

That evening John brought a bottle of champagne to the meeting room, filling each of his friends' glasses for a toast to the momentous occasion.

"Far be it for me to misquote Armstrong's famous line, but *'One small jump for the Scotty, one giant leap for mankind'.*" Although they all cringed and groaned at John's statement, the prospect of the upcoming adventures brought them together in a family camaraderie.

The next day planning for the mission started in earnest. John sat discussing with Jen and Max the first test jump into orbit. The *Scotty* was not going to be pressurized. They thought the Russian-made space suits they had acquired would be sufficient, and the crew would be safe. Extra batteries were installed dedicated to the Bravo Emergency Jump Drive. This could jump them home in a split second. They were eager to make the trip despite the risks. The biggest risk they all agreed, came from the old second-hand space suits they had acquired. If there were decompression from a space suit rupture, they would only have about ninety seconds before there was irreparable damage to the human body, including possible death.

"Is everything locked away? Remember we are jumping to space without gravity." After a few more minutes of tidying and locking down all the loose items, the crew was prepared to jump.

"Are we all systems go?" John asked.

A new console and racing car seat had been installed for Max inside *Scotty*'s large bridge. He took over all the computing and electronics equipment. A new radar system and radio transmitter/receiver were added and linked to Max's console giving him control over communications and sensors. Telescopic light sensors were also included.

Finally, on John's console he had green lights across all the systems, they were ready.

"We jump in five, four, three, two, one... Mark!" The *Scotty* disappeared from the research base and reappeared in geosynchronous orbit above North America. Their bodies and arms were all pummeled as a loud whoosh and squeal could be heard through their helmets. Air rushed out into space from a myriad of holes and the portals on the bridge. The three braced themselves wide-eyed and terrified. Loose items flew around the control room in a chaotic whirlwind. Max held his eyes shut as a circuit board flew through the air striking his helmet only to pass through one of the portals. The *Scotty* was certainly never designed to be space proof. The crew knew they would be faced with massive decompression. However, knowing this and feeling it were two entirely different things. The howling suddenly stopped as all the air vanished. Silence... Blessed silence. They looked and patted at their spacesuit controls checking they were still pressurized and thanked their lucky stars. John watched each of his companion's arms and legs start to lift unintentionally. A sudden giggle could be heard through the comms. Everyone was okay. John let out his breath and grinned with relief.

"Another first for the caped crusaders!" Jen yelled out loud, laughing.

"Make sure you all have your tether lines attached," John said as he checked his own. He swiftly undid his seat belt and pushed his body out from the sitting position. He sailed quickly through the cabin and landed on the ceiling with a crunch. He could hear various thumps and groans through his suit speakers the crew making just as awkward attempts at zero g gymnastics. John made a mental note to practice and to add padding with handholds inside the *Scotty*.

"Make sure you keep an eye on your oxygen and temperature levels. And be careful that you don't snag your suit on anything. They're still lots of sharp bits everywhere."

Max was struggling to gain control. His arms and legs flailed around trying to control his moves. Bouncing from one wall to another only to careen into a bulkhead with the decided thump. The others laughed as they could hear it on their comms. Max could see the others were starting to get the hang of it, but he was still flailing; he was having so much fun he didn't care.

"We should download zero-g gymnastics video, it could become the next Olympic sport."

They definitely needed some sort of training guide for weightless maneuvers and EVA (Extravehicular Activity-maneuvers outside the spacecraft). He knew that NASA would have put something like that out on the World Wide Web.

John checked his oxygen and discovered he had used close to half.

"Playtime is over, please return to your stations, we will be jumping back to Earth momentarily." John smiled at the thought of jumping back to Earth, how strange. John checked the crew, then the board of green.

"We jump in five, four, three, two, one... Mark!"

The *Scotty* appeared outside the familiar cottage with a crack. Suddenly there was a groan, and a part of the wall collapsed in narrowly missing Max's legs. The violent rush of air raced to fill the space within the bridge where there was no atmosphere. John realized too late that he hadn't thought of atmospheric re-compression. The air suddenly stormed into the bridge and filled it with a misty fog as the cold of space mixed with a planet-side air of Texas. It was at that point that Elvis realized that he was thankful for the heat generated by the suit because the bridge had become a crystal ice palace from moist air contacting with the chill of space. The crew had narrowly missed a catastrophic implosion.

Slowly the group exited the *Scotty,* taking in its battered exterior.

"Geez," was all of Elvis could muster.

"Is it fixable?" Jen asked the others.

Large dents could be seen outside on the hull.

They all took a step back, then inspecting each other with their fluoro orange suits and shining helmets, all heartily burst out laughing, as much from the carnival-like display, as from skipping death by the narrowest of margins.

The following week at the base was filled with repairs and improvements to the *Scotty*. Internal structural braces and larger openings were fitted so the *Scotty* looked more like a block of Swiss cheese than a shiny new spacecraft. The larger holes would allow decompression and recompression to proceed with less damage. John also purchased some small remote-controlled rockets and attached them to the outside of the hull giving the *Scotty* some maneuverability in space.

"Are we all set for an orbital jump?" John was answered with cheers and a full board of green lights. Glancing around to the other crew members he said, "We jump in five, four, three, two, one... Mark!"

Once again the *Scotty* disappeared from the research base to rematerialize in geosynchronous orbit. The rush of air into space as the *Scotty* decompressed still filled the crew with fear. John thought to himself, *we seriously have to get a proper cabin.* This time, the crew remained in their seats, strapped in, as they verified their position and systems status.

Jen looked out the larger window and saw the magnificent stars without atmospheric interference, stunned by the brilliance and the vastness of space. She then set to work mapping the next target jump to the surface of the moon. Max had added a few program enhancements to the navigation system. It still took some time to crunch the numbers, but the data entry was much simpler. It had a smooth, crisp interface.

Jen initiated quantum computer start-up for the navigation system.

"Are we ready to trial the thrusters while Jen works on the mapping?" John said looking at Elvis and Max. Elvis just nodded affirmatively while John pressed thrusters and felt the *Scotty* move and slowly pick up speed. John's only point of reference was the pressure he felt into the back of his chair. They ended up maneuvering in all directions. After 20 minutes John brought the *Scotty* to a halt pleased at the results. "You did really well, good work on these Elvis I'm really impressed. Can you now try from your console?" Without another word, the *Scotty* took off at speed once again dodging up and down and around imaginary obstacles.

♦♦♦

Finally, Elvis brought the *Scotty* to a halt because he could hear the muffled groan from Jen. Her face was looking a little green behind her helmet's visor. Suddenly Max took a quick breath in surprise. A contact blipped on his console showing something approaching at incredible speed.

"Oh my God, someone has fired a missile at us!" John slammed his hand down onto the Emergency Bravo Jump drive button. Instantly the *Scotty* jumped back to the safety of home base. The recompression sucked in air from the outside once again disorientating the crew.

"What *was* that Max?" said John.

"I'm not entirely sure, but I think someone fired a ballistic missile at us. I think they must have picked us up on their satellite defense systems."

"Okay. Is everyone all right?" John said, trying to reassure himself while checking the others were okay.

"At least we know the instant home button works." Elvis piped up with a grin. Jen gave the smug bald man a withering look then shook her head at John.

It was some time before they collected themselves after the surprise missile attack. The discussion revolved around keeping away from any Earth forces and out of harm's way. Having the teleporter, distance was their friend.

"Check all the systems. We're going to make a jump to the moon now." The four carried out the system checks including the backup emergency jump drive which, from that point on, was always called the 'Home Drive' (HD). After the heat had dissipated from the heat sink and the batteries recharged John had a full board of green. They made the jump and were suddenly 5000 feet above the moon's surface on the light side. Once again the air whistled out of *Scotty's* command center. When the mayhem had cleared, all aboard took in the majesty of the desolate cratered landscape. "Elvis, do you think that you can land us on this piece of rock?" John waited for his answer holding his hand above the home drive button.

Elvis was thrilled to get the opportunity. "Absolutely!"

They could feel the pull of the moon drag the *Scotty* as it meandered towards the rock and dust covered surface. John touched the landing gear monitor moving it to the main viewer as the ship descended towards the moon's surface. Subsequent thruster bursts brought the *Scotty* down, finishing with a slight bump as dust billowed around the craft from the exhaust. One of the last improvements they had added were solid shock absorbers on the underside of the hull. The crew then set the jump drive on recharge while they took their first tentative steps onto the moon's surface. Elvis did a double take as his first jump rocketed him upwards ten feet only to slowly fall back down. They walked around the *Scotty* peering at the pebbled and jagged rock outcrops.

"Ha, ha," Jen yelled with childlike excitement as she pointed at the blue and white half crescent mid-way above the horizon. They all looked up and saw the blue orb they called home. It looked so alone and vulnerable. After a while, Max bent down and picked up two small rocks as they made their way back to *Scotty*'s hatch.

Chapter Fifteen

Air National Guard Station, 1699th Space Warning Squadron

Brendan climbed back into the mobile ground unit shaking the cold, wet snow from his overcoat. He reveled in the warmth for a minute before taking his coat off fully. Opening the inner door to the control room he almost choked on the heat. Making his way around towards his supervisor console, Brendan sniffed the air. Sam, the NCO, had been eating beans again. The little resupply run to the local store for a steaming cup broke up the long shift not to mention, getting out of toxic range of Sam's flatulence.

The mobile unit was one of a network of missile platforms that linked into the early warning system using satellites and ground radar for missile detection and communications.

The Sam sat at his console playing solitaire on the side screen. Suddenly the biggest bleep he had ever seen appeared on his main monitor.

"Geez, Brandon, can you check your screen for a bogie in quadrant 4J, S by SW, alt 255 miles, heading 270."

Brendan rushed back the last few feet to his console spilling his hot chocolate. "Sam, this better not be a joke!" Bringing the same screen up as his subordinate, Brendan looked wide-eyed at the blinking image with an 'Unknown' tag; briefly checking the distance and vector headings he then reached for the phone in his console.

He was instantly connected to 9451st Air Defense Wing, missile dispatch. Time was of the essence. There was so little warning they had to act straight away.

"Dispatch, Mob 1699. I have a bogey in quadrant four that's a huge sonuvabitch!" The scans were automatically sent to flight operations in USSTRATCOM Nebraska. The call went up the chain of command to land on General Abercrombie's signals queue. The General took one look at the erratic movements of this enormous bogey and its proximity to American soil and spy satellites. He then picked up the phone on a secure line to the nearest missile effective defense detachment near the radar sighting.

"This is General Abercrombie, who am I speaking to?"

"General, Captain Daniels, 201st Missile Defense Detachment."

"Captain this is a priority Red Blast 3. You are authorized to launch. Target X-Ray Zulu Charlie 1. Confirm."

"Launch Authorized. Target X-Ray Zulu Charlie 1. Confirmed," the Captain repeated.

The captain had been involved in many simulated test firings of their missiles. They were never told if it was real or a drill. This was the first target that was space based.

There had been so many discussions at the last Unified Combatant Commanders meeting for USSTRATCOM on the military response to an attack by little green men. Nothing had been resolved. It was left to the individual commanders. That was when the General decided that a clear statement of intent from Earth was required.

At the mobile launch site, the authorization to launch blinked across Brendan's screen.

"Shit, they want us to launch."

The two men flicked through launch procedures... "Turn the launch key, One, two, three...Mark. Launching."

The two airmen felt the ballistic missile rumble and shake their cabin. Wide-eyed that a real launch was in progress.

"There she goes... tracking," Sam whispered. The suddenly grim atmosphere had chilled the room more than the snow outside.

The two men waited for the order to self-destruct the missiles... it never came.

A flash message pushed through e-space to flag the Joint Chiefs, the Secretary of Defense and the President of the successful launch with missile outbound.

◆◆◆

A short time later, Admiral Bryce Tucker, the newly appointed Commander of United States Strategic Command (USSTRATCOM), called a meeting of the Joint Chiefs and General Abercrombie, so the general could explain why a tactical nuke was launched.

General Abercrombie sat stony-faced in front of Admiral Tucker and a board of disbelieving Admirals and Generals. The sensor readings taken of the unidentified object in low orbit were displayed for all to see on a huge wall screen.

Admiral Tucker continued his grilling "... So, run us through your thought process once again on how you decided to open fire on a clearly non-terrestrial ship."

"Well... Umm," the General swallowed. "My original thought was that it was, in fact, a terrestrial ship with stealth technology because it just suddenly appeared."

"The size of the craft just appearing didn't spark off any warning bells or that it was in space in a low earth orbit?"

The general was quiet.

"Please continue General," Admiral Tucker said out loud.

"Then when it made aggressive maneuvers towards one of our spy satellites. I assumed they were there to destroy it or steal it. So rather than the Chinese destroying a billion-dollar spy satellite, I thought to eliminate the threat, and send a Mark X5 ballistic missile."

"General, what was the result of your over aggressiveness?"

"Well, Ummm," the General swallowed again, "just before missile strike, the missile targeted another object and destroyed it."

"... Oh, and pray tell me General, what that other object was."

"Well. Errr... One of our satellites."

"Not just one of our satellites but the billion-dollar spy satellite you were trying to protect! Now given you were attempting to protect the spy satellite, the satellite must've been near the alien craft, did the satellite pick up anything regarding the said alien ship?"

"No. The satellite was being re-tasked to spy on China at the time."

Just then the President walked into the meeting room followed by the Secretary of Defense and the National Security Agency director.

Once seated the President asked, "Admiral Tucker can you explain why we have openly declared war on an unknown non-terrestrial species by sending a ballistic missile as a 'Hello and welcome to Earth'?"

"Mr. President we're just getting to the bottom of that."

Gen Abercrombie just looked straight ahead and gulped.

"Mr. President, given all the recent media attention on reported extra-terrestrial activity that turns out to be bogus, we were taken by surprise. The initial priority was to protect one of our spy satellites. We subsequently believe that the aliens were making an aggressive stance," replied Admiral Tucker.

The President took a long look at the Admiral and the General. There was an agonizing silence till he finally asked, "Well, were we effective in destroying the alien ship?"

"Mr. President, we believe they used their superior stealth technology to avoid our missile."

"Has there been any further contact with these aliens?" Then an air force captain walked into the room and whispered to Admiral Tucker.

"Mr. President we've just had confirmation that the aliens have landed on the moon briefly and disappeared once again with stealth."

"Do we have a picture of the vessel?"

The captain then spoke up, "Mr. President we do have a picture that we're trying to enhance," the captain signaled the projector operator to bring up a very blurred picture of the *Scotty.*

"That's an oddly shaped vessel," the President said, "it looks kind of like the silos we had back on the farm."

"Mr. President, you'll notice nothing that looks like a weapon protruding from the hull of the ship; however, don't let its bulky 18th-century look fool you. The ship was in geosynchronous orbit then three hours later they had landed on the moon. Nothing we have can come anywhere close to those speeds. The only propulsion we detected were minor chemical maneuvering rockets near our spy satellite. This begs the question that their main thrust is undetectable. We would not be able to detect them if they decided to come to Earth."

The President replied, "You mean back to Earth, they obviously know where we are already." The President then directed his words towards the Admiral and said, "I want no further hostilities towards the aliens unless I give my explicit approval. Given the situation now that the aliens know where we are, we need to ramp up any sort of defense we can muster in case they decide to be aggressive," the President ordered as he stared at General Abercrombie. Turning he spoke towards his science and technology director, "I want a report on the latest technologies that are currently available to combat any sort of response. I also want a within reason wish list of the possible technologies available to us shortly. I'm not going to let our nation be defenseless over the price of a few bucks."

♦♦♦

A small office in Strategic Command (USStratCom) HQ, Nebraska

Dan was rubbing his temples while looking at the list of latest research projects undertaken by the Air Force. He was under pressure from a directive he knew had come from the President to find some way of defending Earth, against an unknown alien race, with unknown alien weapons. How could he ever develop something that had so many unknowns? Running through the list of defense contracts he spied the sonic blaster that showed such promise. Dan shook his head. *Although it was unlikely to be used in space, it could possibly be used in boarding operations.* It had been months since Dr. Stevenson had been in contact. He recalled with a slight chuckle the mediocre efforts of his dubious colleague Dr. La Perouse. He thought to himself it's time to pay Dr. Stevenson a visit. Dialing the University, he spoke to the Administrator Mr. Thurston Hughes. The man refused to divulge any information regarding Dr. Stevenson's whereabouts. At that point Dan recalled he had Elvis released, knowing that wasn't his real name but the only one he could remember. They had spoken of a location in El Paso, Texas.

Dan buzzed his adjutant ordering him to dig up the whereabouts of Elvis. A small smile drifted across his face after he made the order. His sister would die of envy if it were the real Elvis incarnate.

Dan rubbed his temples once again then decided he needed to get out of the office for a bit and asked his adjutant to book a flight to El Paso after he met the President in Washington with his latest report.

◆◆◆

Washington DC

Dan was in a deep discussion with the Director of Science and Technology on US space defense capability. They were due in a meeting with DARPA shortly, when his adjutant texted him the details of his flight to El Paso. The director looked at him expectantly. When Dan finally replied, "I'll be checking on one of the contractors for a new sonic weapon, he's moved all his operations to El Paso, Texas."

The director just smiled at him understanding his grief. He'd been a Lt Colonel once a long time ago. Traveling the country was a dull but necessary part of the job.

"Colonel, is that the doctor who you contracted with after the car explosion in DC?"

"Yes Sir, Doctor Stevenson. He's ex-military, working as an inventor now."

The director raised an eyebrow for Dan to elaborate.

"He had a medical discharge from the Army after his helicopter crashed killing two wounded on board. The records don't go into too much detail; however, he was on a COIN (Counter Insurgency) mission when he picked up a squad of grunts. The word is that he could have aborted the mission and returned to base directly. Instead, he chose to continue with the COIN, but crashed on the way out due to a Russian surface-to-air 'cube' missile."

" 'cube' missile! Shit. How?" the Director cursed.

"Russians sold it to the Iraqis for their war with Iran." Both the men paused, reflecting with mutual understanding in their eyes, 'the life of a soldier was always going to be a difficult one.'

"How important was the counterinsurgency mission?" the director queried.

"That's still all classified. I have a feeling it was very necessary given what's not said in his file. Unfortunately, the then Captain Stevenson, returned stateside and had second thoughts about the necessity of it all and requested a transfer."

The Director looked at Dan intensely waiting for Dan to continue.

"Families of the dead Marines did push briefly for an inquiry; however, it was quashed under state secrets provisions."

The director's eyebrows rose higher if that was possible. He then tilted his head at this new information.

"Without knowing what his actual mission was, I'd rather not comment on the necessity of it against the lives of the Marines. Later, Cptn. Stevenson was assigned to the Somalia campaign flying Pave Hawks; combat search and rescue missions. He refused to fly any further COIN missions."

"He can't refuse an order, or a mission," countered the Director.

Dan shrugged, "He resigned his commission instead."

The director sat back in his chair, trying to piece together who this 'Doctor', no 'Captain' Stevenson was.

Another text from Dan's adjutant ended their conversation.

Chapter Sixteen

Research Base, El Paso, Texas

John was sitting at the only table in the cottage reviewing his budget of the project when Max rushed in excitedly pushing some papers in front of him.

"What are these," John asked as the other two team members walked into his office.

"This is the location of that thermonuclear detonation. We finally think we know where it is." The rest of the team looked expectantly at John to give the final go-ahead for their mission.

"How certain are we of the coordinates?"

"Well, it's the best guesstimate."

"Come on John this is what we've all been talking about this past month," Jen put in. Max looked so excited and eager. It was hard to deny him.

"Okay, okay you have my vote. If we go out there, are we sure that we can navigate back home if we lose the harmonics database?" The harmonics database was the three-dimensional map in space of target locations by their harmonics. Each of the different jump locations gets stored in the database.

Max then spoke up, "We have taken readings from half a dozen stars so we can plot our position from those stars. I've picked stars readily identifiable. Once we get to a new location, we will do a scan for those stars, and we should be able to plot a course home. Each time we make a jump the navigation database will automatically record our jump and update the database with our position. At the very least we can reverse the jump settings and return home with the Home button," Max said enthusiastically.

John knew it was more complicated than that.

Max continued despite John's querying look at Jen. "All this extra data will enable us to build a better three-dimensional model of the galaxy. It may take a little time, but eventually, we should be able to jump anywhere from anywhere assuming everything else works... Theoretically."

"So, Jen, can you link the jump drive into the nav computer?"

"Already done," Jen said with a smile.

"Given we only have a guesstimate of its location, how do we home in on it?" The other two just looked at John.

"We could set up some more passive remote sensors each time we jump that can read all the EM frequencies, tachyons, as well as extra light detection telescopes." He paused thoughtfully.

"It would be a bit like leaving a trail of bread crumbs."

John wasn't sure he liked that... *it would lead any alien straight here. Then discounted it... they would already know it if they were that close to Earth already.*

"OK, if we can't find them by passive scans, we can then shift to using active radar sensors and ping for the vessel remotely from the probes. I really want to leave that as a last resort. Pinging their position will give *our* position away too easily. Given we don't have any shielding and only a thin metal hull, we wouldn't last a second against anything sent against us. So the plan I think we should follow is 'jump-out' there using only passive sensors then return home and re-evaluate."

The four of them looked at each other with a tense excitement.

We're they really going to do this? John then spoke up, "Whatever happens, we still need some defenses. The near miss last time in orbit has taught me a thing or two. I've spoken to Scarlet, and she's given me some names of some serious bad ass people."

"What do you mean?" replied Jen.

"Gun runners."

Jen's eyes widened. John could tell that Jen was re-evaluating her impression of Scarlet Riley. The crusty old woman was by no means as harmless as she appeared. "That woman just amazes me who she knows."

John smiled in agreement then turned to Elvis, "I want you to get little 'Paddy'. We're going to visit some of Scarlet's more disreputable friends." Paddy was the nickname of Elvis's magnum revolver. It was a serious weapon that John had never seen Elvis used in anger. They needed to give the impression of a dangerous customer. *If 'Dirty Harry' could use it, Elvis could*, John thought with a wry smile.

When dusk had bitten the landscape, John and Elvis drove out to a remote location of El Paso proper. The warehouse stood off a dimly lit side alley where several indistinct forms walked the perimeter. Next to large crates in the center of the floor stood two immaculately dressed gentleman in business suits, more suited to a bankers meeting then a shady under-the-table arms deal.

John and Elvis had spent their fair share of time in the Army and Reserves and, were familiar with some weapons. They needed to purchase an arsenal of assault rifles, handguns, knives, stun grenades, mines and an assortment of other military hardware quickly without question.

"I think you'll find everything there on the list you asked for," the shadowy figure commented.

After looking over the arms. John handed the man a single sheet of paper.

"I have additional needs. Can you get these?"

The man started reading down the list, "... it will be expensive," he said then halted three-quarters the way down.

The contact seemed stunned at the additional request for a missile launcher and a brochure for other heavy duty weaponry to purchase in the future. The two underworld characters seemed unsure of John and Elvis's credentials, but then told them he would see what he could do to acquire the extra weaponry. Undoubtedly without further background checks and Scarlet's recommendation the arms transaction would not have concluded smoothly.

The quiet business contact seemed almost charming until he posed a simple request of John, "I would like an introduction to meet with your father."

John stood there taken aback. He hadn't spoken to his father in at least five years since he'd revealed the real reason why his mother had left. The man had become more secretive than ever. John had no doubt that it had to do with the company he kept.

"I'll see what I can do," John finally replied with a sigh.

Elvis gave John a curious look but said nothing.

John pulled out two fat brown envelopes full of one hundred dollar bills. John had meant to leave the blood money untouched but succumbed when he realized his friends' lives might be at risk without adequate weaponry for protection. "At least it'll come to some good," he muttered.

After signing over a tidy little sum, John and Elvis started packing all the hardware into the truck. The two sweated while loading their weaponry, it was heavy work. Eventually, when all the weapons and other paraphernalia were loaded, they took off at speed back to the research base.

"Why would he want an introduction to meet your father?" Elvis asked later that evening when the two were alone back at the cottage.

John gritted his teeth and stared directly at Elvis. There was obviously a war going on within.

"My father works for Anton Massionni," John blurted as if trying to spit out an acid aftertaste.

"The crime boss Massionni?"

"Yes." He knew Elvis wouldn't stop probing, despite John's short answer.

John sighed heavily, "I was quite young when my mother left without a word or sign, or so I thought for years." John ground his teeth. "Well, my father just lost it. He was a broken man and tried to raise me on his own. In the end, I moved out and lived with my Aunt Grace. However, my father," John looked down at the ground. "My father wasted all of the money he and Mum had put away."

Elvis was entranced by John story. He had never revealed this seedy side of his family.

"My father was the senior accountant for the ATL stockbroking firm."

Elvis scrunched his eyebrows together in recognition of the firm's name. The stockbroking firm had lost millions when the corporate watchdog accused them of insider trading. There was a serious investigation, which led to some criminal arrests.

"Your father didn't get arrested?"

"No. He was sued by them."

"Well, that wasn't the answer I was expecting," Elvis said.

"I later found out that my mother worked for a pharmaceutical firm that tested their drugs on young families that were too poor to afford the necessities, let alone established lifesaving drugs. The company offered them a ridiculously small payment in compensation for some pretty horrific side-effects; birth deformities, cancer, you name it, and they got it."

Elvis showed his confusion about John mentioning his mother's work and father getting sued by his employer.

"It turned out that my father's firm was 100% stock owner of the pharmaceutical company. So my mother confronted my father that his company was killing people through their drug trials. My father wasn't good at empathizing."

"So your mother left."

It was some time before John nodded and continued his story. "My father tried to buy back my mother by embezzled millions from the firm. He paid all that he took to the poor families that were used as test subjects. Even the money both my parents had put aside wasn't enough to pay for the children's hospital bills or sway my mother."

"She didn't forgive him?"

"No. My mother was still furious with him because he was silent in their board meetings."

John let the implications set in. His father, by his silence was in part responsible. "It was all too late. I found a letter from my mother to my father, she'd said *'the children had died with no arms or legs...* you can't buy that back'.

John shook his head winching. It would be so cliché if he hadn't believed it had happened to him.

"The company knew it was him, but didn't know how he had embezzled the money. They still needed a scapegoat for their financial trading losses. The funny thing was that it wasn't him that had anything to do with the poor share trading. He told me it was his penance."

"So, Massionni the mobster, how does he fit in?"

"My father's name was dirt in the financial world. I don't know, but somehow he was able to convince Massionni that he was good at his job. It turned out that he was brilliant at hiding and laundering money."

"That's quite a story," Jen said as she walked into the room.

John turned at her entrance, surprised.

"I'm sorry John, I didn't mean to overhear... I meant to leave you two alone," Jen continued.

John scrunched his eyes tightly shut. His face flushed red with hurt.

"I just couldn't bear it," She said after an awkward silence.

The comment jolted John; his eyes snapped open. *It was his family history*, and she couldn't bear it ...!

"I can't get it out of my mind, killing Old Man Sykes." Jen bit her lip.

"Well...," John was flabbergasted at Jen's change of subject. "No hiding now...," John said hotly at Jen's insensitivity, but finished up saying under his breath, "I'm from a screwed up family."

"We all have our skeletons," Jen said defensively.

John didn't want to hear her unvoiced reproach, so strode out of the room with Jen's eyes following him.

"You should have stayed quiet Jen," said Elvis quietly.

"But..."

"But, that's the most John's said about his family in over ten years that I've known him," stated Elvis.

Jen gulped. Small tears formed in the corners of her eyes.

The following morning, John couldn't meet Jen's eyes. Instead he and Elvis got to work and unveiled their arsenal showing their two wide-eyed colleagues as they brought out their new toys. The two ex-soldiers went through the mechanics of using each of the weapons with Jen and Max. At first, Jen was uncertain, but as she felt the grip of the .22mm semiautomatic, her demeanor changed abruptly. She'd recalled the close call she'd had with the old man and pursed her lips. She had such a mixture of emotions from the clash and resolved that she would never be helpless in front of such raw aggression again.

The following week they focused on setting up the extra sensors on an extensible arm.

At the same time, they started training in the use of small arms in earnest. Once again one of Scarlet's contacts was able to help. Eric was an ex-special forces type, having toured in some military hotspots. It was obvious by the way he looked, moved and evaluated all those around him. His expertise being a specialist in hand-to-hand and light arms fighting would come in very handy, if they were ever confronted in close quarters. He was mildly surprised at the range and firepower when John brought out a few of the weapons.

John had no intention of allowing that confrontation to manifest itself. Despite Eric's very visible consternation that four apparent intellectuals were learning hand-to-hand combat, he played his role as a trainer with professionalism.

Eric stood before the four in their track shorts and sweats.

"Anyone, meaning the four of you," Eric said pointing at all of them, "that is placed in the position where they need hand-to-hand combat, should be somewhere else. That's best left to the professionals."

"But... That's what you're training us to be, professional, ... or 'more professional'."

"Ha, Ha, that's a good one." Eric said good-naturedly with a deep grin, "To be a professional at hand-to-hand, needs years of practice."

Eric could see the miffed look that Elvis gave, and grinned at his discomfort.

John slapped Elvis on the back, "He's right buddy, can't teach an old dog new tricks."

"Hey, are you calling me old? I'm only 35," Elvis snorted.

"No, I don't think you're old, Rex."

Jen couldn't help giggling at John calling him a dog.

"Right, my best advice to you, if you get in this situation... is to run. That includes you too Grandpa," Eric said with a deadpan expression.

Max threw his arm in the air in victory. "Whoo hoo! The first time I'm great at something physical."

They all just looked at him as if he was insane. "I'm definitely the fastest runner."

The rest of the team burst out laughing. Elvis started to hum, his favorite training song, 'a hunk of love'.

Chapter Seventeen

John could see that all stations in the Scotty were secure, and there was green across-the-board, they were ready. Setting his microphone, he counted down, "Jump in five, four, three, two, one ... Mark!"

The *Scotty* flashed out of existence at the cottage and reappeared light years from Earth. Air bustled out of the ship.

"Mark our position Max. Are our sensors up?"

He ignored the obvious and replied, "No contacts. Computing incremental jumps now. It will take some time." John hoped it wouldn't take too much time as each jump required them to wait for the heat to dissipate and the batteries to recharge. They only had so much oxygen before they would need to return to Earth. The crew could not determine the exact location of the nuclear detonation. But based on the information that they received from TACSA, they did know the direct line of sight from Earth towards the explosion, and they had their new sensors.

"Deploy probe," John commanded.

"Probe away." Elvis and Max had taken turns deploying the basic probes out the back of *Scotty*. They had built half a dozen of the simple machines at El Paso. The Internet was a wealth of information for DYI satellite construction.

"Jump in five... Mark."

The *Scotty* jumped five more times in small increments. Keeping a close eye on their oxygen levels, John concluded they would have to return home shortly because their oxygen would run out in only a few more hours.

"We have a contact!" Max blurted out. "Bearing 5° west, declension 20°."

"Distance?"

"250 miles," Max replied.

"Any other contacts?" John asked with trepidation.

"Other contacts? ... No. Just the one. It's a large vessel, with a significant debris field. They look like bits of the ship," Max said aloud to the crew.

"Do we have a visual on the target?" The *Scotty* had jumped into a planet-less star system. Dim blue light bathed the derelict freighter giving off a light blue ghost like reflection.

"Yes, but there's not a lot to see. There doesn't seem to be much lighting on the exterior of the vessel. I can just make out the shape of it." Max sent the image to the main screen so the rest of the crew could see. They all sat there taking in the view for a few minutes. There seemed to be no life signs, although the ship was so large it was difficult to tell. John immediately got the impression that the vessel was some sort of freighter based on its configuration. He looked at each of the crew directly as they nodded in turn to further investigation.

The four then discussed the situation. They only had two hours left of air. However, they now had a positive location they could jump back to at a moment's notice. They decided to take a few more videos of the external surface of the alien ship, then return home to fully recharge the *Scotty* and their air supply.

◆◆◆

A full two days went by as the crew made a detailed inspection of the pictures and video they had taken on their earlier mission. The four could not readily identify any weapons on the hull of the ship based on the grainy nature of the video and pictures. There was just too little light to make an accurate determination. John made a mental note to seek out any sensor technology including infrared that would help them in the future.

The *Scotty* flashed from Earth and reappeared next to the alien vessel.

"Elvis, if you haven't already can you set the recharge on the batteries."

John was reluctant to move any closer until their alpha jump drive charge had been fully restored.

Twenty minutes later John checked the board was all green before engaging the thrusters.

"Once again Max, check for any contacts while I bring us 500 feet off its bow, please."

Without drag on the ship, they picked up speed quickly compared to planetside transport. Jen roughly calculated when John would have to rotate the thruster unit reversing the ship's speed to rendezvous the *Scotty* with the derelict vessel.

Before them was a monster ship. The four of them released their seat belts floating to the front to crowd around the portal to view their first alien ship in the flesh. It was huge. The rear of the vessel had severe damage. Bent metal and debris were strewn in a spherical field drifting out from the ship. There were stripes of the distinctive fluorescent pattern on either side reflecting what little light there was.

"Elvis, can you take us closer to the ship so we can get a good look. We need to find some sort of hatch or airlock. The tension was palpable as Elvis moved the *Scotty* cautiously around the vessel.

"Everyone, keep your eyes peeled for anything resembling a weapon pointed at us or moving!"

It was difficult to see through the helmet of the old space suits.

"Max I hope you're recording all this." One of the last upgrades to the *Scotty* was to attach cameras to the exterior allowing a 360 view.

"I've set the recorders to immediately start whenever we make a jump. They will automatically download the images and any recordings once we're within range back on Earth."

John pointed to a hatch-like structure on the port side of the vessel near its bow.

"Take us in there Elvis, I think that is the airlock," there was a loud bang as Elvis maneuvered the *Scotty* to kiss the airlock lightly. "Remind me to buy some extra padding near our back door. We don't want the *Scotty* smooching other strange vessels without protection." The other three laughed, breaking the tension.

Max opened *Scotty's* rear hatch to a door like opening with a console to the side. Strange lettering adorned the panel and two buttons within a hand size alcove. Holding onto *Scotty's* hatch, Max reached out and pressed the blue button on the console near the hatch. A small light above the hatch illuminated as the airlock cycled through to end opening inwards. Lights inside automatically turned on. The intensity of light was slightly brighter than what humans were used to so, Max pulled down his visor to cut some of the glare.

"Max, I know that you are eager; however, I want you to sit this one out because we need to know if any other vessels turn up. Looking at the debris and the rear of this ship, I think it was attacked rather than the victim of a horrible accident. I saw what looked like scorch marks near what could be the engines. We need to be prepared to get out of here at short notice."

"Do you mean that you're expecting someone or something to return?" asked Jen.

"I'm not certain. Yet, there still seems to be a vast amount of cargo still on this vessel. Why would they leave so much here, to me that doesn't make sense? Everybody check your partner's weapons and backup oxygen."

Elvis grabbed two lights from the toolbox handing one to John and keeping the other. "Sorry Jen, there's only two."

"Why are you bothering, the lights are on," Jen said. Elvis just shrugged.

John, Jen, and Elvis entered the airlock spying another control panel at the far end. As they traversed the airlock, they gradually felt the tug of gravity within the craft.

"Almost the same gravity as ours," said Elvis. Once they reached the inner lock, John called out for suggestions, "Blue or Red," while pointing to two large buttons on the side console.

"Blue" replied Jen and pressed the blue button. The outer hatch slowly shut then a blue strobe light overhead flashed. After a minute, the strobe was replaced with normal lighting and the inner hatch opened inwards. Passing through the hatch, they were confronted with three separate corridors. John turned and checked each of his crew ensuring they had their weapons at the ready. He then turned left and said, "Let's go this way."

As they moved through the ship, they saw some devices which were obvious but most of which they had no inkling of their purpose. As soon as they came close to any door, it would automatically open. Taking their time, they made slow progress through the ship. An eerie feeling came over them as they realized that the vessel was unmanned. Could this be fully automated or would they eventually find the crew in stasis? As they discuss these questions, it only brought up more questions rather than answers. Eventually, they came to a door that had been cut open. Scorch marks could be seen surrounding the door lock mechanism. "Well that confirms it, they were boarded."

Altering his grip on his pistol, John peered into the large room that only had minimal lighting, unlike the corridor. Unmistakable consoles, controls, and view screens were spaced around the room.

"This must be the bridge," he whispered to the others as he couldn't see all the way in.

"I wonder who must've done this," Elvis pointed out the remnants of the door on the floor. As they moved into the room, John pointed his gun at corners and shadows until he was sure that there was no one on the bridge. He then moved his suit camera in front of each of the consoles so they could get a good view recording them. Elvis looked at each of the controls trying to determine their purpose. Unusual scripts adorned each. Turning to the rear of the room Jen spied an open cupboard. Two weapons hung on hooks, while the rest of the hooks were empty. Jen picked up both placing one in her carry pouch and giving the other to John.

"Sorry Elvis, there's only two," she said with a smile.

Elvis just shrugged.

John watched the exchange and shook his head and moved back out the entrance of the bridge. "Max, anything on the radar?"

"No, we are all clear. How's it going in there?"

"Well, it looks like we found the bridge. Someone or something burnt the door down. So keep your eyes peeled and let me know the minute there's a contact." John knew that Max could see everything they were watching through all of their suit cams.

"Aye, aye Captain."

John wasn't sure whether Max was just joking around. So he just smiled and let it go. Carefully they moved through the freighter's corridors and opened rooms. The three started to get a sense of the aliens that lived there. There were artworks and pleasing colors all over the walls. They would change as they passed from one corridor to another. Landscapes of semiarid environments were portrayed on more than one wall. They briefly stopped in a room that could only be considered as a galley with machines that looked like vending machines you would expect to see at any busy train station. The morsels displayed seemed particularly unappetizing. John wondered if they were freeze-dried native creatures from their home planet.

Elvis stopped at a compartment with various controls and a small portal. Although the language was indecipherable, the pictographs inferred a shield of some sort. Given they were currently in the bow of the ship they concluded it was a shield for navigation. While passing through space, you do not want to run into anything, hence the shield to push obstacles away from the moving ship. John made a note of the location on the 3d mobile mapmaker fastened to the top of his helmet so they could return to retrieve this technology.

Moving on, the trio brushed past more rooms which looked to be set up as entertainment areas. This vessel must've been a long-term home for its crew.

Jen came across what could only be considered a manual control for an external thruster. The pictographs were clear as to its purpose. There was a portal slightly above the controls to which John looked through and saw an enormous maneuvering engine jutting out of the vessels hull. Once again John recorded the location. "Make sure you note the things or tools we will need to salvage this technology."

Chapter Eighteen

Pirate Island Base, Cassiopeia System

Kane, the pirate commander, was enjoying the massage from the two nymph Squishys. The identical twins were masters at tenderizing sore limbs. He couldn't decide which was better as they always changed their designations just to confuse him. Not only was the massage stupendous they had an uncanny ability to change color creating a visual extravaganza as they worked.

"Oh brilliant and masterful Commander, we have completed unloading the spoils and are currently taking on new supplies for the return to the freighter," his tactical officer commented. The Squishy was still brooding after having to look after two little bipedal lizards.

"No need to be so formal, little slug," Kane replied out of irritation. "Have we received an answer from the Carnivores regarding the bio-cargo?"

The crew shifted from one tentacle to the other, "Not yet Commander, they seem to be rather indisposed."

This peaked Kane's interest, "What do you mean?"

"A colony of Furbags was destroyed recently, and I believe the Carnivores are eating their profits."

Kane in his consternation curled his fore-tentacle around the delicate masseur tightly squeezing all blood from the soft sucker. She yelped with pain and reflexively squirted a disgusting inky cloud straight into Kane's face. The crewman snickered under his breath at his Commander's predicament. Kane knew immediately that his face would be marked for quite some time.

"Well, we can't wait any longer, we only left food for a month for that fish-bait Drakmok on the freighter. He will no doubt complain if we're too long." Kane curled his fore tentacle at the memory of Drakmok's response to being left in the freighter medical bay. The fully-grown octopi had squealed like a baby squid squirting copious amounts of ink.

Kane rationalized Drakmok's abandonment by highlighting that the lizards had far better regenerative medical biobeds than the Squishys. It made sense for him to stay and repair his dismembered limb, and prepare the rest of the cargo for the *Kator's* return.

Chapter Nineteen

John, Jen, and Elvis finally reached a hatch that led to the cargo areas. Pictographs advertised the contents on the outside of a larger door. Elvis pressed the blue button opening another airlock. The three moved in through to the small chamber. This time, as the room cycled through their bodies became weightless. Jen pushed herself to the external airlock pressing the red button to open the hold hatch. This time, no lights came on.

"Jen, I think you should wait here or make your way back to the Scotty," said John.

"Why?"

"It's dark out there in the hold. You have no light, besides our oxygen is running low, so as soon as we do a quick recon of the cargo area, we'll head back to the *Scotty*." She looked at the two of them with concern written in her eyes.

John sensing her hesitation, temporized. "I'm sure you'll be okay; we've gone through the bow."

She smiled and said, "I wasn't worried about me, I was worried about you two getting up to mischief."

John and Elvis laughed out loud.

As Jen's outline moved past the corner, Elvis and John turned and floated through the airlock and out into the cargo hold. The hold was a long narrow corridor with what looked like release controls for the containers attached to the hull. As the two moved forward, they could see some had already been released. Someone or something had picked which containers were more valuable. John could see the fourth and the fifth were still actively connected to the cargo freighter. Making his way to the panel release he made a quick study eventually pressing a pictograph with a claw unfurling.

A slight shudder shook the floor as docking clamps released. To John's surprise, the container started to pull away from the freighter. Apparently, each container had its own maneuvering capability. It pulled out from the freighter to park itself 500 feet from the main ship.

Max's distressed voice came over the comm, "Guys, the ship's breaking up."

"It's OK Max, we released a cargo container from its docking clamps."

Elvis smiled as he pushed another controlled release. A shudder once again ran through the floor. Another container on the opposite side maneuvered out into space parking itself ready for pickup. John and Elvis walked further down the corridor holding their lights in front. Suddenly they saw a light in the distance flickering backward and forwards. The men both froze. John really wanted to get a glimpse of the aliens on board but thought better of it remembering the scorch marks.

"Time to go!" he whispered to Elvis. "Max, is there anything on the sensors?! We have a contact here!"

"No, the board is clear."

"Are you okay John?" Jen said over the radio.

"We're heading back; we'll meet you there Jen. Please don't dawdle."

The two raced back to the airlock slamming the blue button and turning to see whether the alien had witnessed their departure. John knew damn well that it would have felt it.

As they waited for the agonizingly slow cycle of the airlock, the two fidgeted with their weapons. The lights strobed on as they raced out of the hatch toward their ship. By the time they reached the *Scotty,* Jen and Max were buckled in awaiting their arrival. "I still haven't seen any other vessel; do you really think it was some sort of confrontation."

"Yes I do, the damage and scorch marks around the bridge door makes it undeniable. I believe they'll be coming back to pick up their crew," Jon replied.

"Jen, do you have the harmonics of this location mapped into the computer?"

"Yes, I did that before we went on board the alien ship."

"Excellent!"

"Jumping in five, four, three, two, one... mark!" The sudden re-compression whistled through the command center again.

The peaceful cottage setting was a welcome relief to the high tension on the freighter. John quickly checked his system board confirming all was clear then adjusted his helmet removing it.

"I think we need to get back there as fast as possible before they cannibalize the rest of the freighter. My first option was to fly it here. But with the possibility of aliens on board, there is no way we should do that."

"But they will be back, John."

John looked at them and said, "Yes, but this is a golden opportunity." Suddenly John thought he hadn't actually asked his crew whether they're willing to take the risk. "I know you're scared, but I believe that if we are quick, we can target those few technologies and be out of there before they return. We can take the containers, the front shield projector, and the thruster. If we hurry, we can keep taking bits till they return. Did you guys mark any other technology we should consider as a priority?"

Jen looked at John thinking over her decision whether to return then smiled and replied, "There was something that was like a medical bay that I've marked."

"There were a few more containers towards the stern of the ship," Elvis commented.

John looked at the other two. Each nodded in turn. "Okay let's get our oxygen refilled and the Uber projector locked down."

One of the improvements that John and Elvis had been working on was a larger version of the jump projectors. This projector, although untested, would comfortably encompass the containers that they launched to a parking station 500 ft.

off the freighter. The projector needed to be connected to the targeting systems.

"John, are you sure about connecting this, we will either have to disconnect our primary jump drive or connect this one to the home drive targeting."

"I think our best option is to disconnect the main drive once we are there. I don't want to touch our emergency home drive. If anything happens while we're doing the conversion or transferring the salvage, then we just jump with the emergency one. We know that works."

"You're the boss," with that Elvis went about setting up the equipment for a quick transfer once they are on site.

◆◆◆

John locked the new alien weapons in his office and return to the *Scotty*.

"Are we ready?" He said to Elvis two hours later. Soon after the crew suited up and the *Scotty* jumped to 500 feet off the stricken freighter. "Status report," John said.

They all breathed a sigh of relief when Max reported, "No contacts other than the freighter."

"Okay Elvis, get cracking, we need that Uber projector on-line pronto." Elvis unbuckled and floated to the rear compartment to connect up the projector to the *Scotty's* targeting system.

"How long do you think Elvis?"

"Give me 20 minutes and it should be done."

"Jen, it's your turn to take the *Scotty* and park us right near that airlock we used last time," Jen unbuckled and moved over to Elvis's console and started to maneuver the *Scotty* towards the airlock. John had forgotten to put padding outside their hatch so was expecting Jen to thump the two vessels. He was mildly surprised the contact was barely noticeable. He smiled seeing Jen's smile from the corner of his eye. He thought just as well Elvis wasn't here to witness this.

"Jen, I'm going to take transmitters and stick them to each of the transport targets so we have a clear signal. If you can start setting up the transporter." John then spoke to Max. "Can you monitor those scanners and radar from anywhere?"

"No, but that's a damn good idea."

"I'm sorry Max, but we need someone on the scanners at all times while we're here," Max could only sigh as he knew that he would not be boarding the freighter anytime soon.

John made his way from the *Scotty* through the freighter's airlock and into the corridor. Once again he was amazed at the gravity control that allowed him to move freely through the ship. John didn't waste time locating the front shield projector and putting a transmitter on it. Then, for good measure, he found the bridge controls. Placing a transmitter on the panel he turned it on then contacted Jen.

"Yes, it's coming in loud and clear."

As he waited for Jen's response, John took another look around each of the controls trying to determine which controlled what. After several minutes, he reluctantly moved on placing another transmitter over the thruster alcove. John then quickly walked past the airlock to the container section holding his sidearm. He walked to the galley and placed another transmitter on the food dispensing machines. Finally, he came to the medical center that Jen had previously mentioned.

John opened the door and yelled out in surprise, "Shit!"

A large octopus like creature stood barely 6 feet from him hunched over some medical device. Its bulbous head turned while its eyes stood erect on their stalks staring at him in surprise. The creature's body turned, and its left fore-tentacle reached around into its pouch to what could only be a weapon.

John quickly jumped backward while pulling his pistol out slamming his hand on the back of the door. Pain coursed through his wrist even though he was wearing his cumbersome orange spacesuit.

The creature squealed, even with his helmet on, John could hear it. It was worse than his heady days of listening to heavy metal music. It must've been a defense mechanism for the creature.

The door swished shut just as the creature aimed and fired the weapon only to score the inside of the door as it closed. Out in the corridor, John moved to the side where he could angle his shot if the door reopened.

"I hope you guys are almost finished! Because I have a seriously ugly alien right next door!"

John started to wonder what the creature was doing in the room when he first opened the door. From his glimpse, all he could tell was that the creature was leaning over some machine with its limb inside. He guessed it was scanning it or something. If the creature hadn't had to take its limb from the machine before it aimed and shot, he knew it would have been a very different outcome.

"John, do you need me to come to you?" Elvis spoke up concerned.

"No. Just make sure you're ready to transport when I get there."

"You be careful," he heard Jen say with concern in her voice.

John backed away from the door keeping his pistol pointed directly at the entrance. Once he was passed the corner and out of sight, John ran like a bat out of hell to the airlock. Pressing the red button repeatedly, John decided it did not make the airlock work any faster. Finally, as he got to the outer hatch, Jen was waiting for him with her Glock in one hand.

"Targets are all set. Elvis is just finalizing the switchover; he should be done by the time we reach the control center."

"All done," they all heard Elvis's pleased voice.

"Right. Jen. Target One, the shield generator on my mark, three, two, one... mark." Jen pushed the engage button. A section of the freighter suddenly disappeared. Sudden decompression ripped through the front of the vessel rocking it into a slight spin while bulkheads shut.

Meanwhile, Drakmok was counting his bad luck that another species had come across their prize. He rapidly changed color from red to blue with trepidation as he realized he was alone on the freighter with an unknown number of aliens. He hadn't seen this species before. It was hard to tell in their bulky orange suits, but he thought it was a mammal given the soft facial skin in the visor. Mammals could be so aggressive and dangerous if they were provoked. It was lucky that the last one he saw seemed more surprised than he did. He aimed his blaster at the door waiting for the alien to enter. He thought how lucky he was that he did not have his blaster set to full power otherwise the door may not have stayed in place. Yes, it may have gone through the door, but he knew how tough mammals could be.

Drakmok looked at his timepiece trying to figure how long he would need to stay here before his school arrived.

Suddenly the whole medical center shook. He thought the freighter must have been hit by a level one phasor. Lights started flashing, and loud noises boxed his hearing. He searched the center to find something to muffle the fear. He rationalized if he can't hear the noise it won't make him fear as much. The only thing he could come up with was a lizard breast harness. Placing the cups over his ears at least, the lethal sound was muffled.

"Can you target the thruster now Jen," Jen replied with a thumbs up. It's been just over 20 minutes since the last transport. Jen had to take into account the ship spinning movement in her targeting calculations. The vacuum of space had the unexpected benefit of cooling the heat build-up faster than in the atmosphere.

A second explosion shook the bow of the ship once again. Drakmok thought, 'Nooo, these mammals are planning to destroy the ship!' All he could do was to brace himself and move into the corner of the medical bay tightly clutching the breast harness with his two fore-tentacles. He used the rest to sucker onto the walls and floor.

The derelict spun even more wildly, making more transports into the ship more difficult. "Now the two containers, let's take the yellow first," Jen adjusted the targeting so that it would fully encompass the yellow one standing 500 feet off the ship. As planned they targeted it to arrive at the far side of the moon.

The container disappeared in a flash without a sound. John calmly waited for Jen to re-target the second container. He knew Max would pipe up as soon as he saw something. Looking over to Elvis he wanted confirmation that the Uber projector was still working fine. The generator ran at high gear to once again recharge the batteries. This was the most intensive number of long distance jumps that the projector targeting systems had made. "Transport in five, four, three, two, one ...mark." The second container disappeared from near the freighter only to reappear on the dark side of the moon."

"Now we can try for more containers or we can go to the Medical Bay."

John then pointedly asked them all whether they should take the medical bay given the alien was still inside. "John we don't have the facility to hold such a person. We don't even know whether it breathes our atmosphere."

"We can't just leave it here. What if the bits that we've taken have damaged the ship's integrity? We don't know how long he'll be waiting for his crew to return."

"Do you think it was left behind on purpose?"

John thought of the various alternatives. They couldn't transport him and leave him in space on the other side of the moon. The medical Bay may decompress as it wasn't designed to be outside of the ship. At the same time, they couldn't transport him to Earth's surface. He might die because he couldn't breathe Earth's atmosphere.

John's mind was made up for him when Max suddenly piped up, "I have a contact on our long range sensors. It's coming in incredibly fast."

They all looked at the main viewer, "Note the direction it's coming from Max before we make a jump home."

Max gave the thumbs up. Then John hit the Home drive.

◆◆◆

Pirate Vessel Kator

The pirate vessel *Kator* dropped out of FTL close to the stricken freighter.

"Commander there is a vessel parked twenty yards from the freighter's port airlock," said the sensor operator.

"What!! Bring it up on the main viewer!" The sensor operator moved to push his readings onto the main viewer when the ship disappeared.

"What the mollusk are you talking about! There's nothing there." Kane said with irritation, his forehead slowly darkened in color.

"I swear on my fifth mother, there was a ship there!"

As the *Kator* closed in on the freighter, they brought the freighter on visual sensors.

"Where are the two forward containers?"

Then the weapons officer said, "There's new damage to the vessel! There's a huge chunk taken from the bow thruster. The bow has had other damage. Look you can see atmosphere venting. The vessel is spiraling."

"Get that mollusk, Drakmok on the comm!"

"You have returned," Drakmok replied with evident relief.

"What's happened? The freighter looks like it's been in a battle."

"I am so happy you're here!! There are some mammals aboard. I thought they're going to scuttle her! I've had to hole up in the medical bay because they're everywhere."

"Drakmok, you spineless mollusk, they've already left."

Drakmok tried to open the medical bay door to the central corridor however it was stuck fast. He would just have to wait for his commander and his wrath. He then quickly removed the breast brace from his ears a little embarrassed. The ribbing from his crew over the lizard bra would be far worse than anything he could imagine. He would wince each time the alarms went off.

Unbeknownst to Drakmok, Kane had decided to leave him in the confines of the medical bay.

"Get back on that freighter and see what those mammals have left us," he told the boarding party. Then with his pinkie tentacle, he pointed to the sensor operator and said, "I want the configuration of that ship and where it disappeared to on my console."

The sensor operator trawled through the accumulated data but found the phantom ship had a tiny energy signature. There did not appear to be any propulsion in the EM residue. There was no obvious trail to follow. There were indications that it used chemical propellant, but that seemed absurd. They were too far from anywhere for it to have been used as a primary drive. The only thing that made sense was if they were used for maneuvering.

Kane sat on his pedestal deep in thought, he knew that this part of space was devoid of any advanced civilizations. He was not aware of any vessel that did not leave a trail. There was no other significant EM signature to identify this craft. It must have excellent stealth technology. He had never heard of any stealth device that could hide a primary propulsion drive. Well, not hide it completely like they'd just witnessed. They had such a low EM signature that Kane had difficulty believing it.

A few hours later when the pirate ship was preparing to return home, the weapons officer was hesitant to remind the

Commander of Drakmok's predicament. Kane had cooled off after his initial anger. He also realized that the mollusk might have some useful information about these advanced mammals.

♦♦♦

Terran Solar System, far side of the moon

The Scotty materialized 300 feet from two large containers parked in orbit on the dark side of the moon.

"Max, can you place a transmitter on each of those containers just in case we need it."

John was conscious that he wanted Max to do a spacewalk, given he'd been left out of much of the salvage operation.

"Make sure you tether yourself because I don't want to be wasting time trying to maneuver the *Scotty* to pick you up."

John could see the childlike grin on Max's face at the prospect of doing a spacewalk. As Max left the rear hatch, Elvis piped up and said with an evil grin, "I hope he's got lots of air because we could be here a while."

Jen chuckled.

"I think he's been practicing," she said with a smile as Max collided with the yellow container.

John quietly asked Jen to ready the transporter just in case Max pierced his suit with the collision. Jen and Elvis suddenly realized the danger Max was in. Before they could get up, Max pushed off from the first container heading for the second one. They were going to need to add a transmitter on their suits for emergency extract. There was so much to learn.

Research Base El Paso

The Scotty flashed into existence with a crack and a loud whoosh of air. Shock absorbers took the weight of the ship as it rematerialized less than a foot above the ground. John looked through the portal to confirm the first two transported items were sitting comfortably on the cement receiving pad. Three huge grins faced him as the import of what they had achieved hit home.

Chapter Twenty

Deputy Sheriff Amanda, El Paso, Texas

That evening John called his favorite local scrounger, Scarlet, to organize a visit the following day. He had some special requirements that could only be conveyed face-to-face.

The following day John sat drinking coffee with Scarlet while he ran through his requirements for two large sheds, labs, and an administration area. He knew that some of the alien-tech would have to wait to be housed, at least until the procured technology was safely secure.

While John bit into his oatmeal cookie, an El Paso Sheriff's car drove up the driveway stopping outside Scarlet's door. A young short-haired blond deputy sheriff waved as she stepped out of the car. Her bright eyes zeroed in on the stranger sitting on the deck as she climbed up onto the porch. A small smile crossed her face when she recognized the rock hard cookies half eaten in John's hand.

"Hi 'Let, how're you keeping?"

Scarlet shrugged with a smile. John looked from one to the other.

"Ole man Sykes has gone missing. No one has seen him for some weeks now, have you heard anything 'bout where he might have gone?"

"I'm surprised anyone missed the ole codger, ... No one's seen or complained about him? That's strange" Scarlet frowned in thought.

The blond officer then said, "Martinez," the real estate agent in town, "has made a formal missing person's request. He said he has a potential buyer for Sykes's ranch." When

Scarlet made no further comment, the Deputy then directed her gaze at John, "Howdy, I don't think we've met?"

Scarlet piped up, "This nice young man is Dr. Stevenson."

John looked towards the Deputy's face, then at her badge and gun. Nonchalantly, he rose from his chair to nod and mumble, "Deputy, pleased to meet you, I was just on my way out. I wouldn't want to keep you from your duties." John attempted to walk around the Deputy to take the front steps.

Rounding on him the Deputy Sheriff asked, "Is that the Dr. Stevenson who purchased the property next door to Mr. Sykes?" which stopped John in his tracks.

"Yes, that's correct Deputy. I bought the place several months ago now from Mr. Martinez."

The woman inspected John from head to toe trying to gauge his character. "Funny you should say that Dr. Stevenson because Mr. Martinez happened to mention that he had a very interested client who had just purchased some land adjacent to Mr. Sykes's block." She then dug out her phone and said, "Mind if I take your picture for identification purposes Dr. Stevenson?"

"I'd rather you didn't, I'm kinda camera-shy, must be my city upbringing..." John stopped mid-sentence, pursing his lips as he realized the Deputy was already putting her phone camera back in her pocket. She seemed not to have heard him.

"Did you ever meet Mr. Sykes, Dr. Stevenson?" the Deputy continued.

John thought about denying any knowledge of old man Sykes, but realized the Officer would check and possibly find the pet delivery.

"Mr. Sykes kindly brought over a delivery for me several weeks ago, but I have not seen him since."

"When exactly was that Doctor?"

"I believe it was a Monday three and a half weeks ago. My two colleagues were also present when he turned up with Scotty and left."

"Scotty?"

"A dog that recently passed away." The Deputy saw that John fidgeted with his collar, which probably meant he wasn't telling the whole story. She needed to check the time frame of the pet delivery. "What are the names of your colleagues Dr. Stevenson?"

John gave the names of his two friends, and his cell number and wished the Officer a good day. He then thanked Scarlet for her kind hospitality and quickly got in his truck and drove off down the driveway.

"What's your take on the man, Aunt Let?" Let was Scarlet's pet family name.

"He's okay, Amanda dear," said Scarlet thoughtfully. "He's a bit weird like all city folk that you would expect, but he's all right."

Scarlet wondered if she should mention the weapons contact she gave to John. But then had second thoughts. Her niece could be so by the book, it hurt sometimes.

◆◆◆

The very next day much to John's surprise, Scarlet arrived in a convoy of trucks at the front gate piled high with building material. Dozens of tradesmen followed in their clapped-out cars. Her smooth talk and familiar cajoling of the tradesmen expedited the construction. John could see Scarlet was a force to be reckoned with. He mused a what she would have been like when she was in her prime.

Within the week, three large expanses of cement were laid in preparation for the labs and two aircraft hangers. Large wooden frames sat close by ready to be installed once the cement had cured. The height of the sheds gave the builders some consternation, which was almost double the height of an ordinary farm shed. The local planning authority had to be suitably encouraged to allow the buildings to progress at such a rapid pace. Scarlet, "the Magnificent," as John started to call her, smoothed ruffled feathers with the contractors and council in every direction.

While the buildings were being constructed, John called Mr. Hughes from the University to enlist some very particular expertise. The Administrator gave John some recommendations to which he promptly searched on the net for their professional details and resumes.

During the construction, the Deputy Sheriff visited twice more before finally giving up and trusting her aunt's judgment of John's character. She had her reservations though. *Who would build a research base in the middle of nowhere? Especially with all this security?*

When the two hangers and labs were completed, John contacted the security liaison to fortify the labs against intrusion.

Meanwhile, the team sat down to plan the retrieval of the two freighter containers. The hanger was large enough to transport one container with space for the thruster and shield on the side. Once the building crews had finished and left for the day, John assembled his team and boarded the *Scotty* then set out to retrieve the large red container.

Dark side of the Moon

The Scotty materialized five hundred feet from the container. Using the transmitters, they steered the spacecraft and homed in on the drifting prize. The dark side of the moon was updated into the astronomical database.

"You're getting good," John said to Jen. She just smiled appreciating the praise.

John thought how quickly he had gotten used to the jump drive technology. Elvis manually reconnected the Uber projector so they could transport the container while Jen input the new source and destination resonance locations.

"Transport on three, two, one, ... Mark!" A bright flash and an after-image flickered in their eyes. The first of the two containers dematerialized from near the moon to materialize on Earth inside the base hanger.

Elvis once again disconnected the Uber projector and reconnected Alpha Jump Drive. Jen reset the target coordinates back to the research base in El Paso. Although they all knew that they could use the Uber projector to transport the *Scotty* as well, John was still reluctant given that the number of jumps the projector had made was still small compared to the well tested Alpha Jump Drive. He didn't want to risk all their lives on it.

The second container would be brought later when they had room.

◆◆◆

Soon after the *Scotty* arrived back at the research base within the hanger, John removed his helmet. An urgent call from the front gate broke the silence. The guard was querying access for a Lt Colonel of the Air Force.

"Please have him escorted to the Admin Office." John rushed to get out of his suit and ran to the admin building as the others made sure all of the hanger and lab doors were locked tight as Dan arrived at the cottage door.

"Dr. Stevenson, it's been a while since we've been in contact. I thought I'd come down while I was in the area and check how you're going." John wondered wryly if the Lt. Col really had been 'in the area'.

"I need to know how you're progressing on your sonic weapon. As you can imagine, we've had quite an exciting time back in Washington with all this talk about aliens."

"Colonel, we've had a slight delay in the testing process. As you can see, we've had to build our own testing facilities." John could see the Colonel grimaced at the news.

"John, if I may call you John? The agreement we made does not include an unlimited time frame. I think I have been more than generous to allow you to continue your research as opposed to sending you to Guantanamo Bay for treason and or terrorism." His words had enough bite in them to give John a chill.

"Colonel, I realize I have tested your patience but please bear with me just a bit longer. I think you will be pleased with the results."

"Given I have traveled all the way here; I would like to see what you have accomplished so far."

John fought hard for an excuse then suddenly a smile crossed his face as he walked over to the weapons lock-up and pulled out one of the alien pistol weapons.

"Colonel, I know we contracted for a sonic weapon; however, we diverted the research into other specialties given your desire for massive mayhem."

The Colonel heard this and was furious. *I don't need this shit from a two-bit science major with a degree from an Internet University,* he thought.

Before the Colonel could make an objection John raised his hand, "Please bear with me Colonel, I know you've traveled a long way."

This better be Damn good, the Colonel fumed.

John had inspected the weapons earlier but had not, in fact, fired them as yet. The truth was he didn't even know if they worked! However, he took a chance and walked outside, Dan following him, away from the cottage and labs into an open area hedged by the valley walls. John looked at the grip of the weapon and saw a small dial on the side with a slide and a pictograph of what looked like increasing intensity. John turned to the smallest increment then raised his arm and aimed the pistol at a tree stump fifty yards away. As he pulled the trigger, a blue beam shot out from the front of the weapon slicing through the stump and into the valley wall beyond. Dan drew in a startled breath. All they could see was the burning remnant of a hole with the circular outline in the stump. They walked towards the burnt cinder viewing it from both sides and determining that the beam continued on into the valley wall. The pungent burnt tree smell followed them as they continued their investigation walking to where it eventually drilled a hole into solid granite to an unknown depth.

Dan was stunned at the intensity and strength of the handheld laser. John had to hide his amazement while assuming he knew of the laser's capability.

"Colonel, that was the mid-range setting for this handgun."

John turned to look at a rock outcrop sticking out of the valley wall more than a mile away. Holding back and showing the setting to the colonel, he reset the dial into the high range then aimed and fired.

The beam struck the wall of the valley, and a sizable crater blew out of the hard sandstone rock outcrop, billowing debris creating an impressive explosive display. The sound of the blast could be heard echoing around the valley as dust and shards of rock fell to the ground.

"I envisage we will be able to develop a larger version of the hand laser for your ships and planes; however, much will depend on the power source and the conversion gasses," John said making as much up as he could. They needed time to examine the laser gun.

Dan was rapidly working through the implications of this new laser technology. It was a far more advanced laser than any he had ever seen. It had major defense applications. He knew of other lasers the government had developed to shoot down surface-to-air missiles used by the Naval Surface Warfare Center. However, nothing came anywhere *near* this for the size to power ratio. This could save him from a tough predicament. At least now he had something to give to his superiors, and ultimately the President.

"As I said Colonel, please be patient and you'll have your weapon."

John then took that opportunity to direct Dan back to his car. "I hope you'll have a pleasant return trip. I will most likely be returning to Washington shortly as I have business with the University. We could talk in more depth at that time. I'll set up a presentation for you and anyone you wish to bring along." Dan smiled at this, his previous anger forgotten with the impressive display of the blaster.

Allowing himself to be shepherded back to his car, the air force officer was halfway down the driveway when he realized that John had provided him with something entirely different to the sonic weapon he was expecting; but, this was so much better.

John returned to the cottage to find Elvis sitting at the table munching on some corn flake crisps in milk. "Did you hear that?" Elvis asked. "They must be doing some sort of blasting around here." John smiled at this but said nothing.

"I need you to find out all you can about this weapon and what it would take to reverse engineer it." John placed the blaster on the table in front of Elvis who looked onto it with a devilish grin.

"And by the way, be really careful, and I mean really careful when you use it because I just disintegrated an enormous hole in the valley wall demonstrating it." John stood up and made his way out of the cottage. When he reached the door he yelled over his shoulder to Elvis still sitting there at the table staring at the alien pistol, "And I needed that yesterday."

Chapter Twenty-One

John arrived at the alien artifact hanger to find Jen and Max poring over the shield assembly unit, but more particularly a dark material. "What do you have there?"

"This is a part of the ship's external hull. It's not robust enough to be a complete physical barrier, and I don't believe that it's part of the shield mechanism," Jen explained. They removed a piece of the dark plastic like material placing it aside on a workbench for further study. Behind the black substance was some palm sized boxes, which looked to be connected to cabling. The other end of the cable was dangling loose where the teleporter had cut its path through the ship. "I wonder if this is something to do with the sensors?"

There were some of the boxes and cables mounted on both the shield projector and thruster assembly unit; however, they didn't seem to be attached or connected to them. The cabling joined together at the edge of the artifact. What it was previously connected to, they didn't know.

"It reminds me of a solar panel I pulled apart when I was a kid," John said.

Jen Thought on that for a minute, "Maybe, we'll know more when we test that stuff and open the cable boxes its connected to."

Jen focused her attention on the shield assembly unit viewing it from all angles before readjusting several video cameras to better document the disassembly.

♦♦♦

John left them to their work as he moved over to view the red freighter container. He walked around the large solid cargo container trying to find an entry point. One of the ends had a small console with pictographs showing a closed and opened box. John pressed the open button. The wall shifted and clicked, then slowly opened out, unfolding and narrowly missing the two working on the shield artifact. Cold fog rolled out over the floor giving it a Transylvanian atmosphere. The top also folded upwards at a 90° angle allowing incredible access to the insides of the container. Boxes of various sizes were stacked to the brim. Larger pieces of equipment of indeterminate purpose were stacked, taking up the bulk of the insides.

On the end was a small briefcase sized box with a handle. Small multicolored buttons adorned the outside in plain view. John went to the case lifting it up and placing it on the workbench and pressed the open button pictograph. He furrowed his eyebrows in thought because within the case were piles of what could only be described as manuals. John picked up a manual and turned what looked like laminated pages of instructions written in an indecipherable alien language. Next to where the suitcase was found was a larger box with a handle John could barely lift. On opening the second box, he was confronted with a computer console with large buttons and a sophisticated array of lights.

"Max, come and have a look at this, please."

The computer specialist dropped what he was doing and sauntered over to take a look at what John was examining.

"What do you make of this?"

Max looked over the box and lights and saw a back panel. Undoing the clasp on the panel he removed it to look inside. He was stunned to find vacuum tubes. His immediate thought was that the tubes had some other highly technical process. But the more he looked, the more he smiled at the relatively antiquated technology used here.

"How can this be? They must be hundreds of years in advance of us and yet they use vacuum tubes!"

"I'll leave you two to it then, find out what this does," John said to Max as he pointed to the alien computer.

♦♦♦

John picked up two of the heavy manuals and took them with him to examine further. He went back to the office and brought up the University faculty listings. Running through the linguistics department, he read each of the bio's settling on Dr. Jerry O'Connor. Picking up the phone John called Dr. O'Connor to be greeted by a rather flamboyant Irish accent. "What can I do for you Mister...?"

"It's Dr. Stevenson, Doctor. I have a rather interesting proposition for you. I have what I believe is an entirely new language that I need you to translate. This language is not like any you would have seen."

"Dr. Stevenson, I know a lot of languages. I doubt there would be one I've not seen or a variant of it." The Irish lilt sounded a little bored.

"Doctor, please call me John. I can guarantee that you have not seen this language before. I'm about to send you a sample of it; however, before I do I will need you to sign a non-disclosure statement."

The little balding Irishman sat back in his chair thinking about a non-disclosure just to view some text. "John, now you have me intrigued. Send me the non-disclosure to my fax and I'll sign it straight away." Within the hour, John had not only sent the statement and received a response; he had also sent a sample of the alien text and a contract to translate the documents. John told the linguist he had a lot more text however he would only be allowed to translate these on-site. Jerry called John back questioning the need to be on-site, and where on-site was.

"El Paso!" Jerry racked his memory furiously trying to recall if he'd heard of any archaeological digs in Texas lately.

"I'm afraid so Dr. O'Connor. We can discuss remuneration when you get here..."

"Right-T-Oh boyo! You've got me there." Jerry responded in his rich Irish accent. He then laughed aloud thinking *John had him with this first sample like sweets to a child*. With that, he signed the contract and packed his bags to leave for the first flight to El Paso.

The second call John made was to a faculty member, one Dr. Fellows, who was a leader in the field of propulsion. "Dr. Fellows, my name is Dr. Stevenson, and I have a rather interesting proposition for you..."

◆◆◆

The various research projects were moving apace smoothly to John's surprise. John knew that deep down, a serious amount of intellect and scientific research would need to be applied to the alien technology. Despite John's desire to remain a small operation, the implications would always push for global change. He needed a business manager who knew technology research. There was one person he had in mind who was perfect for the job. The question was how to get him on board.

John sat down and contacted Thurston the University Administrator.

"John, what's going on there?! Each time you call, I lose more staff! I'm getting to the point of not recommending anyone." John heard an edge to the friendly tone.

"Thurston, I apologize for making this difficult for you. But I assure you, my research is of vital importance." John could hear the consternation in Thurston's breathing.

"Why don't you and Dr. Gardner pop over here to El Paso and we can discuss the situation face-to-face. Having your backing would undoubtedly increase the profile of our work

145

here." With all the resources John was starting to commandeer from the University, the Administrator thought it would be a good idea to take up John's offer. At the very least if he could see if he could stem the tide of intellectual resources being headhunted.

"You want Lucy Gardner, the bio specialist?" John needed to find a bio specialist to analyze the black yeast-like substance from the barrels of goop they found.

"Yes." Thurston's last thought as he put the phone down was, *how odd, a bio-specialist?*

A short time later Thurston and Lucy accompanied by another man turned up at the gate. John had, in the interim, the temerity to enlist yet another specialist, a physicist to join the team. John had ordered all work stopped and lock-down procedures to be implemented as the guests came into the compound. There was a rush around the base to remove any evidence from plain sight of the research being conducted.

John welcomed the three into the cottage and offered them coffee and a couple of Scarlet's oatmeal cookies. He smiled inwardly as the Administrator attempted to bite a chunk of the cookie only to be met with steel like resistance.

"Unfortunately, before we start I'm going to need you all to sign a non-disclosure agreement. I'm afraid that's non-negotiable." The three visitors looked at each other and shrugged knowing they'd come all this way, signing a non-disclosure agreement was not a big thing.

"Okay, the short and the long of it is that we have some alien technology that we are reverse engineering. This knowledge is vital to the defense of Earth." The Administrator and two specialists froze with their mouths gape unsure they heard correctly. Thurston *had* thought on the way over to El Paso, *secret defense contracts, or some such ... but this...!*

"Please come with me and I'll show you some of those artifacts." Without waiting for a response, John moved out the door quickly followed by Thurston and the two specialists.

Finally, Thurston's brain kicked in, and he asked, "Where did you get these artifacts?"

"I can't tell you that, you will need to bear with me." At this point, John was not willing to share all their secrets, especially, that of the jump drive with the newcomers. When the four entered lab number three, they could all see the unusually shaped barrel standing on the bench. Several drum-like containers stood in the center on one on the nearest worktables. Dr. Gardner looked around the lab for any sort of hazmat suit and other decontamination facilities.

She said, "There is no way I can open these barrels here without adequate protection." John stood there frozen a moment.

John nodded, *I thought as much, damn we've stuffed up.* Of course, she needed to verify that it was safe to use on Earth. Doctor Gardner nodded and made the decision there and then to take up John's offer of employment, and said so. The bio specialist then walked out of the lab and started calling on her phone to arrange the use of an appropriate facility to open the boxes and canisters safely.

"Damn John, you just took another..." Thurston said with a small grimace.

Thurston was less inclined to be swayed so easily, so John took him and the physicist on a tour of the alien artifact hanger. His eyes widened when he was confronted with a whole building full of strange equipment. Admittedly one looked like a transport container, but it was like no transport container design he had ever seen.

"Thurston, I would like your help to run the labs and employ whatever specialists that're needed to reverse engineer what we've acquired."

Thurston looked long and hard at John before he came to the inescapable conclusion that he needed to be here more than at the University.

Thurston had had a love of knowledge since a very young age. All his life had been dedicated to finding new ideas and knowledge. It was almost like a drug habit, his desperate need. His work at the University was an indirect avenue that allowed him to be included in the cutting edge research that pushed the boundaries of human achievement. He also knew that his mind was, unfortunately, not wired to think like a scientist. However, that drove him even more to become an incredible Administrator of one of the most prestigious universities in America.

"John, if I am going to effectively manage the lab base and all the supports, you need to be straight with me regarding all aspects of this endeavor." John realized Thurston wouldn't come on board unless he were given full authority to administer across all the research development and acquisition within the group.

It was at that point that Jen and Elvis walked into the room. John introduced Elvis as Thurston got reacquainted with Jen. He then asked his two friends to take the physicist and finish the tour while he had a private chat with Thurston.

John bit his bottom lip unconsciously copying Jen's nervous behavior. Taking a breath, he dove in and explained about the jump drive.

He recounted his initial calibration tests that created the loud noises that so irritated the pompous Frenchman, Dr. La Perouse. John could see the frustration of having to deal with La Perouse flash across the Administrator's face. However when he described his first teleport test to transport an apple. Thurston was flabbergasted. The lab had been destroyed.

"So when the bench disappeared ... the miscalculation sent it and the apple into the middle of La Perouse's new car."

Thurston could only stare at John, till Jen interrupted them as she walked in. Jen looked at the Administrator's facial expression, "You told him didn't you?"

John nodded.

"And the apple?" she continued.

Nodding once again, John looked at Thurston to see how he was taking it.

Jen grinned a wolfish smile. "I love that bit," and burst out laughing. Thurston shook his head trying to keep his cool, but eventually succumbed and joined in the laughter.

"Well, you know the University had to take out an extra insurance coverage at La Perouse's and the DOD's insistence," Thurston said.

John stopped laughing to listen, his head tilted.

"... It's to cover explosive acts of God and apples."

Once again all three burst their sides laughing.

Eventually, after they settled down, John continued his story... How they'd built the first jumpship and used it to acquire the containers and the alien technology. He told Thurston how they intend to reverse engineer the technology.

While John explained how they would recoup their money. Thurston could see the financial implications of the alien tech immediately; it would be worth millions. He also realized that money wasn't their main motivation, it was secondary. John had couched his story within the framework of protecting Earth.

He also told him about the risks and the close call he'd had with the returning ship while he was on station at the freighter. He then showed the administrator the video clip of him in the medical bay getting shot at by the alien. Satisfied with John's openness, Thurston signed an open-ended contract with John and bargained for some of the royalties.

John was relieved when Thurston came on board, as he had a business mind that could be applied to their fledgling enterprise. To Thurston's keen eye the base was in a shambles despite John's best efforts. So he set about to reorganize everything. The biggest problem would be land. The first thing on the list: they needed to purchase the Ranch next door, then expand to accommodate the new recruits and extra facilities. The existing labs needed to be upgraded to handle alien bio-material.

It took Thurston a while to de-complicate his working relationship with the University by taking a leave of absence.

He knew that there would be enormous gains and discoveries to be made with the artifacts. Setting up a corporate structure that would allow them to develop, manufacture or license out and distribute the tech was a challenge that Thurston took on with gusto. In consultation with John, he started to set up the parent and subsidiary companies, which would manage each of the research disciplines of the base. Thurston also began to put together business plans and funding packages for corporate partners and financial support they would need.

Chapter Twenty-Two

The following weeks at the research base were hectic, to say the least. John and Thurston spent much of the time building up the business framework, cajoling venture capitalists to provide funds and tempting specialist scientists to join their ever-increasing team in El Paso. The group now sat around the table in the newly constructed administration building.

John brought the meeting to order, "Elvis can we start with you and your team, what have you found out?"

"The blaster has some flash tubes in an unusual configuration which convert the beam of photons into a super stimulated state. The focusing mechanism I think we can reproduce. The reactive gasses are a little trickier, they are a rare combination of mostly carbon dioxide and other trace elements, which we may need to harvest from somewhere..." Elvis waved his hand out, indicating out there. Elvis looked directly at John in silent mutual understanding, then continued. "We are some way off understanding the materials physics underlying the blaster, we would need a materials physicist. However, I think we will be able to reproduce similar components with a little effort, assuming we can get close to the gasses used by the baster."

John scribbled furiously on his tablet.

Elvis continued, "We've analyzed the initial output of the blaster based on the energy store in the hand grip, and it's off the scale at over 1500 MW. We haven't as yet dissected the power source fully except to identify a small compressed gas cartridge at the base of the stock. To put the output into perspective, a basic nuclear power plant starts producing energy from 8200 MW," Elvis paused for effect, "the largest coal power station produces 5000 MW."

John's eyes widened. He knew the hand blaster was potent, but that was unbelievable. The U.S. Navy had just released their latest shipboard laser beam weaponry at 150 kW. The power supply within the handgun must be incredible, truly alien.

John then spoke up, "So there are two sets of gasses used in the blaster, one in the firing mechanism of the beam, the other in the battery," John said, trying to come to grips with the technology.

Elvis nodded in confirmation.

"Okay good work so far, we will see about hiring a material specialist," John said as he scribbled some notes.

"Max," John nodded in Max's direction.

"I must say that I am absolutely amazed that they are flying in starships." There was a reserved murmur from the group. "The computer technology they employ is quite antiquated by our standards. Think of it as a Commodore 64 and you get the idea. We can revolutionize the use of some of their technologies by our advanced electronics and computing."

"That sounds great. What's the next step?"

"We need to up our IT capability. The scientists need decent machines to model and reverse engineer. I can't be their IT support and do my own investigations."

Thurston then spoke up. "Any requests for IT support come to me. I've already contracted some more IT resources, they should be here shortly."

John then nodded to the Australian. "Jen, what about your team and the shield technology?"

"We've been able to identify the projector screens which create the high concentration of charged plasma that form the energy shield around the ship. It requires serious amounts of energy to initiate. I don't believe we have anything that comes close to being able to generate such large quantities of power, at this point. The good thing is that once the fusion reaction is started, it's easy to maintain. There is a fellow over in Lockheed I think we should try and get on board. He knows a lot more about fusion and fields theory than I do. He will be able to work out the theory behind the shields."

"Okay, send me his details, I'll see what I can do."

"We've also been able to determine the range of frequencies which the freighter used to create their shields."

"So with these sorts of projectors, we would be able to create our own shields?" John asked.

"Yes. All theory aside, I believe we can replicate them. There is a drawback."

They all stared at Jen expectantly.

"When you know the specific frequency of the shield, if you set a laser strike at the same frequency you can shoot straight through it."

"That doesn't seem to be a good defense," Jerry commented, mildly.

"The US military has been experimenting with electrostatic shielding for their tanks, I believe they rotate the shield frequencies quickly enough to prevent just that shortcoming from occurring."

"So why don't the aliens?"

"My guess is because they've only got Commodore 64s," Jen responded. "Our computers should be able to rotate rapidly enough to make that adjustment. All the shield emitters have to be modified at the same time, so as not to lose shield integrity. Given Max's conclusions, I think our computer technology can make a significant impact on this."

They all just sat there stunned at the implication. It brought home to everyone that the aliens, although were highly advanced in some technologies, they were woefully behind humanity in others.

"And now our linguist, Jerry."

"Well, I've been able to take a serious look at the language we have here. I've cataloged quite a few icons that form their language. It's not unlike Egyptian iconography in the way they work. I've been able to make a start on the grammar and syntax and translate only a small proportion of the manuals that were found in the container."

Jerry then pulled out one of the manuals with a picture of several of the barrels and one of the larger machines that were stored in the red container. "I focused on these barrels because the icons clearly depicted barrels as opposed to boxes. I believe that this manual relates to these barrels and other equipment I've yet to fully identify."

The group started to get excited at Jerry's deciphering of the alien language. If they could read the manuals, then so much the better.

"But they don't make a lot of sense, so I'm making a few leaps of faith." They all looked at him expectantly. "What we have here are basically worms." Everyone stared. "As best I can tell, the barrels contain liquids that are not unlike a yeast, where it feeds, grows then poops a substance that is akin to asphalt. They then cure the substance before they use this asphalt as a building material. The manual talks of building transport corridors. Their words not mine. I believe they're some tunneling device or worm that creates something like an underground railway." This surprised the whole team. The bulky machinery didn't look like it could move anywhere let alone tunnel. Somehow they must be missing something. Something so fundamental, that the writers did not need to elucidate.

"Thank you, Jerry, continue on, we have more manuals. How is your progress on creating a translator for us to use?" John said.

"Very early days. It's hard to say how many languages are present. Scripts on the box's packaging look different to those of the manuals. Once I have completed the grammar and syntax rules of the manual's language we should be able to translate the written word at least to some degree if we have the names for things. Of course, I have no idea how it's pronounced. The mouths that created this may have entirely different pitch and amplitude to their language." Jerry said with a smile.

"Thank you all. That's good work," John said, concluding the meeting. "Max and Elvis, please stay behind."

When the rest of the team had filed out of the room, John cleared his throat. "I've been worried over these last several weeks."

Elvis took a more appraising look at John. "The other ship we ran into, isn't it?"

"Yes. Spatially speaking, the Earth is not far from that freighter."

"Are you thinking you want to go back to the freighter?"

"No. The chances are that they're waiting for us to return. We wouldn't stand a snowball's chance in hell if they attacked us."

The three sat there thinking over the situation.

"We need to talk about the deployment of some sort of sensors in ours and other nearby star systems to get some advance notice," John said finally. "Elvis, I need you and Max to come up with a plan of what's required so we can get at least some eyes and ears out there."

John continued on, "We also need to get that blaster reverse engineered as fast as possible. Keep in mind that we will want to upscale it and be able to cycle the frequencies that it shoots."

"We can't do anything without the gasses that it uses to excite the particles," Elvis responded.

"What are these gasses that you need? I'll speak to Colonel Prior and see if we can get some delivered here."

"That will be of no use. I don't believe the gasses are actually on Earth."

John just looked at Elvis. "Are you serious?"

"Deadly."

It was at that point Max butted in, "They may not be on Earth, but they may be elsewhere... We just need to get a spectrograph analysis of the gasses and identify where we can harvest them with the *Scotty*."

John realized that Max's experience in astrogation would be invaluable here. Spectral analysis of various interplanetary bodies told you exactly what gasses were in or surrounding other planets. "Max, you sure you can determine where we can harvest it from?"

"Yes," Max said, grinning back at Elvis and John. "It's simple."

John, Max, and Elvis spent the next couple of hours running through the requirements for the blaster and what was needed for the sensor network.

◆◆◆

Scarlet's Place

John had five spare minutes so he called Scarlet to arrange a coffee and cookie crush session. He turned up at Scarlet's later that day to find the Deputy Sheriff in plain clothes sitting on the porch ruffling the ears of Rufus, the dog. Rufus seemed in heaven from the Deputy's playful scratching.

"Scarlet, I'm sorry I didn't mean to intrude when you have an official here," he said, eyeing the remains of what must have been their lunch.

"John, Darlin', did I introduce you to my niece, Amanda?" Scarlet said with a smile.

Amanda focused her attention on John, smiling as she did. John noticed the cute dimples in her cheeks. The official bravado had been left far behind revealing a beautiful blond with a reassuring smile.

"Umm..." John hadn't been stymied in a long time. All he could conjure was, "Nice to meet you."

Amanda smirked wryly at John's apparent consternation. She was not a vain person, but years on the force had made her more appreciative of her talents that were not physical.

"Nice to see you again Dr. Stevenson," she said.

"I need to find some clerical staff to help me with my labs," he directed at Scarlet, after a quick recovery.

Scarlet smiled knowingly and, with a glance at her niece, replied: "Amanda, didn't you do that clerical course back in Austin this last year gone past?"

Amanda was momentarily taken aback by Scarlet's blatant matchmaking.

"Yes..." Not willing to give any further information, she stumbled to a halt. This time, it was John's turn to smile at Amanda's obvious discomfort.

"She's good people John. She's family." What further recommendation could John need? He trusted Scarlet, which translated into trusting Amanda. With the added bonus that she was cute as well.

Scarlet then rose, not so subtly, and cleared away the dishes leaving Amanda and John on the porch alone.

"She's old-fashioned and wants to see me well placed." Amanda sighed. "She is sometimes unbearable and embarrassingly direct with the matchmaking. However, she does have a good heart."

John looked at Amanda and nodded, and she went on. "If you do need some clerical staff, I know someone who worked as an administrative assistant for a few years. I'm afraid I love my current job too much to return to clerical work," she said with a smile. She then pulled her phone out sending a contact directly to John's mobile. It was a bit disconcerting that she knew his number off the top of her head. She seemed to read his thoughts, then smiled and said, "photographic memory."

John felt like he had dodged a bullet, given the recent events with Mr. Sykes. Having the deputy sheriff on-site, wasn't a good plan. John rose and said his goodbyes to Amanda then yelled in through the door into the kitchen to Scarlet. Scarlet walked out on the porch as John drove down the driveway, Amanda watching him.

"Aunt Scarlet, I know you like him, but there is something about him I'm not sure of."

The White House

The President finished a conference call with the leaders of the five major economic countries of Earth. The most important thing he had to make clear to those countries was a clear and present danger of alien contact. He made sure they all received the images of the spacecraft in geosynchronous orbit and then on the moon. They need to have a serious discussion as to what their political and/or military responses the world could effectively deal out. The leaders were shocked and then furious with the Americans response to first contact. The President was embarrassed by the first strike that was attempted with the ballistic missile, which led to the revelation of their spy satellite. The President thought to himself, General Abercrombie will be scrubbing toilets somewhere in Antarctica for putting him in this position.

◆◆◆

John walked into the cottage where Max sat at the computer scanning the readings from the probe they had left near the stricken freighter. John stood behind Max looking at the scans and shivered at the memory of the octopus in the med bay taking a shot at him. The configuration of the ship looked exactly the same.

"The octopus ship we first encountered, has returned to the derelict freight three times," Max said to John's raised eyebrows.

Max, and Elvis had made several brief data collection tele-grabs bringing the probe back to earth each time to download any new scans the probes picked up since their first salvage operation.

"Has there been any indication that the ship has detected our probes?" asked John.

"Not that I can tell. We tele-put it back in different places each time."

John bit his bottom lip while he stared at the screen. Even if the octopus people took all the cargo, there was still valuable technology and the ship itself.

"Okay, keep monitoring it."

We wouldn't be going back there until they we're satisfied that the octopus people had left the freighter a derelict, John thought.

Chapter Twenty-Three

Traynor, a new Lizard Colony 25 light years from Earth

Shinix Thuwyuum, the colony leader, stood around the situation table with his advisory committee discussing the seriousness of the potential crisis. The freighter from the Unak Clan Homeworld was overdue by more than two cycles. They were counting on the food in its cargo bays to cover them until they were able to set up proper farms on their new world. Their Homeworld livestock herds would take time to establish.

The new world they had taken had a ready supply of non-sentient herd mammals. However, digesting them was causing physiological imbalances that led to nightmares and even sudden death.

The Lizard species, unlike other beings, relied on eating other sentient species to alter their brain chemistry. The food they consumed changed their DNA to such an extent that it created different subclasses within their culture. Eating a particular species' brains would turn a Lizard into a warrior. Others would turn them into scientists, politicians, workers and even egg layers.

The youngest adviser around the table spoke up prematurely, "When can we expect another shipment from Homeworld?"

Shinix scowled, "You know as well as I do, the political situation on Unak won't resolve anytime soon. We're on our own for the foreseeable future."

He couldn't let the youngling distract him by his inexperience. Shinix tapped his claw on the table before speaking up, "I don't think we have a choice. We need to send the frigate *Godzilla* to find the missing freighter."

"That will leave us vulnerable to attack without the warship," advised the Colony War Leader. They had two other frigate class warships in the system. One was captained by an arrogant lizard who thought more about his own reputation than the welfare of the colony. The other captain was young and inexperienced in commanding ships.

Shinix continued, "In the meantime, modify the two freighters we have in orbit, add gun emplacements on them. A least that will give us some extra protection while the Godzilla is investigating the freighter's disappearance."

Once again the youngest adviser spoke up, "But the resources to do that..."

The lizard stopped in its tracks as all the advisers stared at him. They knew the dire consequences of allocating the limited resources they'd brought to refitting the freighters instead of building colony infrastructure.

They also knew that any request for more warships from the Unak Homeworld would question their competence. They wouldn't allow that. Arrogance seemed to run through their whole species.

"Give me any information we have on the original condition of that freighter before it was inbound to the colony," Shinix rasped to a lizard runner.

The smaller clerical lizard rushed out and returned shortly with a laminated page containing the specifications of the freighter.

"Now that's interesting, the family has been recently trading with one of the Ancients. They've traded and installed a new FTL drive and some type of trial plasma shields. Maybe it's a simple case of drive or shield failure." The colony governor had serious doubts about that, any good family freighter unit, would have the problem fixed in short order. The merchants had traded with the Ancients and survived, so they obviously had to be good.

♦♦♦

The Lizards were a species of reptiles that had a confusing difference to Earth varieties, being that they suckled their young after they're hatched. They passed their full genetic species memory through the generations to allow their young to survive as soon as they're hatched.

After millennia in space, the lizards had split into Ancients, and all Other lizard sub species, known as the Others. The Ancients were a pure breed. The purebreds carved out a vicious reputation with their technology surpassing all.

The Other lizard clans instead pursued the art of DNA brain manipulation to progress their species. Their constant need for sentient DNA was not unlike a human 'junkie' needing a fix.

The Unak Lizards at Traynor Colony were brain DNA manipulators; one of the Others Clans, cast out to fend for itself. They needed to be careful that other Clans or the Ancients didn't find them in such a weak state, or they would be nibbles.

The Ancients despised all non-lizard species and to some extent the Others. They were nothing more than food to be crushed and eaten. To the Ancients, the Other lizard clans were considered outcasts, hybrids, abominations to the 'real' lizard race.

♦♦♦

Lizard Warship *Godzilla*

The warship *Godzilla* was orbiting the fourth planet of the Traynor System. Satellites were still being deployed from the freighters to orbit above the colony. There was much to do, their survival depended on this newly contracted freighter family bringing its wares to the fledgling colony. When Rezulin, the War Leader of the *Godzilla* got the news that the freighter was missing, he immediately ordered all leave canceled, and the ship prepared for FTL.

"War leader, I have Colony Leader Shinix on the comm."

"Put him through."

"We need you to find the missing freighter, *Kenuu*."

"It is as I thought. We will leave immediately."

Rezulin signaled his helmsman to take them out of the system at all possible speed. It would take them several hours to clear the gravity well before they could engage their FTL drive and drop into subspace.

◆◆◆

Freighter adrift in Outer Space

The *Godzilla* slipped out of subspace into normal space and closed in on the freighter's dead hulk. It had taken a while to figure out which route the ship had taken to their fledgling colony from Unak Homeworld. This was not the most direct route. Rezulin saw the remains of the derelict adrift in disbelief. A debris field slowly expanded surrounding the spinning wreck of metal. Whoever had done this was going to pay. All the containers were missing, the FTL engine was now only pieces of debris. Deep gouges out of the bow on the port side were visible allowing one to see almost through to the medical bay.

"Get a boarding party together and see if there are any survivors on board." Rezulin didn't like their chances. It had been nearly three cycles since the freighter had disappeared. He then turned to his Sensor Officer and ordered him to scan the whole region for any emissions.

Rezulin had no illusions the search will take time. There were hundreds of stars and stellar bodies within 20 light years from here.

Chapter Twenty-Four

Research Base El Paso, Texas

Over time, the number of scientists in the research base more than tripled. The large variety of projects and the excitement of discovery turned the base into a melting pot of disparate, chaotic disciplines and experimental ideas. The locals did not know what to make of the usually close-lipped group. The morning breakfast at the local diner was fast becoming a tradition, but because of their increasing numbers, they had been encouraged by the waitress to take the tables towards the back of the diner. They could discuss and argue their ideas, over huge plates of waffles and pancakes, in relative privacy, as the locals found their group disconcerting and their language could have been Greek for all the sense they could make of it. Scientists knew well the vagaries of working with non-disclosure clauses and being out in public. Inappropriate disclosure and they would never work on these projects again or worse... scientific exile.

Back at the base, the group was updating their progress.

"Okay, can we get this progress meeting started?" John sat in the main conference area of the administration building surrounded by over three dozen scientists and support staff.

"Elvis, how is the work on the blaster going?"

"We are getting close to reverse engineering the pistol with the exception of the pump and power source gasses. We've located the gasses with Max's help, but it's going to take some doing to get them. I've started searching the net for some appropriate gas tanks for storage.

When we do find some, we'll probably need some structural engineering done to the tanks to make them useful."

The command team knew that Elvis meant other places in the solar system, not just on Earth. They would need to be space capable.

Max nodded his assent, "We are still cataloging potential sources."

"Jen, how is the shield research going?"

"Well, we have a basic prototype using the alien's technique. However, we are stuck in part due to the enormous amount of power which is required to run the system."

John took a deep breath.

"We do have something..." Jen went on hesitantly. "The black substance coating the outside of the freighter is a type of energy collector."

John was about to tell them to stay on the shielding research, but then realized they were at a dead end until they could get the energy problem sorted. He certainly didn't fancy using a fission reactor to power the shields.

"You're saying that the black things are like solar collectors?"

"Yes. The energy absorbed by the devices is unbelievable. Brian can attest to that..."

Earlier that week, Brian had suffered severe electrical burns from been zapped by the energy collector from a small hand sized amount of the black material.

John had a few awkward moments with Amanda when she turned up to investigate the accident. Apparently, the Sheriff's Department was required to do an accident investigation when the injuries were significant enough to hospitalize the victim.

"We have been able to fast charge banks of high capacity lithium batteries easily."

"Do we have any idea how they work?"

Jen shrugged her shoulders. "I'm afraid we only have a basic understanding. There is some quantum entanglement component to the energy storage. We have the material specialist's working with us..."

Brian cleared his throat and glanced at Jen as he said, "The best part is that computer modeling suggests that we may be able to enhance it. We are looking into the possibility of using our miniaturization technology but at this stage, it's a moot point. We don't have a battery storage device large enough to store all the energy.

The collectors can be up-scaled into banks of panels theoretically. Our biggest priority right now is to see what we can do to build our own version of the black collector. The second objective is to enhance the size, placement, and configuration of the energy collectors with computer modeling."

John had to be satisfied with that and turned to Elvis.

"Elvis, it looks like your battery research has become more of a super top priority." Elvis looked uncomfortable.

"No pressure," John said with a smile.

"Next research group, Peter."

Doctor Peter Fellows was a propulsion specialist. He had been charged to reverse engineer the maneuvering thruster they had acquired from the freighter.

"When I first looked at this, I didn't know what to expect. At the very least, it is one that requires no fuel for propulsion. What we have essentially is an electric drive. A lot more work needs to be undertaken to understand it properly."

John knew that pressing Doctor Fellows would not elicit any more progress from him, so he moved on.

"Jerry, how is the translation process going?"

"We've been able to translate quite a lot of information within those first two manuals, although vocabulary and scientific concepts are still an issue. One of the surprising discoveries we've made is that one of the devices is an anti-gravity sled. I've handed this information on how the vehicle works to the 'Fields Research Team'. The user manual, unfortunately, doesn't go into detail as to the theory behind it. It only tells you how to operate the sled. The translation matrix has a rather skewed vocabulary towards road building and worms. Come see me if you want to be bored stiff for hours talking about worms." The room laughed at this.

John then pressed a button on the conference phone in the center of the table.

"Dr. Gardner are you there?"

The familiar voice of Lucy Gardner came on the line. "Yes, hello. The good news is the A-Bitumen like substance has now been thoroughly analyzed. We will be able to use it without contamination. I've given samples to Thurston, who I believe is contracting some local and overseas manufacturers to produce the stuff on-license.

The other items you sent through for testing have all come back negative." John sighed in relief. It had been eating him that they weren't careful enough regarding contamination.

"One thing that did happen when the substance dried. It hardened into a light, tough material like plasti-steel. I'd like to do further tests."

"By all means Doctor, see what you can come up with. It had to be in those barrels for a reason. Hopefully, you will be able to do much of the testing here given we have nearly completed the upgrade of three labs into bio-labs. When we are more established, we will see about specialized mobile labs from a laboratory vendor."

"That brings us to you, Thurston?"

"We now have a new business structure with headquarters including some subsidiaries who specialize in their respective fields. Royalties from any developments will pass through the companies and through to the headquarters and each scientist working on those technologies will receive a small percentage. The remainder will go into headquarters revenue to allow us to start building on more acquired technology.

"Lastly, we have employed a security company to research the backgrounds of all employees, new and existing. As you know, we have the world's most significant technological advances here to be made, thanks to the acquisition of the alien artifacts. You all signed on with John on the promise of being on the forefront of new discoveries. I think we can all say you have been well rewarded. The non-disclosure agreements were necessary to ensure these discoveries remain under our control until we can safely and fairly release them to the rest of mankind. Please expect some interesting questions from the security company interviews. Eric will be taking on the role of head of security, with a team to support him."

When the meeting closed, John and Thurston stayed behind and discussed the future direction of the new corporate structure called T.N. (Terran Navy).

John voiced his concerns about the impromptu alien contact at the freighter, "You should be aware, one of the primary goals of our research is the development of spaceships."

"I had gathered that John. That was not hard to figure out. We need to walk before we can run, to build machines that will build the tools that will make spaceships."

The two had had this discussion before.

"What is the monetary projection for the sale of the A-Bitumen?" John asked. The A-Bitumen was their new name for the black yeast they found in the barrels. They were marketing the A-Bitumen as an all-purpose building material.

"Truly, it's remarkable stuff, John. Aside from the licensing interest, we're going full pelt to build our own manufacturing plant."

John was on the edge of his seat, like a child waiting for Christmas.

"The projections range in the hundreds of millions."

John blew out his breath.

"Okay, on another matter..."

John went on to describe some design firms that he felt they needed to acquire; one which specialized in military oceangoing ships, submarines and such for obvious reasons.

The second built major civil engineering projects such as infrastructure. There was a third that was more radical, developing space-based technologies. Their specialty was converting current Earth-based tech to space based. Admittedly much of their emphasis had been on ordinary everyday items. Common everyday things were going be in high demand in space, just like on Earth. John believed it would be a greater money spinner for them in the long run. There was one other group in particular, the Sage Space Company (SSC), whom they would actively seek to acquire. They had experience in building space stations.

Thurston was initially taken aback by John's vision for the future of T.N. After listening to his arguments regarding the preparedness of Earth to defend herself from space-based attack, which was non-existent, Thurston came to realize the depth of John's commitment to the defense of the planet. Thurston's estimation of John jumped a few notches. He would try his best to make his vision become a reality.

◆◆◆

A week later at the conclusion of another weekly meeting, John stepped aside. "Thurston, Elvis, and Jen, can you stay behind? I would like to discuss a few things please." The room emptied except the four.

John issued his first OH & S directive to Thurston. "I'd like you to organize some medical tests on everyone who's used the jump drive. I would like to be absolutely sure that jumping is not killing us in other ways that we aren't aware of.

"Jen and Elvis, I'd like you to hook up the Uber Drive to tele-grab dirt from underground to create a vast cavern. Not too far from us, as we'll be connecting it to our existing tunnels because I don't think these artifacts are safe here on the surface. The more people who come on board, the greater the security risk we're taking on. So let's build this cavern, reinforce it with the A-Bitumen that Lucy has been testing and transport the red container first; after we've seen what's in it, then we'll move the yellow one from the moon's orbit.

"One last thing, one of Eric's guards approached me about wanting some body armor. I have some designs in mind using Kevlar with the A-Bitumen. Elvis, can you take a look at it?"

John knew that Elvis would be interested given his military background. It was like a new toy to a kid at Christmas. Elvis didn't disappoint, he gave a huge grin that lit up his face.

Shortly after, Jen and Elvis set to work teleporting dirt and stone out from beneath the base to create the new Aladdin's cave to hold the alien artifacts. The research base had been built in the foothills of the Franklin Mountains where there were deposits of granite bedrock, limestone, and gravel. Once they were satisfied with the size, they sprayed several layers of A-Bitumen over the walls, ceiling, and floor to reinforce the structure. Lighting, air, and a power generator were transported into the repository. A narrow secret access tunnel and air recycling tunnel were also tele-built.

When John, Thurston, and Max entered the cavern to inspect Jen's and Elvis's work, they were stunned by its depth and breadth. The two had done a fantastic job. Eventually, the red alien cargo container disappeared from the hanger to reappear in the new repository six hundred feet into the mountain wall. The yellow container winked out of existence from the moon's orbit to reappear inside the cavern next to the red container.

◆◆◆

John, Jen, Thurston, and Elvis crowded around their second prize cargo container. John felt guilty that they'd left it open to the elements of outer space. However, once they'd gotten a chance to really look at the yellow container, he changed his mind.

"This is quite different to the red container. It's almost a third bigger." John said stating the obvious.

There were no external controls to open it like the red one.

"What's this here?"

"It has to be environmental controls," Elvis said, as he walked around a large protected external console with icons dotting the outside.

"Take a look at these!" Jen said pointing to what had to be small thruster units to guide it. "Are they what I think they are?"

John and Thurston walked over to where she was pointing, "Maybe," John said thoughtfully.

"Oh hell, you guys are going to love this?" Elvis said, they could hear the cheeky grin lacing his voice. There was an airlock on one end for access.

"Ok, are you guys ready to look inside. Elvis can you pop back and get our space suits."

The inventor, scientist, and engineer donned their spacesuits and negotiated their way past the airlock and into the main container area.

"Holy shit!" Elvis cried.

All three were stunned at what they found. A dozen different species were hanging like frozen meat in a slaughterhouse. All with grimaces of terror plastered on their faces. At least two of the species were humanoid mammal types. Jen doubled over running out into the airlock, her fingers scrambling at her helmet release latches. Thurston rushed over to help when, to his surprise, she threw up onto the floor, narrowly missing his shoes. Jen's face was pale, turning green. Breathing heavily for a minute, she composed herself, and said raggedly, "They've got frozen people in there … and … they're hanging like gutted pigs."

Thurston stood there speechless.

Over the next several days when their shock had subsided, they determined that the bodies in the yellow container were obviously frozen foods for the freighter species. They removed the bodies sealed within plastic hazmat bio-bags and transported them to the Bio Lab for further analysis.

Thurston made a priority call to his forensic scientist friend, Dr. William Halifax, to see where he was at, and if he could come to the research base as quickly as possible.

William, or Wil to his friend's, was the new head of a body farm in New Jersey. He had been embroiled in a serial killer case with multiple victims. The killing spree had been particularly brutal and sadistic. The whole experience had drained Wil's soul. The killer had been prosecuted several times without success until a particularly gruesome murder exposed his DNA to finally put him behind bars. The thought of bearing witness during the appeal process turned the quiet forensic scientist's stomach. Repeating each shocking truth challenged even Wil's sensibilities. Thurston always felt it was rather ghoulish to study death and the bodies as they decomposed, but his friend generally loved his work.

Chapter Twenty-Five

Elvis and Max looked smug while sitting at the round table with John, Jen, Eric, and Thurston. A cylinder of exotic gasses sat unobtrusively on the table between them. John watched their smiles drop when he asked where they had found it.

"Well, we searched for the exotic gasses in our solar system but couldn't find them in enough concentrations for what we needed, so we looked elsewhere..." Elvis replied sheepishly. "We found the gasses for the blaster at Tau Ceti." Max stared at the ceiling unable to make eye contact.

"What!!" All the team could see John grind his teeth as his anger grew.

"It was just a quick jaunt, we were like, there and back in an hour." Elvis could see John was about to blow a gasket; still, he continued on regardless. "But hold on, the funniest bit of the whole trip was that on the fourth planet they have herds of these cow things with six legs. Guess where the greatest concentration of the gasses came from. The cows, they fart this gas like you wouldn't believe. It was lucky we had our spacesuits, or there is no way we would have been able to get close enough to get even this small sample." Elvis said grinning while holding a second small cylinder. Max couldn't decide whether to be sheepish or grin.

John tried to look angry at the two but burst out laughing instead, which allowed all the command team to erupt in fits of laughter. This caused Elvis to fall over, rolling on the ground holding his chest barely able to breathe.

When all of them had finally settled down, John continued. "I don't want you or anyone to go on these jaunts without my approval, okay? We just don't know enough about the jump drive or the local star systems to be safe about it."

Looking suitably abashed, Elvis said, "The blaster currently works, at a reduced level, using terrestrial power sources. We've got plans on the drawing board now for a larger version that can be used ship-based or platform based.

"The last hurdle has been the power source in the hand-grip of the blaster. It's been tough to dismantle because we didn't want to be blown to bits given how powerful it is. Wallace, the material specialist guy, is looking at that right now and should have a report back within the next few days."

Thurston reported that the first batches of A-Bitumen had been sold on contract for five million.

The command team looked at each other in surprise, they hadn't realized it would do so well.

John then reported that three new design groups had been acquired. They each made an impressive start on an experimental spaceship and space product designs.

At the end of the meeting, Elvis and Max spent the next few hours showing the command team pictures they took of the Tau Ceti system and its 'cows'. It was a beautiful planet within the habitable zone very similar to Earth in size. A massive super gas giant dominated its sky. It was a wondrous sight.

When John and his team of Jen, Elvis and Max, first arrived in El Paso all those months before, they had rented a four-bedroom house not far from the base because the base cottage was in such a state of neglect that Jen refused to step inside. Each of them had a room in the house with Jen taking one of the bathrooms to herself. Although the base now had abundant quarters built and occupied by the various scientists and other employees at the base, the three original members enjoyed the privacy and intimacy of their off-base residence.

"...You had little choice." Elvis cut his conversation short as Jen walked into the lounge of their rent-o-cottage.

John shrugged and changed the subject. "I'll be going into El Paso tomorrow; is there anything you need?"

Jen looked at the two men and waited to see if they would elaborate on their previous conversation. This was not the first time that Jen had walked in mid-conversation, only to have it die a quick death. She decided to push it this time.

"Little choice for what?" she asked.

John avoided her eyes, adjusting and readjusting his jacket. The silence was awkward to the point of being deafening.

"Elvis was just telling me once again about the six-legged cows and how there was no choice but strap balloons to their bums so they could extract the gas," John said with a half-hearted smile.

Jen bit her bottom lip as she looked at John to Elvis and back. She then turned abruptly and walked from the room shutting her bedroom door with a thud.

"John, you had to leave her there. She made her own choices. Even if they were bad ones, they were hers to make." Elvis said taking up the previous conversation.

"I dunno, there must've been something I could have done."

Elvis shrugged his shoulders, "Like?"

John had no answer.

Elvis' eyes glanced at Jen's door.

"Jen, she'll get through it. She's not like Stace at all," Elvis said quietly.

"No, I guess not."

"What do you mean, you *guess* not? Open your eyes! There's no way she's a prescription junkie."

◆◆◆

As the weeks slipped by, Elvis moved out of his room and into a place near a motor mechanic where he could tinker on his Ducati in his off-hours. Max moved to Central El Paso, which had decent cable so he could run his computer network. Jen and John lived on their own with scientists coming and going in the other two bedrooms as the first port of call before they moved onto the base. John wanted to meet and greet, to get to know the scientists before they were accepted fully within the T.N. Corporation. After a while, John stopped this practice because he enjoyed Jen's company without the constant interruption of new personnel.

◆◆◆

"Elvis, look at this." It had taken Elvis's team over a week to figure out how to open the battery pack of the alien pistol. The team had specially machined a tool to match the screw-like fasteners. However, now it was time for the great reveal.

"Okay, now that we have removed the external casing, let's get an x-ray, and possibly an MRI," said Elvis.

"Are you sure that's wise? The emissions from the tests could cause it to explode," Wallace said as he fidgeted, clasping and unclasping the new tool.

"There's always been a possibility of it exploding. Even when we test fired it," the second scientist said.

"Have you go all your wills up-to-date?" Elvis said just above a whisper.

Each of them around the workbench nodded in turn.

"Bring the portable x-ray..."

Soon after they had dismantled the blaster battery, Wallace was able to finally unravel the mystery of the technology. Much of it relied on an unusual combination of elements and what looked like a mini particle accelerator. The only problem was that it was such a unique set of gasses and liquids. The exotic compounds were not found in sufficient quantities to make production on Earth a viable operation.

When the gas was sampled and analyzed it became abundantly clear to John that harvesting resources not only here but in other star systems was cost-effective with the jump drive. Trade would take a turn for the better when jump drives became more plentiful. Max's recent success tracking down the gas for the blaster at Tau Ceti, he put him to work using his spectral analysis to locate a source for the batteries. This was another area where John realized he needed to increase his manpower in the field. Resource harvesting was going to be a big boon when it took off.

◆◆◆

Late one afternoon Max, Elvis, and Dr. Wallace bustled into John's office in the cottage, barely containing their enthusiasm. Max placed a printout in front of John telling him they had found a source for harvesting the gas resource for the new batteries. John was surprised to see the source was not available in the solar system. They would need to travel just under six light years to Barnard Star. He sat back in his chair contemplating the implications. He yelled out to Thurston to come into this meeting.

"Thurston, we going to retrieve an exotic soup of gasses and liquids, and we need to store it somewhere other than Earth. They're dangerous, and they'll be a serious problem if there is any sort of accident. I'm not willing to stockpile them here. I recall that one of Sage's products was an inflatable space station?"

"Yes, I have heard about them. So you want to buy a space station?" Thurston just shook his head knowing that he had to go back to his investors to get more money. "I'll get one for you."

"I need it yesterday."

Thurston looked at him for a minute smiling, then said, "I'll get it done." He knew just which investor he would need to encourage with a bottle of wine, a very expensive meal, and a promise to go on further dates with. As he left the room whistling, John, Elvis, and Max looked towards each other in amazement.

John thought *that was too easy...* and wondered further, *what is going on with Thurston?*

◆◆◆

The Hog's Breath

The bustle of the research base was charged with excited scientists seeking intellectual truths. However, for the non-scientist personnel it was I.Q. overload. Sometimes one needed a break from the geek melting pot so Elvis had taken to riding his Ducati into the Hog's Breath for a relaxing ale in the evenings.

The rough and rowdy crowd was deliberately not conducive to the tastes of the scientific personnel that roamed the base. Especially when local biker patrons frequented the dilapidated bar. Elvis' pool playing skills had been sorely tested when he lost a few wages to BlackEye, the biker leader. BlackEye had a fearsome reputation for extracting his dues.

The biker's latest fling was a stunning brunette with pale translucent skin that made many Harley lovers cry like a baby. Mel's piercing blue eyes would distract Elvis, especially when he lined up pool shots. BlackEye, no doubt, took advantage of her sex appeal to win many a game.

Elvis had felt something the very first time he saw her. She would turn his legs into Jell-O. He was no stranger to dangerous women. He knew that she was, in no uncertain terms, detrimental to his health. Yet despite this, he would return to the Hog's Breath every few nights to get the smallest glimpse of her. Elvis knew that BlackEye was insanely jealous of any rival for her affection. Clenched fists and broken bones were testaments to his gusto in expressing his jealousy.

One evening, Elvis rode into the car park of the bar on his fancy black Italian stallion motorcycle. Unfortunately, twenty feet short of the parking spot his engine inexplicably cut out. Jumping off his bike to push it the final few feet, he suddenly realized there was a small crowd of bikers still hanging around outside. He cringed at the uproarious derisive laughter BlackEye and his cohorts aimed at him. The double row of parked Harley Knuckleheads was proof that biker gangs still thrived in America. Taking a deep breath, he removed his helmet. One of the bikers noticed the permanent 'Jesus lives' sticker covering half his visor. It was the product of his latest vindictive ex-girlfriend. She hadn't taken too well to Elvis' suggestion they participate in a Kama Sutra course. She started screaming at him that she was a God-fearing Christian and grabbed a permanent sticker and stuck right in the middle of his visor. Elvis had tried everything to get rid of that sticker. It had, however, melded into the visors plastic. Once again chortles from BlackEye and his groupies rang out at God's sticker will.

Many of the groupies had road rash and head scars from falls taken from their bikes without helmets. Elvis shook his head at their scars. He was crazy, but not *that* crazy riding his Ducati. He never rode his bike without full leathers and helmet.

Ignoring the crowd's derisive jeers, Elvis entered the Hog's Breath in search of icy, blue eyes. He was pleasantly surprised to see her playing pool by herself. Elvis bought a couple of beers and rocked up to the pool table. Carefully placing the beers on the side-board, he dropped a crumpled note on the table cushion. "Twenty says I can take you in the next game."

"It's going to cost you more than $20," she said turning to him with those dazzling blue eyes. Both of them knew that the extra cost would come from BlackEye. The biker had his reputation and namesake to live up to.

Elvis smiled the best easy smile he could muster, unfazed by her attempt to dissuade him. "In that case, I get a date as well if I win."

Mel eyed Elvis and gave him marks for his persistence but also took some for his death wish. She thought about refusing him his one last dying request then felt guilty not doing her best to fulfill it.

"But I get to choose where we go," she said reluctantly.

"Fair enough!" Elvis said with a cheeky grin.

Blue eyes set the table and smashed the balls causing two to drop in the opening gambit. Elvis saw her shapely legs and looked as if his thoughts were a million miles from the game. Blue eyes saw this and just smiled. She thought to herself, *he is really quite cute. I hope BlackEye doesn't hurt him too much because he's got quite a ruggedly handsome face.*

Elvis took aim at the next ball blasting it down into the pocket to have the white ball line up his next shot. As he was drawing the cue, BlackEye entered and spotted the two in the corner. Snarling he moved his hefty bulk past the bar and aimed for the pool tables.

As if by magic the bar fell dead silent, until he was stopped in his tracks by a sharp voice that pierced the seedy atmosphere.

"BlackEye, you crazy bastard, don't even think about it!!"

Standing ten feet from the bar was a petite blond haired Deputy Sheriff, bold as brass with her hands on her hips. The whole bar stared at the brewing confrontation while the two combatants eyed each other. Everyone could see BlackEye was seriously thinking of *taking down the little bitch pig from the Sheriff's Department.*

Just then a burly man with a large ten-gallon hat came out of the restrooms and stood behind the perky blond. Reinforcements had arrived.

"The game's over," Amanda told Elvis. "You can either stop right now and leave, or I can arrest you for disturbing the peace!"

Elvis looked at Blue Eyes and thought about ignoring the blond Deputy and taking his chances with BlackEye. But sense prevailed as he saw the Deputy's reinforcements and their no-nonsense demeanor. Elvis picked up his beer sculling the rest and left the bar.

"We'll continue this later when the Deputy's not here," Elvis said to Blue Eyes.

"Yes we will," BlackEye said with a snarl.

Amanda left the Hog's Breath and got in her police car shaking her head at the stupidity of men. She picked up the CB radio and called to let dispatch know she was on her way in.

Half an hour later, Amanda was in the station at her computer terminal when an old criminal circular watch list caught her eye. It was for that very same person she had ordered out of the bar as well as for Doctor Stevenson, the man that her aunt had set up a visit with. It mentioned weapons, dangerous untraceable explosives and that the DHS was seeking their whereabouts as a person of interest for suspected terrorism. Amanda felt a chill run through her body realizing that her aunt was messing with a very dangerous crowd.

Chapter Twenty-Six

The yellow container was a decent size. It had all the hallmarks of a very rudimentary interplanetary ship once all the bodies had been removed.

"You think it was designed to be loaded on the planet, then set on a course to rendezvous with a freighter?" Elvis said.

"Yes, the electric thrusters are too big for space maneuvers only. The thrusters were not designed for extended trips, only from the surface to the freighter and back to the surface."

"And the other controls?" John asked.

"Environmental control for especially sensitive goods, limited sensors to enable it to find its parking orbit and a small airlock to allow people in and out."

The command team saw the benefits of using the transport container as the backbone of a new spaceship. To that end, they set about applying the latest Earth-Tech and new alien technologies that they had acquired to the yellow container.

In an effort to force the disparate design teams together, John created a single major project across all the three teams. They were given the current specifications of the container with the requirement to improve on it.

Research Base El Paso, Texas

The yellow transport container had gone through a massive transformation into the first refurbished hybrid spaceship.

"Looking lean, and mean," Jen said as the command team circled the new Earth ship.

"Ha ha. Yes, I suppose so," replied John.

"It's a little creepy..." Jen continued, "The way the energy collectors, turn to face any energy source. They're like eyes in a painting that follow you."

"Except these *actually* move," Elvis said.

The smooth, shiny yellow exterior had been demonized into a giant black and yellow pockmarked scar. The energy collectors taken from around the shield and thruster mechanism from the freighter had been reverse engineered, and the human version set to the skin of the craft. Computer modeling and optimization of the black material made it look even more alien. The little collectors were now vastly more responsive than the original design. They were computer controlled and set with tiny motors to track the strongest energy source they could absorb.

John walked under the bow of the ship examining two of the upscaled hand lasers. "Elvis, you've done a great job on these lasers."

"They may be 10 times the size of the hand laser; however, I doubt they'll be ten times the power as well," he laughed. "Maybe only nine times." Elvis grinned.

"Ha, we shall see," John said without turning. "Let's hope we don't blow up the first time we use them." Elvis had done limited testing of the lasers on the range in the valley. They were too dangerous to test there after their test fire caused a massive explosion that was reported all across town. Fort Bliss sent a Major to see what the explosion was. Fortunately, by the time he arrived at the Research Base the laser had been packed away. They needed to be test fired in space.

The group walked inside the ship. "We've installed cylinders inside the main compartment for water, extra oxygen and the pump gasses for the lasers. Those blue ones are for the battery liquids."

John nodded in understanding.

A jump drive with updated targeting systems was installed midsection of the yellow container ship. This targeting system included a new computer monitor developed by Max that linked the jump drive to the navigation computer. All of the existing astronomical data, based on the readings that had been taken from jumping to the freighter and Tau Ceti, were loaded into the navigation computer to build a 3-D model of local space. Max put together an automatic update to include any new data into their stellar central database.

Jen's new untested shield technology was also added to the nose of the container, crowding the new command center. The hope was that the new batteries would be able to store enough energy to run the shields for a little while at least. Racing car seats and shiny new computer consoles developed by the new design teams adorned the walls inside the bridge. The last new alien tech to be added to the yellow container ship was an electric thruster. It was a smaller version than the freighter's, but just as efficient. This was thanks to Earth's miniaturization expertise and advanced computer modeling by Max. John was understandably nervous, there was a lot of new tech on the ship. They had tested what they could on Earth, however, ...

◆◆◆

"This trip is to be more a proof of concept than anything else," John said to Thurston.

"Isn't it risky?"

"Yes. But we're running out of time."

He realized once he'd retrieved these new exotic gasses from Barnard Star, with a little 'Good fortune from the Gods', his ship would be transformed even more.

The crowd of scientists and engineers gathered around while John smashed a bottle of champagne over the bow of the new ship as tradition dictated.

"We now have an amazing hybrid Earth-Alien tech Container Class vessel. I want to give it the due reverence that such a beast is entitled to. I would like to christen the latest vessel the *Grace Kelly*."

Everyone surrounding John looked at him stunned no doubt thinking '*Grace Kelly*', really?

'*Grace Kelly*'? Jen was the only person who could be heard laughing under her breath, "What the hell? The ship is ugly, creepy as hell, and nothing like the actor Grace Kelly." There were a few muffled chuckles from behind Jen.

John spoke over the top of the chuckles, "I figured that we would name it after one of Earth's favorite daughters, '*Grace Kelly*'. Despite her humble beginnings, she had a real impact on all who surrounded her."

Jen knew John had always liked the movie Rear Window. It somehow struck a chord. She had watched it with him more than once. Jen snorted quietly, *Humble beginnings... I think not, her father was a wealthy businessman, but who was she to say.*

Thurston being the consummate etiquette guru shouted out.

"Here, Here! Three cheers for *Grace* and three cheers for its crew!" John was touched by Thurston's sentiment. Despite seeing Jen in the back roll her eyes.

Chapter Twenty-Seven

Cassiopeia System, Squishy Pirate Hideout

Drakmok was on the beach carelessly playing with the blaster that he had taken from the freighter. It was slightly heavier than most he had used, but it looked dangerous. As he stared out to sea, his eye stalks tracing the horizon on the expanse of water, he was thankful that he could place his tentacles once more in the sand. His right limb had finally regrown allowing him to feel the fresh brush of water and sand against his suckers.

This world was smaller than his home world with only three-quarters of the gravity. The lack of moon meant the tides varied only slightly.

Taking a sideways step to avoid a small wave, his tentacle absently brushed the intensity slide of the pistol. Drakmok smiled at the coolness of the water. Taking another step to avoid another wave he then tripped over a hidden rock and caught his fore-sucker on the trigger setting the blaster off. A blue beam shot out from the business end of the muzzle, ripping through Drakmok's forth tentacle and cauterizing the ends. The beam traveled into Commander Kane's hut narrowly missing him, and out the opposite wall, to vaporize an enormous track of seawater a thousand feet out to sea. Startled, the squishy turned yellow.

Drakmok dropped the blaster onto the sand as he stood in shock, his bulbous head faded to a pale green as he passed out.

Kane jumped up out of the stimulation tank to hide below the hole. Peering through the smoldering gap, he saw the fool Drakmok scream on the beach then pass-out.

Kane turned his eyestalks to stare straight out the hole in the wall on the other side of his room. Steam slowly dissipated out on the flat ocean. Kane resolved to find out more about these weapons, and where the freighter was heading. They could be a serious threat to his hunting grounds.

◆◆◆

"Have you finished loading all the stores, Drakmok?" Kane said tapping his tentacle on the console.

Drakmok shuffled painfully forward on his new limb, his color betraying his nervousness. The stores that the Commander had ordered loaded perturbed him. "You ordered a lot more guns and explosives than normal," he stated.

"That's because we're going into a dangerous situation. We're going to find and confront those mammals that stole our prize cargo. We cannot allow them to invade our hunting territory, we may even get some of their technology."

Drakmok was not impressed. He had lost yet another limb from the blaster and spent the last week in the regeneration pool. He hated that place. It seemed every time he went into space he lost a limb and ended up in the damned pool. His latest one wasn't even in outer space. At least Tela was the medic on duty. She frequently piloted the *Kator*, however, her secondary duties included working in the pool as a medic comfort attendant. She always blushed when he came in without a limb. He couldn't help but get tingles in the other tentacles on seeing her.

Drakmok sighed and said, "We're all loaded commander."

Drakmok fidgeted, "We've had a new addition to the crew, a female called Ceriantharia. She's our new communications officer."

Kane smiled, he knew full well who this officer was. It was one of the twins who gave such fantastic massages. She must have come of age to be allowed on the ship. He still preferred Bella who had sprayed him with ink, however, during the long voyage he doubted if he would be so picky. 'Urges were urges' was a favorite saying that his grandfather used to say. The only problem Kane could see was that he gave his sperm tube to Ceriantharia's sister. She was naturally excited and squeaked and squealed for a whole cycle. Kane smiled knowing that he would have many little squids swimming past his tentacles when he returned.

"Right, let's get under way."

The pirate ship left the Cassiopeia system heading back to the hulking freighter to determine where those cargo thieves had come from.

Chapter Twenty-Eight

John had gone over the inflation instructions of the space station they'd purchased from the Sage company once more before it was loaded onto the Scotty. It had the biggest storage hull for the deployment. Admittedly he could have just transported the inflatable station to Titan's orbit but John wanted to place it himself to see that it was positioned correctly.

With final preparations made, John instructed Jen to jump into orbit just off Titan. Once again the familiar decompression buffeted the four until the air was cleared from within *Scotty*'s hull.

"Okay let's get this space station inflated and aired up from those oxygen and helium tanks the company provided." Max undid his belt and floated to the rear hatch opening it and suddenly losing his grip started to float out and away from the *Scotty*. His arms flailing as he yelped his surprise realizing he had forgotten to tether to the spaceship. Jen saw his predicament and smiled chuckling to herself then pointed to Max so the others could see what she was chuckling about. Elvis started laughing while he tethered himself and pushed off to capture Max by his boot. Gripping his own lead, he pulled them both back to the cargo area of the rear hatch.

"Nice of you to join us, Max," John said. "Since you're so eager to get out into space, why don't you tether yourself and launch 'Space Station Max'." The other three looked at John with grins on their faces at the first space station named after their acrobatic friend.

It took several hours and two refills of the helium from the *Scotty* before the inflatable habitat component of the space station was complete. All four entered the habitat environs to test it and get out of their spacesuits for a little while. Elvis was nearly brought to tears several times because he'd eaten baked beans that very morning. The other three regretted opening their helmets.

After resting a couple of hours, they topped up their air from the habitat's supply, then opened the next module. The larger rooms held a work area sub-module that would be used to join to the gas tank once it arrives. The final modules to be added to the fledgling space station were the docking, airlock, and command systems. Although the habitat modules had an airlock for emergencies, the command module had a larger purpose-built one with decontamination and space sensor control. John didn't think it would be long before they would be adding to the station. As they maneuvered away from the space station, Max noted how it looked like a centipede of sorts. It needed some maneuvering thrusters in case of low-flying asteroids. Max, taking on its guardianship, was going to have fun planning the next stages of its growth.

♦♦♦

Time and again the *Scotty* returned to the research base to attach the energy collectors, battery units, control modules and even plants for the environmental system. It was difficult to keep the Sage company in the dark as to where and how the space station was going. The secrecy regarding the jump drive was still paramount. The only way that John was going to budge on this was if the Sage company was a 100 percent subsidiary of T.N. Corporation. Some weeks passed as the space station grew organically. The energy collectors were attached to the external wings jutting out from the center giving it a centipede look.

Senior research base staff were gradually indoctrinated into work on Max's Space Station through a series of work rotations. Whilst none were given insights on the method of their transportation from Earth to Max's Space Station, it became a badge of honor to be amongst the steadily growing group of T.N. employees selected to go. Experience in setting up, building and working in space was starting to pay dividends when two new space station modules arrived from the Sage Company unexpectedly accompanied by their managing director.

♦♦♦

CEO Ryan Sage was an intense man. He had made an awful lot of money trading shares over the last two decades. Using his profits, he built the Sage Company from the ground up taking a childhood dream and turning it into reality. His company built space stations that would one day allow everyday people a chance at exploring space. To say that he had a lot invested in his company, was an understatement. When Thurston and John first approached him, he had laughed off their assertions and gave little credence to the space going capability of this relatively new player called T.N. Corporation. It was only after his PA had pointed out Thurston's and John's credentials that Ryan started to listen to what they were actually offering.

Despite their credentials, he had seen little from this new company. There were whispers of monumental changes happening and that T.N. Corporation had some part to play. They were rumored to have purchased several space industry design companies, some of them with a military focus.

Ryan drove his rental car into the gated parking lot of the T.N. research base in El Paso. The air was hot and dry, with a slight breeze from the northwest that frayed his temper and fed his pounding headache. He had a devil of a time trying to catch up with the trucks hauling the two latest inflatable space stations being delivered to the research base from his factories in Vermont. This was the second and third space stations that T.N. had bought.

The guard at the gate was polite but very nearly turned him away at his impromptu arrival with the space station delivery. A few frantic phone calls and a security guard was dispatched with Ryan to meet John and Thurston at the main administration building.

"Ryan, it's good to see you," Thurston said with his hand out.

"Thank you, Thurston, John. I hope you don't mind this impromptu drop in. I just wanted to see how all the equipment was faring." Ryan looked around trying to spot where the delivery trucks went on the research base.

John could tell that Ryan could hardly contain his misgivings about selling his space stations to T.N. They were more than just a profit opportunity.

"As you know, we're a relatively new player in the aerospace industry." John said, "but don't misinterpret new for inexperienced."

From the research that Ryan had done on the company, it didn't even have any obvious connections to space-based operations. It seemed they were primarily a research company for construction material.

"I was interested to see your progress in using the first space station. We definitely want to canvass your insights into its usage."

When John and Thurston said nothing, they could see a physical change in Ryan's face. The man seemed to flush before their eyes.

"From my research, all of your operations are geared towards construction material," Ryan said in a short, clipped fashion.

John gave a short laugh, "That's true; however, what is also true is that construction occurs not only on Earth but in space."

John could see from Ryan's face he wasn't pleased with that answer. It was almost as if Ryan was trying to decide whether he would take back the space stations to protect his company's hard earned reputation. John knew that Ryan was passionate about his space stations, but this was ridiculous.

"When do you propose to launch the first space station?"

John and Thurston looked at each other briefly, as if confirming some unknown agreement, before John continued, "The first space station is already in orbit."

Ryan stood there, with his mouth agape. "When did you launch. There has been nothing in the news." He said not quite believing what John was saying.

"We have our own launch capabilities." John still couldn't help wondering where this was leading.

Why was Ryan here?

This was getting awkward. They wanted Ryan on their side because they still needed his company's station building expertise. "Since you're here, do you have time for a tour?"

Ryan jumped at the chance.

"We have a number of different research divisions here, from materials through to propulsion," John said as he started to drive them around the expanded research base.

"Where do you launch your rockets into orbit?" Ryan asked.

"Over here on the right, we have our rocket test facility, we don't launch from here. We're too close to civilization. If anything fell back down to Earth... We have a secret launch facility." John replied as a matter-of-fact.

Ryan was incensed with that statement. Once again John got the feeling that Ryan was here to assess T.N. and whether to continue doing business together. *Could he be worried that their space stations were to be re-branded using someone else's company name? Or worse yet, flounder in some research base only to be junked along with his business's reputation when creditors moved in.*

The three drove out to the propulsion test pad. One of the new electric engines was being tested. It was tiny compared to other rockets that Ryan had seen at competitor's other facilities. His eyes widened when he saw how powerful the thrusters were.

"How many pounds of pressure are you getting?"

"This one is rated at 15 million pounds."

Ryan was stunned.

"I can't see the fuel lines. What fuel do you use?"

This was getting very uncomfortable for John.

"Ryan, why are you here?" Thurston asked straight out.

"I wanted to be sure that my space stations were being used properly and not re-branded or liquidated as some door stop for my competitors."

Ryan's eyes opened even wider as they walked through the buildings where the design teams were creating concept spaceships.

When they eventually arrived at the final hanger, it housed the last components delivered by the Sage Company. Some work crews were making modifications to enable the space stations to link up with what looked to be enormous gas tanks.

"They're yours," John said pointing at the hardened command module. The Sage logo was prominent on its outer housing. One of the modified gas tanks was currently attached providing a clear view for the director to discern what his space station was going to be used for. The other station was being painted with the A-Bitumen.

Ryan stood there admiring the work, while John chatted quietly on the phone.

Ryan's ears had twitched when John spoke the name Colonel Prior into the phone as he said goodbye to his caller. Ryan was familiar with the Colonel, and his name had been mentioned by a couple of his other clients.

"Do you have any outside contracts you're working on?"

John looked back at Ryan, eyebrows knitted together as if his concentration alone could divine something.

"Yes, we have some contracts with the DOD."

John could see the information shook Ryan.

When the tour was over, Ryan thanked the two and beat a hasty retreat. He could see that this unknown company was making incredible strides. He realized that having them as partners could be incredibly profitable for both their businesses. John had taken Ryan further into his confidence showing him the modifications that were in progress. At first, the reasons for attaching huge gas tanks to the space station seemed far-fetched to Ryan until he thought of harvesting resources from space, that was what the research company was ultimately aiming for. His appreciation for their business acumen and long-term planning skyrocketed.

On his way to the research base, he had had an uneasy feeling that he would be deciding to remove his products and support from T.N. Corporation. He had believed they were just another dead end space industry hack company. The impromptu tour had changed his mind. He had a clear sense that they were people of like mind and further he had a sense that their two companies would ultimately be merged. Ryan knew about the offers that John and Thurston were making towards his business. Frankly, he didn't take them too seriously as his company was his life and joy. But having seen what he'd just seen on the tour, made him stop to re-think and re-evaluate. Nothing confirmed it more when a T.N. clerical assistant gave him a flash drive as he left the base. It included requests and modifications to his stations that could realistically only have come from testing and usage of the station in space. He then wondered if the space station was now some military base in orbit.

♦♦♦

John sat heavily in his chair surrounded by the command team for a gas-harvesting mission meeting. The impromptu visit by Ryan had been a wake-up call. They couldn't rely on any one particular supplier. Even if T.N. acquired Sage, they were going to have to organize the manufacture of space-based installations.

"We've got the gas tank shipped into the launch hanger ready to teleport to Barnard Star system. It took a little while to add the collector and converter, but it's complete now."

"Thanks, Elvis. Are there are any problems I need to be aware of before we jump out to Barnard's?"

Elvis was tempted to mention the setbacks they'd had but saw how tired John looked so kept his mouth shut. He would deal with the recalcitrant scientists when they got back. Two of the Brainiac's had almost come to blows over the final tri-chamber gas scrubber design. Elvis broke it up and said they needed both gas purification and delivery systems. The one that works best would be the primary system, and the other one would be the backup or secondary.

One of the new space stations, to be named Wallace Station after the battery specialist, would be teleported into orbit over the larger of the two Barnard's Star gas giants. This would operate as a refining and extraction station, where they would purify the gasses needed for the batteries. Once ready they would be liquefied for transport to Max's Station.

The gas harvest tank was of a curious design. Once it was taken to the appropriate area of concentration of gas or liquid, then valves would open allowing the liquid or gas to enter the tank. It would work like filling a water bottle by placing it under water. Once filled, the mechanism would shut the valves trapping the contents within the chamber. The tank would then be transported taking its newly harvested resources with it to Wallace Station for purification. This was one of the first new resource harvesting applications that were designed by the two new space design teams, converting existing technologies into space-based technologies.

"Jen, Max. How is the *Grace* testing going?"

"I think we are finally ready John. We've added all the new computer hardware, and fixed all the jump drive wrinkles in the *Grace*. We've had quite a few test jumps of twenty feet within the cavern."

"Elvis, is your team ready?" Elvis had been training up a new crew for the *Scotty*.

"They're a bit nervous, but I think it'll be fine. The last three runs to Max's Station, have been with Michael and Carmen, taking turns as first officer. I think Michael should be my XO for the mission."

"Okay," John confirmed. "Right then, are there are any objections to mission go?"

There were none. "We'll schedule it for 10 AM tomorrow. Get a good night sleep."

Chapter Twenty-Nine

Barnard's Star System

The *Grace* disappeared from the research base to reappear in the far reaches of the Barnard Star system. Any planetary body would need to be mapped and with their orbits identified so that for any future jumping into the system they'd have a better chance of avoiding a collision. The *Grace* took the better part of a day to map the system and galactic time stamping the planetary positions. John launched one of the new satellite sensors that Max had been working on. The satellite incorporated the new energy collector technology and miniature versions of the electric thrusters to enable it to circle the inner planets and gather data on the system. They were all happy to see *Grace's* systems start updating with this new information downloaded from the probe. When they returned, it would be automatically added to their growing stellar database. The detailed automatic spectral analysis loaded without a hitch, so they could see what this system offered for resource harvesting.

"Max, have we any leaks?"

"The hull is solid, no leaks." John really didn't expect any, given this was an alien built spaceship. But all the modifications could have created a hole. It made sense to check with the additional sensors fixed throughout the *Grace*.

In the large hanger bay away from peering eyes, the modified gas storage tank they had primed and parked on the launch pad suddenly disappeared in a flash, to re-materialize next to the *Grace* off her port side.

"The tank has arrived five miles off the port side," Max reported.

"The transmitter is reading five by five."

"Doctor Wallace, what's the status of the tank?" John asked.

"Readings all look normal."

Ten minutes later *Grace's* command crew nervously fidgeted as they waited for the *Scotty*. It had failed to arrive on scheduled.

"Jen, do you know if there were any problems with the *Scotty* before launch?" John queried.

"No. The Uber drive and the Alpha Drive were working normally."

"Max, what about *Scotty's* computer?"

"That was all cool."

"How long should we wait?" Jen asked.

"I'm not sure, but let's give them some more time. In the meantime, let's go over the harvest procedures." John bit is bottom lip in sync with Jen, as their concern grew.

Two hours later, the *Scotty* finally appeared a further two miles from the storage tank transmitting their position locater.

"Welcome *Scotty*. Glad you made the rendezvous."

"Sorry about that *Grace*," Elvis said with a smile, recognizing his friend's concern. "We had trouble loading one of the new sensors. The first attempt broke the satellite arm. We've really got to do something about this buffeting from decompression, it's driving me nuts." Then it was John and Jen's turn to smile, they knew exactly what he was talking about.

"*Grace*, we are now deploying the Wallace Refining Station. We'll keep you posted on its deployment," said Elvis as he struggled to get the command module out the rear hatch of the *Scotty*.

"Carmen, can you initialize the inflation process." Carmen made her way off the walls and bulkhead to the rear hatch. Watching the tightly packed space station forty feet away from the safety of the *Scotty* she tethered herself, pulling out her datapad and started the helium pumps. Like a flower opening to catch the first glimpses of dawn light, the station filled. Once it was inflated, Carmen and Mike went EVA to attach the energy collector wings and tri-tank purifier that Elvis teleported nearby. After a couple hours of unfolding flap 'A', connecting valve 'C' and starting Component 'Z', the *Scotty* crew was ready.

"*Grace*, be advised the Wallace Refining Station is open for business," said Elvis with exhaustion in his voice. Although this was the second Station he had deployed, it still took a lot out of him.

"Brilliant work guys. Make sure you hit me for a bonus next meeting," said John with a smile in his voice.

◆◆◆

The giant planet below seemed torn with windswept clouds racing across its surface. Despite the torrent weather patterns, the crew above sat still. The silence of space was deafening. It was accentuated by *Grace's* slow orbit in an unfamiliar solar system.

The *Grace* had been running a detailed scan of the surface gasses for the past several hours.

"How're we doing for sensors, Max?"

"We have the tank at two miles off port side and the *Scotty* circling the Wallace Station deployment a further three miles off our port side. Other than that we are all clear. The spectral scan is bringing up some interesting results."

Max didn't elaborate.

"So when can we transport the gas tank for harvesting, Jen, Dr. Wallace?"

"The new jump drive is good; however there's a slight variation in the calibration targeting that will be fixed before we transport the tank. But other than that, we're in good shape. So I'd say in the next hour."

♦ ♦ ♦

"Dr. Wallace, is the tank ready for remote activation?" Jen addressed Dr. Adrian Wallace, the lead scientist that was allocated to reverse engineer the blaster batteries.

Adrian sat unmoving mesmerized by the main viewer, which displayed a real, but unfamiliar planet. The swirls of cloud along its surface were hypnotic. He and several other scientists were only made privy to the jump drive two days ago. Even then the thought of jumping from system to system was as alien as the world he now saw far below.

"It's amazing the first time it hits you. It's like a gunshot between the eyes," Jen said over her shoulder to Adrian, knowing what he was going through.

"Adrian, the power systems and the tank readiness, if you would?" John repeated.

Adrian, slightly embarrassed by his unseemly distraction returned his attention to his console and spoke up. "The Earth-Tech battery levels are all steadily moving up. The portable power generator is working; however, I will stop it soon, to see how the new collectors absorb the solar energy."

After a few minutes, Adrian spoke up once more. "The collectors have started charging the Earth-Tech batteries," he said with a grin. There were so many new innovations the research group had included in the *Grace;* they all knew there was a very real danger of catastrophic failure.

The researchers and tech staff had set up a de-facto language to distinguish the newly reverse-engineered technologies from the standard tried-and-true Earth know-how or Earth-Tech. The *Grace* had two sets of batteries. Earth-Tech ones, which were currently charging, and the newly manufactured ones based on the blaster battery. Their intention this voyage was twofold: to test the new batteries and the new energy collectors.

"Doctor how long will it take to recharge the batteries?" John asked.

"It's unclear how long the Earth-Tech batteries will take to fully recharge using the new collectors. If we were in closer proximity to the red dwarf, I'm sure the collectors would charge the batteries 'tout suite'," Adrian said with a triumphant chuckle.

"While the Earth-Tech batteries are charging with the new collectors, we should send down the gas tank to fill up." John wasn't sure which form the gas/liquid was in down there, it depended on the temperature and pressure. It was still confusing. He resolved to just call it gas.

"So Jen, my question still stands, how long before we can transport the gas tank to it fill up."

"I'm waiting for the final analysis of the sensing data to come through. I don't want to send it off into that red dwarf," Jen snapped. John turned to look at her realizing he had been pressuring her. This was a new system with new astronomical bodies floating around everywhere.

Jen rubbed her temples trying to alleviate a headache. The quantum computer was still having a few problems, although she didn't tell John that. John would have canceled the mission outright. Jen turned and looked at Max willing him to the make the computer work without crashing. Max just studiously kept his eyes locked onto his computer screen.

John turned his focus back to Adrian and said, "Given the pressures against the gas tank, have you worked out roughly how long it will take to fill and equalize? We will want to harvest the liquid at the earliest possible moment."

"It's difficult to work out how long that process will take given we don't know what the actual concentrations and pressures of the gas giant are. I will be conservative so we don't lose the tank." Adrian then instant messaged Jen to not make it too deep. He'd rather only have a little gas than no tank. Adrian included an icon of the sun blowing gas out of its ass in the text message. Jen chuckled at this and sent back an image of an explosion with a big red X through the middle of it. Just below the icon scrolled 'The force be with you'. To which Adrian then chuckled.

John then opened up. "When you two have finished sending love letters, let's get cracking on this."

Adrian looked suitably abashed, Jen just laughed out loud, which made John roll his eyes at the lack of discipline.

John didn't want to push too much testing in one session so he resigned himself to wait.

◆◆◆

John maneuvered the *Grace* to dock with Wallace Station. Adrian and John transferred over to verify that the refining process was all prepped and ready.

"Once we connect the tank via these hoses the process is automated. The station looks ready for the gasses," said Adrian as he tapped at the nearest computer terminal on the small station.

John nodded his approval. The *Scotty's* crew had done a good job.

The two twisted through the small airlock back to the *Grace*.

When they arrived on the bridge, Jen was setting up the transport coordinates for the gas tank to be transported, by the *Scotty*, to the upper atmosphere of the gas giant. This would be an unusual jump, as she needed to do a tele-grab of the gas tank as it fell towards the surface. The tank would be crushed if it descended too deep into the atmosphere, it needed to be transported before it died a gruesome death under the pressure.

Jen could, if need be, transport a huge cube of the area that included the gas tank, into space if the targeting data from the transmitter was too imprecise. It was a bit of a broad brush and seemed reckless compared with Jen's usually prudent scientifically exacting view on life.

John left Jen to do her magic. He could see the furrowed brow and the pursed lips of concentration on her face. He had gotten used to that face. Slightly freckled, but full of passion.

He sometimes saw a shadow of the horror from the Sykes drama cross her countenance, and he felt the sadness for her loss of innocence. Shaking his head at the conversations he'd had with Elvis about Jen and Sykes he switched his focus from her to concentrate on his mission.

Jen smiled inwardly as she saw John's scrutiny out of the corner of her eye. She usually hated it but surprised herself at how comforting she found it this time.

♦♦♦

"Are you ready Carmen?" Jen comm'ed the *Scotty*.

"Yes, we have the coordinates to teleport the tank," Carmen responded in her staccato Puerto Rican Spanish accent.

The gas tank disappeared in a flash when the *Scotty* transported it into the upper atmosphere of the gas giant where it fell towards the crusty rocky surface below. Adrian connected wirelessly to the small computer onboard the falling tank and waited while it updated his monitor showing the tank's pressure gages.

The seconds ticked by as he stared at the gas tank's internal pressure gauge... it crawled slowly as the tank filled. After a few minutes, he tapped his screen in irritation waiting for the gasses to equalize before he transmitted the auto valve shut-off sequence to trap the gasses within the chamber.

The tank fell. The gauge barely moved.

"Now!" he yelled. Jen executed the tele-get to retrieve the tank, depositing it just next to Wallace Station.

"Jen, Adrian you're up for an EVA," John commanded through the comm.

Adrian suited up in his new personal space suit. His hands trembled as he fastened his helmet clasps.

"You'll be fine," Jen said to the older man. She double checked his suit and ended by slapping his helmet. "Good to go!"

Jen could see the trepidation in his face. She quickly suited up, readying herself at the emergency hatch. The *Grace* was still docked to Wallace Station, but the emergency airlock on top of the ship was clear for use.

She followed him to the airlock, where she attached both their tethers. They exited the *Grace*, linked at the hip by a thin wire. Jen clipped them to the inside safety hook by a tether cable. It was way too flimsy looking for Jen's liking.

Slowly they made their way hand over hand to the Station's exterior external hose housing. Pulling out the flat tube, Jen attached it to the external port.

Through the comm, John could hear Adrian start to hyperventilate. "Adrian, calm down. There is plenty of air."

Jen turned to face the man seeing him wide-eyed and staring towards the surface of the gas giant.

"Adrian ... look at me, not the planet. Focus!"

Adrian didn't move. Jen smacked his helmet.

"Adrian, how much pressure do we need in the tank?"

Adrian turned towards Jen, his face white as a sheet.

"How much?" Adrian was freaking out.

Finally, he turned to face the gas tank.

Without telling him what she meant to do, Jen grabbed the older man and thrust him towards the tank, two miles away.

"Oh my God...Help... Damn you, Jen ... you pushed me!" Adrian yelled over the comm as he flailed uselessly.

The plan was that the two would make their way to the Stations hose port where Jen would spacewalk a hose from the station to the tank and connect the valves leaving Adrian to start the purification process. There was an understanding that you never space walked alone, like the safety precautions practiced in scuba diving.

"Jen, do you need me to suit up?" John asked.

"Negative, John. Adrian is coming with me to the tank." Jen sounded determined.

Adrian finally resigned himself to fly towards the large tank.

Jen clipped the hose end from the station to her belt then pushed off after Adrian towards the tank 50 yards away.

"Damn, ooof... Jen, you bitch..." Adrian spun, eventually thumping into the tank before bouncing off. Ice crystals flaking off the tank's exterior into space from the impact.

Just as Adrian started to spin off, Jen arrived snagging his foot as she hit the tank.

John heard a loud clang over the comm. "Jen, you ok?"

"Fine." She said tersely.

Reeling him in, Adrian was able to grab a handhold near the external port.

"Why the hell did you do that?! I could have fallen into the planet!"

"Hardly, we're tethered," Jen said with gritted teeth. "Here, connect this so we can get back," Jen said as she passed the hose from her belt that was still attached to the Station purification system.

Adrian focused on attaching the hose while Jen shuffled to the valve tap.

Adrian hadn't believed the rumors going around the camp that Jen had something to do with the missing guy. Police had been hanging around asking questions. Now he wasn't so sure.

Jen grunted as she opened the valve.

The hose sprung straight filling with liquid as the precious fluid filled the Station's tanks.

Every few minutes Adrian would curse over the comm. Small things at first, then nastier as he gained momentum.

John walked to the back of the *Grace* to stand outside the airlock. He was surprised that Adrian was alone when he cycled through. The man looked to be in a foul mood. It wasn't surprising given the comms that John had heard over the course of the last hour and a half. Adrian stalked past

John's questioning gaze, he returned it with a scowl on his face and declared aloud, "The tank's full."

It was only minutes later the airlock activated cycling again. John could see Jen move awkwardly out of her suit.

"Jen, what's wrong?"

Jen grunted as she pulled her left shoulder free.

It bulged out in an unnatural way.

John rushed forward, to examine her.

"Ooow," Jen's face was white.

"I think it's just dislocated... hold on..." John, using his army emergency first aid training, wrenched her shoulder into place.

"Oooh, shit!" Jen yelled, then passed out just as John caught her and lay her on the deck cradling her in his arms.

John gritted his teeth. "Adrian, Get in here!"

Adrian stopped outside the hatch with a surprised look on his face.

"What's wrong with her?"

"Explain to me exactly what happened. Leave nothing out." Adrian could see John was furious.

"Well, I was having trouble breathing when she smacked my helmet."

"When she said focus?"

"Yes. Umm, then she pushed me off the *Grace* into space," Adrian said with a slight snarl.

"Why the hell do you think she would do that?"

"Because she's a ..." Adrian started, then stopped at John's expression. "I was freaking out," he finally said.

"Right, so she wouldn't leave you outside on the station exterior alone. Would you have jumped to the gas tank on your own?"

Adrian stumbled over his words. ".. Ummm, no. I couldn't."

"So she helped you over, to keep an eye on you. Then, from what I heard through the comm, kept you focused on your job."

"But she got me so angry..." Adrian stopped as the realization hit him. *Angry but focused, not freaking out.*

"How did she get a dislocated shoulder?" John asked.

"She what... a dislocated shoulder?" Adrian thought about it, "She came in fast on the gas tank and hit hard. Then she took ages to turn on the valve."

"So she continued the rest of the mission with a busted shoulder, without your assistance, except your cussing and bitching. Doctor, you have some serious groveling to do," John said as he nodded down at Jen.

Adrian flushed crimson, embarrassed by his behavior.

"On a personal note, if you ever endanger Jen or any of my crew ever again because of your unprofessional behavior, being fired will be the least of your troubles." John's voice was cold.

Adrian's eyes widened, and his face paled.

When Jen awoke, John heard Adrian apologize profusely, then helped her back to her console after some groveling and basic medical aid.

"Jen, are you OK? Shall we return to Max's station?"

"No. I've taken something for the pain. Let's finish this."

Adrian worked from his console wirelessly remoting into the Stations computers and started the purification process.

It wasn't long before the tank's gasses were purified and pumped to the station's tanks ready for transport. A small amount was pumped into *Grace's* tanks.

John pinged Elvis on the comm, notifying him that the *Grace* had full tanks.

"Elvis, we're going to charge up with our collectors now, so we'll jump in close to the red dwarf. I'm going to get Adrian to add the new liquid to our Alien-Tech batteries onboard to see if we can get them up and running as well. I'm not sure how long we'll need to stay; I suggest you return to Max's space station. I don't want you to be here too long since you don't have shielding to protect you from the dwarf sun's radiation."

"No need to tell me twice John, I'm planning to have kids," Elvis retorted. John just grinned.

The *Grace* flashed out of the geosynchronous orbit of the gas giant to reappear close to the red dwarf. "Adrian, now you're up."

John's console could link into Adrian's to see the progress of the energy collection and the status of the Earth-Tech batteries.

Adrian set filters to purify the new gasses they collected. There was a whole bank of these new alien batteries that needed to be filled. Once the batteries registered full of gas, they switched the energy collection to the empty ones. The electrical charge indicator connected to Adrian's console barely moved. Once again Adrian tapped his console in irritation.

"Is it working? Can you do a diagnostic on the charge sensor?" asked John, trying to mask his impatience.

"It's all working," Adrian replied.

"At this rate, it will take hours to fully recharge the batteries."

"I thought these collectors were meant to be good," John said irritated. The *Grace* had black collectors all over her outer hull. By far the biggest flat concentration of them was on the keel of the ship. The keel was designated as the strong point of the ship, where they had concentrated extra layers of armor and A-Bitumen.

"They *are* really good; however, the batteries are unbelievable. The amount of energy they can store! Although these are reverse engineered from the blaster battery, the size of the ones on the *Grace* is 2000 times larger. We have almost 200 car battery sized storage units under the floor daisy chained in six rows."

"Okay, okay." John put up his hands in defeat. He did know the specs in the back of his mind.

Adrian smiled as he did a small test to briefly switch the power source from the old batteries to the new ones. The power fluctuated briefly but remained strong.

John conceded.

John's mind flicked to the other person most involved in the battery re-engineering project, Elvis. He originally had his doubts about Elvis and his engineering acumen; however, his performance over the last year had been stellar. He had noticed that Elvis was taking some evenings off the base at the Hog's Breath on a fairly regular basis. No doubt it was to get away from the highly, distilled atmosphere of the little scientific enclave they had at the base. Shaking his head once again at the thought of Elvis and the Doomsday Preppers.

He hoped that Elvis remembered to check his oxygen level when he arrived at Titan before he started connecting the gas tank up to the space station. At least he'd be able to take a breather from the spacesuits.

After a few hours, John made the decision to jump back to Earth to give the crew a break. Even though he had done basic medical training and could look after dislocated limbs and other injuries, he hadn't planned for Jen to be out without care for so long. They could test how the batteries worked back in Sol system given the new exotic wonder liquid from the gas giant. A single flash from Barnard's Star and the *Grace* rematerialized back on Earth. John contacted Elvis on Max's station to let him know they had arrived home in the cavern.

◆◆◆

Testing began in earnest on the new batteries. They prototyped several different versions, focusing on sizes not much larger than a regular car battery. It would make the transition from Earth-Tech batteries to these new ones so much easier. The group led by Adrian purified the gasses even further making the batteries longer lasting and more potent. They pushed the design towards different configurations.

Spaceships needed slow extended-release for powering standard necessary ship operations that didn't fluctuate much such as lighting, life support, and sensors. Adrian realized there was also the need for fast dumps of vast amounts of power when the ship would use either their shields or weapons in combat.

Once standardized battery designs were settled upon, Thurston took over the patent application, licensing and manufacturer by the now ever expanding group of companies associated with T.N. Corporation. Retooling by existing manufacturers took time; however, harvesting the gasses for the batteries required regular trips to the Barnard's Star system which also took time.

◆◆◆

John couldn't help but smile as the *Scotty* left the Sol system to set up a third space station within the Tau Ceti system.

Sometimes Elvis cursed his fateful trip with Max to the cow planet. 'Cow Gas', was on everyone's lips. Cow gas and lasers were the butts of many jokes within the confines of the research base. Elvis just knew that the cows and their farting gas would receive an Oscar for their dramatic performance. It was almost fitting that it was the primary economic driver for this latest endeavor, Lasers.

Even Ryan was happy that T.N. had purchased another inflatable space station. He incorporated the tanker valve fittings as a standard feature, with many more features on the way.

"Damn John, why do I have to be the one to launch the station."

"But Elvis it was your discovery," John said grinning at Elvis's discomfort. To be known as the person who discovered the cow farting planet was not his idea of immortality.

"Cheer up, it could be worse," said Max.

"What do you mean it could be worse?"

"Better you than me," Max said tongue in cheek.

"Hurumm."

"In that case, I am going to take Carmen and Mike," Elvis said miffed.

"Ha, ha." John and Max chorused.

To put the icing on the cake, John called the new station *The King's Space Station* in honor of Elvis's namesake. For some reason, Elvis was not impressed.

Max programmed the space station AI with Elvis Presley's voice print.

◆ ◆ ◆

Barnard Star System - Wallace Space Station

John made the jump directly from the El Paso cavern to Barnard's Star, not far from Wallace Space Station. Radioing into the station, John let them know that they were going to be conducting some shields and weapons testing.

Jumping to and from Barnard's Star using the new batteries to power their electric thruster, allowed John to start to get a feel for the basic power usage of the new batteries. As the testing progressed, they moved onto weapons and shields. They had to regularly jump or fly the ship close to the red dwarf facing their keel with the greatest coverage of collectors. Jen pressed a button and arms overlaid with energy collectors extended out of the *Grace* giving it wings.

The wing collectors had reduced recharge times tremendously, but still, it took hours to fully power up. When the new batteries were charged to 80%, John decided to test out the ship's shield generators. That was one new system that took an inordinate amount of power. He hoped that these alien-tech batteries could dump that amount in.

"Okay, Jen let's see what she's got." Jen altered the controls on her console, and suddenly a green tinge showed up on the main view screen.

The external cameras on the body of the *Grace* displayed a green hue with sparkles. John smiled looking at the cameras then the monitor and lastly at Max, "Nice touch," the shield on the screen showed density and thickness based on the real shield levels.

"Shields at 20%."

"Okay, steadily increase the power and let's see if we blow any circuits."

Jen increased power incrementally by 10%. Slowly the green haze around the *Grace* solidified. Outside the ship crackles of energy flew along its length. John was thankful that they had more padding and armor on the vessel now. When they added the energy collectors, they had also added almost a foot of layered A-Bitumen and pressed steel around the outside. If the *Grace* was to be a proper spaceship, it needed protection from the elements without its shields.

Eventually, they reached 100%, and there was a discernible vibration throughout the ship as the generators push the power into the shields.

"How is the power consumption going?" John queried.

"Hold on, I'm opening a tool to graph the consumption for you on your console." Suddenly a chart appeared with markings from green to orange to red. The consumption was well into the green. It was much more detailed than the basic icon on the main viewer.

"Okay, let's cut the shields and reactivate the shields again to full power." It was going to be a long process of testing the shields over and over again. It was their lives at stake, and

John had no qualm about spending the time. Jen just cut them without comment.

After several hours of shields on/off, on/off, they moved the testing to a new phase:

"The next test that I'd like to do is the engines. 5% power please Jen. I'll take the helm." As Jen routed some power through to the engines all they heard was barely a whisper. The small ship gracefully picked up speed making its way towards one of the small moons of the gas giant. Taking the controls manually, was like flying a helicopter. Back in his younger days, John had piloted helicopters for the Army, but more recently for a drug rehab center in the mid-west. The center was a last-ditch attempt at self-imposed exile by the unfortunate drug users. John assisted in transporting the unlucky participants to a remote wilderness ranch in his helicopter. Memories of his ex-girlfriend's intervention splayed across his mind. Just as abruptly John refocused on his flying.

The rocky, airless landscape of the moon rushed towards them. John banked hard left flipping the craft like an old jet fighter.

"Push the shields incrementally, please Jen," John said as he increased the power to the engines. The four were driven back into their racing car seats. The *Grace* rocketed forwards as John powered through some acrobatic maneuvers. All this time they checked the operation of the shields. Until John was satisfied that the craft performed admirably but more to the point he could handle the ship competently.

The last thing on the agenda for this trip was to test the guns with the new batteries and their power-dump capabilities. John had been reluctant to fully test them on Earth given how powerful they were. Any significant disturbance would undoubtedly be picked up. They needed to test them in simulated combat. John smiled to himself knowing that Elvis would have died to do these tests. They pulled the craft a few miles from an unsuspecting asteroid.

"Jen, if you would target the asteroid please and fire the left fore-turret at 5%." The small asteroid sheared in half. All four crew were stunned at the power.

"I said 5%, Jen," John said a little annoyed.

"That *was* 5%!" Jen snapped back.

They flew to a much more substantial asteroid. "Left fore-turret at 10%." The gun sheared off a sizable chunk. They continued the tests on one asteroid after another. After several hours of firing and recording the settings and results, they had a much clearer idea as to the power and range of shots they could achieve. They all discussed various firing patterns that they could pre-program into the system. In combat, John knew you don't have time to explain, so preprogrammed combinations were essential.

Although he hadn't intended to spend so much time on the testing voyage, he was feeling much more comfortable with the capabilities of his new ship.

Making their way back to Wallace's station to check on the operations, and refill their air, all four were tired from the days testing and recharging.

Chapter Thirty

Max's Space Station

Elvis was decidedly unhappy with the time John was taking to test *Grace's* systems. The Scotty had returned to the Sol system after going on another harvest mission to Tau Ceti. He was getting very sick of the damned cow fart gas. There is only so many ways that you could laugh about farts. He and his crew had begun to connect the gas tank to the second Work Module of Max's station.

The command team had discussed each of the different gas resources that were now being stored at the Station. So far they had only the two large tanks, but a newly attached third was set aside for fuel. Titan was basically a huge ball of ice, which they could harvest. They had plans here for a free fall manufacturing area where they could manufacture the battery cells much more safely. After an accident where the exotic gasses escaped into Earth's atmosphere, Thurston pushed the safety concerns. The other reason was to ensure the manufacturing processing stayed under their control. Thurston had been tougher in his setting up of the business and legal structures, but still, unscrupulous companies were hanging out the door just waiting for any opportunity.

"*Scotty*, this is Max's Station Control, we've picked up a sizable signature of a ship entering the solar system."

Elvis quickly disembarked from the *Scotty* and made his way to the space station communication and sensor control.

"It's moving pretty fast!" Elvis watched nervously as the ship speed towards the Kuiper Belt and stopped on its outskirts.

"What's it doing there?" Elvis queried after an hour and a half. The ship just sat there on the periphery of the system.

216

"We think it's scanning the system."

"Damn, OK, I want everyone in their suits, with your helmets handy," Elvis ordered.

"Then power down any systems not absolutely necessary." *Hopefully, they hadn't noticed them, but that was an unlikely big if.*

◆◆◆

Space Command, Peterson Air Force Base

Lt. Colonel Prior placed the phone down after a frustrating conversation with the loud-mouthed Dr. La Perouse. The last several months had seen little progress. He was having second thoughts once again about contracting the Frenchman. The only good thing that seemed to have come out of it was the discovery of the real deal. He was referring to Dr. Stevenson. The blaster demonstration had blown him away. The few early prototype lasers that had been delivered had lived up to his expectations. Any aircraft or ship based blaster with an equivalent energy source of the same order of magnitude would be truly frightening. The only issue now he could envisage would be to power it. A dangerous amount of energy would be needed. His thoughts then drifted to nuclear-powered lasers, when his phone messaged him with a priority Red Flag situation. He was required to report to the Comms Center immediately.

He ran down the several flights of stairs at space command into the bunker. The lower levels had the situation room (SITCOM) with links to NORAD, space missile command and various space observatories. The recent alien contacts had forced the upgrading of the communications center. A new SITCOM war room was being built in Nebraska, but until then, the combined Missile Defense Command and Space Command (MDSCOM) were based at Peterson Air Force Base. Running past the marines guarding the entrance into the war room, Dan gulped air for a second before he questioned the Duty Captain on the threat board.

"We have two contacts, one active contact and one we are still trying to confirm as it's intermittent."

"The active bogey is inbound to Earth; it's currently sitting at the Kuiper Belt not doing anything. Tachyon scans have it as a warship and not a freighter configuration."

"The President has been informed of the alien contacts." The President's standing orders still apply. They were to attempt comm contact only, nothing was to attack the aliens unless the President gave the go-ahead signal. Staff were glued to their view screens showing a model of the Sol system with the bogey flashing on its rim.

When the warship started to move, it was estimated that it would take two hours for the ship to traverse the Sol system. The Star Wars anti-satellite laser system had been re-tasked to point outwardly as opposed to down-to-earth since the last alien incursion. Hundreds of missile silos and mobile launch platforms on Earth were charging and preparing for a confrontation.

"Have the other Nations been informed?" Dan asked.

"Yes Sir, we sent them a priority packet."

Numerous aircraft including Air Force One scrambled with the Vice President. America set its alert condition to DEFCON 1, which meant the armed forces were ready to deploy and engage weapons including nuclear missiles.

The US military was a beehive of activity. New laser-based aircraft took off, warships fired up their reactors while nuclear subs dived under the waters. Mobile Army Missile Defense Platforms checked their camouflage and were fully manned and operational.

NATO Response Force and the other major powers around the world set similar alert readiness conditions.

Max's Station off Titan

Elvis was in two minds as to how to approach the building situation. The Scotty had no defenses. If the enemy only had a pea shooter that shot wads of paper, it would probably destroy them. Getting in close and targeting the warship was going to be very problematic without getting shot at. The alternative was to jump to the cavern to fight the battle via transporter, targeting the alien ship from there had its own problems.

Just then in a flash, which temporarily blinded Elvis, the *Grace* materialized off *Scotty's* port side. "Damn," Elvis mouthed while flicking his eyes through the after image of *Grace's* appearance.

On the *Grace*, Max piped up and advised of the alien contact in-system moving towards Earth's orbit from the Kuiper Belt.

Chapter Thirty-One

The Lizard Warship *Godzilla* halted on the edge of the Sol system scanning for signs of life. Unbelievable amounts of EM comm traffic were broadcast from the third planet. It was a jumble of radio waves, microwaves and even some gamma radiation.

"Have you deciphered the comms traffic?" Rezulin asked of his comms officer.

"There are multiple of languages being broadcast. We have just decrypted some video. Although there is still a lot of pulses that are gibberish."

Rezulin brought up the video on his console. "The dominant species are chaotic hyperactive lifeforms." Rezulin concentrated on the moving pictures.

Pulling up the lifeform infra-red scans, "They are endothermic. They must be mammals." Rezulin scowled. Lizards have enslaved mammal species before, but they can be tricky. They were so unpredictable.

"Sir, there are still many different species on the planet. Even some ectotherms. Although, they seem to be non-sentient. Most are restricted to non-urban swamp or jungle areas."

Initially, Rezulin thought they must have stumbled onto an interstellar trading hub. But it soon became apparent that all the transmissions were being made by one species. There were no interstellar communication transmitter arrays that would have been needed. His smile broadened showing his saw like teeth as it became evident that the civilization was barely space faring. There were scores of satellites and junk orbiting the planet, almost to the point of stupidity. All that space junk would be hazardous to regular space bound traffic. There were no bases further in the solar system. There was not even a base on their moon.

The mammal population would be an excellent source of food for their fledgling colony. They may even be trainable to perform some menial tasks. He wondered what these creatures would add to their brain chemistry.

The Unak Lizards had highly malleable brains. If they ate intelligent creatures, then they would gain in intelligence. If they ate warriors, then they became aggressive. The downside was if they ate slothful creatures, they became more lethargic and indolent. Eating herd animals was problematic long term. Their race would degenerate into mindless beasts.

At the very least, if these mammals were incompatible, they could be used as slaves.

Thoughts of being rewarded with an estate for this find drifted through Rezulin's head. He could take some of the mammals as slaves to serve his every need.

The lizard military on the Unak home world had been over populated for the remaining food sources. Regular mass protests pulled the Lizard society to breaking point. The Lizard aristocracy denied the smartest food species to any but themselves. The Lizard worlds were starving. Even slaves were few and far between as the meaning of slave and food became more and more interchangeable.

The Unak Lizards needed to find a sentient food source before they devoured themselves.

♦♦♦

Rezulin's decision was an easy one. Before him floated a planet loaded with resources for the taking.

"I have a shuttle size new contact War Leader. It must've been behind the gas giant's moon. It's only now appeared, or it's fitted with stealth technology." Rezulin waved his arm acknowledging the sensor operator.

A ship that size should be no problem, he thought.

The *Godzilla* powered towards Earth reaching it in just under two hours. As soon as the warship came into range of Earth's satellites orbiting the third planet the *Godzilla* launched a blistering attack that destroyed all of the satellites that registered as weapons and many that weren't. The warship easily destroyed the international space station with a single missile.

"War Leader, I have an unusual reading from the surface on my scanners. We're picking up on some; Furbags, Bunny Bears and Mortcatts on the continent south of the desert region."

"Send our harvesters down there and see what you can find out." Two transports flew out of the *Godzilla's* hangar bay towards the planet's surface.

Rezulin had a sinking suspicion that not everything was as it seemed. How could an apparently advanced civilization with so much EM traffic not have expanded into their own solar system? It was unbelievable, yet here they were.

The bigger question, *how did Furbags, Bunny Bears and Mortcatts get here? They are from Erandi Five sector.*

Chapter Thirty-Two

Space Command, Peterson Air Force Base

"Colonel, that ship has just taken out 95% of our military satellite assets and the international space station, what are your orders?"

"Was there any response to our hails?" Dan asked.

"No response!"

"Get me NORAD on the line. I want the satellite buster targeting that ship."

Admiral Tucker, Dan's immediate superior, commed into the war room querying the status.

"Admiral Tucker, is on the line, sir."

Dan picked up the phone, "Sir, we are tasking the satellite buster to target the alien vessel."

"You have a 'Go fire order'."

Dan then turned to his subordinate and ordered them to fire the Satellite Buster.

"Sir, the Satellite Buster was one of the 95% destroyed. I'm getting two new smaller contacts separating from the warship. Bandits Charlie and Bravo heading towards the West Coast of the United States... Correction, towards San Francisco... Correction, Texas."

"Are they heading for Colorado Springs?"

"Negative, there's been a course correction to El Paso, Texas."

"Bogey three is currently holding position near Titan."

Dan thought to himself, *it's too much of a coincidence that El Paso is where Dr. Stevenson has his base of operations for the laser testing.*

"Scramble 120th fighter squadron from Buckley to intercept those two ships on Admiral Tucker's Authority."

Dan thought to himself, *they are sending shuttles, why?!*

"I also want some Predator and Osprey attack helicopters on standby, and let Fort Bliss Armor Division know to expect company. I have a hunch, and I want them to send some M1 tanks to this address in El Paso." Dan passed the coordinates of the research base to the comms officer.

Lt Samuels of the Cougars sat in the cockpit of his F16c fighter jet watching the clouds shoot by. The word over the wire was a full-blown alien invasion. He steeled himself as he flew on an intercept course towards the two alien craft. He straightened out the picture of his sweetheart he'd jammed into the side of the forward control panel for luck. Samuels took one quick look then refocused on his mission. Orders were to hold fire until told or fired upon. The brass wanted to determine what their purpose was. Geez, blowing up all of our satellites and the ISS (International Space Station) isn't purpose enough? The lieutenant just shook his head in disbelief.

♦♦♦

"Okay Elvis, taking the *Scotty* anywhere near that ship would be suicide. That looks like a warship because it's certainly not a trader, the hull is not big enough, and the guns are a bit of a dead giveaway. This is what I think we should do..." John explained.

The *Scotty* disappeared and materialized within the cavern below the Research Base. Elvis then went about connecting the Uber transporter drive and a booster to their targeting system.

At the same time, John ordered Jen to bring up shields and set the course for Earth at flank speed. While they moved in-system, *Grace's* jump drive was recharging and still needed a good half hour before it was ready.

Chapter Thirty-Three

Sheriff's Offices El Paso, Texas

Amanda had waited long enough for the apprehension warrant and extra officers from the nearby El Paso SWAT and Albuquerque Police Department to come through to her offices just outside of El Paso. She wanted a dozen law enforcement officers at her back when she went to confront Dr. Stevenson about the disappearance of old man Sykes as well as some heavy weaponry.

She had checked with the postmaster regarding the delivery of a golden retriever. The delivery boy had given the dog to the old man to pass on to the Dr. Stevenson. No one seems to have seen him after that point, except Dr. Stevenson and his friends. The whole community had been bamboozled with all the secrecy. Each person she spoke to had been very tight-lipped about the goings-on at, what some of the locals had started to call, the fantasy lab.

Amanda had contacts of her own in the criminal underworld where gun running and people smuggling were a seedy part of her job. According to her informant, Dr. Stevenson had definitely bought high-powered weaponry, which included of all things missiles. Given the military base and gunnery range was just down the road, the likely-hood of the doctor getting the weapons was, unfortunately, high.

When Amanda spoke to the Police Chief of the raid on the research base and her concerns with high-powered weaponry, the police chief did a double take and immediately ordered her to contact Homeland Security to have them participate in the raid.

♦ ♦ ♦

Homeland Security, Washington DC Branch

"Got you finally!" Agent O'Brien smiled as he saw the incoming message from a small town Deputy Sheriff outside of El Paso, Texas. For the past twelve months, he had been fuming that the Air Force had gutted his investigation into the two terrorists, Dr. Stevenson, and his friend Randy 'Elvis' Watts. He had suffered the indignity of justifying to his superiors the expense of SWAT teams and bomb disposal units against these so-called Department of Defense contractors. Words like *inappropriate resource allocation* were bandied about, raking his reputation through the mud. This report from the Deputy Sheriff outlining the purchase of heavy weapons from known criminals was the golden bullet that he needed. He grabbed his kevlar vest and raced off to the airport to catch the first flight to El Paso.

♦ ♦ ♦

Sheriff's Office El Paso, Texas

Agent O'Brien flashed his DHS badge at the petite blond Deputy.

"I'm glad you contacted us when you did, Deputy Riley, who knows what sort of trouble these two terrorists and their paramilitary organization are getting up to. They've eluded me once; I don't intend for them to get away a second time. I see the El Paso SWAT has come, excellent!"

Amanda was slightly taken aback by the rather rough looking agent. His crumpled suit and bleary-eyed look had the hallmarks of something more than just being tired. She could tell that he was fixated on Dr. Stevenson and his group. From her own conversations with John, she had trouble thinking of them as a paramilitary organization as described by Agent O'Brien and yet they had purchased those missiles.

The nine men and three women piled into their sheriff vehicles and headed out to the research lab with a SWAT truck following behind.

Amanda couldn't believe that Scarlet had tried to set her up on a date with Dr. Stevenson! If he could hoodwink Scarlet... She stopped that train of thought, not wanting to pursue it to its logical conclusion. And yet, she thought again about looking into nursing homes for Aunt Scarlet. On the brief times that she had spoken to Dr. Stevenson and his associate Elvis, they had seemed reasonable. Trying to get a handle on his associate's character and their working relationship, Amanda thought, *who would name themselves Elvis?!* She knew his real name was Watts. She had enjoyed their company, and yet, they were definitely hiding something. Years on the job had given her some insights; the old man's disappearance just didn't sit right.

As the sheriff's convoy turned into the driveway of the research base, two huge, impossibly dark shapes flew over them, heading directly for the buildings. In disbelief, the occupants of the cars and SWAT truck stared, mouths agape, as they sped towards the gate. How could they even be flying! They had no real wings.

Flashing their badges at the nervous guards manning the gatehouse, the carloads of officers were let through. The guards, who hadn't seen the flying craft, pointed them to wait at a spot just outside of the administration block.

Amanda thought, *Yeah right, as if!*

As they approached the administration block, all hell broke loose. Giant six-foot lizard creatures with red body armor had exited a craft that had landed near the labs. Without warning, they started firing weapons that looked like some kind of ray gun, dropping anyone in their sight within the compound area. Their weapons projected wide beams of blue light.

Amanda jumped out of the car drawing her weapon and firing at the nearest lizard. She had no choice, she couldn't tell if those ray guns were killing or stunning people. Her two quick shots flew out of her gun, bullets striking the Lizard in the head, ripping a hole through the skull and out the back.

Other officers took Amanda's lead and drew their own weapons, firing as she did. An all-out pitched battle ensued as the flames of light issued from the Lizard's guns changed from blue to a deadly bloody red. Their ray guns might look impressive, but their armor didn't stop armor-piercing shells made of tungsten with copper jackets.

The lizards were startled by the accuracy of the mammals with SWAT on their torso. The giant creatures scurried further towards the bio labs as SWAT shot down another two lizards despite their clan body armor. These inferior mammals didn't even use to auto-target on their weapons.

The patrol car behind Amanda suddenly exploded with a roar. Hot smoking debris billowed high into the air scattering everywhere. A piece of hot rubber landed on Amanda's exposed arm sending rivers of pain shooting through it. Rolling on the ground, beating her arm with her free hand in an attempt to put out the flames, her burnt flesh reeked of singed meat and rubber. The pain bit ever deeper into her forearm. Next to her, the top half of an Albuquerque officer's body disintegrated into a mess of useless flesh. His legs and pelvis stood for a few seconds before falling lifelessly to the ground. Amanda turned her face away from the horror, shutting her eyes and trying to expunge it from her inner sight. Blackness took her vision as she lost consciousness from the pain.

Chapter Thirty-Four

The comm officer of the Godzilla flagged Rezulin's attention. "The landing party has met with some resistance War Leader. I've authorized the use of deadly force. The harvesters have retrieved the Furbags and Bunny Bears; apparently, the mammals have been experimenting on them. They dissected half of them but had not eaten any." It was a horrific waste of food.

"I'm afraid the two warriors that found them killed some of the mammals in their rage."

Rezulin waved his claw dismissively. "Bring all the food you can, and I want a selection of the local mammals so the cuisine officer can test them to see how fitting they will be for our colony."

The warrior smiled and turned to issue Rezulin's orders knowing that his war leader was considering taking this world as a slave world.

◆◆◆

Lt Samuels guided his F-16c in with his wingman beside him as they rocketed past the research base.

"HMN, this is Knife. We have contact with two alien bandits on the ground. They look like some sort of shuttlecraft. There are unidentified troops in combat on the ground," said Lt Samuels into his comm. "HMN, be advised, I have seven M1 tanks approaching from the south in traffic."

Normal flight operations required pilots to contact the local military flight control tower, in this case, Holloman Air Traffic Control Tower. However, Space Command at

Peterson Air Force Base could tap into the military ATC communications anywhere around the globe.

The comm officer at Space Command pointed to the monitor. "We should be getting Knife's, umm ... Lieutenant Samuels', targeting video feed shortly."

Dan held his breath as the monitor screen resolved from white noise static to a live video feed from the nose of the F-16c fighter jet. Unmistakable blue then red laser light lit up people and buildings. Two cars had already been destroyed and were burning wrecks.

Dan was shocked at the chaos that unfolded before him. Giant lizards were firing on what appeared to be uniformed sheriff officers and SWAT.

The radio crackled again, "HMN, Knife, Dam Buster has been tapped. I say again Dam Buster has been bounced by a red beam and bought the farm, there's no chute," Samuels cried out over the radio. A red laser had hit Samuels' wingman; he had no chance to eject.

"We have no other bandits on the scope," said the Sensor Officer to Dan.

The strangled voice of Lieutenant Samuels continued, "HMN, this is Knife, beams came from the shuttle craft."

Dan grabbed the mike from the comms officer, "Cougar Squadron this is KCOS, pullback I say, pull back, take high cover." Dan had to use the call sign for Peterson airfield military air traffic control.

"Is Knife the FAC?" Dan asked the captain who was monitoring the threat board. The FAC was a forward air controller, which was the aircraft that directed the airborne attack from the front lines. The captain nodded his confirmation.

"Knife, this is KCOS, continue video recon of the research base," said Dan to the Lieutenant. He wanted the squadron away from the alien shuttle craft. But he still needed Lieutenant Samuels to record as much video as possible.

"Captain, how long before the attack helo's from Fort Bliss arrives?" Dan said looking directly at the Captain.

The Captain took one look at the threat board, "Four minutes."

"Hold all of them high and out of the line-of-sight except one for recon," Dan ordered the captain, then turned and held his microphone at the ready.

"KCOS, this is Cougar Squadron, we are looping back for a closer look. So far there have been no enemy locks."

"Cougar Squadron, this is KCOS, negative. Take high cover patrol of the alien shuttle, until bingo." Dan said confirming his order for the rest of the squadron to remain on patrol above the shuttle in a holding pattern until their fuel ran low before their return to base.

On the second pass, Lieutenant Samuels was shocked to see aliens herding people into the shuttles.

"HMN, Knife, I have ET loading people into the shuttles."

There was crackle on the radio.

"HMN, Bear, Knife has been hit." One of Cougar squadron flying high above reported.

"I see a chute. HMN, I see a chute."

"Bear, KCOS, you are now FAC."

Dan could see other officers breathing heavily just like him after holding their breath in anticipation. Dan looked at the clock. Two more minutes before the attack helicopters were in sight.

"HMN, Bear, ET is bugging out."

Space Command, Peterson Air Force Base

"Launch those modified ICBMs at the larger of the alien craft ASAP."

"How many?"

"80% of them," Admiral Tucker ordered as he started to receive reports from the El Paso and the research base.

Similar orders were being issued in other countries. For the first time, a genuinely unified world response was taking shape against the alien threat. All the countries with ICBM missile capability launched a space attack in unison. Even the Chinese were among those that fired their missiles.

Chapter Thirty-Five

Space Sol System, outside of Earth's orbit

"War Leader, we have hundreds of missiles launched from the surface; from land and from water locations."

"Get those harvesters back on board! Raise shields." Rezulin watched with apprehension as their point defense warriors took their stations at the gun emplacements all over the ship.

"Fire rain on those missiles and make sure you keep enough off our harvest teams to allow them to return! Ready the main guns for orbital bombardment."

As the missiles raced towards the warship, they started to spiral, making targeting even more of a challenge. The lizard warriors were initially startled by the missiles haphazard maneuvers but were secretly delighted. Deep in their makeup was a warlike species that enjoyed the vagaries of war.

"Lowering shields for harvester entry."

"All harvesters have now docked," announced flight control.

"Raise Shields!" Rezulin let out a breath.

Missiles started to explode as the point defense smoothly detected and targeted the inbound missiles for the gunners to fire at. The lizard Sensor officer set about recording not only each missile's flight path but also its initial launch location for later bombardment. Competition and boasting between the warriors were beginning to distract them from their primary task, point defense. Who could target and destroy the most missiles? This species superiority complex was unconsciously taking control of their actions.

Even Rezulin was enjoying the show of force his warship could display as more missiles were destroyed. The warriors cheered and cajoled their fellows as their feats were exaggerated in the telling. The destruction of these weapons would be remembered in the history cubes.

One of the last few modified ICBMs sat stalled in the launch bay, the Chinese tech pushed the big red button on his launch console... nothing happened. He pushed it down, again and again, hoping that doubling his efforts would change the launch status of his entrusted missile. Finally, after the tenth attempt the blockage cleared and the missile skyrocketed towards its target. It's programming hiccupped at the last minute causing it to deviate from its original course then re-target back on the Lizard warship. The warrior aiming for that missile missed it at that split second. The nuclear warhead exploded against the shields knocking the ship sideways. System alarms blared for attention.

"They have enhanced nuclear warheads!!" Rezulin grimaced as he recovered from being flung against the sides of his command chair.

The warriors manning the point defense guns were startled as the last two warheads landed in quick succession onto the same shield knocking it out. The *Godzilla* was pummeled.

"Damage report!"

"Port shield down," cried the Tactical Officer.

After all the missiles that had been taken out. What happened...? Thought Rezulin.

Luck was with the *Godzilla,* had any more missiles gotten through, they might have been just floating debris!

"I want that shield back up! Where is that other ship?" Rezulin demanded.

◆◆◆

The *Grace* had picked up substantial speed en-route towards the alien warship. Jen pushed the limit on their systems dumping as much power as she dared into the engines.

Max chimed in, "They've taken a battering from those missiles. One of their shields must be down because the EM reading is non-existent."

John said, "Put me through to the *Scotty* right now!"

"Go ahead."

"Elvis, we are sending you some target information, make the transport as soon as possible, they currently have a shield down. I want this dispatched to the far side of the moon for collection later." Elvis knew exactly what that meant. The transporter could work straight into their ship.

Elvis needed no further incentive as he connected the last of the cables to the Uber Transporter. "Carmen, have you finished targeting?"

"The target is in and locked." Elvis punched the green start button. The whine of the generator echoed around the cavern. The drive executed its transport and depleted the power reserves. It would be 20 minutes before they would be able to rejoin the fight.

◆◆◆

Suddenly the *Godzilla* was rocked to its core by an explosive decompression within the ship itself. Stunned, shield engineer S'sank stood with his mouth agape. The bow shield reactor had disappeared from its housing. Hoses and cables whipped through the air like headless snakes. Loud alarms started blaring warnings of impending danger.

The engineer was roused from his shocking discovery by Rezulin's voice coming from the comm. "Engineering, why is the bow reactor off-line?"

"Well... It's off-line because..." the engineer tried to think of an excuse as to why the reactor had disappeared but in the end decided to tell the truth "...it's disappeared."

"What do you mean it's disappeared?! Get that reactor back on-line now! We're in the middle of a battle!"

The engineer knew that his life was over. The colony credits he had amassed during his service would all be for naught. He turned and walked aimlessly out of engineering down the corridor. He could still hear the comm blare out Rezulin's words.

"If it's not back online in the next two minutes I'm coming down there..."

The engineer didn't hear the rest as he turned into the kitchen stores area. Reaching out he picked up a delicious looking fruit from the stores reserved for the War Leader. Taking a deep breath, he sat down by the portal and looked out at the expanse of space and the beautiful yellow sandy world with large amounts of blue and green. Biting into the juicy fruit, he cleared his mind.

♦♦♦

The *Grace* continued inbound towards the warship. John could see the arrival and docking of what looked like two transports that had come up from the Earth's surface. "Has the jump drive fully recharged?"

"Yes, we're green across-the-board," Jen said, as she bit her bottom lip.

♦♦♦

Rezulin strode into engineering and was struck as if with a hammer as he stared at the empty space where the bow shield reactor should be. All his anger at the engineer disappeared in an instant as he looked around the empty room that sparked with torn wires and conduits but still seemed all too empty. He'd never come across a weapon that could take a reactor from inside a ship. Fear gripped his body shaking him to the core. Quickly pressing his comm he rasped into it, "Have the harvesters returned?"

"Yes, War Leader."

"Helm, take the ship out of the system at flank speed."

The *Godzilla* turned outward bound showing its massive engines to the telescopes on Earth. The main thruster burn put on a light show as the powerful engines lit up the night sky. Rezulin returned to the bridge just in time to see the *Grace* coming into range.

"Roll the ship to bring the other shields between us and that small transport vessel. Main guns target that vessel and fire when ready."

◆◆◆

"They've powered up their primary weapon and are preparing to shoot," Max said, eyes wide in disbelief. A warship like that would probably swat *Grace* like a fly to a flyswatter. John started evasive maneuver patterns. The *Grace* couldn't accelerate too fast in any direction, as the G-forces would kill them.

"Shields at maximum and prepare to target and fire main guns, Pattern Alpha three, target their engines."

The two ships converged as the lizard warship's main guns spat out their deadly laser fire directly at *Grace*. Her shields flared a brilliant white, the power dissipating around the ship and crackling as they barely held.

Many of the shield emitters exploded with that one shot. The halo of green surrounding the vessel on the main view screen had evaporated, burnt off by the laser bolt. They all knew they were lucky that the A-Bitumen armor plating had protected them this time.

Jen yelled, "OMG that was close." The Home jump drive status light started blinked on and off.

"They took out our shields and home drive!" Jen yelled, fear making her voice unrecognizable.

John quickly re-evaluated their options, sweat beading his temples.

"Change of plans, full power to the lasers and target their main guns!" shouted John.

"What?! You can't be serious?! We have no shields!" Jen was starting to panic.

John whipped his head around pointing to Jen's console; "Damn well do it!" John yelled at her.

"Done!" she yelled back, after completing the switch.

"Fire!"

Jen pressed the fire button and watched as the two lasers fired striking the warship's shields, flaring light green without any other effect.

"Cycling the beam frequencies."

Jen set the beam frequency to cycle.

Suddenly the beams passed through the Lizard warship's port shield, to rip through their armor into the main gun housing. John had seen their shields and thought they were at 60% before they penetrated the armored hull.

◆◆◆

Rezulin and the bridge crew were thrown from their chairs as the force of *Grace's* onslaught bit into the ship. The main guns were a mess.

How did they get through our shields? He thought.

Rezulin pointed at the weapons officer, "Launch a spread of missiles targeting that ship!"

The whole bridge was a chaotic mess. The main viewer flickered to eventually display the outside view.

Rezulin coughed and spluttered as he noticed a large chunk of the *Godzilla's* main gun pass by his forward view screen.

The wrecked gun emplacement flew through space twisting and tumbling with its housing a jumble of twisted burnt metal. Bolts of electricity flared through the whole emplacement. He could see jagged bits of half-melted metal spinning away indiscriminately.

Air vented from the *Godzilla;* it triggered alarms and the automatic closing of bulkheads throughout the warship. Danger pheromones leaked from the crew. The ship's life support sprayed pheromones into the air hyping up the Lizards to reflect higher battle posture.

The only bridge officer to remain seated from the last onslaught was the helm. He swiftly set the ship to roll, once again placing the strongest armor between the *Godzilla* and the *Grace.*

Rezulin ordered the crew to reset the shield frequency. He was reluctant to order this because it took the time to modify all the emitters throughout the ship. Somehow the enemy knew their shield frequency. They had no choice.

♦♦♦

John directed Jen, "Use the jump drive to target another of their reactors!"

Jen's eyes widened as she realized what he was ordering.

John knew he was taking an awful risk. They could safely jump away from danger right now. Who knew what other weapons that warship had to throw at the *Grace*. There was no way *Grace's* shields were coming up anytime soon. Using the jump drive to tele-grab another reactor would seriously cripple the warship, however, it would remove their ability to jump for twenty minutes while the one remaining drive recharged.

She hated John's order and recoiled in dismay! She knew damn well that they would lose any chance of getting away from the battle at hand before it was too late. John was being an ass!

Jen saw the look on his face. His eyes bulged wildly from their sockets. Every line in his body stiffened as he tried to take everything in at once. He was determined to go after another reactor. She knew they wouldn't get a second chance at this, but her hand refused to push the button to activate the jump drive targeting!

John saw her hesitation and said, "I'm sure our armor can hold up to their other guns if they fire."

Jen replied under her breath, "On what planet!"

John had been their leader for so long, and she had taken his orders since they had first met so she trusted him once more, yet at the same time, she hated herself for it.

She entered the coordinates, but then she paused and couldn't bring herself to execute the tele-grab command. She was so scared ... of dying.

John saw her struggling with his decision, so he took it out of her hands and slaved her console to his, then pressed the execute button. Jen glared at him in shock.

Like a hot iron rod burning her insides, there was nothing that she could do now. John had decimated her decision-making process, effectively trampling on her free will. She would never forgive him for that. He was just like her father, destroying her self-determination!

John turned back to his own console and the action, seeming to ignore her frigid glares.

◆◆◆

The Lizard warship lurched, suffering a massive shock as another section inside the craft disappeared in a blaze of bright light. Exposed conduits flashed burning the nearby Lizards who were suddenly thrown off their feet by the blast. Two warrior lizards flew off into space suitless and flailing from the explosive decompression ...

Explosions could be seen through the wrecked gun emplacement. An area of the ship's bulkhead crushed in as more gas vented. Finally, the tactical officer was back on his clawed feet targeting and pressing the launch of a dozen missiles. He could tell that the little shuttle had no shielding left. There was no way the small ship would last after all these missiles.

"Shields reconfigured," rasped the chief engineer through the comm.

The helm held a flight pattern keeping the strongest shield facing the little vessel.

The engineering officer S'sank, walked further into the galley store in a daze. He had gone there to eat more delicious fruit before he died, whether by the War Leader's hand or these aggressive mammals, when all lighting failed.

♦♦♦

Rezulin was astounded that the little ship had survived a salvo from their main guns. They not only survived but also launched two more devastating attacks crippling his lifelong love, the *Godzilla*.

Missiles shot out of the Godzilla missile racks aimed directly at the *Grace*. The two ships were still closing into close range so the missiles would take only a few moments to reach their target.

"Time to target, 3, 2, 1 ... target destroyed," said the Tactical Officer.

♦♦♦

Elvis watched the battle on the tachyon sensor scope.

"Oh my God!" he cried, as he slammed his hand down onto the emergency jump button.

He had ordered it programmed to teleport the *Grace* down to the base, just as one of the missiles slammed into *Grace's* armor. A white glow surrounded the ship as it dematerialized from the space battle to rematerialize a split second later in the huge cavern under the research base next to the *Scotty*. Smoke billowed from the side of the yellow and black craft. Twisted metal fused with pieces of melted and broken A-Bitumen. Debris lay strewn across the cavern floor. Elvis counted his lucky stars that he asked Carmen to program a third source to auto target, the location of the *Grace* just in case they got into trouble.

Elvis shook his head, *of course they'll get into trouble.*

He and his crew jumped out of the *Scotty* to look at the scored warped metal. The outside was a wreck. Smoke billowed from the hull; while a pungent smell of burnt metal and A-Bitumen gave them a horrific preview at what it must be like inside. The *Grace* was a disaster.

Elvis reached for the airlock controls, but pulled back from the heat. Pulling has jacket over his hand he pulled on the emergency manual release; it wouldn't budge. The airlock was jammed shut. A-Bitumen on the hull started to burn profusely with the addition of oxygen in the underground hanger Bay.

"Quickly! We need to put the fire out before it overloads the life support systems down here," Elvis said in his best command voice.

Mike and Carmen rushed off towards the fire extinguishers. Elvis returned to the *Scotty* to try and raise the *Grace* over the comm. The external aerial on the *Grace* had been melted clean off. He hoped that they didn't need it given the proximity.

◆◆◆

The Lizard warship staggered out past the Kuiper Belt leaving a small trail of twisted metal fragments and battle debris. Rezulin sat heavily in his command chair looking at the chaos on his bridge. Warning lights and alarms still rang. Order was slowly restored. His nose and tongue were being overloaded with fight pheromones pumped out by the air conditioners.

"Cut the pheromone conditioners," Rezulin said to his operations officer. Too many pheromones could send the warriors into berserker mode.

Setting aside his immediate concerns he sat in thought. It seemed impossible that the mammals on the planet were the same ones that controlled the little shuttle-sized ship.

If, and it was a big if, they were the same species, then there was much more to this species than he first imagined. He had badly underestimated them. *The cuisine officer needs to test these mammals as soon as possible*, he vowed...

Their brain chemistry would be a staggering addition. The slaves will give Unak's their much-needed intelligence. He wondered briefly from eating the mammals, whether the leap in lizard intelligence would create a whole new class of Lizard to emerge.

Rezulin shook his head chiding himself for believing the planet dwellers and those beings in the small ship were the same species. There was too much disparity in their technology levels.

He then wondered if the small ship was from a patron race. They had lots of technology they didn't share with the younger species. If they were a patron race, the lizards would be in serious trouble. He had to get back to warn the colony.

Looking around at the chaos on the bridge, "Engineering, I need everything you can from our engines!"

Chapter Thirty-Six

The Oval Office

The confrontation between the two ships was witnessed by worried eyes from Earth. Who were these aliens from the small ships and what did they want? Dan was summoned to the Oval Office to provide a report directly to the President regarding the situation in El Paso. Admiral Tucker had found out that Dan had ordered the Hornets and other craft to intercept the shuttles from the large alien warship. Not only that, he had directed them to the exact location of where the warship shuttles were to land before they landed. Admiral Tucker also wanted to know what was going on in El Paso.

◆◆◆

"Mr. President we believe the lizard ship came down to stop some research into new laser technology that was being conducted by Dr. Stevenson," Dan said nervously. Images of the ferocious lizards firing blue and red hand lasers at El Paso police officers were etched in his mind. Dan couldn't be sure, but the laser pistols looked similar to those designed by Doctor Stevenson. *Surely all laser pistols look the same,* Dan told himself.

"Where do I know that name from, Andrew?" the President directed a look towards his assistant.

"I believe he was on one of the latest internal terror threat boards, Mr. President." The President looked back at Dan with a raised eyebrow.

"Mr. President, that was a misunderstanding, Dr. Stevenson is a patriot. He was attempting to develop a ground-breaking sonic weapon when Homeland Security got involved in a car explosion in Washington DC. Since that blast, I personally negotiated a contract with Dr. Stevenson for some weapons development. In his bio, he served in the Army as a pilot to the rank of captain. He flew helicopters on COIN ops in Iraq and relief operations in Somalia, then resigned his commission. Since leaving the service, he has become a successful inventor and is a serving reservist."

The President looked at his assistant, "COIN ops?"

"Counterinsurgency Mr. President."

Dan then continued his report, "Two months ago I visited Dr. Stevenson's labs in El Paso, Texas, where he demonstrated a remarkable hand laser. Frankly, it blew me away."

The President recognized the name of the labs and the location of the shuttlecraft's surface activities. "You think they want to stop Dr. Stevenson from producing these lasers?"

"It's very likely, many of the labs and surrounding buildings have been destroyed. There is some confusion, however. It appears that the DHS and the local police enforcement had a raid in progress at the same labs when the aliens attacked."

"Are you telling me, that Homeland Security was in the process of raiding a government contracted defense facility when the aliens happened to attack?"

"Yes, Mr. President," Dan said with pursed lips.

General Abercrombie looked sharply at Dan and broke in on his report. Knowing full well that Dan had requested support from the Major General Commanding Fort Bliss, he said, "I ordered 1st Armor Division posted to Fort Bliss to secure the area. We still have not located Dr. Stevenson."

The President turned around to look at who had spoken. "General Abercrombie, you're still here. It seems your initial gut reaction was, in fact, correct. The aliens are dangerous and no quarter should be given, however,..." The General smiled smugly at the President, who frowned and turned towards Dan. "I want you to make finding this Dr. Stevenson your top priority. If the aliens want the 'good doctor', then we definitely don't want to lose him."

The President turned back to Admiral Tucker and the Joint Chiefs, "What are the ships up to at the moment?"

As if by design, a Captain raced into the room and saluted the President. He then went and whispered into Admiral Tucker's ear. The Admiral whispered back with some orders. The Captain nodded and moved back quietly passing the orders on through his comm.

Admiral Tucker then addressed the President, "Mr. President, it appears the small ship was destroyed after being hit by a wave of missiles."

"If that little ship's been destroyed, what is the Lizard ship doing?" the President asked the captain.

"Sir, the Lizard ship is continuing out of the system. The tachyon sensors show it's quite heavily damaged, their energy readings have been fluctuating, and they left a significant amount of debris behind. The feeling in the war room is that they don't want to take the chance our X37s will capture it," said the Captain nervously.

"X37s?" The President asked.

Admiral Tucker then spoke up, "Mr. President, after the last battle with the two alien spacecraft, I launched two X37 space planes. They are unmanned drones."

"To what end?"

"The hope was Mr. President, that the space planes may pick up some useful technology in the debris."

The President nodded.

This latest development only brought up more questions. *The two races obviously didn't like each other. The President wondered what this small ship's race was like and what they wanted.*

Would their race send another ship? The battle had the result that the lizard ship was leaving the system. Every favor has a price. He wondered what the price was for the second race's intervention.

♦ ♦ ♦

Jen awoke and stared daggers at John's profile. She was sure he could feel her wrath. His decision to try and grab another piece of the alien ship, when they could have withdrawn safely, was in her opinion, reckless. What really grated on her, however, was his forced takeover over her console, and leaving her with no choice. Leaving her powerless.

She'd never been this *angry* at him before.

Her neck still hurt from the impact of the missile.

She looked down at her and Max's consoles. The shield and the long range comms consoles flashed red. Glancing at the sensors, her first thought was the readings must be wrong, the alien ship was now out near the Kuiper Belt, and they had somehow ended up in the cavern.

She had expected to die... instead, there was a terrible crash and nothing, she had blacked out.

John sat in his bucket seat, nodding his bloody head silently in thought, *we transported ... then they fired missiles ... he had blacked out... it must have been Elvis.* A grin crawled across John's face.

The ship had performed remarkably well given that she had her armaments installed just before the voyage. The *Grace* was banged up, but they could repair her. They had stopped the alien incursion, which was what they were all there to do. It then occurred to John that the others didn't actually sign up for that. This was not a military operation. John put those thoughts to the back of his mind to deal with later.

He did have to go and check the damage they had suffered in the last attack. He also wanted to get out of the bridge because it had turned icily cold. He knew Jen wouldn't easily forgive him for this one.

John didn't regret what he had done. Because, in his mind, it was the right thing to do despite Elvis having to save their asses. He knew on some level that he should feel guilt at slaving her console, but couldn't quite feel it. John had hoped the tele-grabs were more successful in shutting down the ship. However, he did regret that by not being successful, Jen was suffering the indignation of losing control of her console.

John found Peter, the new crew member who specialized in propulsion, pouring over the drive engines checking and rechecking the power systems with Adrian.

"The power that warship sent through the shields was absolutely mind-boggling. It would be a shame to waste it when it hits the hull, there must be a way to trap and recycle it." Peter was thinking and talking to himself out loud. His forehead wrinkled in concentration, trying to work through the problem. He walked away deep in thought, without even glancing at or acknowledging John's presence.

John remembered that it had taken Peter a week when he had first arrived on the base to feel socially comfortable and act relaxed around him. Often people who live in scientific spheres were struck with ideas then forgot the normal social protocols. It wasn't surprising, John mused. Recently it had become the norm at the research base.

John moved over to the energy cell collections control console, bringing up the current energy absorption status. They would need to park the *Grace* close to the sun to allow the energy collectors to recharge the battery cells as quickly as possible. He made his way to the stern of the ship and pressed the button to open the inner airlock. Nothing happened. John pushed harder several more times, but it still didn't open.

Max walked into the stern. "Elvis has been trying to contact you, he was worried that we're all dead. He said the stern of the ship was totally busted."

"Aaah, that's why I can't open the hatch."

"He said he is going to have to cut the door off to allow us to get out. It might take a little while."

It was nearly two and a half hours before the crew could exit the *Grace*.

John found Elvis sitting on some container boxes hunched over with his hands covering his face. "Elvis?" John said with concern lacing his voice. He just looked up into John's eyes with a look of despair plastered over his face. John placed a comforting hand on his shoulder and squeezed.

"I just can't go through it … the suicide threats, the counseling … not again," Elvis pleaded.

John frowned trying to understand. The only thing that made sense was one of his ex-girlfriend's had committed suicide, but that was years ago. Suddenly John was alarmed at the absence of Mike and Carmen. They wouldn't have left Elvis like this. Leaning forward he saw Elvis' soot covered hands and clothes, "What's this?" John asked, pointing to the black marks. Elvis gave John a blank look.

John turned to see Jen move forward to sit by Elvis wrapping her arm around his shoulder with a questioning look on her face. John signaled her with his eyes to take care of him. Elvis saw Jen and started to cry.

John pushed his sadness for his friend aside; he had a bad feeling about the soot. He retreated from the two and walked up into the *Scotty* wondering where Mike and the others were. When John reached the bridge, he noted the last few jump coordinates; one to the surface and a second from the hangar above down to the cave. John then returned to the two and said he'll be back shortly. With that, he re-boarded the *Scotty* and set a transport to materialize within the hangar above.

◆ ◆ ◆

John rematerialized in the hangar and walked to the outside. He was disturbed by the lack of people, especially the security that should have been guarding this particular hanger. He made a mental note to have a word with Eric Manders, the security head. John then stopped in his tracks. The smoky, acrid stench of burnt flesh and rubber hung in the air. Turning towards what was left of the artifact hangar, he saw a broken, crumpled hulk of destroyed twisted struts and spars.

In the distance, he could see Thurston talking to what looked like Colonel Prior and an army Major, surrounded by troops. Several M1 Abrams tanks were parked in John's drive and compound pointing towards what was left of the bio labs. They must have come from Fort Bliss. John knew that there was an armor division based just north of El Paso not far from the research base. A roar of half a dozen Osprey attack helicopters flew over followed by a Squadron of F16s fighter jets that could be heard flying off into the distance.

Soldiers were milling around and over all the wreckage, avoiding interfering with staff from a medical and military ambulance that stood on the side. Some people in sheriff's uniforms were being treated near the makeshift triage area. John made his way slowly around the base in a daze taking in all the death and destruction. He was flabbergasted by what was left of what looked like an alien. At least, not one they had discovered in the yellow container. The scientist part of John's brain took the details of its discovery in with amazement. This one looked tall and lanky. There was no doubt that it was of Saurian (Lizard) makeup. Unlike those depicted on the Hollywood silver screen, this lizard had a fine facial bone structure. Its mouth hung open displaying sharp cutting and ripping teeth. The teeth were too uniform, too perfect for the being not to have had dental work. Its skin almost glittered as the small snake-like scales reflected the sun. Red and yellow plated scales on the torso had huge holes in them from armor piercing rounds. The army was packing up the bodies apparently taking them for study.

John fell back into his army ways, putting aside the carnage to be dealt with later, and started to make a critical situational assessment of the base. Eric exited out of one of the huge smoking holes with soot and grime covering his face and hands. His clothes were marked with blood and charcoal burns. The whites of his eyes were a stark contrast to what was left of his burnt fatigues. Two other men walked behind him with the same grim professional expressions.

"John, if I had known the party goers you were planning to host, I would have definitely advised running faster," he said in a deadpan face without any jovial timbre.

"What happened here?"

Eric stared at him perturbed. *Where has he been?!*

"There was a lizard alien invasion. It seems that they came looking for their friends."

"Food," John corrected him.

Eric looked back confused. John wondered how Eric knew about the other aliens.

John continued, "Food... the aliens were after food... I'm only guessing, of course."

John could see Eric process this new information as he stared back, reassessing his boss. John just knew that Eric had made a mental note to have a conversation about the real risks of the job.

Eric nodded as if something made sense and then said, "They were loading up some alien bodies as though they were sides of meat. Then they started on the humans, any human they got their hands on. We now know that they were only stunning the people until we fired back. Their ray guns changed color. Then they started killing everything in sight... they were quite efficient as you can see." Eric nodded at the smoking hole he had just exited. "They forced people into their shuttles."

It was John's turn to be surprised. *Oh my God!*

"It gets worse."

How could it get any worse, John thought?

"In the middle of this mayhem, Homeland Security, and the local Sheriff's Department arrived to arrest you guys. Apparently, they thought you were making some fancy weapons."

"We *are* making fancy weapons, *for the U.S. Air Force.*"

Eric just looked at John for a few seconds before he gave a short bitter laugh, "Those goddamn idiots were going to arrest the good guys, but ended up getting arrested themselves, by the aliens."

John couldn't see the humor in it.

He then spied half a dozen motorcycles near the entrance to the admin building. Eric shrugged and said, "They were looking for Elvis ... some unfinished business?"

John shook his head; *Elvis did mention a run in with Amanda and the bikers from the Hogg's Breath. I wonder if it's connected? Elvis had been close-lipped about a biker girl he'd been secretly seeing, according to Eric, for what? ... quite a while for Elvis. If she's one of the 'Taken', no wonder he's cut up.* John took a moment and bit his bottom lip while he stared at the motorbikes.

"How many did the lizards get?" After all his trouble with homeland security already, they were still after him. *Damn them.*

"We are still counting, but we figure around 35," Eric replied.

"All the wreckage has been searched?" asked John.

"Yes, but we somehow missed you. I will order another search," Eric then turned and spoke quietly with one of his colleagues behind him, who immediately walked off enlisting men for the search.

◆◆◆

Eric started to list aloud those that had disappeared like on an honor roll, each name piercing John's soul like a hot poker. He looked at all the devastation and thought of all the people that had been taken. They came here because of him. Somehow the aliens knew.

The three other crew from the *Scotty* walked out of the wreckage that was the admin center with their faces tear stained and soot covered. John tried to order his thoughts.

The aliens already knew about us.

Then a cold hard truth boiled in him, *Mankind is still defenseless, one ship is no defense. Humanity has just fallen headlong into the big bad galaxy, and we had better learn and learn fast if we are to survive.* It was no fun being food for some advanced alien lizards.

Suddenly he could see the hopeless humor in Eric's comments.

"DHS used the local Sheriff's department and SWAT?"

"Yeah, they put up a reasonable fight. Unfortunately, the Lizards took all the bodies with them except a few charred ones. They didn't even take one or two of their own."

"I didn't hear Amanda's name among them from your list?" Eric looked surprised that John asked about Scarlet's niece, "Her first name is really Doris, not Amanda," John stared at him.

"Wait a moment," Eric scanned the list again. His face was grim when he said, "Sorry. John. There's a Deputy D.A. Reily on the list the sheriff's department gave me."

John felt it like a punch in the gut. Pulling himself together he took a deep breath.

"Eric, if I had known the aliens were to come and do this..."

"I believe you John, we've trained together, and I think I got a pretty good handle on your character now."

John took a hard look at Eric and evaluated bringing him in the loop of his small command team. He had been impressed with Eric's professionalism and competence ever since he first started. Any rescue attempt would undoubtedly need Eric's special forces skill set. In the end, knowing Amanda was missing, decided it for him.

"We need to have a talk. Not right now but soon when they all leave," he said waving his arm at all the military.

Eric seemed reluctant to let it go. "John, I know that you have your secrets, but there are a lot of good people missing. We need to do everything we can to get them back."

John was relieved with Eric's response and felt even more confident that he had made the right decision.

"Eric, I plan to go after our people. I'm going to need your help."

"I was hoping you'd say that." John was surprised at Eric's confidence in him, given the enormous odds against them. The kidnappers were aliens and on another planet, but Eric just smiled knowing John did have his secrets.

"I have to talk to Colonel Prior now, however, as soon as that's done: you, Thurston, and I need to have a sit-down planning session." Eric then moved off to check on the progress of the latest search.

As John walked over to the group of military officers, he could hear Thurston's usually calm business-like voice was strained. Thurston showed uncommon relief when John walked up to the group, briefly giving John a gentlemanly hug. This took John utterly by surprise. Thurston was never very animated when it came to expressing his feelings.

"John, it's good to see you made it through."

"Yes, I was testing some of our latest equipment and missed the whole thing."

♦♦♦

Jen sat on the large crate in the cavern opposite the *Scotty* with her arm lightly around Elvis' shoulders. Red rims surrounded his eyes telling a story of pain and suffering. He wasn't the type to be easily affected by ordinary everyday inconveniences. Whatever he had just seen must've been emotionally charged enough to set off this atom bomb of a reaction. There was no doubt it rocked him to the core. The lizards had come into his personal space, his home and messed with his own people. It had been evident from the start when Elvis returned to the surface the destruction of the base was like a war zone. He had run around the compound with the rest of his crew trying to identify who was still alive and whom they could help. It was immediately obvious that there were much more people than were typically gathered in the compound area. There were sheriff cars strewn at the entrance to the cottage administration building. The unmistakable hog bikes, at least half a dozen of them, were also parked near the Administration entrance. What had been going on!

It was then he saw Mel's blue bike right next to BlackEye's unmistakable Harley fat boy with eye-patched skulls on the tank. There were one or two bikers that survived, they all confirmed Elvis' fear. Mel was one of the taken.

Elvis had a girlfriend once who had been kidnapped from her house one dark night by some unscrupulous people. She had dabbled in drugs before she'd met Elvis and, when under stress, still occasionally slipped back into that old life. It only took a few benders for her to fall back into debt to her old dealer. She was too ashamed to tell Elvis how deeply she was in trouble. He'd only found out when her dealer came knocking on their apartment door in the middle of the night. Before Elvis' had a chance to help her out of it, her dealer had passed her name on to his collection people, and the next week she'd been snatched.

Her family hadn't liked Elvis in the beginning. They were grateful in the end, Elvis had sold his bike to pay the dealer and handled all the arrangements to get her back. When she returned to her life, she struggled dreadfully with the residual trauma and guilt, only to end it all. He had tried desperately, but in the end, couldn't see any semblance of the person she once was before the kidnapping. She had returned a shadow of herself, lifeless and unable to reconnect. Countless sessions in counseling, and all the care that Elvis and her family could provide was still not enough. Not nearly anywhere near enough. It had taken her a year and a half, but she did it. In the end, she killed herself. It was one of the longest relationships Elvis had had. The year and a half seemed a lifetime to Elvis. And now Mel's disappearance...

◆◆◆

Outside the administration building, the two officers discussed the security arrangements with John and Thurston. Earlier, by command of the President, Colonel

Prior had hightailed it to El Paso from the Oval Office to personally oversee the search for Doctor Stevenson and 'safeguard' him from alien abduction.

"This is Major Matthews," Dan introduced. "We're placing some soldiers and some armored support to help protect your labs," Dan said without any discussion. "Major Matthews will be in charge of this contingent. John this is not a request... So the latest prototype is safe?"

John nodded his confirmation.

"I don't want to seem callous right now; however, we need to get your laser weapons into full production as quickly as possible," Dan said to both of the civilians.

Thurston piped up, "I was just telling the Colonel, that we should have the weapons avaliable within the week if all goes to plan."

"And the power store for the larger versions?" Dan asked.

"You can use power from anywhere, even the grid. Although the lasers will also be fully integrated with the new power cells. All that's needed is for the batteries to be recharged before it's fired. We've been running tests on them, but I think given the circumstances we'll fast track it if I can get your assistance with another matter."

Dan looked at John with raised eyebrows.

"The power cells that we've developed have been road blocked with red tape," John explained. "It's not yet been fully approved by the patent office. I'd hate for the manufacture of these weapons to be delayed by red tape."

"I think we can help you there. We can set up a Special Patent under the Homeland Security protocols that will expedite the process. The President has been informed of your project and wants to make it a high priority."

"Our power cells are highly specialized and difficult to produce, but they have a myriad of other applications. Its manufacture will be very restricted given the materials involved."

John could see this piqued Dan's interest.

"Well, let's have a meeting Wednesday to hammer out the details. That'll give you time to tidy up this mess."

John looked at Thurston, then the devastation around them and shook his head in dismay.

Chapter Thirty-Seven

Once the military had left the research base to set-up camp in the national park opposite the base. John and Thurston picked through some of the bio labs that had been destroyed. At least one of the labs was still standing untouched.

"Thurston, I don't know what to say."

"John, I don't think there is anything to say. This is not your fault. The aliens were the ones to fire on us. We are just lucky that you came back when you did."

John filled Thurston in on the battle that took place in orbit between the alien vessel and the two Earth ships, the *Grace* and the *Scotty*.

"If you hadn't ..." Thurston shivered. "I'm sure the Colonel suspects something... John, they're scared. They're really frightened. Colonel Prior is desperate for some sort of weapon to use against these aliens."

John was flabbergasted, "We're all scared! ... We have to get serious about producing these weapons because I have no doubt those lizards will be back."

Right then Eric walked over to the pair to report that no further survivors had been found.

John looked directly at the bespectacled administrator, "Thurston, I haven't run this past you yet. I'm planning to go after our people."

"I'm going to need your help even more than I have in the past to manage our operations. Eric is going to put together a military team to help us." Thurston nodded realizing that John was bringing Eric into the loop. He had expected something like this, given the attack on the base.

John had spoken to Thurston previously about his plans to build a space-based Navy. Thurston hadn't really taken much notice of it, until now.

He then explained to Eric about the jump drive and the retrieval of the alien technology from the freighter. Each new revelation stunned the usually composed ex-special forces.

"And you have two spaceships?!" Eric shook his head in disbelief.

"Eric, I want you to start putting together a list of military personnel and their specialties for us to look at. It may be some time before we can track ..." Suddenly John's eyes took on a far-away look. Turning away from the two he activated his comm calling Mike.

"Mike, I want you to jump the *Scotty* out past the Kuiper Belt to try and track the direction the warship takes from there."

Mike responded with the affirmative. "And Mike, the *Scotty* is not a warship so don't endanger her," John warned.

Mike returned shortly after with the *Scotty*. There was no trace of the warship.

"Damn!" John chastised himself for not thinking of tracking the warship before it was too late.

◆◆◆

When John finally returned to the cavern, he found Elvis and Jen in the office. The three of them looked at each other in a mutual understanding of grief. Uncertainty hung in the air, as John's mind drifted.

Had their salvage actions precipitated this attack? The question was left unanswered.

The following morning Elvis reluctantly, still half in shock, set to work with Jen expanding the cavern to accommodate the new technology they had swiped from the lizard warship. They tele-excavated the bedrock with the aid of *Scotty's* Uber transporter. The new large section was separate from the existing cavern. A connecting tunnel was then carved out between the two caverns.

Once again they spayed the quick set A-Bitumen on all four walls, floor, and ceiling, giving the cavern the extra strength it needed to prevent cave-ins. When they finished, they transported the two pieces of alien tech, which they had moved to the far side of the moon during the battle, into the new cavern. Under closer inspection, the fusion reactor had set itself to standby mode. Amazingly there were no plasma leaks from the housing. There was a remote possibility that it may have been damaged given it had been exposed directly to space. Human understanding of fusion reactors made the control icons and symbols on the reactor easily identifiable with some careful investigation.

♦♦♦

Walking around the second snatch and grab was disappointing. They'd hoped to have acquired another reactor or something just as important; however, what stood before them was some sort of small room because a door jutted out on the side. The controls were still lit. John realized the door must have backup power.

Just as Elvis was about to push the door open button they heard a soft bumping noise coming from inside. Elvis jumped back colliding with John and Jen in the process. Looking at each other, *that was definitely not a machine noise.* They all hastily backed away. Elvis raced to one of the cupboards in the office and pulled out a firearm. Checking it was loaded, he returned to the doorway.

"Elvis, you keep guard while I get some back-up," John said as he ran to the *Scotty*.

On the surface, Eric sat with three other men taking a break from the clean-up of the bio-labs when John found them.

"Eric, we have a situation." Eric immediately stood up scanning the surrounding area. The other three men also stood seeing their leader's tense stance. "Are these men...?" John left the word, 'trustworthy' unspoken. Eric nodded.

"Grab some weapons, then meet me at the hanger." John turned and loped off towards the cottage. A few minutes later, the five men gathered outside the two-story hanger. John spoke in short clipped words like on a battlefield, "If you pass this door you will be assenting to a contract to work for me for at least two years. What's behind the door is top secret, and you'll be bound by our non-disclosure agreement. Make no mistake, I mean to enforce it!"

It was clear to the men what John meant with his threat.

"Do you agree?" The trio gritted their teeth. They didn't like being talked to like that by some science puke, even if he was paying the bills. They all looked at Eric for guidance. He just nodded ascent and moved aside. Each man passed through the door saying, "I agree" and signed the document that John put in front of them. Eric was a little put off by this but then decided not to make a fuss. It was not the time.

Once they were all inside, John led them to the rear hatch of the *Scotty*.

"Strap yourselves in and make yourselves comfortable, were going for a trip." The four men looked nervous as they inspected the inside of the ship. A DIY converted silo wasn't their idea of transport. They all looked at their leader. In the end, Eric took the lead and walked nonchalantly to the nearest seat and belted in, daring the others to do the same. John secured the hatch then raced to the command console and started the jump procedures. The four men heard the whine of the generators, mentally crossing their proverbial fingers. A loud muffled crack echoed outside the *Scotty* in the hanger.

John quickly clicked his seatbelt open and climbed out of his racing seat. Eric hadn't felt a thing. John walked past them and opened the rear hatch waving the four men to follow him out. All four were speechless as it was obvious that they weren't in the hanger they were in a minute ago. The walls were solid, and smelt of wet A-Bitumen.

"John, we *really* have to have a talk," Eric said staring around in disbelief.

John sighed, realizing he neglected to fill Eric in on the caverns below the base.

"I promise Eric. We have one or more Lizard people inside a bit of alien tech we seized in that last attack." Eric gave John another look rolling his eyes. "Remind me later to tell you about the battle," John said slightly abashed.

The other men looked at each other with trepidation, this was so not what they were expecting.

"How brilliant is this!" one of Eric's men said aloud.

The four men followed John to the doorway guarded by Elvis. Eric nodded to him, then signaling his squad to take position. Eric counted down with his large hand... Elvis pushed the button, and the door slid sideways. Chilly air escaped from within. Eric entered with his squad followed by John and Elvis.

The room was brightly lit with flickering lights. Three sides housed compartments while the fourth side had an array of different machines. John couldn't guess what they were. In the far corner sat a uniformed lizard shivering as he watched their entry. The alien looked in a bad way, slumped with its legs bent beneath its torso and its tail limp. John noticed the air was putrid and toxic with carbon dioxide. The lizard just sat there watching. Compared to the lizard bodies John had seen on the surface, this one was much smaller than the others, with a yellow front plate, and smaller mouth. Its pink skin was drawn taut and pallid, its mouth gasping for air. After a brief hesitation, the men lifted the alien up checking it had no concealed weapons and brought it outside into the cavern where it was warmer. Its color immediately started to return as it breathed in the oxygen-rich air in the cavern. John ducked aside taking out his phone.

"Thurston, has your friend from New York arrived yet?"

"Yes, why do you ask?"

"Well, I have this live lizard here, who doesn't seem to be in great shape. I would prefer it didn't die."

263

There was a pause at the end of the phone line.

"You're serious aren't you," then Thurston answered his own question by saying, "I'll meet you in Bio Lab six."

Bio Lab six had escaped the carnage wrought on the other labs. It was the only lab that had no alien remains inside. Remnants of the A-Bitumen development project were still strewn across the benches.

While the group waited for the *Scotty* to recharge its jump drive, Eric put two guards on the lizard and then went to check with John the contents of the store. John wished he had Jerry here. He really could have used his linguistic skills right now. He shook his head as if it would change the lost status of his friend and colleague. He could only hope that he was still alive on the alien ship.

Chapter Thirty-Eight

Lizard Warship Godzilla, Cargo Bay

Amanda woke to find the blue-eyed biker chick from the Hog's Breath leaning over her wiping her face with a damp cloth.

"By the way my name is Meredith, but everyone calls me Mel. You've got a pretty nasty burn on your arm and some awesome bruising on your head. But you'll live," she said with a half-smile. Amanda just looked at her with incomprehension written all over her face.

Looking around the dim room, she attempted to understand how she got there. Mel pointed over into the dimness with a nod of her chin. There were armed lizards near the door. It was hard to miss them as they held some sort of baton. The large room was nondescript except for the thirty odd people milling around in clusters. The far corner had what looked like a ghoulish pile of body parts. Most were not human. The scene shocked Amanda to her core. She thought, *how could this nightmare get any worse!*

"You're one of the lucky ones," Mel said, while she spoke, she nodded towards one of the lizards. "They were starting to carry the bodies to their ships, those that were too heavy they just cut up and carried them in. It didn't matter to them if they were just unconscious or dead. You're lucky that BlackEye was there to carry you."

Amanda took another look at the pile of body parts, crinkling her nose and upper lip in disgust. She had gone to the Jewish Museum in Nuremberg and seen the horror that the Nazis had inflicted on the Jews, gays and anyone else in their way, but this was somehow worse. She turned away and fixed her gaze on BlackEye, mouthing the words, "Thank you!" BlackEye just stared back at her with a vacant look on his face.

"He's got good strong arms, and he does what he is told," Mel said with a smile, that didn't touch her eyes.

Amanda fell back unconscious.

Mel sat back staring at the pile of dead bodies. In a moment of weakness, her cheeks stained with tears. She quickly brushed them away before anyone saw... *Yes. They're going to need more than strong arms to get out of this bloody mess...*

◆ ◆ ◆

Amanda winced as she sat up, her back resting against the wall. Her arm was in tremendous pain from the prolonged burn. She had already passed out twice since waking upon the alien ship.

"Well, sleeping beauty awakes," Mel said as she saw Amanda's eyes flutter open.

"What, your still here? I thought your boyfriend would have punched his way out'ter here," Amanda counted with a wry smile.

"Well maybe if I show a bit of leg he might just do that. Then again, I don't know if I've got enough leg to make him take on Scales over there... he's pretty ugly," Mel nodded towards the nearest Lizard guard.

"They are pretty ugly. I'd hate to be their dentist. One slip and it could be your last."

BlackEye had regained some of his composure and was starting to bark orders at the others. The scientists all huddled in a group in one corner while the enforcement types stood around daring the Lizards to fight them hand to hand(claw).

The last group of humans was made up of locals under contract, who had a supporting role at the Research Base and a few bikers.

The lizards kept a close watch on each of the groups and how they interacted. No one touched the body parts as the stench started to permeate throughout the large hanger.

Mel had seen dead bodies and even smelt a few as a criminal attorney in a life long gone; before she went rogue with the bikers. The mixture of human and alien body parts made a particularly potent odor, even though the Lizards had set up a transparent force field that must work as a bug-kill sanitizing screen. She just wished it also stopped the smell, she could barely keep from gagging.

Two smaller Lizards, armed with sacks, entered the large enclosure and spoke to the two guards in their slithering raspy tongue.

All the humans stopped mid-sentence to watch their captors.

After some animated discussion, the smaller yellow plated lizards walked in their swaggering gait over to the disgusting pile of body parts, sniffing, then picking parts from the remains and scurrying off out the door. Amanda seeing this for the first time turned her face away in horror, redness rimmed her eyes as she bit her bottom lip to keep from crying out.

Mel stared at the picky captors with a steely gaze saying nothing.

◆ ◆ ◆

The lights flicker on brightly to almost blind the humans. Four lizards entered with batons and a mean disposition. The leader yelled an unintelligible order pointing for the mobile humans to line up. Several of the slower scientists received an electro-baton shock for not moving quickly enough. Mel could almost feel the charge in the air through her own skin.

"Come on Amanda, we need to move. BlackEye, grab her other arm," Mel said as she struggled to get Amanda on her feet. The three of them shuffled to an imaginary line, under the watchful gaze of the Lizards.

One of the yellow plated lizards walked down the line of humans inspecting them, swinging its baton. Halfway down the line it stopped at one of the El Paso contractors and pointed the baton at him. Two larger red plated lizards strode forward and grabbed the man by the arms.

"No. Please, I have a daughter!" the man yelled to no avail.

The giant lizards easily lifted the struggling man out the door.

The humans stood rigid, grinding their teeth and balling their fists. This was not the first time the lizards had taken someone from the line. The first few times, they viciously battered any resistance with electric shocks till they were unconscious, then took who they wanted."

◆◆◆

It had been some time since the lizards had taken anyone. The next time they entered, several of the smaller lizards carried barrels of sloppy liquid porridge like substance. The last lizard stacked food bowls on the top of the barrels. The lizard leader grabbed a bowl and held it near the barrel, then pressed a button on the barrel that dispensed a serve of the porridge out a spout on its side.

Once the lizards left the humans gathered around the barrels.

"What's this goop?" Agent O'Brien said as he held up a bowl of gray substance to his nose for a sniff.

"They're full of all the nutrition we need, with the exception of taste," one of the scientists said.

"I'm not eating this shit!" O'Brien retorted.

"Suit yourself, more for the rest of us," another onlooker said.

"Is it safe?" Mel asked.

"My guess is that they're from something like yeast grown in vats. It's unlikely to be poisonous" The group around him stared at the little bald scientist. "Once they autopsied the stomach contents and made a bioscan of the rest of body they should be able to tell what's poisonous to us." To make his point the little man scooped up a handful of the goop and ate it before them.

Mel's stomach growled, she hadn't eaten in what seemed like days. So she copied the scientist and tasted the goop. By the time the little man had finished his bowl, the rest of the group were smelling their food and scooping handfuls into their mouths.

Chapter Thirty-Nine

Research Base El Paso, Texas

Doctor Halifax, the criminal pathologist, closed the door from Bio Lab six.

"I was a bit perturbed when Thurston told me that he had an alien that needed to be examined. I thought excellent, how exciting. I'll be able to see exactly how they tick. Only to find that the alien is not only here, but is still alive. I have not practiced live medicine for a while now." He coughed apologetically.

John stood there, waiting for Halifax's report on the condition of the alien.

"Doctor, it's not human, so how relevant would your recent non-practice on humans be. At this stage, we want to make sure the alien isn't going to die on us from lack of basic care. It is entitled to necessary care, and that is all."

Dr. Halifax looked at John frowning.

John continued an explanation, "The lizards have kidnapped over thirty-five of our people and killed many more."

"Well, I can say after drinking several liters of water, *he* seems to have bounced back. The food that you brought me, I believe he can eat. His teeth suggest that he is an omnivore. As to his mental health, I have no idea."

"So it's a male. Can we talk to him?"

"You can speak his language?" Halifax asked with a furrowed brow. "Yes, he is fit enough, once he's had a little to eat."

The Doctor's words struck John right between the eyes.

♦♦♦

Max set up the interview room where the lizard was to be interrogated where it had recorders and monitoring gear that would have put police TV programs to shame. The whole setup was monitored from Max's operational center. He liked to call his little cubbyhole, meaning his desktop computer, the 'Operations Center'.

The lizard looked at the two tablets in front of him without a word. One of his two sets of eyelids folded back into his skull in a most disconcerting way, as his tongue made a nervous clicking noise against the back of his front teeth. Although not as large as the warriors, his tall thin frame sat down on a stool making it look child sized. His head bobbed slightly in time with his tail flicker as he sat waiting. Even sitting, the creature was tall, tall enough to still be at John's eye level when John stood.

"Release the prisoner, make sure there are three guards in here at all times," John said to Eric.

Eric sized up the alien then motioned to the corporal to cut the Lizard's bindings. The corporal moved forward pulling his large bowie knife from its scabbard.

"This will be my present to you if you don't co-operate. Believe me, I so want to play Santa Clause," the Corporal said with menace. Waving the serrated knife slowly in a macabre threatening motion before the lizard's face, then quick as a flash, cut the bonds. The lizard, on seeing the knife tensed his muscles and took a deep breath. Rubbing his hands and arms slowly to return circulation to his claws. The movement brought three guns to aim directly at him. The lizard stopped dead, not moving a muscle. He then slowly rubbed his forearm some more, while eyeing the weapons.

John made a hand motion placing his open palms on the table. Then pointed to the lizard's claws. The lizard took a moment, then placed his own claws onto the table. Eric leaned forward and handcuffed one of them to the table.

John placed a fruit he found in one of the storage holes onto the table. The lizard eyed the fruit and licked his lips. Otherwise, he didn't move a muscle. John then spoke into a communicator while Max wirelessly connected to the data pad from the next room. In front of the lizard an image displaying a picture of the fruit on the desk. Below that image were pictures of the icons and graphics in the lizard language taken from where the fruit was found.

The lizard gasped in surprise and blurted out an incomprehensible sound. The microphone recorded the lizard's speech. When the lizard finally stopped talking the data pad repeated exactly what the lizard had said. The first eyelid retracted back into his head. His nostrils flared in what John thought was amazement.

The device could repeat what he had said! S'sank thought. *The pictures on the device are so clear and life-like.*

The program under Max's control not only repeated what the lizard said but recorded the sound against the fruit that was displayed. John removed the fruit and placed a small piece of seed also found on the alien store. Once again the picture with the lizard writing below appeared on the data pad. The lizard looked at the seed then looked at the data pad and repeated the word on the screen while looking at John. The data pad repeated the Lizard speak. John removed the seed and placed the third item, a piece of meat. The lizard then glanced at John, closing one of the two protective eyelids on his eyes. John could see the lizard's jaw tighten. As if on cue, two guns moved as one towards him.

S'sank then spoke a single word out loud in his rasping slithering voice, "Hippashh."

John frowned.

Watching the Lizard he got up and left the room, leaving Eric and the guards to continue the word association exercise.

♦ ♦ ♦

S'sank watched the mammal leave the room. He was obviously an officer or an administrator based on the respect the other mammals gave him.

S'sank was confused about how the galley from the *Godzilla* had gotten into a cave on the planet? It was impossible! And yet, here he was a prisoner. Sighing, he had expected to die when his War Leader reached engineering and found no reactor.

He had never seen this species of mammal before, not that he had met too many mammals. He's sure he would have remembered these ones, which are mostly hairless and come in all different colors. These creatures obviously didn't know standard trade language.

♦ ♦ ♦

John walked out of the Bio Lab to find Jen and Thurston discussing the reactor down in the cavern.

"Thurston, we need someone with linguistic skills to replace Jerry O'Conner," John said interrupting the two.

Jen stared accusingly at John's heartlessness, *they had just been kidnapped and it's business as usual?*

Her eyes cut him deeply, so he did what he could to ignore her and continue, "But right now we need someone to get as many pictures that will help us to learn the lizard's language." Thurston looked a little confused given they'd been learning the lizard language for quite some time now. "I'm talking about pictures of spaceships, people, food ... you get the idea. This lizard is going to give us our dictionary in that room right now!"

Jen just stood, wrapped her arms around herself and walked away. John watched her go feeling dread. He should comfort her but given her anger towards him right now, he knew it would be a lost cause. He pushed that dread into a cold hard ball into the pit of his stomach.

Thurston watched the two in silence, as sadness crossed his face.

"How soon can we get the labs back up and running?" John and Thurston talked for several more hours thrashing out logistic details.

♦♦♦

Scarlet's Place

It was getting past noon when John finally had a chance to duck out to see Scarlet. In all truth, he had been avoiding it. His truck pulled up outside the front door as the porch light came on despite the hour. John could see as soon as he got out, red rims circled Scarlet's eyes. She had been a strong, confident person, a hardened Texan rancher who'd seen life in the raw. But as John closed the distance he saw the fragile Scarlet, that had been through hell when her Frankie passed on, and now had to face a whole new reality without her niece, Amanda. John was about to say he was sorry when Scarlet lashed out and slapped him across the face.

"John, I don't want to hear you're sorry! You betrayed my trust! The lizards obviously came to your place for some payback. You're not welcome 'ere no more!"

The sting in John's face camouflaged his hurt feelings. With nothing more to say he made an abrupt about-turn leaving Scarlet standing there watching him drive away. Another tear rolled down Scarlet's face and dropped to the parched ground. She looked down and wished death could swallow her up quickly, it was better that than this slow agonizing torture.

John took a slow way home, reeling in anguish over what he could have done to prevent Amanda's kidnapping. There was no answer.

♦♦♦

1st Amour Division, Mobile Command Post - El Paso, Texas

"Get me Colonel Prior on the horn," Major Matthews ordered his first lieutenant.

"Yes, sir," the Lieutenant saluted and left the room. The other two men in the Major's Command tent stood at ease as they recounted what they witnessed at the research base they were charged with babysitting.

"So Sergeant, how many lizards did you see entering that building," the Major queried the two men.

"Sir, only one. It looked to be quite ill. It was Mr. Manders and his group, sir."

"The ex-special forces?"

"Yes, sir."

A light flicked on the Major's comm, signaling a call waiting.

"Yes, Major?" Dan's voice came over the phone.

"Colonel, sir, I believe you need to get back here. Dr. Stevenson is hiding a lizard."

"Damn!! I'm on my way. Major, I want no one coming or going from that research base until I get there." Dan was more than just a little pissed, he was furious. He had been more than generous with John, and now he pulled this stunt. If he wasn't so goddamn smart, and that we needed him so much... He fought against wringing John's neck the first chance he got.

Research Base El Paso, Texas

When John turned into the research base parking lot, military vehicles were parked outside of the administration building. Thurston was once again having a lively conversation with Colonel Prior and Major Mathews. John thought to himself *too bad I didn't go to the house tonight!*

Thurston had stood his ground, and he even had Eric and a few of his men with weapons in plain sight to enforce his claim. John could see this could get ugly very quickly. Ultimately he knew that the Air Force would have control over the alien. But they needed time with the prisoner to determine the lizard ship's exit location to affect any kind of rescue. Thurston knew this and was doing all he could to prevent Dan from taking the alien, there and then. Although Eric and his men were on John's payroll, ultimately they would probably not stand in the way of US Armed Forces. John knew it was wrong to put them in that position, dividing their loyalties.

"Colonel, Major, Thurston, you seem to be thoroughly engrossed, maybe I should come back later," Dan gave John a serious look that would snap freeze an insubordinate under his command. The Major tilted his head with a curious frown, while Thurston gave him a withering look, which only made John snort forcing Thurston to smile in relief after he rolled his eyes.

Before Dan could speak John continued on, "Colonel, I fully expect you to take this alien we have found to a safe, comfortable place for it to live out its short life in the height of luxury." The Major snorted and briefly smiled noting the scientist's sarcasm.

"However, I would ask you and the Major to see for yourselves what progress we've made so far, and then judge when to take it into custody." Thurston threw a sharp look at John and raised a single eyebrow as he was prone to do. Eric, overhearing John's comments, quickly radioed the Bio Lab to advise them that they were getting visitors and for them to put on a good show.

Dan had been fuming all the way to the base. His thoughts flashed here and there as he wondered whether the aliens had in fact returned for one of their own, given this latest development.

"We found this fellow after all the confusion of the invasion," John commented as they walked towards the Bio Lab. Dan was not entirely convinced. Yet, it was possible.

The lizard took notice when the group walked into the lab. John noticed the alien straighten up as soon as he saw Dan and Major Matthews in military uniform.

"We have determined that the lizard is a male from one of their engineering areas," John said filling in some of the details.

Some of the men felt a slight shiver as they watched the lizard's tongue flicking in and out of his mouth sampling the air. It made John's flesh creep. He could see the lizard recognized him, most likely from his scent. Doctor Halifax had mentioned how sensitive their tongues were. The lizard then made a curious motion, he sat up straight and bowed his head, and spoke out a rasping slithering sound.

Dan and Major Matthews stepped slightly backward their eyes pinned to the lizard sitting before them. John noted the shocked look on their faces from either the mere fact they were talking to an alien, or the data pad drummed out the words 'respect, respect'. John could hardly mistake the impressed look on their faces.

"What is your name?" The data pad then brought up a graphical representation of the question on the first pad.

"Engineer S'sank, of the Dido Clutch."

"Engineer S'sank, where did your ship go?" John asked.

The lizard said in his slithering tongue, "I know nothing of navigation." The data pad then chirped out the response in English.

"Which direction did your ship go?" John repeated.

"I previously answered ... question. Your machine here must ... broken"

"How fast is your ship," John queried.

"I cannot tell you this."

"How long did it take to get here?"

"Our brood grows very far from here. We travel many cycles to be here." There was an audible collective exhale of relief from some of the guards.

"Did you come directly here?" John asked anxiously.

"No, we travel many star systems near here first."

"Why are you here?"

"We lost brain food, we come here for food," all the men in the room stared directly at the alien. Fear was creeping into the room like a stench. It was at that point the lizard unknowingly made his greatest mistake.

"Will you eat me when ... finish the word list?"

John slammed his open palm onto the desk making a loud cracking sound. The lizard jumped in surprise.

"We don't eat sentient beings!!" John yelled.

He stood abruptly before the translator had time to work. He could not stomach been in the presence of the alien anymore. Thoughts of Amanda being eaten piece by piece tormented him. A deep guilt ripped and tore at his heart.

Did the salvage on the freighter bring this nightmare to Earth? Was the technology really worth it?

In the room, John stood leaning forward almost touching the lizard's snout. The scaly leather smell wafted into his nostrils.

"We want our family back ALIVE!" The lizard cringed at John's outburst, repeating the word 'respect' over and over, obviously not understanding the mammal's outburst.

Dan thought he needed to re-evaluate John. He didn't think he had the balls to stand over the lizard like that. One swipe of the lizard's claws would end John's life. With a snarl, John stormed out of the room leaving the alien cowering and panting heavily.

John met the two officers outside catching some air. "Dr. Stevenson, you have two weeks. However, you will forward on any, and I mean 'any' Intel. We will also be sending our negotiators to sit in on the interrogations." John knew that he was lucky. He half expected Dan to remove S'sank there and then.

That night John fell into bed exhausted, the events of the day came back to him in excruciatingly explicit detail. Amanda's face among others haunted him. The scaly leather smell and S'sank's sharp teeth lent vivid detail to his self-recrimination. Even now he could feel the sharp sting of Scarlet's anger and open-handed slap. It was just as painful as Jen's angry disappointed dagger stares, or Elvis' tormented hollow eyes. Sleep didn't come at all that night.

Chapter Forty

Godzilla, Deep Space

Eventually, the Lizards removed all the body parts from the corner of the prison. No one wanted to ask what happened to them.

Slowly Amanda's wounds healed leaving a raw scar. Mel had been a strong positive influence on the locals. Her leadership helped to debate the pros and cons of their captivity versus escape.

The huddled groups of humans seemed to solidify their members. The most outspoken, the enforcement types, who were joined by the bulk of the bikers despite Blackeye's presence.

Blackeye had lost some of his standing after his zombie impression post kidnapping. Hanging out with the Deputy and Mel didn't help.

The goop the lizards provided was sufficient for the human body to survive; however, it did nothing for their mental state.

"Is this normal?" Mel asked one of the scientists.

"The time it takes to travel between the stars?"

"Yes."

"I don't think so. Because the Lizards didn't bring enough food. My guess is they're repairing the ship."

"So, we're not far from Earth in astronomical terms?"

"No."

A slow smile spread across her face.

"The longer we can put up with this goop. The longer we stay alive."

"What did you do at the research base?" Mel asked of the diminutive scientist.

"I worked on materials."

Mel and Amanda looked at each other.

"What things are made of and how to manufacture them. I was in the middle of this new energy collector that could replace fossil fuels."

"Solar energy has been around for donkey's years," said Amanda.

"Not these ones. A bank of these put on the roof of a car and you won't need petrol."

"That's impossible."

The scientist just shrugged. "It exists. John gave me the stuff to reverse engineer."

"He already had it?" Mel pursed her lips.

♦♦♦

"Report!" Rezulin craned his neck to see the status on the repaired front viewer of his bridge. The weekly meetings were getting tiresome with no real change in their status.

Engineering was still trying to fix one thing or another they deemed critical before the ship went FTL. Rezulin knew they were still weeks or possibly months away from being fully FTL capable.

Tactical was no closer to determining the makeup of the multidimensional weapon. They did have some results in the construction of their drone.

♦♦♦

The human prisoners slowly fell into a routine. The days melted into weeks and months. The enforcement types maintained their fitness with rigorous exercise and hand to hand combat.

The scientists would endlessly debate the pros and cons of the technology employed by the Lizards.

While the rest told campfire stories to pass the time.

"So where in Ireland are you from?" Amanda asked of Jerry, the linguist.

"To be sure, t'was born in ere village called Donegal." Jerry smiled at Amanda's interest. He sometimes slipped into his strong Irish accent when he wished to impress.

Privacy within the human enclave on board was virtually nonexistent. The slow pace of the repairs had an agonizing, interminable effect on their mental state. The four women that were captured were vastly outnumbered. Their celebrity status came crashing down when several of the aggressive men try to force themselves on Sarah the kitchen hand one night. If it weren't for Agent O'Brien and Jerry O'Conner coming to her rescue, they would have had their way.

Bodyguards seemed to be the only answer to protect the women. Jerry was more than happy to hang around Amanda while Mel and Blackeye were inseparable.

"Don't you get creeped out by all the leering?" Sarah said to Amanda one evening as she stared at the group of her attackers.

Amanda looked over at her concerned. "As long as that's all they do. You and Robert seem to have hit it off." Robert was one of the SWAT team. He was more than capable of fending off several of the others until help arrived.

Sarah didn't seem to have heard her.

Mel had an ongoing discussion with Amanda about the single partner relationships they were used to back on Earth and whether they would still apply in this situation. The men had to be doing it tough. She no way condoned what happened to Sarah although they hadn't come to any conclusion on relationships. All they knew was time could be very short. The lizard lineups could restart at any time.

Chapter Forty-One

Research Base El Paso, Texas

John and Thurston were in a heated discussion as to whether to change the location of the research base. The aliens had found the facility using their superior sensors. Working under the constant threat of a repeat of the attack would not help John and his team's productivity. Not to mention the ever-present US Air Force interrogation squad. John was of the opinion that a change in location on Earth would not make it safe. Removing the base totally from Earth was logistically possible, however, they really only had two jump ships. This would strain the resources to breaking point, John thought. In the end, they compromised by leaving some research facilities there but started preparations to develop another site on Earth.

When Thurston left his office, John chastised himself for not following up on the jump drive manufacturers. They needed these new drives to be built quickly. Yet, he still had huge misgivings about providing the technology to any manufacturer or even the US government. He couldn't separate thoughts surrounding 'total power and how it corrupts' and passing the technology on. This whole argument to limit giving this technology to anyone including the government was inherently hypocritical. Could *he* be trusted with this "total power"?! The irony of this was not lost on John. In the end, he did not trust others with the jump drive technology yet, so he took steps to ensure its safety.

John redesigned the drive technology into component parts; each on their own was meaningless. This had the unfortunate effect of having to contract lots of manufacturers to provide the components. Add to that a variety of delivery addresses, purchasing methods, and a complicated process of transferring the products between companies before it reached its end destination. The cumbersome process created significant delays. John added one final step in the design/manufacturing process, and that was to include an auto-destruct in the drive. This would activate if there were any type of tampering or if the unit was not serviced in the proper way within a specified time frame.

After calling some manufacturers to get the process moving forward again, John set his mind to the prospect of a new base.

◆◆◆

John was still receiving dagger eyes from Jen whenever they met. So as part of his self-preservation, he asked her to look into gravity fields that were fundamental to the tunneling device. He knew that she would take up the challenge because of her remarkable aptitude for field technology. Well, that was the plan. He halfheartedly chastised himself for the sneaky act. To make it even more official, he asked Peter the drive specialist to work with her.

Maybe his calm will settle her down a bit.

Since the release of A-Bitumen, demand for the product was still outstripping supply. There were now quite a few plants producing the product with most under license. A myriad of uses was being discovered every day for the material. Everything from building construction to art, and now shipbuilding. Elvis's idea of spraying the inflatable space station covering it with the A-Bitumen was inspirational. It would give it structural integrity but also provide protection against radiation.

The infiltration of these products into the economy sent shock-waves through the steel and construction industries. The auto industry was rushing to test cars fabricated with A-Bitumen. The financial markets hesitantly climbed as they saw the potential growth of T.N. Corporation with the use of this new material.

"Thurston, we need our own shipyard to start building proper spaceships. I don't want to face the next lizard incursion with such small ships again! The hull and major fit out could be done there. However, we would still need to add the critical systems like the Jump drive ourselves." Thurston had a far-away look as if weighing up his financial options. John went on, "I've sourced an inexpensive shipyard on the net in Indonesia, and I'd like you to look at it. It has a large dry dock hanger that can fit a frigate sized ship with sea-access for materials deliveries. It's located on a separate island so we can easily manage security." John sent him the details.

"I would also like to create a spaceport somewhere out of the way from populated centers in case we are visited by our friends from space again. My initial thoughts were somewhere in Western Australia. We could set up some of the more classified production there and have access to the spaceport."

"John, I hate to point out that with the jump ship, we don't actually need a spaceport. All we need is a big hanger."

"Thurston, I know... I've been struggling with this issue for quite some time. Whether to gift mankind with this drive technology or not. You saw how devastating it was when we used it against a vastly technologically superior warship. I'm not prepared to be the person who introduced the destruction of our world based on the development of the teleporter. My plan at this stage is to get technology that will allow us to develop human civilization quickly without killing us. I know this may sound hypocritical; however, it's one thing to hand a baby a nuclear warhead, but quite another to give it a loaded gun. The gun would only kill a few, whereas the nuclear warhead could destroy the world."

Thurston thought about this for a long time. He eventually replied, "I want your promise if it all goes to shit, you will pass this technology onto the military."

They had both heard the latest news reports that India, North Korea and Pakistan had set off test nuclear weapons. They couldn't forget the links the Pakistani government had with terrorist organizations. And now the war on IS. The whole world was becoming more dangerous.

John sighed, "Thurston it's more a matter of timing, that's all." John knew that Thurston was not convinced and they would be having this conversation again.

It was at that point that Eric walked into the foyer. John waved, glad for the interruption. "Eric, come join us."

"To make any rescue attempt, we're going to need a decent force that is trained. I need you to start putting together a proposal for training sites and a list of personnel."

Eric knew this was coming, as John had previously broached the list of personnel with him. "How many people are we talking about?"

"My first thought was to start with a company of Marines and an equivalent number for the Space Navy. Thurston and I were just discussing the possibility of setting up a new research base and spaceport in Australia."

"Giving up El Paso?"

"No, we're going to expand. Having the Armored Tank Division just outside our door is rather comforting; however, it's also a bit unnerving with all those guns pointed this way. Besides, we'll involve the military in our operations soon enough."

Eric stared at the two weighing up his next statement, "I don't understand why they aren't involved right now, especially their Special Ops, given that's what they're trained for. To extract American citizens from foreign soils."

"It's going to take some time to track down where the aliens have taken our people. You have until that time to build up whatever forces we can to take along with us. Mark my words, we will use the Special Ops, if you're not ready by that time. This is a private business, and I'd like to keep it within the family. We are going after our people, and I want to make sure that's done correctly with the best people we have at the time." Eric nodded that this. "You will be on the pointy end of that operation," said John.

"Once we have a definite site in Australia, I'd like your security input."

♦♦♦

The lizard manuals had described various forms of anti-gravity transport carriages that were used in their tunnels. Their whole understanding of the lizard language was based on the manuals, until now.

Max bustled into the cottage with a grim look on his face.

"The manuals that we have and the language that this alien speaks are different."

"What?! What you mean?" John asked.

"He can't read the manuals. He said that it's the language of some group called the Ancients."

John just looked at Max dumbfounded and rocked back on his chair appalled. He had hoped that S'sank could help them with the gravity fields. But it seemed these lizards were in the dark just as much as they were. It also meant that there was possibly an even more dangerous lizard species out there. He didn't know which dismayed him more.

♦♦♦

Tidying up the research base after the carnage had been a mammoth task. John, Thurston and Eric had used up many favors to get the personnel and security reestablished. The devastation that had been unleashed on the research base gave Eric the impetus to address some of the blatant safety issues. The base was so much more than just an ordinary research facility; it required decent security and more, given possible future alien threats.

Eric had thought once he retired to civilian life, his world would be boring. The security contract that he had with John invigorated him. Over the last several months he knew that monumental things were happening here in El Paso. The carnage before them was proof of that. It struck Eric that, his life since leaving special forces was more important than when he was in the military.

Eric resolved to tighten his daily rituals. Being SF was a personal commitment to oneself, to be the best they can at precision mayhem. Loading and holstering his weapons, Eric made his way to the Administration cottage.

"John, there is one person I would like you to meet in Washington. Bill Withers, ex-intelligence smart as they come. Has the most damnable join the dots brain I've met, present company excepted of course." John just smiled. "He would be a serious asset, and not just for his intelligence skills but in the field of security, he's one of the best I've seen."

The next morning John looked gravely at his friend sitting in the diner opposite him. A full plate of three eggs, two sausages, two pieces of toast and pancakes left untouched. There was definitely something wrong with Elvis. He seemed utterly despondent which, given the current circumstances, was quite natural. Elvis had only spoken a little bit about his relationship with a girl that had been kidnapped in the past. This was before John first met Elvis. He could tell that that relationship had a life-changing effect on him. John had always believed that keeping oneself busy was the best distraction to a lot of pain and grief. So later that day he called Adrian, the battery and power specialist, into his office.

"Adrian I want you to look at the lizard reactor we have downstairs."

"That's not my specialty."

"What do you mean, you're in power," John countered.

"Well... Yes, but not fusion reactors." Adrian said as he shook his head.

"You've seen what the lizards did?" John said more as a statement while pointing outside the window.

"Yes." He said almost in a whisper.

John pulled open the top drawer of his desk and took out one of the laser pistols they had acquired in the freighter.

Adrian stood there, confusion across his face, with a little bit of fear.

John then put the gun against his own temple, "This is where we are at right now, except it's the lizards that are holding the gun." John watched Adrian's reaction intently.

Adrian stood there staring into John's eyes, then at the gun and back. Slowly Adrian inched forward as if preparing to dive for the pistol.

"What do you need me to do?"

"Just make a start on the reactor, you'll need Elvis's help," John said without emotion.

Adrian stood there for a minute, "OK, I'll make a start."

Coolly, John slowly put the laser back in his top drawer. Adrian turned and left John's office shaking his head.

When the door closed, John took a deep breath letting it out slowly. *When had he become so aggressively manipulative?* Standing up, John walked to the window where he poured a whiskey neat. Downing the whole shot, John watched Adrian outside talking to his troubled friend, Elvis.

Finally, Adrian made an animated pistol shooting his own head with his hand in front of Elvis, who then turned to stare at John.

The following weeks saw the research base come back to life. The wreckage was cleared, and the numbers of base personnel steadily grew. Eric's guards now patrolled the area with assault rifles. Small towers were erected to house hidden automated laser cannons. Alien shuttles coming close would receive a special 'Welcome to Earth' message if they got too close to the base without permission. On the far side of the fence, US soldiers also patrolled with armor support.

Regular visits by Major Mathews, and his specialists for the interrogation briefings was intrusively disconcerting.

Across the road from the research base in the makeshift military base, Major Matthews, and Colonel Prior stood casually chatting in the officer's wardroom tent. The M1 tanks on maneuvers made a dull rumble as they passed close by.

"So, Major, let's have it," Dan said.

"Well, there's been no resistance within the research base to restrict our access to the alien and his interrogation." Dan nodded.

"All the base personnel seem to embrace the idea that they are there building weapons or supporting the goal to defend Earth. More than one person has reiterated Doctor Stevenson's claim that the alien was not there before the attack. There is definitely a hierarchy within their organization where a small command group dictates the scientific development.

"There is, however, a side group of military types. I know they are building up their security, but this seems more than that. It's more like para-military."

Dan stood there looking at the Major. *What is going on there! Had he been wrong about Dr. Stevenson and the survivalist link to Elvis Watts.* Dan nodded for the Major to continue.

"I've been able to determine that they have dealings with the Sage Corporation."

Dan was surprised at this. He knew that Sage was heavily into space-based technology, mainly space stations.

"Continue."

"The research base itself is very well run, I believe Thurston is more than just a good administrator. They've had visits from the State Department regarding the development and sale of arms to foreign nations."

Dan raised an eyebrow.

"The State Department wants to restrict the sale of the lasers, whereas John and Thurston are pushing to provide it to nations committed to the defense of Earth."

Dan blew out a deep breath. *Thank God that's above my pay grade.* "Are they saying that they will stop production of the lasers unless they are available to our Allies?"

"That and more... to the Chinese."

Dan shook his head, *It's never a dull moment with John and Thurston. He wondered how the President would take the news. The question is not just how we stop the sale but should we.*

"There is another thing. You may have noticed that there are a high number of foreign scientists contracted there. Even if we did put sanctions on the company, I don't think they would be effective given the make-up of their development group."

"So once again it comes down to how much we can trust John in his goal to defend the Earth, without bias," Dan summarized.

"Yes, I'm afraid so. But if it's worth anything, I believe Earth's defense is his highest priority. He's a bit unconventional in his approach; however, I ... I would trust him to do the right thing," the Major said with all seriousness.

The Major reached down to his desk and handed Dan a list of personnel and their specialties, "Have a look at these specialists that are coming and going from the base."

"Mmmm," Dan said with a frown. "That is interesting... maybe they are looking into making the lasers nuclear powered?" The Major shrugged.

"Talk to some of the locals and see what they say," Dan said. "We need to be absolutely sure he's not going to go rogue or worse, communist."

Major Matthews saluted, leaving Dan staring at the list of specialists deep in thought.

The Major left the base on the nature reserve avoiding the deeply furrowed tracks left by the heavy tanks and headed to the small diner outside of town. He had had word that it was a favorite eatery for the group. It was a place to start canvassing the locals' opinion of the research base.

The more he spoke to the locals, the more he got confusing and contradictory information. The locals had no idea what they were doing at the lab and were supportive of it until the aliens. Now, there was fear of their operations and the possibility of the alien's return. Some had a grudging respect for the scientists and underlying pride of their own contribution to the weapons development despite all that happened. It seemed everyone had a different opinion.

His biggest surprise was from an older Texan rancher called Scarlet from a nearby ranch. He was sure she would have few opinions of John and his team; especially since her niece was one of the ones' kidnapped. When she spoke, her hard shell was impenetrable as the granite in the hills nearby. The Major resigned himself to eating plates full of rock cookies in an attempt at gaining her trust.

Against the odds, the Major saw the research base start to heal itself by being infused with new staff and an intense new determination.

◆◆◆

Washington DC

Dan returned to Washington to a storm of questions and cross-examination. He stood before Admiral Tucker, the Joint Chiefs, and the President, detailing how Doctor Stevenson was found alive, and the discovery of a live alien to which Dan had given permission for Doctor Stevenson to interrogate before it was to be transferred to Area 51.

Dan felt like he was on the torture rack being stretched. For nearly two hours he had been trying to convince his superior officers of the validity of his decision to give the doctor access to the alien. He showed video footage of the progress they'd made in the first few days they'd had him. General Abercrombie spoke up then,

"How do you know they've only had the alien for a few days? That alien may have been the reason why their warship turned up!"

The Joint Chiefs all swung towards Dan waiting for his response.

"I suppose it is possible, but going over the footage of the interrogations, and comments made by the base staff, I think it unlikely. The Lizards don't seem to have the same respect for life we have," Dan said as he shifted his weight from one foot to the other.

"Well ain't that just dandy, you're expert in video footage as well," the General snorted. "Mr. President, we should remove this lizard, S'sank from Doctor Stevenson's hands. I believe we can do a better job."

Dan responded abruptly, "And I suppose you know how to speak lizard!" The General's chest puffed out towards the Colonel who could see the anger growing in the General's face. It was then the President intervened.

"The Colonel has a point. No one here knows lizard. The only way we're going to find out is to send our people there to El Paso pronto."

"Mr. President, I have already assigned trained investigators to sit in on all of Doctor Stevenson's interviews with the alien. We have been receiving their reports on a daily basis."

The President looked at Dan, "Make sure the summaries get to my office. I want to know what the lizard is saying."

"Yes sir."

The General wasn't to be put off so easily, "What of the rumor that they had other aliens, frozen in their bio labs," the General sneered.

"Is there any truth to those rumors Colonel?" the President asked.

"There is a macabre story going around the townsfolk that they were experimenting on weird animals. But no one has seen anything."

The President zeroed-in on Dan, "I would say it's more than a rumor Colonel, the warship went directly there. Most people would consider alien's weird animals. I need to think about this a little, whether our Dr. Stevenson is a Doctor Mengele or Doctor Do-little."

Dan then countered, "There is another rumor going around which seems to have more substance in my view Mr. President, and that is that the aliens went there for food." The President sat back and thought about this for a minute.

"Colonel, how did the aliens get into Doctor Stevenson's refrigerator in the first place?" Admiral Tucker asked.

Dan clenched his teeth, "That I don't know Admiral. I will re-interview the base staff and relook at all the footage from our F-16's during the attack."

"Colonel, I want you to go back to El Paso, and search that place. It is now a matter of national security. I want confirmation as to whether they harbored aliens before the warship attacked," said the President.

"Sir, I would advise extreme caution at this point because Doctor Stevenson seems to be providing surprising discoveries with his team of experts. As you are fully aware, we will have our new laser technology in no small part due to him and his team. The aliens already know we're here. Their return, is in my view only a matter of time. Having Stevenson work with the backing of the US government, rather than against, locked in a cell due to crimes against unusual animals, would curtail our chances at obtaining more technology that would be useful for our defense."

The President hadn't forgotten Stevenson's role in weapons development but having it spelled out to him reminded him of its importance. His latest strategy to provide the technology to other nations had grave consequences for the

US. He then breathed out a heavy breath. "Very well. But I want him to delay the laser technology transfer to other countries till the US has fully implemented them."

"Yes sir, I'll see he's notified."

The President stared at Dan. "Colonel, I want him on a tight leash."

Dan saluted then turned to leave as a President made one final comment. "Colonel, I want to see you in my office after this meeting!" Dan's heart sank as he'd thought he might be finished with the grilling. Apparently not.

◆◆◆

Dan had been to so many high-level meetings with Admirals and Generals but had never been openly defiant as he had towards General Abercrombie. He felt nervous meeting with the President now. When the President walked into the room, he waved away Dan's salute.

"Colonel, that was a gutsy move you made in the Joint Chiefs meeting, confronting General Abercrombie like that. It's likely to get you sent to Antarctica or somewhere equally unpleasant. Especially at the rank you are."

The President reached into his top desk and said, "You can take those oak leaf's off" as he handed him silver eagles. "Dan, I want to know if Doctor Stevenson brought the aliens here."

"Mr. President. I would like to know that as well, however, at this point I believe it's irrelevant. The aliens are coming no matter what."

"Perhaps you're right, Colonel." The President gave Dan a worried look. "That will be all."

Dan was stunned at what the President had just done. He'd jumped to the rank of full Colonel. He hadn't been a Lt Colonel for very long either. This was either 'really good', but more likely than not, something 'really bad'. Still, he couldn't help grinning as he left the oval office.

Chapter Forty-Two

The T.N. Corporation and its business partners as a whole had continued on regardless of the difficulties the troubled research base had been faced with. The licensed technologies and manufactured products raked in enormous amounts of money.

Looking to the T.N. expansion plans, John and Thurston were astounded when they found large parcels of open cut mining and cattle grazing land in Western Australia, selling for unbelievably low prices. They settled on a cheap area of land called, 'Dragon Trees', for the new spaceport they had discussed. The exhausted bauxite mine was remote enough from the rest of the world, but still had road and rail access to the coastal port of Broome. The spaceship's hull could be made in Indonesia and shipped by sea and rail to the spaceport.

The Australis Research Base (ARB) would be constructed on an old Kidman property they bought at a bargain. The political fallout from over aggressive Chinese investment in Australian grazing land made the property irresistible.

Research Base Australis, Western Australia

Adrian pushed the 'Product to Market' team to develop racks of collectors and batteries for large-scale energy harvesting and storage. The new base was in North West Australia, called Pilbara, and was surrounded by the Great Australian Desert. It was an ideal location to set up the first energy collection farm. Not far from the base, they started construction of a new spaceport near the Dragon Tree Reserve.

Elvis and Jen's construction technique using the transporter was a marvel to watch as they built massive underground facilities within days. The excavation and lining of the caverns with A-Bitumen. The internal spaces around the underground hangers were filled with Ryan's and other transportable modular units of accommodation, labs, workshops, etc. It was an impressive start.

Something that would have taken months to achieve without the jump technology was completed in mere weeks. There was still a mountain of things to do, but they had the bare bones done. There was room enough for all the research, design and prototyping crews to move in. Staffing the base with all its personnel including the supporting trades was now the issue. Although they had the old mine rail from Broome to the spaceport, a fast transport network was needed.

When it came time to construct the fast train, they started with three terminals; the Research Base, Dragon Trees Spaceport and T.N. Corporate offices on the outskirts of Darwin. Under John's direction, Jen and Elvis stretched the capabilities of jump technology. They configured the jump drive field into a long tunnel shape, large enough for a train to pass through. It took weeks to remove the dirt rock by tele-grab. The tunnel was built several miles below the surface in a stable layer of sandstone. It snaked its way in a loop from the new Research Base all the way to the NT capital, Darwin.

The second stage of the fast train construction was to use the jump drive to line the tunnels with a mixture of compressed A-Bitumen and iron. Thousands of gallons of A-Bitumen laced with metal alloy were tele-compressed into hundreds of tubes. The teleporter combined the mixture into smaller pipe-like shapes, making it harder and denser. These tubes, once placed end to end, would allow the train to run through them at high speed. The metal in the tube lining when magnetized, would work like the repulsor rails for the maglev train.

Eric and his company of soldiers provided manpower to install the terminus connections and placement of the modular components from the T.N. subsidiary, Sage Corp. and modular manufacturers. Many of the components were based on modified habitat modules. The research base, spaceport, and terminus were testbeds for components designed to be used on other planets far from Earth.

The cylinder-like train carriages purchased from the UK were then mounted with repulse rings on the hull to levitate them away from the tunnel walls. Unlike other maglev systems, it used electric rocket engines built into each end of the carriages to propel them at high speeds.

The Trans-DragonTree Railway was born.

Repairs to the *Grace* hadn't taken as long as John had expected once they had removed the broken twisted metal and scorched bitumen. The greatest concern was the seal around the airlock. Once again fresh A-Bitumen came in handy after welding extra plating.

"Right, let's take the old girl for a spin," John said to his crew as they boarded the newly repaired *Grace*.

The *Grace* blinked out from inside the cavern to materialize near Titan. John was always impressed when he jumped to Titan, one could almost guarantee one of Saturn's many moons was bright with splendor, tinged with the reflected blue tint off Saturn herself.

They had more tests to perform on the *Grace*.

◆◆◆

Space Command, Peterson Air Force Base

Dan sat in his office running through the latest reports he had received from Dr. Stevenson when his comm beeped.

"Sir, we have a new contact that just appeared near Saturn's moon, Titan," the Comm Tech said.

"Right, I'm on my way."

Just as Dan was leaving his desk another message popped up on his screen, his adjutant had placed a reminder note of an appointment to see Dr. Stevenson Friday. The doctor had been cagey this past week inferring some new product he wanted to canvass with him. No doubt to get special treatment. Dan sighed while he locked his screen and rushed down to the USSTRATCOM war room.

"Sir, they don't seem to be approaching Earth," said the duty officer.

"Have the President and Joint Chiefs been informed?"

"Yes, sir, as per standing orders."

This was the third sighting in as many weeks from near Titan. *There's definitely something going on out there.* Like each of the other times, Dan contacted Admiral Tucker personally.

"Keep me informed Colonel," was all he said.

Dan thought about the implications of the new sighting. *The aliens must have a base there.*

After the second positive sighting. Dan arranged for an X37 drone to be sent on a flyby of Titan. It would take several months for it to arrive. The first sighting was when Earth's and Saturn's orbits' were on opposite sides of the sun. The drone would have to use a gravity assist to slingshot around Venus, picking up velocity to once again slingshot past Jupiter and on towards Saturn and its moon, Titan.

The flashing icon of the ship on the war room monitors jolted Dan back to the present. At least another small ship had appeared in the system since the last one was destroyed by the lizard ship. Although he worried that he didn't know if that was a good thing or not.

♦♦♦

Research Base El Paso, Texas

S'sank was having the time of his life, since becoming a captive of these mammals. He had never eaten so well and yet he hadn't even eaten any sentient beings dead or alive. He was fully aware that the information he provided led to the lifestyle that he received. He knew he had no hope of getting home so he resolved to do the best he can. He had received bonuses of meat when he provided them with 'good intel'. Although they had never given him any live meat. He supposed he could not afford to be too picky.

Many times did they ask where he was from, he could only reply, "I am not a navigator." He could only think; *they do not believe him.* So he would try harder to be more accurate with their word association game. He had seen many pictures now of their home world, and he longed to be out there basking in the desert sun. Ever since leaving his home he had been ship bound. Now, he was in an underground cell where they let him out to the desert above under guard for brief periods. Even though much of the planet has water, they do have some nice dry deserts, perfect for lizard bathing.

A short, balding human called Elvis, often entered to ask about the *Godzilla's* forward shield reactor. This particular alpha male secreted many danger scents and was always impatient. Especially when he showed pictures of the *Godzilla's* engines asking about their performance.

S'sank could tell when the mammal was angry; the veins on his face and neck became red. Sometimes, Elvis stank of bitter danger pheromones, so much so, that all S'sank could do was hold his sensitive tongue to the roof of his mouth restricting his taste sense. In desperation one time, S'sank purposely, farted. The soldiers on guard duty had to call in a doctor to check that Elvis wasn't dying of toxic gas inhalation.

S'sank knew the pictures were of the bow shield reactor from the *Godzilla*. The yellow colored coolant access panel didn't match the blue housing. He recalled replacing the unit with spare parts from engineering stores. All their parts were yellow.

Late in the evening after all the questions. In the quiet of night, S'sank's mind drifted to the inevitable... *a sublime fear of these humans. If they could take any piece of a ship from a distance, there would be no stopping them. He wondered if the Ancients could even stop them. He had his doubts.*

♦ ♦ ♦

Research Base Australis, Western Australia

Once the *Grace* had completed her testing, they jumped back to the Australis Research cavern.

"That went perfectly, Jen. I was half expecting another alien invasion since we were testing the ship," John said goofing.

Jen's smile disappeared, John belatedly realized once again he had made a gaffe with Jen.

At least Jen had settled into a research routine with Peter over the anti-gravity fields. She looked tired and withdrawn.

John looked into Jen's eyes squeezing her shoulder reassuringly. Despite John's display of concern, she was still distant.

John worried that Jen would never get past the lizard battle. It seemed wistful thinking they would ever return to the earlier carefree days, where the worst they faced was Eric's torturous hand-to-hand combat training.

◆ ◆ ◆

Bill Withers, the security specialist, was a forgettable man so typical of a secret agent. His dry nondescript appearance belied a quiet confidence born from years of experience blending into a crowd. John stuck his hand out to a soft, clammy palm designed to distract a person from eyeballing his face.

"I'm looking for someone experienced in security and intelligence gathering," John said by way of introduction. "You come highly recommended by Eric Manders." It was clear that Bill saw John's uncertainty.

"John, I took the liberty of checking over your operations in El Paso and Australia, and I was impressed that you had acquired so much alien technology."

John was dumbstruck. He knew that Eric would not divulge that sort of information. Then he quietly reminded himself that Eric was one of the best in his field, and he recommended Bill as the best in intelligence. He shouldn't have been surprised, and started to chastise himself.

Bill just laughed, knowing exactly what John was thinking.

"I guess that takes care of the interview," John said. "Welcome aboard."

From their brief chat, John set in motion the transfer of the bulk of staff and technology to the Australian research base and Max's space station. In his eyes, their remoteness was their best defense.

John conceded they needed to work hard to increase the security of their bases and the ships. John hadn't really thought about the arrangements much before the alien attack. It wasn't that he didn't trust the government or his people, exactly, but Bill pointed out that the government already knew the El Paso base intimately from their interrogations of the lizard and constant satellite observation, and more personally from the army living and working on the base.

John was mortified that he had not set up lasers and scanning technology which would have prevented, or at the very least, slowed the aliens down in their kidnapping of his friends and colleagues from the base. John vowed that laser cannons with auto tracking would be installed at all T.N. bases.

The aliens won't find it so easy next time they try.

As a last-minute extra precaution, he got Jen to pre-program a jump to the Australian Research base to be applied to all jump ships that were operational. If the Captain of the ship didn't acknowledge the security protocols every few hours when the ship was operational, the ships would return to a warm reception at the Australian base using the Bravo Jump drive, like homing pigeons.

Elvis and Max walked into John's office carrying a star chart interrupting John and Eric's progress meeting. John could see straight off Elvis had been working on the rescue plan. Ever since the lizard incursion, Elvis has been spearheading the rescue efforts with John's oversight. Their first priority was to get Intel, on the possible location of their people and the lizards that took them.

"I'm telling you that lizard, S'sank, knows more than he's saying," Elvis said.

John looked at Eric sitting opposite him for confirmation.

"He's a minor techie that has no clue about navigation." Elvis gave Eric a dirty look.

Eric continued, "If you sat in the back of a bus with your head down looking at the engine all day, would you know how to get from Sydney to Darwin? In case you're wondering, it's two and a half thousand miles." Since they had all spent only a brief time in Australia, Eric knew that they had no idea how to get to Darwin by road.

John felt conflicted. He agreed with Eric but desperately wanted to extract the information from S'sank. "Fine, ease up on him a little Elvis." John knew that Elvis visited the lizard a lot.

Elvis gave John a stabbing look.

"Max, based on S'sank's description of their colony's star system, can we narrow it down?"

Max was reluctant to get into the middle of the unspoken battlefield. "Well, we are slowly getting there, but translating astronomical terms is a slow process. Our definition of visible light color is different, so all of our measures are different."

"Ok, well keep at it. How are we going with the pocket satellite sensors?"

"We've contracted an Indian firm to make them. The first few should be arriving in the next week. I've started a short list of star systems to search. We'll jump to the system, drop off a couple of the satellites to start scanning while we move to the next one on the list."

John was nodding with each point. "When we return for the scan data, don't jump back but tele-grab the probe to Barnard star. Just in case it's booby-trapped."

Max smiled at John's precautions, he could almost do it all from his operations center.

John turned towards Eric.

"I've got the men practicing boarding actions and SAR (search and rescue) operations. I have two squads fitted out with space suits. It's early days yet. Assuming we find them on the lizard ship...?"

"Elvis, can you help with the space based training? They'll be next to useless in zero G if they don't get some space-time."

Elvis stared at John, wondering if it was a distraction tactic, but then saw the truth in it. He let out a breath. "Sure." At least he'll be doing something.

♦♦♦

Abigale and John sat in the admin building eating a snack.

"John, some of the locals have been running regular support meetings for the friends and family of the taken. A few base personnel have been attending."

"Have they broken their non-disclosure agreements?"

"No, but there's a feeling of hope that is not entirely unfounded."

"We are doing all we can for now."

"I know, it's just sometimes so hard not to say anything."

"You have been attending these meetings?"

Abigale turned red.

John softened.

"Would you speak to the locals?" she asked.

John sighed. "I... wouldn't know what to say."

"Just what you tell yourself every day... you promise you will do everything in your power to get them back."

John opened his mouth to retort, but what she said was the truth of it.

"When is your next meeting?"

Chapter Forty-Three

The Pirate Ship *Kator*

Commander Kane of the pirate ship *Kator* rubbed his elongated head with a wet cloth stuck to his tentacle. They had spent literally cycles searching for the container thieves. The boredom of it forced him to dally in Delar's succulent tentacles more than once since leaving their hideout. The crew naturally spewed ink all over at the lack of female companionship on the vessel. Only three females were currently aboard, of which he had had to confine two of them to their quarters when they were off duty. It was an anti-mutiny tactic to limit the amount of damage the competing suitors and their berserker ink spurts caused when vying for female attention.

The sensor operator broke the Commander's latest train of thought with a snort and a whistle, advising they were slipping out of subspace. The Alcubierre drive (A-Drive) powered down as the vessel sped to the boundaries of the Sol system using sub-light engines. The helm had little trouble navigating through the Oort Cloud.

The sensor operator puffed up and expelled red warning ink in alarm at the amount of EM traffic he had been picking up.

"What's all the chatter?" Kane asked.

"Commander, from video chatter it appears to be a mammal system with extreme EM clutter."

"Are they trying to jam us?"

"No, Commander, I believe they're just a lot of insistent communications. Their bandwidth is quite low."

"How many ships are in the system?"

"There doesn't appear to be any."

"Check your system is working correctly," said Kane with a squirt of irritation.

"It is confirmed, there are no ships in the system. There is significant debris and some comm satellites surrounding the third planet and a larger one which could be as big as a station near a moon of the sixth planet, the one with the rings."

"We will continue on for the moment, continue to gather more information ... this," Kane said shaking his head, "doesn't make sense."

The Pirate Commander squeezed back into his command chair after standing behind the sensor officer. He just didn't know what to make of this system.

Space Command, Peterson Air Force Base

The USSTRATCOM war room duty officer called Dan.

"Sir, we have a new contact on the edge of the system. This bogey is larger than the ones we've seen at Titan but smaller than the lizard warship."

When Dan arrived and stared at the screen, a worried look transformed his face. "Get Admiral Tucker on the line."

♦♦♦

Research Base Australis, Western Australia

John wondered if Jen would ever let the issue drop and forgive him for his single-mindedness to grab the alien technology. He knew slaving her console and locking her out in mid-battle was drastic, but he had no choice, she was paralyzed with fear. Jen had barely said two words to him about the incident, sending him looks of nothing but frozen eyes laced with betrayal. Now, as time drew on, he had never felt so alone. She had been an important confidant. John's eyes cast down, trying to make sense of everything that had happened.

He switched his thoughts to his longtime friend, Elvis who was still emotionally gutted from the attack, and subsequent kidnapping of Mel. They'd all started this adventure together, and now this dysfunctional relationship could be the very end of it. He felt helpless that Jen and Elvis were disintegrating before his eyes.

He knew it wasn't exactly a loss of confidence in his leadership, but a lack of mateship, buddies having each other's back. John corrected himself, *him not having their backs*. After all, Jen was the sensible one, and Elvis saved their asses'.

Then as if on cue, a message from Max's Station reported an alien contact entering the Sol system. The same configuration as that of their first encounters with the octopus looking people at the freighter. Jen looked at John with a sad 'not again' look.

"I need you on this one Jen. What if they take more people? We can't just let them do that." John tilted his head in emphasis. He could see the conflict warring behind her hazel eyes. He then put his hand on her shoulder. She scrunched her face up and with her eyes closed, took a deep breath. Eventually, she opened them with sad resignation and nodded almost imperceptibly.

"Let's get this done," John said with an encouraging smile. It was all he could muster. John wondered how he could do this to Jen, how could he ask this of her? The sad look on her face ripped at his insides, tearing at his soul. It was as if the words just popped out, it was beyond his control to stop them. But even then, he didn't dare take them back. He felt sick and disgusted with himself, and his single-mindedness.

The Oval Office

"Another ship? We seem to be the tourist capital of the galaxy of late. Is it a class of vessel like the other ships we've previously encountered?"

"No Mr. President, it's an entirely new configuration sized between the last two combatants," Dan said.

"Does anyone else here feel like we're the hapless grand prize of some sort of gladiatorial space match?" The grim faces of the Joint Chiefs stared back at him.

♦♦♦

Jen, Max, and Peter exited out of the lift and into the large cavernous hanger to find John in a heated discussion with Eric. Ten of his soldiers were standing surrounding them loosely. Each had a suit on that looked like it was made with A-Bitumen plates. Their suits had a dull gray sheen with an emblem on the left breast. The soldiers held clear plastic bubble helmets and wore an unusual weapon slung over their other shoulder. Stun grenades, knives, and other equipment adorned each of the men like a comfy warm jumper.

Eric was negotiating with John, "This is an excellent opportunity to practice the skills that we've been training for these past months. We have our new stun weapons." The new weapons use a micro amount of the high energy batteries put it into a rubber shell with a metallic rubber tip making the 'Bullet Tasers'." Eric showed John his gun. A broad smile meandered across his face. He could see it was a simple design, yet would yield powerful results. It would change the course of tactics used by many policemen and military. The slick design had two barrels, one for the larger shells and another for a smaller .22 caliber semi-automatic. He was pleased with the non-lethal inclusion on the weapon when he saw all the men had it slung over their shoulder. It would give Eric options.

"I can't guarantee where you will materialize in that vessel. You may end up in the reactor core," said John.

"I believe if you target the hanger bay, we will have a much better chance."

John stared at the determined faces surrounding him. It was true they had been training hard these months. The A-Bitumen plated suits were hardened with layers of Kevlar between more layers of A-Bitumen. The plates had then been pressed hard to reduce their bulk.

Jen was shocked to hear John say, "Have you all made out your wills?"

Each of the men nodded in turn. It was a way that John could acknowledge the sacrifice these men may be asked to make. John was glad when the company of soldiers was being hired, John and his growing military contingent had decided on a more formal military structure and gave Eric the rank of Captain. The men understood the military rituals and the framework of sacrifice that came with the profession. He then turned to Eric, "Captain, if you load your men in two hours, we will get underway shortly after that." Eric saluted smartly and ordered his men to prepare to board the *Grace* in two hours.

"What's going on?" asked Jen.

"Eric wants to board the alien vessel." Jen opened her mouth to object, but John held his hand in the air and said, "I'm sorry Jen, the decision has been made."

Jen immediately bit her lip at the thought of having to transport those men unprotected into an alien ship.

John saw Jen's trepidation. "Jen, there's a high probability that we won't even get the chance because the alien's shields need to be down to make the transport."

Jen didn't look too reassured.

◆◆◆

"Is it ready?" John asked of Elvis when he caught up with him.

"Yes, all the controls are linked in." John walked around the new space tanker class ship, *HeavyLifter*. The tanker was to be their next addition to the King space station merchant services. Ryan had put it together, it was little more than a large gas tank with an engine and maneuvering thrusters. Within its belly was a large airtight container with half a dozen live kangaroos.

The Australian government had recently released control measures to start culling kangaroos. In some areas of the outback they were considered a pest, their overpopulation was having a devastating impact on the environment.

John was just as surprised as Elvis when they were notified of the culling efforts by the Australian Northern Territory government. The large property they'd purchased, was only one of the areas that were required to cull some of the kangaroo population. The kangaroos would be used as live bait.

The tanker was larger in size than the *Scotty*. The exterior of the tank was coated in A-Bitumen to give it strength. *HeavyLifter* was a remote controlled drone ship.

"The heater and cameras?"

"Yes, they're all fitted, we have a 360 view in all planes," Elvis replied.

John didn't want the kangaroos to needlessly suffer in the cold of space. As a final touch, large barrels of water and oil, and several bins of old electrical components were placed at the rear of the ship.

"This tanker is almost better than the Scotty," Elvis said joking, "All it needs is the jump drive."

John smiled at his friend.

"Okay let's transport it to Makemake," John said. Makemake was one of the dwarf planets of similar size to

Pluto in the Kuiper Belt. "The aliens should pick it up on their scopes, once we start transmitting."

"What do you want to transmit from the tanker?" Elvis asked.

" 'Who are you, and what are your intentions?' We should send the transmission as a direct beam of the ship so Earth doesn't pick it up. We don't want to cause a panic."

"Three, two, one... mark." The freighter winked out of existence from the cavern below the Australis base to materialize in orbit around Makemake asteroid in the Kuiper belt, out past Pluto.

The two men made their way to the communications room.

"Remote control activation codes for the tanker are being sent. Confirming remote control with the *Heavylifter*."

"Ok, let's move *HeavyLifter* towards the alien vessel and start transmitting the welcome message."

The two watched as the ships were drawn to each other like moths to light.

"I better check the base is secure with the new laser cannons," John said and left Elvis to maneuver the freighter through the Kuiper Belt, while he sought out Eric to ensure that their laser cannons in the towers at the two Research Bases were prepped and ready. They had kept them in standby mode to ensure no accidental shootings.

◆◆◆

Pirate Ship *Kator*, Sol System

The *Kator* comms officer turned to Commander Kane and whistled. "Commander, I have a vessel on comms sending a direct beam communication. The language is unknown."

Kane looked at his Sensor Officer, "Where did that ship come form?"

The officer looked back dumbfounded. His scans were clear a moment ago. His eyestalks stood straight as antennas.

"They're not sending in any of the basic trades?" the Commander asked.

"No. It isn't one of the seven trade languages," replied the Comm.

"Excellent. Then the ship falls outside of the merchant space code. They're free game, they're not protected by the Patron Trade Accord," the Commander summarized.

The mood of the bridge dramatically shifted from mild apprehension to buoyant optimism. They could legally take the vessel as a prize.

"Battle stations, helm flank speed. Charge main laser battery, Kazorr, try not to destroy it this time." The Commander squirted a fine jet of ink which splattered on the back of Kazorr's head. Even though it was annoying, Kazorr grinned with the prospect of a new prize.

The pirate ship *Kator* zeroed in on the defenseless human tanker ship the *Heavylifter*.

◆◆◆

Elvis sat watching the sensor readings from the freighter, "John, the alien ship is charging their weapons."

John stopped outside *Grace's* hanger listening to his earpiece. "They didn't respond to our hails?"

"No," Elvis shook his head unconsciously.

"Turn the *Heavylifter* around, get it out of there."

It was always a possibility that the aliens would not respond to their hails. It didn't invalidate their plan, but it made it more difficult. The human tanker ship was small compared to the *Kator*. The two ships flew through the asteroid belt, dodging in and around the spinning ice and rock asteroids.

♦♦♦

Aboard the pirate ship, Kane asked the Sensor Officer, "Are you scanning that ship?"

"Yes, there's very little EM signature, much like the one we encountered at the Lizard freighter." It was small compared to any other spacecraft they've encountered. The human freighter was running off batteries that were charged before leaving Earth. Unlike other spaceships, it did not have a reactor or major power source to recharge the batteries or power the craft.

"We need to get that ship." The Commander was under no illusion that the power source had no discernible EM. It would be invaluable to a pirate allowing them to sneak up on their prey. "Are there bio-signs?"

"Yes, they're some sort of weird mammal. They're like a mammal version of the lizards with a tail." The scanning officer had scanned the kangaroos.

The two ships continued their frantic race through the asteroid field to Orcus, another dwarf planet in the Kuiper Belt. Weaving around and over its surface hugging the rugged lifeless terrain.

"Fire a warning shot," Kane ordered.

Kazorr sucked the main gun battery fire control.

When the weapon discharged the freighter plowed headlong into the Orcus's cratered surface. Kazorr sat dead still with his mouth agape. His eye stalks sprung to attention making his eyeballs bulge out of their sockets with fear.

"Kazorr you idiot! You've destroyed the freighter," Kane yelled.

♦♦♦

Elvis sat there stunned. All the preparatory work they had made blew up in a brilliant ball of plasma. The aliens were supposed to capture and board the *Heavylifter* after a little desperate attempted fake escape ... by the kangaroos. The freighter would sense when the alien craft dropped their shields and message the *Grace*. With nothing left of the freighter, the aliens won't drop their shields ... *unless.*

Thinking quickly while he raced to the pre-flight ward room where he grabbed the rest of his crew for the *Scotty*. Gritting his jaw tight he said, "We need to jump quickly out to Orcus."

He then filled them in on the destruction of the *Heavylifter*. Would the alien ship stop and investigate the remains of the *Heavylifter*? They had to get out there to spot when aliens lowered their shields long enough for a shuttle to exit their ship. Time was of the essence. Elvis said they still had time to complete the first part of their plan to get them to lower their shields, and message *Grace*.

Elvis stopped in his tracks. *It was unlikely there was anything left of the Heavylifter. It had no armor at all. It didn't stand a chance running... But if the Scotty didn't run?* ... He had another plan.

The cavern was a hive of activity for the next hour as the two human ships prepared for the upcoming battle. Elvis cursed himself for not spending the time to cover the *Scotty* with extra layers of A-Bitumen. He told Carmen to grab any loose old outdated electronics and dump it inside the back hatch just in case. He sprinted to his lab, grabbing all the old and outdated computer parts as well as his trusty beanbag. He then ran to the kitchen and into the cold storage to pull out two large legs of lamb, much to the kitchen staff's surprise. Hurrying back to the *Scotty* breathing heavily, just in time to see Carmen dumping a whole lot of her old unwanted things onto the *Scotty's* back deck.

When they had all finished the prep work, and the crew was walking up the ramp about to enter the *Scotty*. Elvis stood at the entrance, barring their way.

"No. You guys stay here," Elvis said to his crew.

Carmen and Mike looked at Elvis with trepidation. Over the weeks they had seen a man crumble: his skin slowly turned sallow, his eyes hollow from sleepless nights, and worry lines crisscrossed his face. But now, with an actionable purpose, Elvis' complexion cleared, as if a tremendous weight had been lifted. The *Scotty* will become the bait alien's instead of the *Heavylifter*.

Mike and Carmen looked at each other with the only question that mattered. Turning to Elvis, "You can't do this on your own," Carmen said in a whisper to Elvis who stood frozen scrutinizing the two for an agonizing few seconds before relented.

"I thought *I* was crazy, but you two…" Elvis said as he shook his head. "Come on, get on board before I change my mind."

◆◆◆

John and Jen made their way through the *Grace* to the bridge passing ten steely-eyed armored soldiers. Peter and Max were already seated, both of them breathless ignoring Eric's jibes about their fitness.

"Grab a seat and buckle in Eric," John said over the comm, "we will begin transiting in a few minutes after we get word from the *Scotty*."

Eric looked over the cavern and spoke out with concern lacing his voice, "I'm not sure that sending the *Scotty* to meet with this spaceship on its own is a good idea. I thought they could transport from any distance?"

"That's true on both counts Eric. The *Scotty* shouldn't be anywhere near the alien spacecraft. It's a forward spotter, the *Heavylifter* is the bait which we'll hopefully use to get the ship to lower their shields."

John had no inkling that the *Heavylifter* had been destroyed an hour before.

"We need the *Scotty* close enough so we can accurately target the shield generator in order to tele-grab it, then transport the boarding party from the *Grace* and Australis Base into the alien ship shuttle bay. We will then jump the

Grace near to keep the ship busy while you give them a 'Hello and welcome to Earth'.

"If they don't take the *Heavylifter* bait or can't get them to lower their shields then we'll jump the *Grace* into battle and drive them off the hard way. If we can, we will transport you aboard mid-battle.

"Max, can you open a comm to the *Scotty*."

♦♦♦

Once again Elvis had his crew working frantically aboard the *Scotty* in used Russian spacesuits.

"Elvis, how are you set?"

"We'll be ready in five John, just setting up the Uber jump drive so we are prepared for an instant change over."

One of the changes to the *Scotty* that Elvis had insisted on, was a second power source so that the backup jump drive could be used immediately in case they ever got into trouble, effectively giving them a double jump if that was ever needed.

Elvis scanned his command console on the *Scotty's* bridge while the crew plugged their suits into the ship's air. The *Scotty* blinked out of existence from the cavern making that hallmark thunderous crack as it did, to materialize within visual range of the *Kator* pirate ship. Decompression ravaged the insides of the silo spaceship, buffeting the crew as they sat strapped into their racing car bucket seats. This time, the loose items that Elvis and the crew had left on the back deck exploded out of the hatch which was left open. The *Scotty* seemed to burst, spewing atmosphere and flotsam.

"Passive sensors only," Elvis ordered.

All the electronics within *Scotty* powered down except the minuscule amount through the sensor array.

♦ ♦ ♦

"Elvis, what have you done," John cried out as he saw the latest scans, it showed the *Scotty* had jumped right near the alien ship. Both Max and Jen were similarly stunned.

John commed the *Scotty*, "Elvis, what the hell are you doing? Was there a malfunction?" John demanded. Without waiting for a response, "We're on our way!" John turned and yelled down *Grace's* cabin, "Eric, we have to go now! ... Jump in three, two, one.."

"John, wait!" Elvis commed.

John held his hand above the jump button.

"John, the *Heavylifter* was destroyed, we are the bait now," Elvis said, "It'll still work. We'll just be a little closer than we were expecting."

"But, there's no guarantee they won't destroy you too!" John said, concern lacing his voice.

"They haven't yet," Elvis responded.

"Don't do anything, as soon as you charge the jump drive, they'll sense it and raise their shields or worse," John said.

John could hear an audible gulp through the comm, he didn't know who from.

"But we need this Alien-Tech," Elvis said.

John thought quickly then spoke to Jen and Max, "Can you guys connect into the base's transporters and remote the base's teleporters from here on *Grace's* bridge?"

The two looked at each other then chorused back, "Yes."

Turning his comm back on, John said, "Send us the coordinates of the shield generator when they lower their shields, and we'll tele-grab their generator from the base's transporter. We'll then jump between you and the alien ship before you scat back here."

Jen bit her lip. *First John, now Elvis, all the men are flipping crazy around here,* she thought.

319

◆◆◆

The stunned look on the *Kator's* Sensor Officer's face was mirrored by Commander Kane. The second the *Scotty* appeared proximity alarms rang out throughout the ship.

"What the barnacles?!" Kane yelled while pointing at the appearance of *Scotty,* "Where did that come from?!"

"Commander, ... that's the ship! It's the one we've been looking for!"

"It looks like it's in trouble," spoke up one of the bridge crew.

Kane wasn't convinced. He had been around the quadrant more than once.

"Scan that ship," Kane order.

"Commander the ship is dead, there is no shield, no engines online, and there is no atmosphere on that ship."

"Scan for biomass," He retorted, still not taking any chances.

"Commander, there is some biomass within the vessel. However, there are two more dead outside the ship in the flotsam." The sensor officer had scanned the two legs of lamb that Elvis had included on the back deck of the *Scotty.*

Kane started snorting, spraying yellow ink everywhere. "What luck we have. Drakmok, get out there and salvage the ship!" Kane yelled.

Drakmok raced to the hanger bay as fast as his rubbery legs could carry him. Yelling out to Tela, that he needed her to pilot the shuttle once he had jumped across to the small vessel.

It took Drakmok only a minute to suit up and make his way to the edge of the hanger bay. A thin shimmering curtain of energy held the air safely within the hanger. Kane ordered the ship turned so the hanger bay was facing the *Scotty.*

"Please lower the ships' shields Commander, I am ready," Drakmok commed. He then took a flying leap from the hanger, jumping through the air curtain into space towards the *Scotty*.

Using his jetpack, the octopus set a course with his thrusters to intercept the struggling human ship.

♦♦♦

"Have they lowered their force field yet?" Elvis asked nervously.

"Just now, when that person in the jet pack flew out of what looks like a hanger bay," Mike replied.

"Carmen are you ready with the alien's shield generator coordinates," she looked up smiling with the thumbs up signal.

Elvis punched the transmit button that flicked up flags on John's comm console! At the same time, it sent the targeting coordinates of the shield generator and alien's hanger bay directly to Jen's console in the *Grace*.

♦♦♦

The *Kator* sensor operator changed to a crimson color and spoke out, "Commander, there is an energy buildup in the dead ship." The sensor had picked up the energy for the *Scotty's* tachyon comm signal transmission.

"What! Raise shields," Kane yelled.

"But, Drakmok..." the sensor operator countered.

"I said now!" Kane screamed squirting a potent emphatic.

Suddenly, the bow of the *Kator* imploded with a flash of light. The ship was jostled several meters tossing its crew like candy in a jar. Ship-wide alarms set off blaring warning clangs of decompression.

Chapter Forty-Four

Space in Sol System near the Scotty

"Jump in three, two, one, mark!" Jen pressed the jump button transporting the *Grace* from the cavern and materializing her between the Scotty and the pirate ship. John signaled Jen to execute the next phase of their operation. A flash and crack echoed through the rear compartment of the *Grace* transporting Eric and his platoon into the hanger bay of the pirate ship.

Jen hadn't anticipated the shocking movement of the alien ship from the explosive decompression brought on by the transport of the forward shield section. The elongated bubble of the target transport flashed into existence placing two of the soldiers in the Shuttle Bay Control rather than on the hanger deck.

Tela was suddenly knocked off her feet as she collided into a bubble of force when she entered the control room. The traffic controller sat stunned as the two soldiers materialized and pointed their guns to fire in one smooth motion. Electrically charged bullets shot out of their weapons striking each of the Squishys, stunning them. Both the Octopi melted to the floor spraying ink over the soldiers as they did, "Aaaarrgh, just my luck to get slimed."

The other soldiers chuckled over the Comm while they ran to the next door, each covering their squaddie.

Eric radioed back to the *Grace* after checking green life signs from all of his men on the heads-up display inside his helmet.

"Alpha-1 Actual to *Grace*, transit successful, I repeat transit successful, Alpha-1 Actual out."

The rest of the team ran to the hanger door with smiles on their faces, which were soon framed with determination as they moved stealthily through into the unknown.

Eric pointed to the other exit, "Johnson, take five men, move aft and secure the engineering area. Remember stun, unless you have no other option. We want to keep the ship intact as much is possible." Turning his attention to the other men, "Maz, check the shuttles then hold the hanger bay clear with Roberts, we may need it. Roberts, see what you can do about interfacing with their computers in the control room. The rest of you are with me."

Eric and his team cycled forward covering each other as they went. Their quick, stealthy movements the hallmark of any elite human force. The hanger bay was located not far from engineering. Eric and his team would need to head in the opposite direction and pass through most of the ship to get to the bridge. He hoped that John would be able to create enough of a diversion for him to get a good foothold.

"Shields up!" Jen activated the shields at full power because they didn't know how powerful the pirate ship guns were. The familiar green haze enveloped the *Grace* almost entirely hiding the *Scotty* behind her bulk.

"Max, get me the *Scotty*," John said in a gruff commanding manner.

"Elvis, where's the *Heavylifter*?"

"It was destroyed near the surface of Orca."

"You need to get the *Scotty* out of here now! We'll cover your retreat," John said.

"No, you need to create the diversion so we can take the ship. That's what we planned," Elvis snorted wondering why they were having this discussion.

"Your lives are more important. Eric can hold for a little while."

Jen turned and faced John with a concerned frown. The tips of her mouth threatening to smile.

While Kane struggled back into his chair from being knocked by the blast, he looked up at the main viewer and was startled to find an entirely different ship where the *Scotty* was.

"Raise shields!!" He yelled.

The shields operator sat dumbfounded because half his console was dark. He was reluctant to say anything because he knew the Commander's wrath.

Finally, without a choice, murmured, "The shield console is dead."

Kane turned and stared at the shield operator before he yelled, "Damage report!!" Then in the very next breath, "Where did that yellow ship come from!! Where is the other ship?"

Elvis was wild. Tapping his comm furiously hoping to reconnect to the *Grace*.

"*Grace*? John, we're in trouble! All the jump drives have stopped working!" Elvis' crew were working frantically to try and fix the problem, but nothing seemed to make a difference, the drives were dead. They were sitting ducks out there without shields or armor. Elvis pushed the thrusters too full. The *Scotty* turned away from the pirate warship all the while they kept the *Grace* between them.

Carmen opened up cursing with a plethora of Spanish-Mexican swear words while she pulled off the external casing of the home drive.

Elvis held his breath while the electric engines pushed the *Scotty* forward. Despite all that was going on, Elvis had a brief mental spasm remembering his shock when Spanish curses poured out of the comm from Max's automated space controller program. Max's station computer would swear in Spanish at spaceships just like Carmen.

The *Scotty* sped away from the battle.

◆◆◆

The *Kator* sensor operator spoke in soft tones, "It's still there, but behind the ship that looks like a transport container."

"Charge weapons... Where are my shields?"

"We're getting reports from the bow shield station, there's been massive decompression around the shield generators."

"Tactical, target that ship with the main guns and fire! Helm, get us out of here. We won't last long in a fight without shields."

The weapons reactor zipped into overdrive releasing enormous amounts of energy through the main guns. A thick beam shot out from the pirate ship directly at the *Grace*, electrifying her green shield turning it almost white. The energy discharge generated at this close range crackled, sparking smaller discharges. The *Grace* lit up like a Christmas tree, while the rest of the energy speared off into space narrowly missing the *Scotty*.

The pirate ship shunted energy into its large engines to move its vast bulk. Drakmok's tumble-turned himself to face his own ship, his face tinged with orange in surprise as he saw air bleeding from the bow. Blue flares of light blazed out the back of the *Kator*. It could mean only one thing. The engines were firing up. Drakmok frantically flailed his limbs at his ship to no avail. He knew the Commander. Fear crossed his face at the realization that there was no way he could return in time. His usually pale skin turned a dark crimson. Judging the distances, his only option was to continue onward to reach the dead ship, which also seemed to be firing up its engines. Desperation wracked him, tightening his tentacles. Gripping hard on the rocket boosters of his jet pack, he strangled the EVA thrusters up to maximum. Anxiously he shrunk his body form, the malleable lower forelimbs curled into a shock absorber as he slammed painfully into the side of the *Scotty*.

Rebounding off the hull from the silent space thump, Drakmok struggled, he stretched clasping for any tentacle-sucker purchase on the hard surface. The small ship began to pull away. Still dazed, he reached out once more for a metal spar as it slid by only to have his limb chopped cleanly off by the thin metal wiring that cut like a knife through butter. Wincing he reached out once again, this time grabbing the sill of a window portal. Air and blood spewed out of his severed limb until the suit's auto-sealer kicked in.

Drakmok scrambled to grab his discombobulated limb spinning away while the *Scotty*'s electric engines thrust out the back of the silo in an incandescent blue. The pressure on his limbs increased with the thrust as he struggled to maintain his grip. Straining to pull himself inside the portal with only his two forelimbs, his EVA jet canisters bashed against the sill too large to fit through the opening. He reached down fumbling desperately to release the buckle. Glimpsing sideways he saw the jetpack tumbled off into space. He cursed silently at the loss of the EVA's oxygen supply. Pulling his focus back he concentrated on gripping with all his remaining strength to slide into the portal. Drakmok had had close calls in the past, but this was different.

His ship had left him behind. They had abandoned him!

He was lucky that his suit morphed with his body to quickly close and seal the tear caused by the spar. Painkillers automatically pumped into his system disgorging relief and giving a small amount of ecstasy. Losing a limb or two in a salvage operation was not unusual for Drakmok. He had been through this many times before, even on an alien ship;

however, this was different, it was the first time he felt terribly and utterly alone.

♦♦♦

Aboard the Squishy vessel on their way to the engine room, Johnson with his fire team, struggled to make headway down the dimly lit corridor. Colored suckers on the decks and bulkheads grabbed at their armor and boots to stick fast like velcro that would only release after a concerted strain. The gooey floor squelched when their boots landed on the mushroom shaped steps. They could feel the vibration of the engines firing, knowing that time was running out. The weight of each step seemed to increase as they arrived at what looked like an elevator.

In the opposite direction, Eric could only wonder why the Squishys were changing the gravity levels. Staring through heavy night vision goggles, he saw his men silently moved forward. His plan was to quickly push to take the bridge, then come back and clean up any enemy stragglers. He had pressed John into this, and now he wanted more than anything to prove the men's training and skill were up to the task.

Squishys started to appear in the doorways and within the side rooms, only to be quickly dispatched using the electro-bullets. Those first few fell without much more sound than the background buzz of the engines under thrust. Then surprisingly the lights flashed, strobing on and off in all colors, making it tough to see.

Ink spurted out of the walls and floor like fire sprinklers in a burning office. The once pristine body armor the team wore, turned slick with the ink sprayed through the life support of the ship. The soldiers, for the most part, ignored the psychedelic colored mist, until a high-pitched staccato squeal reverberated off the walls to bash through their helmets.

♦♦♦

All this time while listening to the radio chatter, Elvis turned his ship around and trailed the two ships on their way out of the system. He didn't want to be left too far behind if he needed a jump because the drive still didn't work. In the end, Carmen resolved the issue by kicking the Uber drive in the guts while swearing in three languages. Suddenly, all the lights came on. None of them could explain it. However, the first order of business was to jump back to Earth.

In the time it took the crew to buckle in, it took almost as long to get back on Earth from the Kuiper Belt near Orcus. The ship flashed and materialized inside the larger hanger bay of the Australis Base. Elvis resolved there and then that he wasn't taking the ship out until it had been thoroughly overhauled, and updated with real windows and armor surrounded by bucket-loads of shielding. He also wanted a laser, the biggest one he could find.

♦♦♦

"We've been boarded!" said the squishy at the sensor console. "Internal bio scans indicate mammals are moving through the ship. Three groups; two in the hanger standing still, one group of five near engineering and the last group in corridor 4 deck 3. I think the last group is coming here!"

Kane had trouble hearing the sensor officer over the loud clang of alarm systems on the bridge.

"Turn that awful sound off, it's hurting my inner drums! Open the ship-wide comm."

Kane took a moment to compose himself, "You worthless Squishys, you had better harden your bladders and camouflage your bods, we have intruders claiming our ship as theirs. Squeeze the life out of these mammals so we can return to our calm seas and not end as crunchy soup."

Johnson and his squad rushed out of the lift into an empty room. Pushing forward, the walls suddenly changed color and morphed into Squishys with razor sharp beaks. Many swarmed forward slashing down at the men's arms and legs, the Squishys took the fight to the humans. Johnson reacted without thinking, raising his weapon to deflect the spear-like serrated beak aimed at his heart.

Banjo wasn't so lucky, a toughened pincer skewered him through his armor plating. The sharp tip found the neck joint of his suit and ripped it and him with it. The two men beside him were able to deflect their attackers narrowly missing the pincer beaks. Ducking sideways, Johnson butted the next Squishy with his gun, knocking the attack wide.

"They're coming off the walls and ceiling," he yelled in warning.

Johnson depressed his finger on the auto-fire trigger of his semi-automatic. A barrage of .22 caliber bullets ripped into the Squishys, knocking them down from the walls and ceiling. The yellow-banded leader ran forward striking Davis backward, then grappling with him. Tentacles slapped his arms wide, as Davis fought to retain his weapon. The scuffle allowed the Squishy time to blind him by wrapping its tentacles around his helmet and body armor. Johnson kicked another in front of him, then using his gun as a bat, hit the head of the yellow leader that was squeezing the life out of Davis. The blow forced the Squishy to release its steely grip. Davis staggered back with deep teeth marks scraped along his visor and armor. The yellow leader rolled into a ball and spun across the deck to drop like a pinball down into a hole. There was no way a cat could fit down there let alone a human. On seeing their leader leave, the rest of the Squishys melted down the walls to roll across the floor into the very same hole.

Johnson inspected his remaining squad and commed Eric, "Bravo Squad to Alpha Actual. We have contact with Squishys! One man down, two with minor injuries. The primary form of attack was deadly strangles, beak pecks and teeth bites. Be warned; excellent camouflage, enemy drops from walls and ceiling! Continuing to objective, Bravo out."

"Bravo squad, Alpha Actual. Confirmed. Alpha out." Pecking, biting and strangling, Eric warned his squad. "And watch the walls and ceilings."

♦♦♦

Kane sat on the bridge watching the *Kator* struggle along without her shields. They needed to get out of the gravity well quickly so they could see to the shield repairs and activate their FTL Drive. The sensor operator yelled, "The small container vessel is pursuing us."

Kane thought suspiciously, *why board us rather than attack us? They had to at least kill the shields to get the troops aboard.*

Shaking his head, Kane spoke to the bridge, "Tactical, target that vessel and try to destroy it this time."

The *Grace* took off in pursuit of the pirate ship spiraling as they did to avoid being targeted by its prey whilst covering the *Scotty*. Despite *Scotty* leaving the immediate area, they were still in range of the *Kator's* guns.

"Target and fire one rack of HR missiles," Kane said sure that that should be more than enough.

♦♦♦

John was waiting for something like missiles or torpedoes.

"Jen, point defense!" he yelled as he saw missiles inbound.

330

Just as quickly, Jen activated the targeting and acquisition computers to direct the laser fire at the oncoming missiles.

In a split second, *Grace's* point defense had the quantum computer calculate the trajectories of all the inbound missiles. Target locks were passed onto the defense laser with beam intensity and duration settings to ensure their efficient destruction.

◆◆◆

The view screen on the *Kator's* bridge lit up with explosions. The little yellow and black container ship soldiered on through the flashes that hit the shields.

Kane's eye-stalks bobbled and changed color. But still, the *Grace* followed. "Launch anti-point defense missiles and the second full rack of HR missiles," Kane ordered. "These mammals are more stubborn than I thought."

Once again the flashes splashed across his screen, "Will these mammals die already!" The anti-point defense missiles separated into hundreds of false EM signatures for each missile launched. Their purpose was to mask and confuse *Grace's* point defense to allow real missiles to penetrate through.

While the false EM signatures started to disappear from the *Kator's* view screen, the Commander cursed out loud, "These mammals can strangle like a Grand Master Squid... *What! They're still there!*"

◆◆◆

The *Grace's* point defense reactivated, although now thousands of missile EM signatures screamed towards them creating a whirlwind of targets. *Grace's* sensors struggled to keep up with the targeting and dismissed as many false images as possible. *Graces* shields faltered and flared white under the deluge of missiles that got though PD.

Abruptly the ship was rocked aside with the impact strike of the pirate's latest few missiles able to pass the overtaxed point defense, depleting the shields each time.

"Twenty percent shields, we can't take much more of this!" Jen yelled out knowing full well that John could see it on his own console.

John's hand hovered over the break contact signal for Eric. The red button was supposed to be a last-ditch attempt to retrieve the boarding party from the hanger bay in five minutes after button press. John wasn't sure whether they had five minutes to recover them. Even if their shields went, they still might have a little time with the A-Bitumen armor surrounding the *Grace*.

◆◆◆

Eric was hyper-conscious that this was a ship with unknown dangers, and he'd split his forces against military doctrine. Thrice he felt the vibration from the launch of missiles.

They needed to get this done! He thought.

Eric whispered to the Marine on point, "I am not taking any more chances..., Briggs, start using flashbang grenades."

Eric pressed the blue open button while Briggs walked up to the door pulling a flashbang from his chest harness, priming it, and throwing it through the hatch in one smooth motion. A second later, blindingly bright flash and a loud bang detonated from next door. The thumps could be heard as Squishys fell from the ceiling to land on the deck, flailing in agonizing starfish patterns. The men behind Briggs charged in and stunned each of the octopi with bolts of electro-bullets. They quickly moved to the next room blasting with flashbangs and stunning their way to the bridge. The new strategy was working, they picked up speed as they progressed, Eric checked his watch. He hadn't heard back from the *Grace* so continued on as quickly as possible.

Periodically, sprays of what felt like ocean water created a misty, foggy environment. The men's suits of armor were dripping with this salty liquid substance. Eric belatedly tested its makeup on his sleeve environment tester to determine if it was corrosive to their suits. It was very similar to the normal saltwater of the Atlantic Ocean. The tester was a simple dipstick attached to their sleeve. It wasn't brilliant as testers go but it was better than nothing. At least they knew it wasn't strongly acidic to melt their armor.

The boarding party continued on, tasing and flash-banging their way while moving from room to room. At the last door, Eric held up two fingers pointing at Briggs and Sampson, the two men who stood each side of the opening. Both men drew their last grenades from their kit, holding two flashbang grenades each. Eric signaled the countdown with his gloved hand. Briggs snapped the door open with an elbow jab to the control, then all hell broke loose.

The Commander was in the process of ordering more missiles, to be targeted at the un-killable container ship, when the bridge lit up like a neutron star. Four painful flashes blinded him and the crew. Shockwaves from the grenades disorientated him further as he slumped cringing to slide from his pedestal chair onto the deck. His tentacles started to flailed. The stringy tentacles jerked wildly in uncontrolled starfish patterns. Ink spewed in all directions from all the command crew. Eric's team rushed in re-shocking unconscious all of the octopi. The Commander's colors earned him two taser bullets.

All of Eric's team looked at him. He was suddenly dumbfounded. He asked no one in particular, "How do we stop this thing?" Slowly at first, each of the men laughed. They had done it!

◆◆◆

Johnson finally reached what he thought was engineering. It had a big donut shaped cylinder thing that had several large consoles. *Hope this is it. He regretted not paying more attention to the scientist puke Adrian ... when he described what it 'may' look like.* It may have been their entertainment suite for all he knew.

The Squishys had been particularly vicious defending the room, with three yellow banded ones. He set up a perimeter covering all the entrances and exits with particular emphasis on any holes they could see. Reaching for his comm he called it in.

"Bravo team to Alpha Actual. Bravo team has secured engineering. No further casualties."

"Alpha Actual to *Grace*, priority objectives are secure. I say again priority objectives are secure!"

Cheers on *Grace's* bridge broke the serious concentration of its crew. "Acknowledged Alpha Actual, *Grace* out."

Jen let out her breath without realizing she had been holding it, while John moved his hand away from the big red button, placing the fireguard over it. He then slowed the ship to trail the *Kator* out of short range just in case any nasty surprises were still sent towards them.

◆◆◆

"You three men stay here, while we start clearing the Squishys from bow towards the stern.

"Alpha Actual to B-4 Maz, report!"

Startled, Maz pulled up his weapon ready, he was crouched behind a crate with his weapon tracing his view to each of the entrances. The hanger had been quiet, a little too quiet for his liking given the warnings that Bravo team had been issuing. Holding the rear guard alone was making him look at every wall twice and twice again. He was sorely tempted to set off a flashbang just to make sure. Only the thought of the mens' ridicule on being a scaredy-cat prevented him. Being the youngest team member had its drawbacks. "B-4 Maz to Alpha Actual, all clear and secure."

"Alpha Actual to A-4 Roberts, talk to me, have you been able to get into their computer system?" Eric had been doubtful that Specialist Roberts would succeed even that far, it was an entirely alien system in a very real sense.

"A-4 Roberts to Alpha Actual, I'm in, but I have no frigging idea what I'm looking at. This is definitely not lizard language. I could make some wild guesses like..."

"No guesses at this time. We don't want you dumping the reactor core by mistake?" Eric said with a smile because he knew that Roberts was a dedicated sci-fi fan. "Keep searching for ship plans or specs. Take a download of whatever you can, just in case, and start transmitting it to *Grace*. Alpha Actual out."

Chapter Forty-Five

Captain Eric Manders onboard the pirate ship *Kator* pressed his comm on the side of his helmet.

"Alpha Actual to *Grace*."

"Go ahead Alpha Actual," John responded.

"We are now running sweeps to remove the remaining pockets of resistance. We need reinforcements and some tech heads to stop this ship."

"Roger that Alpha Actual, We'll be transporting in ten minutes from RB Australis."

Jen looked at John, "It's too risky, they are going too fast to target adequately for people." The two had set basic safety standards regarding transporting people directly. The accuracy of targeting a moving object and the distance was an important factor. This was the reason they didn't transport Eric and his squad directly from the base on Earth.

"*Grace* to Alpha Actual, belay the transport, we will be landing on Alien ship in one-twenty minutes."

"Copy that *Grace*, landing at Alien LZ in one-twenty minutes. Confirmed."

"*Grace* to RB Australis, Sergeant Wilcox."

The sergeant, back on Earth in their Australian Research Base designated RB Australis, responded after a few seconds delay, "RB Australis, go ahead *Grace*."

"Transport will be in ten minutes."

"RB Australis, transport in ten minutes. Confirmed," the sergeant replied. He then turned and yelled out orders organizing his men ready for transport.

John reversed course sending the *Grace* at flank speed towards Earth. When they'd reached a safe distance for human transport, he slowed the ship to a full-stop and cut the engines to allow for easier transports. The cargo area could only take 20 soldiers given the space restrictions and designated transit area.

The soldiers stood on the transport platform in the hanger Bay of Australis Research Base. Checking their equipment for the third time, the men stilled and said prayers to their God and waited for final orders. The atmosphere was charged like paratroopers preparing to jump from a high-flying plane into flak. Their training had not yet included actual space travel, certainly not teleportation! Not that there was anything for them to do, but psychologically it was a whopper.

"Brace yourselves boys and girls." Sergeant Wilcox smiled when a blinding flash lit up the hanger bay. Quiet descended on his men as they marveled at the spacecraft around them realizing they had survived their first teleportation. Some of the more anxious started feeling each and every part of their body, just to check that all the parts arrived safely. Nervous chuckles rang in relief at surviving their incredible teleport.

Sergeant Wilcox had the men move off the transport platform in the *Grace* and call off. So he could check all his men were settled in. The men could hear the change in pitch of the engines as they fired up while John turned the ship around, once more heading out of the system. This time, it took a little over 50 minutes to reach the *Kator* as it sped further out of the system. It took time for John to match the vessel's speed precisely to allow him to dock.

"*Grace* to Alpha Actual, we are ready to start landing procedures."

Eric had had to return to the hanger bay to make sure all was ready for the arrival of the *Grace*. He had ordered three men to stay on the bridge and the rest to return with him. The hanger bay area available was clearly not huge, as there were two other shuttlecrafts crowding the flight deck. Eric took a picture and flashed it to John.

"Alpha Actual to *Grace* you're cleared to land. Be aware, two shuttlecraft are docked towards the nose of this ship." It was going to be a tight fit. He had to reverse in like a rhinoceros trying to reverse park into a disabled spot. When he finally came to a halt, the back three-quarters was flat on the flight deck leaving the nose of the *Grace* sticking out the side through the hanger's light air curtain force field. Max raced back opening the airlocks to allow the soldiers to troop through.

◆ ◆ ◆

John watched as Eric manhandle the first of the five aliens on the deck into the back of the *Grace*. Their unconscious forms seemed unreal. They were wearing no clothes except what looked like bioimplants.

John could smell the salty tang from the Squishys as they were secured to the seating.

"Do you have any idea how long they are going to be unconscious?" John asked.

Eric just shrugged, "We put enough into them to drop a rhino."

"Sgt Briggs, you and two men guard the aliens." The Sergeant saluted and pointed to Maz and Davis, "You two are with me."

Jen, Peter, and Max stood wide-eyed near the entrance to the bridge of the *Grace*. The Squishys had a strange smell that made one balk at going too close. The salty sea smell clogged their noses.

Four of them were a similar color with the last having bright yellow markings. Just then Rogers came limping down through the hanger to the hatch. Spotting no seats, "Sir, I'm okay I'll catch the next one. Looks like you have a full bus there anyway."

The sergeant replied before Eric could step in, "Maz, make room for Rogers. You will take his place on Alpha team." Maz smiled at this implied promotion to the top team.

Eric ordered the new arrivals, "Sergeant Wilcox, you will take Charlie team and make a sweep from engineering through to the bridge to pick up any stragglers."

"Yes, sir!" The sergeant saluted then abruptly turned around and started ordering his troops to get their butts into gear and be lively for any, 'drop-in unfriendlies'.

While they finished loading the Squishys, John commented, "Eric, you did good." Eric barely nodded his acknowledgment, then turned back to his troops unable to hide his grimace. *Not good enough for Banjo and Pele though!*

◆◆◆

The *Grace* made three more trips depositing the Squishys in the Australis Research Base (ARB). Some of them started to wake on the return journey and were summarily stunned again. The most notable were what looked like the captain, as his body was adorned with the most colors of all the Squishys. He did have a strange ink marking on his face.

"Elvis," Jen grinned as she spotted him walking down the ramp of the *Scotty*. She ran up to him giving him a small hug.

Just as quickly he turned and pointed at the *Scotty*, "Old girl nearly gave me a damn heart attack when the jump drives failed."

Jen looked at Elvis with concern. He had never openly criticized the *Scotty* before.

"What happened out there?" Jen asked.

"What *didn't* is more to the point. There was a catastrophic power failure within the system. I know the power was getting into the drive projectors, but she just wasn't doing anything with it. We tried everything to coax the old girl back. If it hadn't been for Carmen, we'd still be out there," Elvis complained as Carmen made her way down the ramp smiling.

Jen's forehead scrunched in concentration. "Did you try adjusting the power control con..."

"Tried that," Elvis said interrupting her.

"What about replacing the projector phase..."

"Did that," He said cutting her off again.

Carmen just kept smiling at the two playing their verbal joust while problem-solving *Scotty's* hiccup.

Jen was about to ask another question when she spotted Carmen there grinning. Jen's face lit up with a smile of her own. "How did you fix it?"

Elvis barked a laugh while he pointed at Carmen to finish the story.

Carmen's eyes narrowed not sure whether Elvis was laughing at her or the situation. "I kicked it," she said in a staccato Spanish accent.

"You kicked it?" Jen repeated, surprised.

"She kicked it with her metal-capped boots cursing like a 'Lizard in Heat'," Elvis repeated laughing again. The lizards had been the butt of Elvis' jokes a lot lately.

Making their way back to the wardroom, Jen smiled at Elvis' long laundry list of improvements he was loath to make. She was relieved that they were all safe, giving each of them a quick hug before she tottered off towards her own ship thinking on what changes she should make to the *Grace*.

When she returned to her ship, John was waiting at the hatch. "Elvis?"

"They're all okay." Jen then proceeded to tell John of Carmen's exploits in jump drive maintenance.

"Oh my God," John said, then joined Jen and burst out laughing. It was good to hear Jen laugh again. He had missed that laugh like a warm summer shower.

John knew that Jen was nowhere near over the damage that he had caused her and their relationship. But he did see a little hope. He rationalized

if he could make her laugh then ... Who knows what's possible.

Taking a deep breath, John said with half a smile, "Let's get back out there and stop this Squishy ship." The final trip back to the warship included excited scientists itching to get their hands on the alien technology.

Roberts had been dumping all manner of data and transmitting it directly to the *Grace*. There was some logic to how the system was set out which allowed him to make sense of the alien computer system. He had located some diagrams, outlining the ship and various compartments. The IT tech specialist took snapshots of the screens which he forwarded to Eric. It was useful for the final sweeps that included chambers they had missed on the previous runs.

Chapter Forty-Six

Space Command, Peterson Air Force Base

"What are they doing now, Colonel?" Admiral Tucker asked Dan.

"The two small vessels appear to have driven off the middle size warship after it destroyed the third small ship. There was a brief battle, it seems like the larger ship is making a leisurely retreat. The first Angel ship must have gone stealth as it's disappeared again."

"Keep me informed if there are any further developments."

Dan just shook his head, *everything about this whole business between these three ships was unusual...*

Eric dismissed his troops and walked over to John who stood near the catafalque watching the reveille ceremony on the parade ground. The men had had a service for their fallen comrades earlier in the week. Two names were chiseled in gold prominently and displayed on the wall behind the memorial.

"How are the men doing?" John asked.

"The boarding action has polarized the group. It has turned the men into a real band of brothers. Once they got past all the technology, one alien is like another. It was a real confidence builder. They are now settling into training for the task of rescuing the abducted."

John could see the serious faces that practiced before him. He knew they all still had a lot to learn and prepare before they would be ready. So he said a silent prayer that the abducted stay strong till he could rescue them and give the lizards some payback.

◆◆◆

Research Base El Paso, Texas

John sat on the wooden deck of the cottage admin building eyeing the champagne on the side table. Dusk had set. He could clearly see the stark red colored air contrails that zig-zagged across the sky from the latest hornet top gun pilots assigned to Buckley Air Force Base. The sight was disturbingly familiar these days.

Eventually, he sighed and rocked back in his chair to look around and survey the research base. It had come a long way since the ramshackle transport containers and derelict cottage. The slow, deliberate movements of the security guards patrolling the fence line were a stark contrast to the M1 tanks from Fort Bliss just beyond the fence.

The lizard attack shook the very foundation of Earth. But it especially catalyzed the transformation of the research base and his colleagues into what ...? A highly motivated center for technology infusion. The good nature of the locals, was on a knife edge, swaying between the victim and angry berserker, not really understanding the machinations of the attacks. These major humanist events were driving their usually peaceful lives far beyond their control.

Most were scared but proud of their contribution in supporting the base, however small. They were confused about what the research base actually did. However, it did seem clear that it was dedicated to the defense of Earth. The army parked just outside their door confirmed the importance of it.

John's thoughts on the last several months crystallized in his mind. They needed to get serious about space defense. He came to the conclusion that there was very little time, much less than he initially thought.

Earth had to develop a credible Space Force, or they would be subjugated as a feeding ground for the lizards or some other race.

The crack of the *Scotty's* return, a reminder of the power born of new technology. If they could only harness that power safely, then maybe, humanity might have a small chance after all.

◆◆◆

Elvis walked into Johns office for their weekly star scan. They had fifteen probes out there now being dropped at nearby star systems in search of the lizard ship *Godzilla*. S'sank had provided some intel on his shipboard crew. The more that John heard the more he cringed.

The small shake of Elvis' head said it all. No *Godzilla*.

"What are the next star systems targeted?"

Elvis and Max pulled out the latest   stellar map. At least their intel network was being built.

◆◆◆

Jen walked onto the deck dropping into the chair next to John. The two sat in silence, listening to the wind rustle past the desert scrub.

"You really hurt me you know," Jen whispered.

"Yes," he said with a pained look on his face.

"I do understand the need to defend the planet and acquire new technologies..." Jen said.

"But not at your expense," John put forward completing her sentence. Once again the awkward silence returned.

"How are your night terrors?" John said.

Jen frowned, "I didn't think you knew about them."

She could see a sad look shadow John's face while he tried to avert his eyes.

Jen turned to stare at him, biting her bottom lip. Something had changed in him, but what? She thought frowning.

John took his time before speaking, "I'm sorry about Sykes. I know what it feels like to be responsible for another's death, even though it was self-defense. I am not going to tell you that you will ever get over it. It may seem like it was morally wrong to take his life, and on some level that's true. However, we are at war. Our enemy is coming for us, whether they be lizards or mad old buggers that can't mind their own business. If we don't prepare to defend ourselves, the whole human race will end up as slaves on some forgotten planet, or worse."

"You're being a little over dramatic aren't you?" Jen countered.

"Am I? We've already had two incursions with over a hundred people either dead or kidnapped. They know where we live. All they need to do is nudge an asteroid and bye, bye Earth."

Jen looked unconvinced.

"Who else can do what we do right now? Not even the combined governments of Earth could do what we did."

"That still doesn't mean that killing Sykes was justifiable."

"So what would have happened if he had killed you, Elvis and me?" John asked.

Jen stared back at him.

"More than just a hundred people would be dead or abducted." John continued, "We are soldiers here. We're fighting for our very survival. I'll do what I can to try and protect you, but we both have our roles. Unfortunately, you need to be the one to convince yourself that our work here has meaning. That you believe within the context of saving humanity, and that our actions are in fact moral. The alternative is to be eaten from within with shame, anger, and helplessness... They say, 'War is hell', unfortunately, for you, it is indeed cruel and unrefined."

Jen's eyes teared with the realization that she was never going to be innocent again. Did she hate John for that? Well... Not exactly. She scrunched her eyes tight. She would have to think heavily on his words.

John chastised himself. It wasn't the best apology he had ever given by a long shot. Hell, he didn't know if Jen even saw it as an apology. He really didn't want to hurt her, but he couldn't say to himself that he wouldn't do it all exactly the same given the same circumstances. She needed to understand they all had no choice.

Fortunately, the tense moment between the two friends was shattered, when Elvis, Max, Thurston and Eric jumped onto the porch from the grass. Gathering up the champagne flutes from the side table, John stood before the team. Two glasses remained prominently placed on the table in honor of their fallen 'comrades in arms'.

"Well guys, a toast to a successful snatch and grab," John said as he charged his glass.

Eric nodded in appreciation for those that lost their lives under his command.

John continued, "With this new technology we are one step closer to returning our family, and protecting our own."

The small group knew they still had a long way to go, but for now, they had grasped in two hands one small victory. The conversation flurried around the treasures to be unearthed on the fascinating ship made by, of all things, Octopus people. Eating squid would never be the same.

"Well, John," Elvis piped up when there was a break in the conversation, "did you ever build that sonic weapon you were always promising the Colonel?" he said with a wink to Jen.

John groaned.

"What weapon?" Max perked up. The rest of the team just laughed, clinking their glasses, while Eric shook his head giving John a, 'We need to have a talk, look'.

The End

Hope you liked the book!

If so, please give it a positive review on Amazon.

Try the next book in the series coming soon,

Humans on the Menu.

Titles by A.K. Brown

"Champagne Universe Series Book 1: JumpStart"
Available Now
"Champagne Universe Series Book 2: Humans on the Menu"
Coming Soon
"Champagne Universe Series Book 3: Traders Bluff"
Coming Soon

Cover Art

Includes:

© Abidal - Planet Earth with sunrise in the space.

www.Dreamstime.com

Connect with A.K. Brown

Website
akbrown.info